TIME FOLDS FOR US

Natalie Sol Gallagher

Poppy & Olive Press

Published by Poppy & Olive Press

2897 N Druid Hills Rd Ste 211

Atlanta, GA 30329

Book cover art and design by Caitlin B. Alexander

Names: Sol Gallagher, Natalie, author.

Title: Time Folds for Us / Natalie Sol Gallagher

Description: first edition | Atlanta : Poppy & Olive Press, 2026

Identifiers: ISBN: 979-8-9957590-0-3 (trade paperback)

Subjects: Romance fiction. | Novels

First Edition: June 2026

For Shannendoah, my great love in any century.

"Time is not a line but a dimension, like the dimensions of space."
-Margaret Atwood, *Cat's Eye*

PROLOGUE

ATHENS, GEORGIA • JULY 2020

GEORGE

I attended my father's funeral wearing a bespoke suit I found in the back of his closet that fit me disturbingly well, accessorized with a medical-grade face mask and purple rain boots. Unfortunately, I could not anticipate that my estranged wife would be wearing a thrift store pillbox hat and black veil from an old Halloween costume. The symmetry between my vintage suit and her hat made us look like we'd coordinated our outfits. Which she made sure to tell me she hated. More than once.

Rhiannon and I stood next to the display the funeral home had set up on the sprawling front yard of my father's house. A plastic tent arching over us protected my father's photographs, urn, and flowers from the uneven drizzle that had been plaguing us all day. The rain created divots of grassy water all over the yard, forcing me to swap my leather dress shoes for the rain boots after I stepped in an ankle-deep puddle. Any time the downpour paused, steam wafted up from asphalt and kudzu, creating a musty sour smell that stuck to our skin and permeated our clothing. It was like standing inside of a mouth.

A short, socially-distanced queue formed to offer condolences. Guests watched from their cars for the line to move, and when it dwindled to just a few people, the next group trudged across the sodden grass to pay their respects. Because I was terrible with names and partially covered faces, Rhiannon stood at my side and greeted people before I could embarrass myself, placing an emphasis on the person's association with the recently deceased, Dr. Albert Rosen.

"Dr. Kommareddi, thank you so much for being here," she welcomed the next person in line, bowing slightly to avoid shaking hands. "Albert spoke highly of your work at the University." Rhiannon added pointedly, knowing I had no idea who this was. But given the right clues, I was usually able to piece together an appropriate response in time. Though if I didn't catch on quickly enough, she'd give me the side-eye from beneath her morbid veil.

A man neither Rhiannon nor I recognized made his way to the front of the line. I could feel Rhi tense up next to me because she hates not knowing things, especially if not knowing something makes her look like someone who doesn't know the right things—like every single mourner at her father-in-law's funeral.

She was spared when the man gave us a small, awkward wave from a few feet away and introduced himself. "Mr. Rosen? I'm Steve Cunningham, Dr. Rosen's attorney?" The question in his tone made it sound like he needed me to verify this fact.

"He had an attorney?" I asked, caught off guard by this development. I knew nothing of an attorney.

"Oh yes, and he left me specific instructions on how to execute his estate."

It never occurred to me that my dad had a will, much less an "estate." He never once mentioned it, or the attorney, to me, his sole surviving family member and only child.

I stepped a few feet away from the receiving line. Rhiannon gave me a sideways glance but maintained her post greeting the stream of colleagues and friends who'd come to pay their last respects. There was a time when she would've taken the lead with any conversations pertaining to attorneys and estates.

But at that point, she was working to extricate herself from my life.

Steve stood a safe few feet away from me. I spoke as loudly as I could to be understood from the distance, through the mask, but low enough not to reveal all our business to the neighbors. "What estate? Dad had nothing at the end. It all went towards paying for his medical bills." I thought I knew everything about my father's final assets. We had liquidated everything we could, drained every account, and tapped into our meager retirement to stay ahead of the mounting medical bills from the months he was in a coma, on a respirator, and receiving experimental treatments for the novel disease.

"Well, he held on to one thing. Do you mind speaking with me somewhere private?" Steve extended a hand, indicating he wanted me to go to another part of the yard where we couldn't be overheard. I jerked my head towards the wraparound porch of the house. He followed me up the steps to a secluded corner, still in view of the funeral, but protected from the spluttering rain.

Under the dry cover of the porch, Steve placed his briefcase upon the rail and opened it to reveal a single sapphire blue jewelry box. He handed the box to me as casually as if handing me a napkin I'd asked for. The velvet covering looked old and worn, buffed down on the corners, and stained on the bottom. I stared at it for a moment, convinced I should know what it was. But like with the people waiting in line, I couldn't seem to place where I knew this thing from.

It was added distance between me and my father. One more instance where I didn't really know him and he never tried to get to know me.

Steve cleared his throat. "I have strict instructions to wait for you to open it and answer any questions I can. Though I must warn you, I have very few answers."

I rolled the velvet box around in my hand, tempted to pocket it and inspect it later, just to spite Dad and his dumb rules. But the desire for clarity won out in the end. I pried the lid off the top.

Inside the box was a precisely folded letter. The paper it was written on looked like an ancient piece of parchment, or (most likely), was styled to look like an antique. It was bound with a frayed red ribbon (also suspiciously antique in appearance) that I slid off without untying and shoved in my suit coat pocket. I unfolded the letter and read the brief message scrawled with what was clearly a quill and ink, as evidenced by splotches at the end of certain letters and pools of ink in the crevices of the folds.

My father had been an esteemed professor of history at the University of Georgia and his love of both the past and theatrics meant he was constantly planning elaborate melodramas rooted in historical treasure hunts—like the one I suspected I was about to find myself in.

Beneath the letter was a single, slightly rusted skeleton key, crafted from black iron. Deeply confused, I glanced at Steve. "Dad had a cottage? How? *What*? And, most importantly, *where*?" I picked up the key and examined it. "How did I not know about this already?"

The attorney seemed both unsurprised and uninterested, as if he bestowed secret cottages to unsuspecting heirs every day. "Dr. Rosen insisted it be kept secret until the right time. That is all I know. Oh, and there is a family who have been maintaining the property. De Ros, if I recall correctly, is their name. They're the stewards. While you own the cottage, it technically sits on their land. In England, somewhere north, I believe."

I walked to the other side of the porch, pulled down my mask, and took a deep gulp of moisture-drenched air. "Okay, I have many, *many* questions!" I called out to Steve.

He acted as if he hadn't heard me. "That reminds me," he said while pulling a piece of paper from the inside pocket of his blazer and waving it at me. "This is the address."

I pulled my mask up, headed back to where Steve stood, and snatched the paper from his outstretched hand. The address was written on the same old parchment as the letter, also folded several times. And it wasn't a modern address, so much as a list of cryptic directions.

Kendal, England

Park at end of Sunnyside Road

Head East, Castle on your left

Follow the dirt path 600 paces

I sighed. If nothing else, Dad was infuriatingly predictable.

"Is there anything else I can help you with?" Steve inquired.

"Yes! Many things!" I exclaimed. My exasperation with the entire situation burned in my chest. "This hardly constitutes an 'address'," I said while shaking the note with one hand and making air quotes with the other. "What am I supposed to do with this?"

Steve leaned forward and awkwardly patted my arm with the tips of his fingers, trying to offer some performative comfort while maintaining a safe distance. "Mr. Rosen, all the paperwork has been completed, so you and your wife are now the proud owners of Plierton Cottage. If I were you, I'd book airfare as soon as you can and go see it for yourself. Best of luck."

Before I could ask him anything else, the attorney hopped down the steps of the porch, into the steaming rain, using his hand to shield his eyes as he headed back to his car.

"Oh okay, I'll just fly across the ocean during a goddamn fucking pandemic to go see a mystery cottage in fuck-all England," I muttered in his general direction, muffled by the layer of papery cotton covering my face.

"What was that about?" Rhiannon asked as she came up behind me.

"Well, while we were contemplating selling organs to pay for Dad's medical bills to keep him alive, it turns out he owned property in England that we now own. But in typical Dad fashion, instead of selling it to help us out a bit, it's now part of a scavenger hunt from hell we must do to even find the thing." I pressed the note with the so-called address into Rhiannon's palm. "Wanna go to England?"

She closed her hand around the parchment but didn't look at it. I could tell her desire to know what was in the note was at odds with her desire to not be tangled up with me anymore. Which, fair.

"I'm not sure this is really the best time for taking a trip together," Rhiannon replied gently.

"Because of the pandemic? Or because we're getting divorced?" I asked.

I was done with the people I loved never saying what they meant.

Rhiannon gazed out at the lawn where the funeral guests had dissipated, leaving us alone. "Both?"

"I understand. Though if nothing else, we're still legally married. Which means this is your property too. He even addressed you by name. Aren't you at least a little curious what it's like?" I pressed the velvet box into her hand, on top of the note she was still clutching, unopened. "Look at the letter he left. I can't make sense of it, so maybe you can. You were once his favorite student, after all."

The little telling twitch of her left eye gave me hope. If one thing is certain, it's that Rhiannon Rosen likes to know things. Once she is faced with the unknowable, she will do everything in her power to understand it. For her, winning means being at the top of the class, the most valuable trivia team member, the best teacher with all the answers.

And the solver of cryptic notes related to unexpected inheritances.

If leveraging this compulsion got her to go with me to see this cottage, if it meant I got a little more time to make things right, then I would use it to my advantage.

"Damn it. You win," she sighed. Rhiannon pulled back the veil that obscured her vision, opened the box, unfolded both notes, and examined each carefully for several minutes without looking up or saying a word.

I leaned against the porch rail, watching her. One strand of Rhi's curly auburn hair came loose from her bun and fell across her cheek; I resisted the familiar temptation to tuck it back behind her ear. As much as I wanted to touch her, I suspected she'd feel it was a violation.

This version of myself wanted to punch Past George in the face for being so stubborn and so stupid as to land us in this situation. Past George foolishly thought he'd never lose Rhiannon, that her well of patience and understanding would never run dry because it was constantly replenished with her immense capacity for love.

Present George knew this was a fallacy—all wells run dry if you cut off their source.

Rhiannon sighed and snapped the velvet box shut, notes tucked neatly inside. "All right, George. I'll go with you. But not until September as your dad instructed, okay? There's a reason he wanted us to go then, so we might as well follow his directions."

"Of course," I agreed. "I'll take care of everything. All you have to do is show up at the airport when I tell you to."

"I'll believe it when I see it," she exhaled. There was no hint of sarcasm or fight, only exhaustion in her words. "And, to be clear, I'm only going to see it with the intention of selling the thing. God knows we both need the money. But nothing else. Understood?"

"Absolutely," I nodded. "That is a solid plan."

PART 1:

A CASTLE IN RUINS

1

RHIANNON

"Rhiannon, don't panic."

Though the words were meant to be comforting, I found them ridiculous because I never panic. Panicking is counterproductive; it shuts down your cognitive function and leaves you helpless to your base fight or flight instincts, making it impossible to solve problems. To panic is to yield control over the situation when maintaining control is paramount.

However.

The voice belonged to someone whose funeral I'd attended only months earlier.

And I heard the words as I was falling through complete darkness.

Before I could determine whether this was a rare and possibly valid time to panic, I slammed shoulder-first into what felt like a pallet of dense fabric, before tumbling onto the floor and landing on my hands and knees. Gasping for breath, I carefully lowered myself into a sitting position. When my bare bottom pressed against a frigid slab of stone, I realized I was completely and utterly naked. Wincing, I pulled my rapidly bruising knees up to my chest and glanced around, trying to get a bearing on what, exactly, had just happened.

Don't panic, I reminded myself. Because, let's face it, most people would agree this was a panic-worthy situation.

Moments earlier I was fully dressed, snuggled into a couch with a blanket tucked around my legs, gnawing on a partially unwrapped piece of chocolate. As I sunk my teeth into the dense bar, the entire room tipped over, as if I was on a capsizing ship.

Then, I was plunging through darkness.

From my position sitting on the floor, a quick survey of my surroundings revealed I was in a room comprised of stone walls, a long fireplace full of ashes, a grimy little window, and a slab of a wooden door—the only entrance or exit I could make out. Above me was a thatched roof, and though it was thinning in places, it certainly didn't have any holes large enough for a fully grown human to fall through.

The smell of soil, wet wool, and dried grass clouded my already addled senses. I rubbed the bridge of my nose; a headache bloomed between my eyes and my joints ached with the impact of my fall. While shaking out my arms and taking deep breaths, I shifted up onto my knees to get a better look at the room.

The pallet I'd crashed into was in fact, a bed—though no more than a rickety wooden frame topped with what appeared to be a straw-filled mattress, a crusty wool blanket, and a dingy sheepskin. And George, as naked as I was.

The situation was truly testing my resolve not to panic.

He was groaning and gingerly examining his forehead with his fingertips. As the bed was pushed up against one of the walls, it appeared that while the force of the fall had sent me careening onto the floor, it had slammed George into the stones, face-first.

"Are you okay?"

"Yep," he winced, stretching out one arm and rubbing his neck. George rolled onto his side, so he was facing away from me. The muscular lines of his body shifted as he pushed himself up into a sitting position while shoving his long hair out of his face. He glanced over his shoulder at me. "And you? Are you okay?"

"Maybe?" I was shaking and sore and deeply perplexed by the situation. "What just happened?"

I stayed huddled on the floor beside the bed. I couldn't make eye contact with George. I hadn't seen him without clothes in months, nor had he seen me in this state. I was inexplicably bashful.

"No idea," he replied. "But I'm sure there's a good explanation. Here." He yanked the wool blanket out from underneath himself and tossed it to me.

Standing on wobbly legs, I wrapped the blanket around myself, rolling it under my arms like a towel. A crusty, filthy, scratchy towel. I rolled my shoulders and tried not to think about the history of the blanket that was touching my bare skin.

George scooted off the foot of the bed, holding the sheepskin in front of himself, wincing as he moved. When he stood, the slight sound of a piece of metal hitting rock clanked below him. He touched his neck before looking down, then knelt to pick up a silver coin from the floor.

"That's weird," he remarked. "My coin is here, but the chain disappeared." He glanced down at his body. "Along with the rest of my clothes." He stared at the little piece of silver in his hand, fingers trembling. George always wore an old Norman coin his father had given him on a chain around his neck. He never took it off.

There were too many unexpected and alarming developments stacking up; I didn't know where to begin figuring out a solution. Though the shock of the fall was wearing off, confusion set in, which was just as disorienting.

George and I stared at each other. He had a red welt forming on his forehead from where he'd hit the wall.

"Are you sure you're okay?" I asked again, reaching out to touch him instinctively.

His eyes widened but he didn't move. Rather, I stopped my hand midair, clenched my fingers into a fist, and dropped it to my side.

He noted my shift. "I'll live," he said stepping away from me. "Getting back to what the hell just happened, I'd also like to know, where the fuck are we?" George walked the perimeter of the room slowly, one foot placed carefully in front of the other, as if the trek would yield information our eyes could not. When he reached the point where the edge of the fireplace and the corner of the room met, he made a choking noise before looking at me with horror. "Rhi, look at the designs carved into the mantle. And ... and the corner," he pointed, "look at the tree trunk."

I stepped closer to the fireplace so I could see what he was talking about. A pattern of vines, books, and birds were carved into a unique design along the mantle. It was alarmingly identical to the design carved into the mantle of the cottage we'd just inherited. The cottage where I was snuggled into the couch, moments before. Beyond this, to the right of the fireplace a tree trunk supported one corner of the cottage, with the stones masoned up against the living wood. Though this tree was smaller than the one our cottage was built around, it was such a unique architectural feature that the similarity made me queasy.

Despite the chilly dampness of the air, I was flushed with anxious heat. My heart pounded and my hands grew sweaty. "I think we should get out of here," I whispered. "Something feels ... off about this place."

"Do you have any recollection of how we got here?" George frowned, ignoring my concerns. He was absentmindedly flipping his coin over his knuckles while gazing around the room.

"No. I just felt like I was falling. Then, this." I decided not to tell him about the voice I heard. I was so anxious to get out there, I did not want to distract George by giving him something else to ruminate on.

"Do you think we were drugged or something? Do you recall going anywhere? Meeting anyone? Could we have been robbed and dumped here?"

"No. The last thing I recall was sitting on the couch, waiting for this supposedly magical equinox everyone kept going on about. Then," I gestured towards the bed, "this. Besides, if we were robbed, they were the dumbest thieves ever because they left the most valuable thing of all." I pointed at George's coin. It was over a thousand years old and certainly worth more than our phones or clothes.

"True. But then *what just happened?*" His voice hitched at the end, expressing his own growing fear. "And where are our things?"

I shifted on my feet. The stone floor was like an ice block on my bare soles. "I'm sure there's a reasonable explanation for all of this. And we will figure it out. But for now, can we get out of here? This place gives me the creeps." I was fidgety to get moving. I felt certain the answers we sought were somewhere else, somewhere that was not this dark little stone room. Like if we stepped outside, all our questions would be answered, a solution would present itself, and I could get down to the business of solving this problem and not panicking.

"Okay." George clutched the sheepskin around his waist and used his free hand to push his ash-blonde hair out of his eyes.

For once he didn't argue with me, just followed me to the door. I tried pulling it open, but it was stuck. I pulled as hard as I could, and though the door creaked, it didn't open.

"Here," George reached around me, braced one foot against the wall, and yanked the door with such force, it popped open with a cloud of dust and leaves scattering about. A thick, dried vine fell across the doorway, swinging from where it had been attached over the door frame.

The path leading out of wherever we were was piled high with undisturbed dried leaves. Like no one had walked through the entry in years.

"Oh good, another weird mystery to solve," George sighed.

2

RHIANNON

Once outside, we saw that we'd fallen into a small stone cottage standing in a copse of overgrown trees. Ivy vines wound their way through the crumbling masonry of the walls, as the forest slowly swallowed up the structure and reclaimed the land. Though a dirt road passed by about twenty feet from the cottage, there was no obvious path leading from the cottage's front door to the road. Only leafy overgrowth, mulched foliage, and dead vines lay before us. A gray sky overhead obscured what time of day it was, letting only a bit of light through the tree branches.

We carefully picked our way through the overgrowth to get to the road, mindful of each step where our bare feet sunk into mud, ankles tickled by dried leaves and prickly vines. The cloudy skies morphed into misty rain, then to a full downpour, soaking us both. My hair clung in clumps and stuck to the side of my face, the disgusting wool blanket I'd secured under my arms was slowly growing heavy with moisture, and my feet were throbbingly numb.

George looked equally miserable as water ran down his shoulders and he tried to keep the sheepskin secured around his waist. "I've had enough rain on this trip," he grumbled.

The road itself was narrow, nothing more than packed mud rutted with unfamiliar tracks, and the tree canopy overhead swallowed up the view, obscuring any information about what was in either direction.

"Which way?" George asked, tightening the bulky sheepskin around his waist. He was clearly trying to ignore the frosty breeze across his bare torso, but the shivers he could barely contain gave him away.

I considered each direction, biting my lip, hoping for a clue as to what we should do next, as if there was even a slight possibility that one way may be warmer than the other. The rain felt like ice cubes tumbling down my bare shoulders and back, pooling at my ankles. Standing on the road, I realized that wherever we went or whomever helped us would see us in this state of undress.

George grabbed my upper arm. "Listen."

Coming from a distance, I heard the distinct rhythmic clopping of what sounded like a horse trotting. As the sound increased, it was clear the animal was heading our direction.

"Let's get off the road." George pulled us behind an oak tree's thick trunk, so we were partially obscured, but could still see in either direction. We watched the point we heard the noise coming from, waiting for a visual to give us an idea of what to do next. Through the rain-soaked tree branches, I caught glimpses of a massive black horse ridden by an oddly dressed man. I nudged George with my elbow.

"I see him too," he confirmed.

Though the rain eased into a light drizzle, it didn't matter—we were already soaked and cold enough I worried about what would happen if we stayed out there much longer. A chill wracked through my body, reinforcing my concerns.

"Should we ask him for help?" I whispered. "Maybe he knows where we are?"

"We don't seem to have any better options."

"Do we have a plan?"

"Other than jumping out and begging for help? None that come to mind. Why?"

Before I could reply, I realized the rider had gotten so close that if we were going to get his attention, we only had seconds to act. George must have understood this as well, as he darted into the middle of the muddy road.

He held his hand up and exclaimed, "Wait! Please, we just need some directions!"

The rider startled, causing his horse to stop short and rear up with a frightened neigh. The horse—a massive black stallion whose hooves looked like they could crush bones into dust without much effort—whinnied and flared his nostrils. The horse side stepped back and forth a few times as the rider pulled on the reins and said something calming in a voice so low, I could not make it out. When the horse calmed and stood still, tail swishing impatiently, the man regarded us from the saddle.

He stood roughly fifteen feet from us, one hand at his side as if to make a quick motion for a weapon, staring us down, before he cupped a gloved hand over his ear and glanced around. But the breeze carried only the sounds of birds in the distance and drops of water splashing on leaves and in puddles. The rider stared at us for several drawn-out moments, his expression relaxing from shock into curiosity. He seemed to be mulling over his options before swinging one leg over the side of the horse and dropping to the ground as softly as a cat.

As the rider approached George, one careful step at a time, he pulled his gloves off and held them loosely in one hand. His eyes were fixed on George, mouth twisted in a frown, making no attempt to hide the fact that he was sizing him up.

I scurried to George's side from behind the tree, hoping my presence was less threatening. He tensed up, gripping his sheepskin covering.

The rider was average height, perhaps only an inch or so shorter than George. He wore a hip-length black cloak with slits for his arms, a long-sleeved velvet tunic in a deep shade of blue, and black leggings with polished black leather calf-high boots. The boots, strangely, had toes that elongated into an exaggerated pointy tip. Across his chest was a chain of silver, stretching from shoulder to shoulder, each link a carefully wrought design that I could not make out. The rider's wavy shoulder-length brown hair was topped off with a black velvet cap, adorned with what looked like an emerald brooch set in silver.

Despite the storm, he looked impeccable. Apparently the rain was respectful enough not to cling to these fine—and stupidly weather-inappropriate—garments. It seemed we were being rescued by some kind of medieval cosplayer who enjoyed riding horses while wearing velvet in the rain. I sighed inwardly, annoyed that this day was about to get even weirder.

When the man stood about three feet from us, gloves in hand, one eyebrow lifted in curiosity, I spoke. "I'm so sorry to bother you, but we're in some sort of ... predicament." I looked to George for support. He nodded at me. "We're from out of town and ... and we seem to be lost." I shifted from foot to foot, unsure how much to share without sounding totally insane.

The man's mouth fell open in surprise, though he quickly regained his composure. He furrowed his brow and scanned the woods as if he were expecting someone—or something—else to appear at any moment.

"Pray tell, where have you traveled from?" he finally asked.

The rider spoke slowly and carefully, as if working to ensure his words were appropriate. What struck me though were the underlying sounds that accompanied his voice. It sounded as if he was speaking one strange language but was being dubbed over with words that I could understand. A slight echo, two words for every one spoken.

I glanced to my right to see George's face twisted up with uncertainty, one eyebrow cocked, apparently trying to work out the same odd phenomena of the dubbed words that I was.

How on earth was he doing that? Was it some sort of translation device tucked under his cloak? Was he so deep into his cosplay that he was speaking what could be Old English?

A cool, damp breeze rustled the leaves and lifted the hem of my blanket, sending shivers up my spine. I clutched the blanket tighter under my arms while considering how to answer the man's question, because I truly did not know how to answer where we'd traveled from in a way that would get us the right directions. Would the non-address of the weird cottage we'd inherited be enough information for him to help two hapless Americans?

My head throbbed. I could have murdered for some coffee and dry clothes.

The rider took a step closer, his attention turned fully to me. He tilted his head to the side while making no attempt to hide the fact that he was scanning my entire form while I trembled in the wind. I felt exposed, though I did not think my flimsy blanket was necessarily to blame. I glanced away, uncomfortable with the attention.

The man must have been in his mid-to-late thirties and he was stupidly good-looking. He had warm brown eyes, a sharp jawline, high cheekbones, and full lips. Something about him seemed familiar, but like any memory of how we ended up in our predicament, the information about who he was remained elusive.

"Well?" he asked. "I am disinclined to help common thieves posing as weary travelers if they cannot provide the requested information." Despite his assertion that we could be thieves, nothing in his demeanor indicated he felt threatened or afraid of us. He spoke with the same deliberate cadence, as if he had to consider how each word should be formed in his mouth before saying it aloud. And like before, each blurry-sounding word was layered with clear language I understood.

"Look, we're just trying to find our way back to the place where we're staying. It's past Sunnyside Road, kind of close to the castle ruins, so, if you could give us directions that would be very helpful." George finished with a helpless shrug.

Hopefully it was enough information for this guy to help us.

The man's eyes widened in surprise. George looked at me, appearing stricken with the notion that our situation may be much worse than whatever we were initially thinking.

The rain stopped, fading out into a few drops landing on my cheek. All three of us looked up at the sky, as if to confirm it was done soaking us, before glancing at each other.

Without asking, the man grabbed my right hand and examined each of my fingers before flipping it over and running his finger over my palm. His hand was warm and rough. When his thumb stroked the inside of my palm, I held my breath.

"Hey now," George warned.

Unfazed, the man sunk down on one knee and lifted one of my feet, wiped the mud from my big toe, and lightly caressed my heel before he slowly stood again. "My lady, it appears you have not stood a moment in a field, much less worked in one."

"What?" I stammered.

"Perhaps you are a very long way from home, then." He unfastened the silver clasp holding his cloak closed at his throat. With one swift motion he removed the cloak from his shoulders and draped it over mine. He gently fastened the clasp at my collarbone, holding my gaze the entire time. It felt strangely intimate. I clutched the fabric tightly, grateful for the added warmth, regardless of the unabashedly appraising look the man was giving me.

I looked to George, whose eyes were narrowed and jaw clenched at this exchange.

The rider moved to examine George. He stared at him, his face inches away and unblinking. George didn't back down, didn't relax the fury already written on his features. Seemingly satisfied with the standoff, the rider grabbed one of George's hands and examined only a few fingers, carefully inspecting the nail on his ring finger, before appearing content with what he found.

I think George only refrained from saying something or yanking his hand away because he knew we needed help.

The rider turned back to me, clicked his tongue a few times, muttering, "How interesting," to himself.

"What is? What's going on?" George was impatient with the apparent inspection. "What does it matter if she's ever stood in a field, or whatever? What does that have to do with anything right now?"

"You must be relatives of Lord de Ros. That is the only explanation." He said it low, almost under his breath, as if this revelation was mostly for himself and not for us.

"What are you talking about?" George demanded.

But the man only glanced to his left and appraised him for a moment before turning on his heel and striding back to his horse. "Do you think we should we follow him?" George whispered to me.

Before I could reply, the man grabbed a rolled blanket from the back of his saddle and walked back towards us. He tossed the blanket to George, who caught it in one hand.

George turned so his backside was facing us while he dropped the sheepskin, wrapped the rough wool blanket around his waist, then picked up the hide and draped it over his shoulders. "I suppose this is moderately better," he sighed.

The man led his horse to where we were standing and patted its muzzle while whispering calming things under his breath. When the horse stilled, he turned his attention back to us. In the same deliberate cadence, he introduced himself. "I am Lord Edward of Kendal." He placed his hand on his chest, giving a small bow as a show of courtesy, then waited for us to introduce ourselves.

I shifted from foot to foot, trying to shake the cakey mud off my toes. "I'm Rhiannon and this," I thumbed at George, "is my," I paused before choking out, "*husband*, George."

George held his right hand out to Edward. Edward seemed to consider it for a moment before placing his hand in George's. George gave it a firm, decisive squeeze and a quick shake before releasing Edward's hand. He had some audacity for someone wearing only a sheepskin and a stranger's old horse blanket, I'd give him that.

Edward smoothly pulled his gloves back on his hands, seemingly unfazed by George's aggressive greeting. "Do you have any recollection of the brigands who put you in this predicament?"

"Brigands?" George raised one eyebrow.

"Yes, it is quite common this far north of London. Merciless thieves—Scots, usually—hide in the brushes," he gestured to the ample foliage surrounding us, "then pounce on unsuspecting lords and ladies passing through, stripping them of all possessions and coin. Often, they render their victims unconscious in the process. Or worse." Edward paused and looked at me meaningfully. "Given your current state, it is even possible that a member of your household was part of the nefarious plot. Do not be surprised if we run into a humble servant, suddenly enriched by some of the jewels you may have lost in the attack."

"Servants?" George blinked several times, like he was having a hard time wrapping his mind around this possible explanation. I doubted he could conceive of a situation where another person was his servant.

While George was distracted by the idea of servants, I was annoyed. This cosplay thing had gone too far, and though we needed help, my patience was wearing thin by the unrelenting method acting of "Lord Edward." I resisted rolling my eyes.

Edward grabbed his horse's reins. "You will accompany me to Kendal Castle, the seat of these lands." He glanced at George. "You certainly bear more than a passing resemblance to the baron. Though I do not recall any word of distant relations making the journey north, many do travel here for the equinox. The king himself has even journeyed here for the spectacle." Edward scratched his chin for a moment. "Regardless, it is clear from the state of your fingers and toes that you are no common peasants, scratching out a living in the hills. Come, Lady Rhiannon, let us get your delicate feet off this damp soil." Edward held his hand out to me.

Unclear on what I was agreeing to, I placed my hand in his but stood still.

Edward tilted his head at me and smiled curiously. "My lady, do you not recall how to mount a horse?"

"Oh! I didn't realize I was getting up on it." I looked up at the massive beast standing beside me. It snorted and scratched the mud with one hoof, startling me. The horse's sinewy muscles rippled as it tensed up beside us. I took a step back hesitantly. I'd never ridden a horse before and was completely unprepared to start now, soaking wet, wearing only a wool blanket and a strange man's cloak.

"Come, I shall lift you."

I looked past Edward to where George was standing, looking alarmed with every aspect of this batshit crazy interaction. He was grimacing, clinging to the sheepskin around his shoulders, brows furrowed.

But he made no move to help me. Per usual.

I nodded to Edward. He clasped his hands around my waist and with one motion floated me up into the saddle, where I grabbed the horn and clumsily pulled myself the rest of the way up. I tried sitting turned to the side to keep the blanket wrapped tightly around my legs, but I did not know if I could maintain this position the entire ride, on the slippery curved saddle. The fluid motion of being tossed up onto the horse made me temporarily lightheaded and I struggled to hold on.

"This, of course, is not the right saddle," Edward mused as I fumbled about. "Though it will be more comfortable for you than being on foot for the journey up the hill."

I adjusted the cloak so it closed in the front, then pulled the hood over my head to ward off the cold. Inhaling deeply, I caught the scent of cedar smoke, cinnamon, and cloves emanating from the warm fabric. I shook my head. The alluring scent was a distraction. I needed to keep my wits about me. I needed to figure this all out so I could fix it.

Before I could acclimate to being on the horse, Edward hoisted himself up into the saddle and settled behind me with one arm hanging lightly around my waist while the other clutched the reins. I could feel warmth emanating from him, could feel his thighs tense as he guided the horse forward, could feel the strange sensation of being pressed up against this man. I tried to scoot forward in the saddle to put distance between us.

"Careful, my lady," he said softly. "We cannot have you slipping off and falling."

George looked up at us dumbfounded. It was clear that this latest turn of events was beyond his comprehension, and he had no idea what to do.

"'tis but a short walk," Edward called down to him. "Follow us." He snapped the reins, and our little procession began making its way up the muddy path.

3

RHIANNON

After trotting along in silence for several minutes, we emerged from the edge of the forest. A large castle came into sight, looming over us from the rise of a steep hill.

A curtain wall circled several towers built of deep gray stone; the largest of the towers rose four stories tall into the cloudy sky. A red and gold banner flapped in the wind above the castle's tallest turret, a splash of color amongst several plumes of smoke rising from within the walls. I could make out distant sounds of metal striking metal, sheep bleating, and the creak of a wooden wheel turning.

As we ascended the path, a village built into the valley below came into view, bisected by a river, dotted with thatched-roof buildings and distant fields of sheep.

My heart hammered beneath my ribs. This wasn't right. When Edward had mentioned Kendal Castle earlier, I dimly processed it as using the ruins of the ancient structure as a landmark. Not an actual, standing, living castle.

I glanced down at George to see if he noticed what I did. He was staring up at the castle, pale, jaw slack, hand twisted so tightly around the sheepskin draped over his shoulders that his knuckles were white.

When we approached the castle's bridge, Edward dismounted. I breathed a sigh of relief to no longer be pressed against him. He'd spent the ride with his arm around my waist and his hand on my hip to keep me from sliding off the horse; though his intentions seemed clear and relatively innocent, something about the interaction left me feeling even more off-balance than I already was.

A stone bridge arched over a muddy moat dug deep around the perimeter of the castle. At the other side of the bridge was a humongous wooden door, well over twelve feet high, nestled between two large towers and guarded by men wearing leather doublets, keeping their hands on the handles of the swords hanging at their sides.

Again, it was a sight I understood—I'd seen movies, read historical fiction, and studied history, after all—yet it was painfully strange. Had we stumbled into some sort of historical reenactment? A movie set where each actor was committed to method acting? A weird cult where people lived like it was still the Middle Ages? God, I hoped not; I didn't have the energy to deal with a cult on top of everything else.

I gripped the horn of the saddle and inhaled slowly. I wanted to rub my temples, to close my eyes for a bit and open them to find it all made sense again. Yet perched precariously atop the swaying horse, I didn't dare move a finger—much less close my eyes—for fear of falling.

Before we stepped onto the bridge to proceed through the gate, Edward paused, halting the horse's steady trot. In a low voice he said, "This is very important. We will tell the servants you are distant relations of the baron who met significant misfortune on the road while traveling to witness the equinox." He patted the horse's snout. "There will be questions, of course, but this should calm the suspicions until Lord Henry returns from court." Edward tugged the horse's reins, resuming the procession before we could respond.

Edward's mannerisms, from the moment he slid off his horse when we first encountered him on the road, to now, indicated he was used to being obeyed without discussion.

George glanced up at me, face knotted with worry, appearing increasingly helpless with each new insane development.

As we ambled over the bridge, the guards on either side of the door pulled open the hulking wooden slabs, allowing us to pass through. I looked up as we passed under the stone arch of the doorway to see a menacing, spiked iron gate held open above us.

Once it closed, we would be trapped inside.

"My lord," the guards bowed to Edward. As we passed through the entry, the guard closest to me gave me a slight bow, but kept his sight fixed on my bare feet peeking out from underneath my blanket. I curled my toes under, trying to shrink my feet out of reach of his gaze.

Through the gated entrance, our trio entered a bustling courtyard. Within the courtyard were structures you'd find in an average medieval castle: a small chapel, lean-tos full of hay, a blacksmith's shed, and stables. Scurrying all around were women wearing woolen dresses that brushed across the muddy ground and men wearing tunics and hoods, all in varying shades of green and red and yellow. They carried baskets of bread, linens, and vegetables or hauled stacks of wood and pails of water from the well in the center of the courtyard. A stocky man with leather braces on his wrists and several tools hanging from his leather apron led a horse across the expanse. He narrowed his eyes at us as he passed but did not say a word.

"What in the actual fuck," George exhaled next to me.

I could only nod.

I startled when Edward touched my leg to get my attention. He helped me slide off the horse and steadied me as I stumbled a bit, still disoriented, like I was waking up from a haphazard dream in the middle of the day.

"Wait here," he instructed before heading towards a man walking in our direction, with long black robes billowing in the wind.

"What ... uh," George ran his hand down his beard. "What do you think is going on here?" he finally choked out. The pallor of his skin and trembling hands mirrored my own growing panic. That's right, I was starting to panic.

I clutched the cloak tighter around my body. Beyond the strangely dressed people in the courtyard was a bigger problem: yesterday, Kendal Castle did not exist. It was nothing but a pile of stones and a few signs depicting life in medieval Kendal.

Life that looked disturbingly like what was happening right in front of us.

4

Kendal, England · September 2020

Rhiannon

George shivered as rivulets of water streamed down his neck and shoulders, soaking through his jeans and water-logging his completely weather-inappropriate leather jacket. Under a sodden red wool beanie, his long hair was plastered to his face, making him look like a miserable wet cat.

"I should've picked a castle with a roof to explore," he grumbled while pulling his useless jacket tighter against his body.

George's style is eclectic and varies. Most days it can best be described as "punk band bassist attends a poetry slam in Los Angeles." On a sunny day in Atlanta, his ripped jeans, thrift store cardigans, silver jewelry, and various band T-shirts with the sleeves cut off make perfect sense. But on a rainy autumn day in northern England, he just looked uncomfortable.

While George struggled, my feet were cozy in fleece-lined rain boots and my head remained dry under the hood of my impermeable rain jacket. Though we brought an umbrella on this trip, the stiff winds on the castle's hill rendered it unusable.

We stood in the ruins of Kendal Castle, a relatively obscure pile of black stones overlooking a quiet town in England's Lake District. Most of the castle had been dismantled over the centuries, its stones pillaged to build new, more useful, structures for the inhabitants of this gorgeous landscape.

However, there remained a footprint of what it once was. A low ring of stones—remnants of the curtain wall—circled a wide plane of smooth grass that used to be the courtyard, giving us a clue as to the castle's significant scale. I stood in the middle of the ring, imagining the grand lords and ladies who walked in this place before me, wondering what they discussed and how they felt and whether any sunlight shone through the windows of the castle in this spot.

"Why didn't you pack a raincoat?" I was annoyed. I'd wanted to spend time exploring the ruins but had a feeling our time would be cut short due to George's lack of preparation.

"I was trying to pack light. And I thought we'd be spending our time hanging out in pubs and what not."

"In a pandemic?"

He just shrugged.

"It's not like you don't know how to dress for rain. And you've been to England far more than I have. I don't get it."

"I wasn't thinking ahead," he sighed while turning away from me.

"Of course you weren't," I snarked under my breath. This was George: never planning ahead, always trying to make things easier on himself, which somehow made things much more difficult in the long run.

He wandered over to a set of signs detailing life in medieval Kendal, the only indicator this place was still being tended to as a historical landmark. Unlike other British castles, this one had no parking lot or gift shop, no admissions or lines, no docents wearing period-appropriate costumes taking you on tours and letting you know what famous historical figure was born in what room. We were the only people standing in the rain, letting the quiet of the steady drizzle envelope us.

I found I rather liked the solitude. I enjoyed getting to dip into my imagination about what this place was like without the hum and crush of tourist crowds breaking the spell.

When George ambled back towards me, head down in a futile effort to keep the rain off his face, I fought the urge to criticize his poor clothing choices again. Before we even left on this trip, I'd written and deleted numerous texts reminding him to bring rain gear and hiking boots. A force of habit from when we were together.

But it was no longer my business what he wore. He could live his life as he wanted, as I would live mine.

"I really hate my dad right now," he muttered.

"Why?"

"Because instead of having just one basic conversation about anything important, anything real, he's once again sent us on a stupid quote 'adventure' with few directions and a questionable purpose. Even on his deathbed he couldn't be straight with me about anything. Why are we here, Rhiannon?" George waved his arms around, indicating he meant more than just the castle ruins. "Why did we come all this way for some stupid, shitty cottage? I mean. I mean," he hesitated. I could tell when he wanted to cry but was working to hold it back. "I mean he couldn't just leave me a nice letter and some money like a normal parent? Why does it have to end like this? And this is so, so like him. I mean, he couldn't have sent us to a cottage in a booming tourist trap so we could make some money off it? I've never even heard of this place before."

Though he tried to hide it, I could tell George started crying then. The rain drops running down his cheeks may have obscured the tears, but his red-rimmed eyes and halted breath gave him away.

I shifted awkwardly from foot to foot, hands kept dry in my jacket pockets, unsure of what to say. My capacity to be the one who comforts, the one who plans, the one who takes care of everything, had long been spent into a deficit.

Despite this, despite everything, I still loved George—the kind of love that may wane but never ceases—and somehow that love filled the well again... if only for a moment.

"You and your dad are so alike," I said, shaking my head. "Your dad liked to dress up his avoidance and call it an 'adventure.' I mean, why have a deep conversation about something real when you can plan a scavenger hunt instead? But at least it was interesting, wasn't it?"

George laughed wryly, then tried in vain to wipe his wet face with the back of his sopping sleeve. "Is this how you feel all the time? Incredibly frustrated with me?"

"You mean like right now, where instead of exploring these interesting ruins, we're spending our time worrying about you, because you didn't think to bring a raincoat to a rainy climate? Because you're stubbornly committed to doing it your own way, regardless of how it affects anyone else? Yeah, you could say it's frustrating."

He winced and crossed his arms over his chest. "Maybe I took your detailed packing lists for granted."

"Amongst many other things," I sighed. "But it doesn't matter now."

The trip had gotten off to a rough start, testing the limits of my patience with George. While he'd planned the entire route from Atlanta to Kendal, when we got off the train, he realized he had not planned a way for us to get from the tiny train station to the cottage itself. Maps said it would be a twenty-minute walk, but it failed to show us the rocky and steep paths around the castle's hill to the general vicinity of our cottage—which wasn't even on the map.

With the sun setting, starving and cold, we dragged our suitcases along the precarious path to avoid spending anything on an Uber as we were both mostly broke and looking to save money in any way possible. When we finally tore through a significant amount of foliage to find the cottage, I was so angry with George and his absolute resistance to planning anything ever, I almost turned around and left.

But being tired and hungry shut down any escape plans. The bright spot was in finding that the stewards of our cottage—the lovely strangers who were maintaining the thing before we even knew it existed—had left a welcoming note for us and a fridge stocked with food. George baked frozen pizzas while I showered, both of which improved my mood significantly.

For our first full day here, we decided to explore the castle ruins as they proved to be one of the more interesting attractions (especially given how much was closed due to the pandemic), but the rain was wreaking havoc on our already challenging trip.

"I'm sorry I drove you so crazy." George murmured. It was almost imperceptible through the gusts of wind washing over us. "There's nothing more humbling than finding out you're just like all the worst parts of your father."

My own tears came in hot, unexpected. I turned my face up into the rain to feel the cool water wash down my cheeks. "It isn't just that. You haven't asked me how I've been doing even once since he died. He was my family too, you know. And I know he wasn't perfect, but I really miss him," I choked out. "He was more of a parent to me than anyone else. And even though this trip has been nothing but weird so far, it feels like we're retracing steps he took, which makes me feel closer to him. Like he's still with us. Like," I wiped my face pointlessly. "Like he can still help us."

George winced. "God, I'm really, really, sorry Rhi. Every part of this is so fucked up and I know I'm making it worse. But I don't know what to do to make it better." He looked around at the ruins of the castle circling us. "Wait, I do know one thing I can do."

He grabbed my hand and pulled me towards what remained of the castle's main living quarters. One part of the structure that still had any semblance of a roof was a tiny alcove that had possibly been a fireplace or storage room. It reeked of years of cigarette smoke, most likely from kids sneaking up here to take drags during their brief periods of freedom before curfew.

Though it stank and we both had to crouch a bit to keep our heads from striking the stones above us, the little space in the last vestiges of what was once a great castle was at least dry.

George took my hands and gazed into my eyes. "Rhi, in all seriousness, how are you doing right now?"

His clammy fingers lightly holding mine were the first significant human touch I'd had in...well, a long time. Too long.

I regarded my estranged husband, unsure how to answer. I was perfectly okay and a mess at the same time. I was functioning and falling apart all at once. I didn't think I could depend on him, but out of force of habit and a lingering bit of love, I still wanted to try.

"I don't know," I replied. "I don't know what I'm supposed to make of any of this."

He nodded. "It's been a wild year, hasn't it?"

"God, has it ever! It's been a wild few years, really." I wiped a fresh tear from my cheek. "Brutally hard years, too."

George looked down at our hands, fingers intertwined, and I could tell he was trying not to cry again. "Brutal," he agreed.

The rain let up, turning from a steady drizzle to a pressing mist. George shivered in his sodden clothes, huddled against the stones.

I gave him a weak smile, one last gesture of camaraderie.

He returned my smile, but it was tinged with sadness. These days, everything seemed to be wearing a coat of sadness. "What now?"

I squeezed his hand and released his fingers. "Come on, let's get you inside before you turn hypothermic."

5

GEORGE

It is a truth universally acknowledged, that a married man in possession of a good wife must be in want of a fortune. And if he fails to secure said fortune—plus does some other dumb shit along the way—he will be in danger of losing his wife.

That is the situation I found myself in when things began to get weird.

After returning to our cottage at the base of the castle's hill, I took a hot shower to regain some feeling in my extremities. My hands were so numb from the cold that I could barely grip the soap. Yet the feel of Rhiannon's fingers on mine lingered—I'd missed her touch so much, I found myself clasping my own hands together just to mimic the comforting contact.

Post-shower I changed into sweats and headed downstairs to wrap myself in every blanket I could find, leaving only my hands exposed to turn book pages. The cottage only had one bedroom with one bed, so I'd opted to sleep on the couch so Rhi could have the comfort of a mattress. While she was upstairs soaking in a bath, I settled in to read.

I sunk into the lumpy velvet couch cushions, grateful for the warmth of the crackling fireplace that took up almost an entire wall of the cottage, and cracked open *The People of the Book*—a novel Rhi had been bugging me to read, for like, a decade, but I'd never gotten around to. Right when I hit the point during reading when you're fully immersed, when the words automatically become images in your mind and the story starts to take off, someone knocked on the door. Quick, steady, forceful raps, as if they would not be deterred from me simply not answering the door. Which I seriously considered.

This would be aggravating in most settings, but to have it happen when you're on vacation in a secluded cottage in northern England—where you don't know a soul and a pandemic is raging—is a bit unnerving.

I ignored the door, but the rapping persisted.

"Fuck off," I muttered.

As Rhiannon was occupied, the task of extricating myself from my toasty cocoon and dealing with the interrupters was left to me. I tossed my book on the coffee table, shoved off my blankets, and stumbled to the door.

I fully expected to be greeted by a solicitor, some ambitious salesperson who was undeterred by the fact that this was an incredibly isolated house set far from the road. Instead, two people stood before me: a woman holding a giant picnic basket and a man clutching a bottle of wine. Both looked like they were in their early fifties, tall, blonde, and dressed for what my imagination assumed Brits always wore while traversing the English countryside: knee-high rain boots, wool sweaters, canvas hunting jackets, and herringbone newsboy hats.

Most unnerving though was the fact that the man looked alarmingly like my father. He had the same gray-blonde hair, pale blue almond-shaped eyes, straight dark eyebrows, and pointed jawline. Every question I had had about my vague lineage rose to the surface of my thoughts. And once again, I cursed Dad for never having given me enough information about anything regarding our family history besides vague platitudes about "distant English relatives."

We stared at each other for a few beats, as the blonde couple looked as stunned to see me as I, them.

Finally, the man clutching the bottle of wine spoke in a wavery baritone with a light scouse accent. "My name is Henry de Ros and this is my wife, Gwen." He rested his free left hand on her shoulder. "We're the stewards of this cottage. We came to meet you as Albert's barrister informed us you had come to visit and get the lay of the land, as it were."

Gwen held out the basket. "And we brought goodies." Her eyes welled with tears as she said this.

I ignored the outsized reaction and took the basket (which felt heavy enough to contain a few spare bowling balls and lead weights) and set it on the floor next to me. They stared at me expectantly.

"Oh. I'm George, Albert was my father—" I began to introduce myself, but hearing my name caused Gwen to place her hand over her heart as her tears flowed freely. Henry wrapped his arm around her waist, pulling her closer to his side.

"My apologies, but we were devastated to hear of Albert's passing." Henry explained while rubbing his wife's arm.

"Of course," I replied with as much empathy as I could muster. "Dad had lots of friends so it's always nice to meet people who knew him."

"Yes," Gwen replied through stifled sniffles. "You bear such a striking resemblance to him." She reached out as if to touch me, but Henry gently pulled her back by the wrist. "And you're here for the equinox, yes? It's marvelous, it really is. No rain predicted for tomorrow, so you're in luck!"

"Yes, I have heard the equinox is ... interesting." We stared at each other awkwardly before it occurred to me they were expecting to be invited in. Which, fair, seeing as they had managed this place for who knew how long.

"Do you ... do you want to come in?" I asked, stepping back to give them space to enter. "I apologize but my ... wife ... is occupied, otherwise she'd come down to meet you."

"That would be lovely!" Gwen clasped her hands together and stepped in without hesitation, pulling her wet boots off just inside the doorway. Henry followed her lead, pausing to remove his boots before the door had closed. Behind them, a gray cat with a white patch in the shape of Texas on his chest, who seemed to appear out of nowhere, waltzed on in as if he'd also been invited. (My fellow Lit majors, don't read too much into the shape of his white patch—it was literally in the shape of Texas, which is a very specific shape.)

I reached for the cat to toss him back outside, but Henry pointed to him and explained, "That's Gustav. He comes and goes as he pleases."

"Oh, okay." I got the impression the cat had as much right to the cottage I owned as I did.

Gustav trotted over to the fireplace, stretched out with a wide yawn, and curled up on the rug. The couple took seats at the dining table without hesitation, and Henry fished around in his jacket pocket to withdraw a corkscrew. "Wine glasses are in the cabinet by the fridge," he nodded his head towards the small kitchen.

I stood awkwardly in the middle of the room, trying to figure out who was the host in this situation. But ultimately decided to be helpful, grabbing the glasses while working out how to get Henry and Gwen to leave so I could get back to my book.

Rhiannon would probably be extremely irritated to have her quiet afternoon interrupted by strangers. And I was trying to relieve her stress—not add to it.

Henry popped the cork on a bottle of Bordeaux and poured four glasses. Gwen fetched her basket from the floor and pulled out various cheeses, crackers, and some chopped up fruit. "Just some nibbles," she explained.

"Now then, I expect you want to know about this cottage, yes?" Henry asked.

Upstairs I could hear water draining out of the tub. "Sure." I mustered as much enthusiasm as I could. Not only did this guy look like my dad, but he also apparently loved holding people hostage for unsolicited historical lectures—just like my dad. I slumped into a chair and reached for a glass of wine.

"Marvelous. Well then, to start, this land has been owned by our line—the de Ros's—for almost a thousand years." Henry launched into a full history of the lands, Kendal, how the cottage was considered part of the castle's estate, but when the castle fell into disrepair, then ruins, the cottage became its own independent property, which they had tended to for years.

I kept one ear tuned on him, nodding politely, while also listening for Rhiannon upstairs.

When Henry paused his lecture, I asked offhandedly, "What happens if we want to sell it?"

"Sell it?" Gwen asked, verging on horrified. "Oh no, no, I'm afraid you cannot do that. But, oh, you won't want to!" She reached across the table as if she wanted to grab my hand before Henry shot her a look and she withdrew it, looking chastised. "That is to say, be here tomorrow to witness the equinox and you will see you absolutely do not want to sell it. That's all."

She looked to Henry and he gave her a short nod of approval.

"Okay ... but, like if we really wanted to sell it, how would we go about doing that?" I needed to know we had options. Especially given that Rhi and I were too broke to even file for divorce, it seemed necessary to see about selling this unexpected asset we'd just inherited.

The cottage was small—only a large main room consisting of a living area, dining area, and kitchen, plus a bedroom and bathroom upstairs—but it was well-maintained and could easily be a second home or vacation rental for someone. Given our lack of funds, it'd be dumb to not at least consider selling it.

Henry sipped his wine and fiddled with the stem of the glass. "You can only sell it to us. And I'll entertain an offer. If—and only if—you let us know what you think of the equinox."

Before I could follow up on that absolutely bonkers requirement, Rhiannon came down the stairs wearing leggings and an oversized sweatshirt. *My* sweatshirt, I realized with a stab in my heart.

"Hello?" she paused on the bottom step.

Henry and Gwen both rose, and from the corner of my eye I could see Gwen's tears starting up again.

"My lady," Henry put his hand on his chest and gave her a little bow. "Please, come join us."

"My, look at you!" Gwen said breathlessly, as if she knew Rhiannon. Which, she did not.

Rhiannon gave me a confused look while she made her way to the table. I shook my head. I had few answers.

"This is Henry and Gwen de Ros," I explained. "The stewards of the cottage. They were just telling me what we would need to do to sell it."

"Which you should not," Gwen interjected.

"Right," Rhiannon replied. "And why is that?"

Henry and Gwen gave each other a look that seemed to contain a multitude of meanings. Gwen nodded, and said, "Because tomorrow you will see during the equinox what an asset this little cottage truly is." She extended a hand to her husband. "Come now, Henry, we have intruded on these young people long enough."

The tone shifted so quickly I wondered if I had offended them with this talk of wanting to sell the cottage. They had settled in as if they were going to stay for a bit, only to abandon half-drunk glasses of wine and an uneaten cheese spread.

The de Ros's pulled on their boots, gave us a strange look before smiling at each other, then breezed out the door calling out one more reminder to be home to watch the equinox.

After they left, Rhiannon spread some sharp cheddar dip on a cracker and commented, "That was weird. What's this obsession with the equinox? Also, did you notice that Henry looks a heck of a lot like your dad? And like you, for that matter." She popped the cheesy cracker in her mouth. "And what's with the cat?" she asked around her mouthful, nodding her head towards Gustav, who was now belly-up and purring by the fire.

"I did and I have no idea about any of it. Only that if we want to sell this thing, it can only be to them, and we have to watch this magical equinox first to make the deal."

"Well, that's easy enough," Rhiannon mused while rummaging around in the basket of goodies. "Ooh, chocolate!" she exclaimed, pulling a Cadbury bar out. "At least they brought good snacks."

The next day was clear, though windy and cool with the early autumn setting in. Rhiannon is nothing if not great at following directions, so she set a clock timer to let us know when the specific equinox time was. Despite this, she also insisted we stay close by, just in case.

When late afternoon rolled around, we were both bundled in blankets on the couch, books in hand, feet to feet, eating the last of the chocolate the de Ros's brought us the day before.

Sunlight shone through the window, moving at an angle that cast a shard of light across the room. Roughly a minute before Rhiannon's equinox timer went off, she sat up and noticed that the beam of light was almost perfectly lined up with the oak tree that supported the northeast corner of the cottage.

"Hey, look at that," she pointed as the shard of light hit the tree, lining up perfectly right as Rhiannon's timer went off.

The tree itself started glowing. I watched, in awe, as I felt myself somehow being turned upside down.

Which was the last thing I remembered before plummeting face-first into a stone wall.

6

GEORGE

We huddled against the castle's outer wall, waiting for Edward as he spoke with a man who kept shooting us hostile glances, still clad in the cloak and blankets we'd been offered earlier, feeling exposed and absurdly out of place. People in the courtyard were giving us more than just a cursory glance. Some stopped and stared, unabashedly, jaws slack. A few made the sign of the cross over their chests as they scurried past us, gazes averted, frowning. And others glared at us before hurrying away to whatever it was they were doing before we showed up and disturbed the peace.

I supposed that if I saw us in my castle, feet muddy, hair soaking wet, wearing only blankets and a sheepskin, I would stare too.

"Cover your tattoos," Rhiannon hissed.

"What?"

"Pull your sheepskin over your arms. I think that's why people are glaring at us."

I rolled my eyes but followed her directions. Tattoos were common, though it occurred to me we were in strange territory and I should cooperate.

Edward parted ways with the man he'd been speaking to, who flashed us one more suspicious glance before stalking away.

When he approached us, Edward stopped several feet short of where we were standing and called out, "Wait here for Clifford, the steward. He will ensure your care."

I gave Edward a thumbs' up and he flinched, narrowing his eyes before turning away.

"It was completely different," Rhiannon said out of nowhere.

"What was?"

"This castle. It was empty. Ruins. Yesterday we were here, walking around the ruins. This is Kendal Castle, is it not? Isn't that what Edward said? We were here yesterday, when it was a pile of rocks. How is this possible? Is there more than one Kendal Castle? Is this ... like, a replica? Is that even thing?" She shook her head. "I don't understand."

"It's okay. I'm sure there's a reasonable explanation for all of this." I instinctively went to wrap my arm around her shoulder, but hesitated, unsure that's what she wanted. We had gone from being an affectionate couple who constantly held hands and cuddled, to awkwardly navigating chaste hugs and unexpected brushes against each other. Since my raised arm was already mid-air, I settled for patting her on the head.

Rhi gave me a confused look before taking a step backwards, away from me. Which, fair.

After mulling over multiple possibilities as to what could be happening, I'd moved past the part of denial where I thought this was surely a strange dream and settled on one obvious—yet impossible—explanation. An explanation so outlandish, so inconceivable, I barely allowed myself to consider it.

"I can't shake this feeling we're someplace we should not be." Rhiannon mumbled. "Even though I still have no memory of how we got here. It was just, couch, then this. How?"

"It'll be okay," I answered with more confidence than I had any right to feel. "I'm sure we'll get answers soon." The words came out sounding false. Even I didn't believe them.

Before we could discuss it further, Edward emerged from one of the castle's massive wooden doors and strode purposefully towards us. Trailing behind him was the same man he'd been talking to earlier, a lean, gaunt young man with close-cropped black hair and blue eyes. His face was drawn into a grim expression, accentuated by the black cloak he wore, held tightly to his body. Securing the cloak was a silver brooch, adorned with simple jewels—a similar but less extravagant design as Edward's brooch. I glanced up to see the same design, a ram's head with some sort of tree, on several of the flags flying from the castle's turrets.

"This is Thomas Clifford," Edward gestured to the man before him. "He is the castle's steward and thus will tend to you. Clifford, these are relatives of Lord Henry, who met misfortune on the road when they were robbed and left with nothing. Assure our guests are well-cared for."

Clifford bowed slightly to Edward but didn't say a word. His eyes had not left Rhiannon since he first emerged from the door, trailing behind his lord. I stared down this Clifford. It was not lost on me that the men here were blatantly ogling my wife, which both irked and concerned me.

Rhiannon's dark auburn curls, hazel eyes, full lips, and tawny skin made for an unusual—and alluring—combination in northern England. She was clearly not from these parts, and as such, was attracting unwanted attention.

I took a step to my left so my arm brushed her shoulder. Rhi was trembling, and I felt an instinctive need to protect her from both the cold and the malicious gazes.

Edward addressed us. "I have business that cannot be delayed. We shall meet again at dinner in the great hall. You will join me at the family's table." He turned on his heel and strode off towards the chapel in the courtyard.

"Follow me," Clifford commanded, heading towards the doors he had just emerged from, not looking back to see if we followed him.

As both men spoke, I marveled at the odd phenomena of hearing two languages at the same time—one rough, guttural, and vaguely familiar. The other a standard English with a British accent that, though overly formal compared to what I was used to, was still understandable as my language. The clear words I knew were layered over the quieter, softer guttural language. So soft, that every time I heard it, I thought I was imagining things. One glance at Rhiannon's scrunched up face told me she heard it too.

"Go ahead, lay it on me." Rhiannon held her arms out, letting the massive sleeves of the garment they'd dressed her in flap like sails in the wind.

"Lay what on you?"

"Whatever insane theory you have as to what's going on here. We both know you have one. Let's hear it."

I crossed my arms and leaned against the post of the bed in our newly assigned chambers. "To be fair, given the evidence, would my theory really be that insane?" I pointed to her flowing velvet gown. "I mean, look at what you're wearing. Look where we are!"

Agnes, the ladies' maid Clifford summoned, had dressed Rhi in a velvet dress the same color blue as Edward's tunic. The dress had long, wide sleeves—so wide they almost dragged on the ground. I touched the collar of her dress, which was lined in what appeared to be a dark brown fur (mink, perhaps?). Beneath the velvet, Rhi held up her leg to show me she was wearing a white linen undergarment, almost like a nightgown, with sleeves cuffed tightly against her wrists with ties.

"You look beautiful, but this is kind of crazy, isn't it?" I placed my hand on my own velvet-clad chest. "As is the fact that I'm currently wearing tights and a cloak. And all of this is attached with laces and ties. Not a single zipper or button to be found."

Rhiannon fiddled with the laces on the side of her waist that cinched the dress close to her body. "Agnes said this belongs to Lady Gwendolyn, so they had to adjust it for me."

"And I'm wearing the Baron of Kendal's garments, so at least we're a matching set." I cleared my throat. "So, how much more evidence do you need before I lay out my so-called insane theory?"

Rhiannon didn't answer for what felt like several minutes. She bit her bottom lip, fidgeted with the fabric of one of her gargantuan sleeves, and gazed around at our bedroom—all signs she was considering before answering.

Rhi is a science teacher so she's all about the evidence. Whenever I make an assertion about anything, she chortles, "Show me the evidence!" The only way to persuade her is to build a case of indisputable facts and substantial data that can withstand the scrutiny of peer review.

And I felt like we'd been here long enough that the evidence spoke for itself: we had traveled back in time.

We'd been led up a twisty, narrow stone stairwell to a room on the third floor of the largest of the castle's towers. In our quarters within the mysteriously reappeared Kendal Castle, a giant four-poster bed occupied most of the space. Two stuffed armchairs faced the long fireplace—the room's only source of heat. A narrow window cut into the thick wall allowed in a bit of light. A few woven rugs were tossed over the clay tile floor, and several colorful tapestries depicting various domestic and romantic scenes (all of life in the Middle Ages) hung along the white-washed plastered walls. In one corner a massive wooden armoire stood, where Agnes had stored extra garments that she had scrounged from around the castle.

Rhiannon patted the white silk headdress wrapped tightly around her head and gave me a resigned sigh. "Let me guess. You're going to theorize we traveled back in time. Right? And God help me, because there's lots of evidence to support it. Like, a stupid amount of evidence. So much so, I'm almost relieved because it means I'm not having a stress-induced psychotic break. Is that what you were going to say?" She twirled around, causing her skirt to float a bit before facing me with her hands on her hips.

My shoulders relaxed and dropped. I hadn't realized I was tensed up, waiting for her to come to the same insane conclusion. "Well, yeah. I mean, look at this place. Look at us! I'm glad we agree that this is happening. I thought you'd need more convincing."

Rhiannon cocked her head and stared at me. "I mean, how could I not even consider it? This is a literal castle. Not ruins, but a fully alive medieval ecosystem.

Science says it's impossible, but science also says to look at the evidence. And this has gone on way too long to be a dream. Plus, it's too elaborate to a be a prank or some historical village. I was hoping it was some kind of re-enactment, like a Renaissance fair on steroids, but no one has this kind of funding."

I chuckled. "When Edward led us over the bridge, I was looking everywhere for cameras or something to indicate this was a movie set. But there's nothing like that. Plus, that doesn't explain the whole falling into an old cottage thing."

Rhi's eyes widened and she smacked her hand to her forehead. "Holy shit. *The cottage*. George, I don't think we fell into some random cottage. It's *our* cottage."

Several seemingly unrelated pieces fell into place. Obvious pieces we hadn't even considered putting together when our focus had been entirely on figuring out where we were and what happened to our clothes.

We stared at each other, wide-eyed with the terror of understanding.

"Oh fuck. You're right." I started laughing. Desperate, painful, I'm-losing-my-grip-on-sanity, laughing. I sunk to my knees, clutching my sides while trying to catch my breath. Because I understood all at once what we were up against. I'd been so concerned with the castle, and trying to understand what was happening, I'd totally forgotten about the cottage. And everyone's weird preoccupation with making us watch a stupid equinox. I gasped, still trying to breathe. "I get it now."

"What?"

"Everything. All of this," I gestured to the room around us. "It's on purpose. We were dropped here on purpose." I exhaled a slow breath, wiped my eyes, and calmed myself. "This is real and it's on purpose. I think ... I think my dad did this on purpose."

Rhiannon sunk to her knees beside me, her skirts pooling around her like a cloud. She looked gobsmacked. "The cottage. The weird letter." She looked at me, wide-eyed. "The goddamn equinox."

Breathe in, breathe out.

I had to think clearly.

"We have to get back to the cottage. Hopefully it'll send us right back home." Even as I said it, I understood the flaw in the plan. The critical piece of information that everyone from my dad to Henry and Gwen de Ros had emphasized repeatedly: the equinox. "Except ... the mother-fucking equinox," I whispered.

"I wish we had the letter," Rhi mused. When we'd inherited the place, we were given a cryptic set of directions that were now missing. It's not like we were dumped here with pockets or anything.

Rhiannon stood up and extended her hand to me. I could tell she had moved past shock and was quickly gathering her bearings. This was simply another problem for her to solve, a conundrum that could be resolved with enough determination.

I grabbed her hand and pulled myself up, shaking dust off my black wool cloak. "Me too. But seeing as we were dropped here completely naked, I have little hope that the notes made it with us."

"Listen, there's no way your dad sent us here without a way home. We just have to figure it out. I'm sure it'll be obvious once we give it some thought." Rhiannon stood in front of a polished piece of metal hanging next to the armoire that served as a mirror. "What do you think of this headdress thingy?"

Rhi's hair was twisted into two buns, each wrapped in white silk, like a medieval Princess Leia. I came up behind her and squeezed one of the fabric-wrapped bundles on top of her head. "I like your usual braids better."

Rhiannon typically wore her long, curly auburn hair in a revolving series of braided hairstyles, meant to keep the unruly strands out of her face as she worked with Bunsen burners and formaldehyde-preserved creatures while she taught high schoolers chemistry and biology. And though I loved it when she let her fiery hair fly free, her braids were her signature style for when she meant business.

"I'll admit, the head wrap isn't very comfortable," she paused to scratch the side of her head through the fabric. The silk was even wrapped around her throat, completely covering everything but her face. "But all the other women are wearing them, and I was getting tired of people staring at us, so I'm willing to endure … just a little longer." She gulped, the first sign she wasn't as confident in getting this resolved quickly as she'd initially appeared to be.

I rubbed my face. "Honestly, I'm still in shock. I don't know how you're so cool about it all. I can barely process a thought right now."

Once the possibility of time travel had settled in my brain, it interrupted all other thoughts. It was like a flashing neon sign in my head blaring: YOU TRAVELED BACK IN TIME! HOLY FUCK TIME TRAVEL IS REAL! Who could think about anything else under such circumstances?

"Honestly, I'm barely holding it together," Rhiannon whispered, eyes wide as she looked at me from where she stood in front of the mirror. "I feel numb. Like, I should be terrified. And that will set in. But right now, all I can process is that we *traveled back in time*!"

I nodded. "You have the same neon signs flashing in your head that I do."

Her eyebrows rose. "These thoughts are inescapable! It's hard to think through it. That's why I'm focusing on the headdress. How is this even possible? And if this is possible, then what else is?"

"I don't want to go there. I think I'm like, one more surprise away from a heart attack. I need to think about something else, if possible."

"Okay," Rhiannon nodded. "How about this," she held up her flowy sleeves. "This type of dress is called a 'houppelande.' Agnes said Lady Gwendolyn would not mind that I'm wearing it, seeing as we're apparently kin and all. But it still feels weird. It's not terrible, though I think getting used to the full skirts will take some time. They're awfully heavy and drag on the floor a bit. Lady Gwendolyn must be taller than me. While I wish I was wearing jeans and T-shirt, maybe a nice sweater given the cold, at this point, I'm just happy to be dressed at all." Rhiannon's chattering about her wardrobe calmed me, distracted me to the point I could catch my breath.

Things had been so strained between us, I'd almost forgotten what it felt like when we were clicking, when the bond between us glimmered with tenderness and care.

"Why don't you tell me about your clothes," Rhiannon requested, continuing her helpful distractions.

My own garments, also made of thick blue velvet and fur, were almost as cumbersome as Rhiannon's outfit. Clifford sent me a valet named Barrow—a nervous boy no older than maybe eighteen—who arrived with arms full of Lord Henry's clothes as he was the only one tall enough to provide garments that would fit.

Once Barrow had dressed me and Clifford got a good look, he took a step back, putting his hand to his chest. "You are surely a de Ros," I heard him murmur, but his tone did not indicate he thought this was a good thing. Which increased the ever-present uneasiness that resided in my gut. Edward had mentioned the baron and his entourage were away, and I hoped we would be gone before they returned from wherever they were.

"Well, like you, I'm happy to be wearing actual clothes," I told Rhiannon while holding up one foot, clad in a calf-high black boot with a long pointy toe. "And shoes. You take shoes for granted until you have to walk barefoot up a rocky, muddy hill in the rain."

Rhiannon glanced at my new footwear. "Did you ask about taking a shower like I did? They had no idea what I was talking about but offered to fill a bath when I kept mentioning bathing, washing, and so on. Though I cringed when I saw how much work went into it. I asked before I even gave the time travel theory much weight, and now I feel bad for creating all the extra work."

We traveled back in time and Rhiannon was more concerned about not being a burden on the people working here than her own wellbeing.

I didn't have the same concerns. "Yes, I also asked for a shower, but I felt no guilt over it. Even when I saw that baths were the only option and it was going to be a whole thing. There was no way I was putting muddy feet in these boots. They also were keen to shave my beard, but I wasn't letting them near me with that razor."

"Hmmm," Rhiannon hummed without making eye contact with me. I knew I'd let my beard get too long, but it was my business. I could tell it was killing her not to say anything about it.

I cleared my throat, eager to change the subject. "Now that we're properly attired, should we explore?"

Rhiannon nodded.

I held out my arm and she slipped her hand into the crook of my elbow. "You know, yesterday when I was complaining about this castle not having a roof, this isn't the solution I had in mind."

Rhi laughed. God help me, she laughed at that stupid joke. And for the first time in months, despite the insane situation we found ourselves in, I began to think maybe, perhaps, somehow, we could be okay.

7

RHIANNON

Dinner in the great hall was an overwhelming, chaotic—yet strangely rhythmic—experience. Through the din of roughly a hundred people occupying massive dining tables spanning the length of the room, there was a clear pattern and protocol everyone seemed to follow. I watched in awe as the kitchen staff brought in huge platters of food, while gracefully dodging heads and hands and kicked out legs, and placed them on tables in a practiced order that looked like a choreographed dance. There were no plates or utensils, only huge slabs of bread people piled high with steamed cabbage and pieces of ham. Most people carried knives, with which they used to eat, before wiping them off and stowing them back in the pouches they wore attached to their belts.

I was grateful we had an invite to the family table, as it was a much smaller, elegantly carved walnut table sitting upon a dais at the front of the room, away from the fray.

Especially as the whispers and glares aimed at us from the crowd in the hall made me uneasy. They seemed to know we did not belong. Their animosity was palpable.

Edward was the only one who joined us at the head table. A servant followed him up the dais and pulled his chair out for him, then poured him a glass of wine from the carafe already on the table. "My wife has briefly joined the baron and lady in London, so as of late I have been dining in my private quarters." He took a sip of his wine and continued. "However, I could not leave such company to dine alone."

We both waited, without answering, as it seemed like Edward had more to say on that matter. But he did not continue, and before I could comment on what he'd said, the first course arrived. The only course of the meal that didn't make me want to die.

I would not say that I'm a picky eater (though George certainly would), but I am a particular eater. I like what I like, unapologetically, and I loathe what I don't like. Just when I was feeling good about sitting at the head table, I remembered enough of the history classes I took during my undergrad to recall that the medieval diet of the affluent was an erratic array of adventurous, decadent, and outright gross foods. I prayed those accounts were wrong.

Servants handed us damp cloths to wipe our hands. While everyone eating at the main tables went without plates and had to bring their own knives, I observed our table was set with silver plates, goblets, and what looked like wide-bladed butter knives. But not a fork in sight.

We started with a first course of cheese, almonds, and dates. These were all good, relatively safe choices for me. The cheese had an unusual funk to it, but tasted incredible so I didn't think too much about it.

The second course was a small pie filled with kidneys and liver. It smelled like blood and dirt. George gave me an alarmed look as they put the monstrosity on my plate. He knew I couldn't handle organ meats. He loved offal, so this was a treat for him. Normally, he'd eat what I couldn't (or wouldn't), but as he sat across the table from me, there was no discreet way of giving him my uneaten food.

But I also remembered the various draconian punishments for a wide-ranging list of offenses in the Middle Ages. A mild insult could rapidly escalate into being accused of being a goddamned witch, and I didn't know how Edward would respond to me snubbing his hospitality. Food in this time was a limited and precious commodity—it's not like you could just run to the nearest grocery store if you ran out of something. If I didn't eat the food, would it exacerbate an already perilous and awkward situation? I decided I couldn't risk offending him.

From the corner of my eye, I observed as Edward used his knife—and only a knife—to eat his kidney pie. We followed suit, mimicking his handling of the sole utensil on the table, but often clumsily dropping pieces of food back onto our silver plates before scraping them up again.

I ate the soggy, copper-tanged monstrosity, holding my breath between bites, chasing it down with copious amounts of watered-down wine, all while controlling my considerable gag reflex.

After Edward finished roughly half his pie, he asked as casually as if he were asking about my shoe size, "So, what do you recall before you ended up on the side of the road?"

My head was growing light with wine and the lingering effects of shock. But I needed to think clearly. We had traveled back in time, and the only person helping us needed a believable backstory for him to continue doing so.

George responded before I could. "We—or at least I, as I cannot speak for my wife—only remember that we were traveling from our home … in Germany." I gave him my most alarmed-looking face, my face that said, *this lie can get out of hand because we don't speak any German!* But he continued. "Where our destination is, we do not recall." He gestured to the darkening bruise on his forehead from where he'd smacked into the stone wall earlier. "However, I assure you that we will not overstay our welcome, nor wear out your hospitality." He put his hand on his chest and gave Edward a respectful nod. "As soon as we've recovered from our ordeal, we shall be on our way."

I may have been slightly drunk by then, but when George interacted with Edward, he looked and sounded so different from how I knew him.

My George veered from being a bit sarcastic and irreverent to completely disconnected, like he was often in his own little world. Sometimes to the point I felt like he didn't take very much seriously.

But this George came across as confident, refined, and quite serious.

As if he were speaking from one lord to another.

The performance worked because Edward smiled and nodded in return to George. "Please, do not fret about such things. As I said, I am certain you are kin of Lord Henry's, which, when you see the remarkable resemblance, you will agree." He poured himself some more wine. "And as such, there is no boundary on the hospitality we are prepared to offer you, until winter has passed and it is safe for you to travel again with your delicate wife." Edward turned the full weight of his gaze to me, unblinking, over the rim of his silver goblet.

Something fluttered in my stomach when he looked at me like that. I decided to ignore the feeling, pretend it hadn't snagged my notice at all.

"Yes, winter," George murmured, eyes boring into mine.

We both heard it: if we didn't figure out how to get home, and fast, we were about to endure a winter during what looked like the late medieval period. Year unknown. Pretending to be Germans with amnesia.

Holy mother of God.

I gagged and covered it up by pretending to cough, the reaction completely unrelated to the food in front of me. Though the food was obviously making the situation worse.

I closed my eyes and inhaled slowly, willing myself to shove this ever-encroaching panic back into the depths of my psyche. There was no need to panic because there was clearly a solution and I was going to find it and all would be well again. I could do this. I opened my eyes and gave George an overly confident smile. He looked relieved.

The third course—wild goose stuffed with dried fruits and some other suspicious ground meat—broke me from my reverie. It tasted like rancid lake water, cardamom, and rotten apples. I struggled through each bite, trying to chew just enough so I didn't choke, but not so much that the food had to stay in my mouth any longer than necessary. And I chased each bite with a gulp of wine. At least the texture was familiar, like baked chicken.

Which I could not say about the final course: boar baked in a mixture of its own blood and barley. Like a nightmare version of sausage. The texture was both tough and slimy in my mouth. It almost broke me. I clenched my shaking hands into fists and took slow, deep breaths between each bite and mouthful of wine.

I became envious of the simple cabbage and ham everyone else was eating. The head table—with its multi-course horror menu—didn't seem so great after all.

George looked deeply concerned for me and my abysmal progress with this meal. While he'd finished each of his courses, I was struggling to choke down even the smallest bites of mine. Though I was ravenous when we'd sat down for dinner, my appetite dwindled with each bite of food that tasted like blood. So. Much. Blood.

By the time they'd cleared the last course, I was decently drunk and one deep breath away from vomiting. I rose, unsteady on my feet, desperate to get out of the stifling, loud, smoky dining room.

George immediately stood with me, followed by Edward, as I realized was protocol for when a lady stands.

"Are you okay?" George asked.

"I'm fine," I waved him off. "I just need some air. Please," I motioned to their seats, "sit down. I'll be back soon.

Edward nodded, giving me a curt salute with his goblet to signal his regards.

George sat back down, frowning. "Are you sure—" he started to ask as I waved him off.

"I'm fine, really." I gathered up my ample skirts with one hand, stumbled off the dais and headed for the nearest door to the courtyard, while pressing my other hand to my mouth, trying not to panic.

8

GEORGE

Rhiannon was gone so long, most people had cleared out of the great hall and the fires had been left to dwindle. Edward had long since retired for the evening. As I sat, watching the embers in the massive fireplaces crackle and glow, my unease grew. I was torn between waiting for her in the great hall so we wouldn't miss each other, or going to find her in case something had happened.

Rhi had looked ill, if not totally drunk, when she stumbled out of the hall. And it's not like anyone had handed us a map to this labyrinthine castle. We were in strange territory, the sun had set, and we were surrounded by unfriendly faces. What if she was hurt? Lost? Or being bothered by one of the creepy men leering at her earlier? I would not forgive myself if she needed me and I wasn't there for her.

Decided, I went in search of my wife.

I found Rhiannon in the courtyard, bent over next to the well, retching into the trampled mud.

"Water," she croaked at me between gags, gesturing towards the well.

I grabbed the rope, praying there was a bucket at the end, and pulled. I was relieved when the rope strained against the weight, meaning water was coming.

When the bucket reached the lip of the well, I grabbed it from where it hung and handed it to Rhiannon, supporting the bottom while she drank, water sloshing over the sides and down her pale face. After she finished, Rhi inhaled a big gasping breath, coughed for a couple minutes, then seemed to calm a bit, regaining her composure.

"Are you okay?" I started rubbing her back with the light touch of my fingertips—something I used to do for her often to help relieve stress.

She gave me a wary sideways glance but didn't move. "I think I'll live," she coughed, leaning against my hand. "But if we stay here much longer, I'll need to figure out how to survive meals."

I didn't want to think about how long we could be stuck here. Without having a clue how the cottage worked, an escape plan was slow to form.

From across the courtyard, Agnes—the rotund and angry-looking ladies' maid they'd assigned Rhi—came scurrying over.

"Don't let her near me," Rhi wheezed, hand on her chest, still recovering.

"We're fine," I called out, waving her off. I made a mental note to ask about that later, when Rhi was feeling better.

Agnes halted her steps and glared at me. "Does the lady require assistance?" she demanded more than asked.

"No, I'm taking care of her. All is fine." I called out.

Agnes looked perplexed. She narrowed her eyes at me, wiped her hands on her apron, then stormed off back in the direction she'd come from.

"We can worry about how to get home tomorrow," I said while gazing up at the sky. The wind had blown the clouds away, revealing a pristine blanket of twinkling lights. Without the obscuring glare of city lights, we could see trillions of stars surrounding us.

When I was a kid, my dad spent hours trying to get me to learn how to navigate using the few stars we could see. But I was always more concerned with looking for shooting stars. I clung to the idea that they could grant wishes, and boy, did I have some wishes I wanted to come true. Any time I saw a flash of streaking light, thinking I got lucky, Dad would correct me and say, "No, that's just a plane/satellite/meteor, can't you tell the difference?" Which, I could not, given that I was just a little kid.

I never did learn how to star-navigate; I only learned I should stop wishing for anything.

But here ... these were all stars. Not an airplane or satellite in existence.

"Look up," I wrapped my arm around Rhiannon's shoulders and pulled her into my cloak to ward off the night's frigid air, gambling that she'd prefer the warmth of my contact over nothing at all, as she'd rushed out of the great hall wearing only the velvet dress.

Shivering, she leaned against me and turned her gaze up towards the sky. "Wow."

We stood like this for several minutes, awestruck with the scene above us, leaning against the only other person in the world who understood what this experience was like.

We should not have been there, it was not our time, and everything was wildly uncomfortable for people who were used to electricity and running water and eating with forks. But seeing those stars made all those concerns temporarily vanish.

"No matter what happens next, I'm glad I got to see this." I breathed.

"Me too," Rhiannon sighed. "No matter what happens next."

9

RHIANNON

I woke up that first morning aching from the tumble into the cottage and wracked with stomach cramps, certain I wasn't going to make it to the bathroom. Excuse, me *the garderobe*. Or worse, the chamber pot.

The bed beside me was empty. It was still dark outside. And it was impossible to tell what time it was as our room had no clocks. Out of habit, eyes still blurry with sleep, I fumbled around for my phone before realizing I had no such crutch. Sighing, I tucked my arm back under the covers. Our fire had dwindled to embers and the air in our room was so cold, I briefly considered just staying in bed and hoping for the best.

But another wave of urgent cramps twisted up my guts. I slid out from under the heavy wool blankets, stifled a groan from the wracking pain in my abdomen, and grabbed my cloak. The stone passages linking the castle's rooms were without fires save for a few interspersed torches, which meant I might as well have been heading outside given the frigid temperature. Clutching the cloak over my linen nightgown, with my feet shoved into floppy leather shoes, I trudged down a level to where the garderobe was.

I shoved open the door with my shoulder and was greeted by the worst sight imaginable: George, sitting on the plank, looking pale and miserable. The only light in the tiny room was a sliver of a window, casting us both in shadows, emphasizing the twist of his frown.

A garderobe (in case you've ever wondered how people in medieval castles used the bathroom) is a small room with a bench, with holes cut into it, that drop into any number of situations, depending on the castle. And that's pretty much it.

"Oh god, no, please," George whimpered when he saw me.

We understood then that our failing marriage was about to undergo the worst kind of intimacy test: there was no other bathroom, and our situations were clearly too urgent to figure out another plan or for me to wait for him to finish. We were in this together. In sickness and in health, as they say.

"If it makes you feel better, I'd rather die than share this garderobe with you," I groaned as I carefully sat on one of the precarious open holes that dropped into a void below, wincing as a crisp breeze caressed my undercarriage.

"Honestly it feels like I *am* dying," George muttered in reply.

I closed my eyes, visualizing a happy place with central heating, a bidet, 3-ply toilet paper—and blessed privacy.

We sat like this for several minutes, the quiet punctuated by an occasional whimper, both of us working to not make eye contact.

When my legs were falling asleep and every part of me felt like it was on fire despite being drenched in cold sweat, when I was hunched over and trying not to move for fear it would stir the pain, George rasped, "Do you think we have the plague? I mean, this is probably the plague time, right?"

"No, we'd have those black things at our neck," I gestured to my lymph nodes. "I think it's something we ate." Through the pain and nausea, I'd been working out what must have caused this, desperate for an answer that would yield a solution. The most obvious answer was either the (unwashed, unpasteurized) food or the (unfiltered, unboiled) well water—or both—were the source of our distress. I rubbed my hands over my face. Without looking at George, I explained my theory. "I think ... I think it's gut biome stuff. Nothing here is pasteurized and our systems are not used to the bacteria from this time." I took a deep breath and clutched my sides from the ensuing cramps. "Also, all we've been drinking is wine ..." I grimaced at the thought of any type of booze. "And not enough clean water."

I would have killed for clean, filtered, running water right out of the tap. I hadn't been able to brush my teeth and all the wine left a sour coating in my mouth. Which meant in addition to being sick, I was terribly thirsty. While the water from castle's well was most likely safe enough given the natural filtration the sand provided, the buckets it was transported in and the people transporting it were absolutely filthy. Plus, water was in short supply given the large population living here. There was only one well serving the entire castle. It's not like I could just fill a glass whenever I wanted.

"Right," George sighed. He leaned down and tore a thick strip of linen off the hem of his nightgown. "Here," he handed it to me. "For when you're done."

I took it, grateful he'd figured out a solution to the lack of toilet paper (besides the rag tied to the end of a stick, resting in a bucket of what smelled like vinegar). "Thank you."

"Hey, want to know a gross fact?"

"Sure," I agreed.

"These holes drop right into the moat. This castle is literally protected by a river of shit. I think the wind was the only reason we couldn't smell it yesterday."

I snickered, despite the disgusting revelation. "I mean, that's a good plan. What soldier would want to die, drowning in the feces of his enemies? I'd certainly think twice before attacking this place."

George laughed too. "It's a war strategy they conveniently leave out of textbooks. But sounds effective."

Another wave of cramping seized my sides. "Time travel sucks," I moaned while using the rough fabric to clean myself.

"Indeed," he agreed quietly. "We need to figure out how to get home as soon as possible. This is my only nightshirt, so I'm not sure what a long-term solution to the toilet paper thing will be." We both looked at the bucket in the corner. "I mean, we do know, it just seems... unhygienic." He shuddered.

"Which kind of describes everything here, if you think about it." I mused.

We glanced at each other then, squatting on those dank holes in a dark stone room, considering just how unhygienic—and unsafe—everything here was. George's brow was furrowed, his skin pale and slick with sweat, and the look of horror in his eyes matched what I was sure reflected in mine.

All my earlier bravado about not panicking was gone.

"Is it okay if I panic now?" I asked quietly.

He nodded. "I think this is as good a time as any to panic."

10

GEORGE

It took us about five days to fully acclimate to the food and drinks—long enough that Rhiannon and I got over our aversion to sharing the garderobe during our worst moments. Edward had various broths and teas sent to our chambers, plus some bread that was a soothing change from the elaborate meal that had gotten us both sick. He seemed unsurprised by our illness—though the servants were wary of us and avoided us like the plague. Trays of food were shoved into our room and the door slammed shut behind whoever had left it. Which, fair. They were literally trying to avoid what could be plague.

We also got used to sharing a bed again, after months of living separately. The first night Rhiannon clung to the edge of the small mattress, trying to keep a respectful space between us. But the fire only warmed so much of the room, and it dwindled through the night, taking the heat with it. As we lay awake, terrified and confused about our predicament, still in shock that we'd stumbled through time, Rhiannon shivered so hard the bed shook.

"Come here," I pulled her into my embrace.

"George," Rhi started to protest.

"You're so cold you're shaking the whole bed. You used to complain that sleeping next to me was like sleeping next to a bonfire. Why not take advantage of my excessive amount of body heat?"

She sighed and scooted back against me. "Fine, but this doesn't mean anything."

"Of course not," I whispered. But my body was already reacting to her pressing against me. Especially as she moved around, trying to get comfortable.

"I can feel that," Rhi complained.

"Sorry. Try not to wiggle so much."

She stilled herself, and before long, I could hear the rhythmic sound of her breathing indicating she'd finally fallen asleep.

From then on, we slept wrapped around each other, wool blankets heaped over us, desperate to keep every bit of heat contained.

Despite the hard mattress, despite the illness and itchy clothes and never-ending damp cold, despite the lingering shock of time travel, I found I slept more peacefully than I had in ages.

"Do you think we will eventually laugh about this?" I asked Rhiannon late one night as we clung to each other, winds howling outside.

"Depends if we make it home or not," she whispered.

Our persistent illness, combined with days of nonstop freezing rain, made getting back down to the cottage impossible. As each day passed, we grew increasingly uneasy that perhaps we'd missed an important window to get home. I tried not to think about the possibility we were going to be trapped here for the rest of our lives.

Based on the clothes, we seemed to be sometime in the early 15th century. If I let myself worry, my brain would dredge up my knowledge of English history: the various wars that destabilized the country for decades, combined with the occasional resurgence of bubonic plague, plus the usual oppression, filth, lack of technology, and general roughness of the late medieval period. There wouldn't even be coffee or chocolate or potatoes for another couple centuries or so, at best.

To occupy my thoughts, I took to hoarding all the pieces of linen I could find. If it wasn't for our horrendous trips to the garderobe, then it was because I knew Rhiannon—my germaphobe wife—needed them to maintain her cleanliness and her sanity. While we were in the practice of tossing the used strips into the rubbish pile, I knew this practice wasn't sustainable. Everything here was used multiple times, in a multitude of applications. Every scrap of fabric was precious and soon someone would notice how wasteful we were.

But I'd rather swallow my own eyeball than use the communal vinegar-soaked rags on sticks everyone else used.

Despite the cold and lack of sanitation, not everything was terrible. Once I felt well enough to leave our room and explore, I was gobsmacked by the experience of the world we were in. Without the constant bombardment of synthetic scents and industrial noises, my senses were reset. The air smelled of fresh earth, roasted chicken, dried herbs, cedar smoke, and clean wool. Water retrieved from the well in the middle of the castle's courtyard tasted crisp and mineral-fresh. Ripe apples were pulled right from the branches and served to us, their dense flesh sweet and tart and unlike anything I'd ever eaten before. We began the day lured downstairs by the smell of bakers hard at work producing loaves of fresh bread, served with butter churned right here in the castle.

The castle itself was its own little world where everyone had a role and everyone contributed to the well-being of everyone else who lived there, like a well-conducted symphony. Bakers made bread day and night (course-grained loaves for the servants, finely ground wheat bread for the baron and his family and guests) to feed the vast number of people living and working in the castle. Blacksmiths shoed horses; hammered out pots, pans, and various tools for the kitchen; and forged weapons for the cadre of guards. Cooks roasted pigs, wrapped dried fruits into pies, and stirred porridges and stews. There were servants who simply went from room to room tending to the fires: adding wood, cleaning out ashes, replacing the beeswax candles that were too precious to let burn for long. There were servants who cleaned out the chamber pots, others who did the considerable amount of laundry, and yet an entirely additional group who, we were told, followed the baron and his family around all day long, tending to their every request.

Agnes and Barrow were part of this staff, and they made sure we were dressed properly and in the right places at the right times.

Most servants owned only the clothes on their backs, plus perhaps one other outfit, and that's it. They slept wrapped in their cloaks propped up in corners or curled up by communal fires, as most didn't have beds—much less bedrooms. During their free time they drank ale and mead, told bawdy jokes and stories, played homemade instruments, and enjoyed each other's company anywhere they could.

Rhi and I—bored from the lack of constant information stimulation we had grown accustomed to—had taken to eavesdropping on conversations, collecting gossip and information about the workings of the castle. At night, we'd tuck into bed and share notes like we were discussing a reality TV show: "Did you know Agnes has a twin brother named Angus, and he's in charge of the horses? Anyhow, Cook was telling one of the bakers that Angus and one of the milkmaids were seen together in the stables, if you know what I mean." And so on. Castle gossip became our main source of entertainment. Without television, movies, magazines, books, podcasts, music, and social media, our content-starved brains clung to any form of external stimulation we could grasp.

While I loved getting to witness this lost history firsthand, and I certainly enjoyed my fair share of castle gossip, I had a more important motive for my observations: we needed to know what year it was. This seemed to be a critical piece of information for solving the mystery of how we got here—and how to get home again.

As there were no calendars hanging on walls, no phones packed with important information available with just one swipe, no daily newspapers with a printed date on the page, my only methods were watching and listening. It finally paid off.

11

RHIANNON

As I shuffled down the corridor towards the great hall for lunch, hoisting up my considerable skirts, George snagged me by the upper arm and pulled me into a side hallway. Before I could make a sound, he held a finger up to his lips and nodded his head in a direction where I could pick up the faint sound of voices.

When the voices faded, George smiled at me and whispered, "I know what year it is."

"How?"

"Did you overhear what they were saying?"

I shook my head. It was all echoes bouncing off the walls, nothing decipherable.

"The baron is returning from court where they were celebrating King Henry's wedding as part of the Treaty of Troyes."

George looked at me expectantly, with a smug smile. But I couldn't place a specific year based on that information alone. England had a lot of King Henrys.

"That's all?"

He made an exasperated noise and scratched his beard before continuing. "You, the person who likes to know all the things, don't recall what year that treaty was signed? Come on now, at least guess. Pretend its bar trivia and everything is riding on this answer."

I rolled my eyes. "There were lots of treaties and I've had a few things going on in my life since I last took a history class. Will you please just tell me?"

I had no capacity for time travel guessing games. We had spent the past several days getting our bearings: recovering from what felt like endless bouts of food poisoning, learning new manners and protocols about who could do what and when, remembering the layout of the castle, ignoring the fact that neither of us had bathed since our first day here roughly two weeks earlier, and desperately trying to stay warm in a damp stone building with no central heating. All while slightly drunk since the main beverages being served were ale, wine, and mead.

Given the rough lifestyle we were thrust into, trying to figure out what year we'd stumbled into came second to staying alive.

But I also understood that without knowing what year it was, it hampered our ability to figure out how to get home. Perhaps there was significance to the year we'd come to, or a pattern that would be revealed if we knew. I appreciated George's efforts; I just didn't want to overthink it.

He exhaled and dropped his shoulders, clearly disappointed I wasn't invested in this game. "Fine. It's the year 1420. That treaty makes England's King Henry the Fifth the legal heir to the French throne as well. We're in the midst of the Hundred Years' War."

I grabbed his upper arms. "George, how do you remember that? That's not even especially cool history. Also, holy shit! 1420? That means we went back in time *six hundred years*!"

"Shhh!" He looked both directions, making sure we were alone. I'd spoken louder than I realized. "I know," he nodded. "It's insane that this is happening. And I remember it because my dad talked about this treaty all the time. Like, he literally taught this lesson every semester in his medieval English history class, so I heard about it at least twice a year." George scratched his chin, dragging his fingers through his beard. "You know, I thought I did a good job of tuning him out because it was so boring, but lucky for us, apparently I hadn't."

I felt lightheaded with this revelation. Evidence aside, part of me still hoped this was a dream or some elaborate prank. I leaned forward and placed my hands on my knees, feeling like I was about to keel over. "I cannot believe this is happening," I moaned.

George held me by the shoulders to steady me. I'd been holding it together this entire time, fighting the panic like the champ I am. But panic was winning. Every time I thought I got my bearings, panic slugged me in the jaw and knocked me down again.

"What do we do? How does this help us?" For once, I didn't have a plan and didn't know where to start to form one.

None of my chronic overthinking prepared me for traveling back in time to the late medieval period.

"Well, we need to be careful. Very careful." George pulled me up and wrapped his arms around me so he could speak quietly into my ear. "If you recall, in this particular time and place you are considered my property as you are a woman and my wife." I immediately tried to jerk out of his embrace, ready to protest on multiple fronts, but he held tight. "Relax, you know I'm not going to be shitty about it."

I took several deep breaths, working to calm myself. Though my arms were hanging down at my sides, George made no movement to let go of me. The steadiness of his heartbeat calmed me, and I found myself wrapping my arms around his waist, returning his familiar embrace. The logical part of my brain demanded I let him go, lest I feel things I shouldn't be feeling. But my heart was longing for comfort and his specific, gentle touch. So I clung to him.

George caressed my cheek with his thumb and tilted my chin up until I met his gaze. "Rhi, seriously. You know me. I'm not going to let anyone hurt you. Nor will I abuse this awful situation. Okay?"

I knew he was right. I knew he wouldn't use this to put me in a bad situation, no matter what state our marriage was in.

"I know," I sighed. "It's just one more reason to panic. Which I'm trying not to do. Panic, that is."

For the first time in a long time, I had to rely on George again. Time travel aside, that also made me want to panic. Relying on him hadn't exactly gone well in the past ... or future, as it were.

George gazed at me, concern knitting his brows. "Maybe let yourself freak out a bit before getting it together? I feel like this situation warrants panicking. It's probably counter-productive to hold it in."

"Okay, but later, when I can scream into my pillow. People here already think we're dangerous weirdos. No need to confirm it." The fact that everyone pointedly avoided us and made the sign of the cross when we got too near, was not lost on me. Only Edward treated us with kindness and continued to emphasize we were welcome—even if no one else got that memo.

"Good. Speaking of not looking like dangerous weirdos, everything we say and do has to be completely aligned with what the other does. Our stories must match and we need to behave like a proper married couple. We're a team. Any discrepancies could raise suspicions—suspicions that could get us kicked out of this place. Or worse. Agreed?"

"You mean like your crazy story that we're from Germany? I can't believe Edward hasn't followed up on that. You're lucky no one has tried to speak to us in German."

George stroked his beard. "Yeah, that was kind of a knee-jerk reaction. I honestly didn't think we'd be here this long. But yes, to your point, we have to stick to it and be unified Germans." He cleared his throat. "And Spaniards."

"Wait, what do you mean, 'and Spaniards'?"

"So, I may have overheard Barrow commenting on your darker skin, and later when he was dressing me, I explained to him that you were Spanish. Which seemed like the best explanation, given Europe and all."

I rubbed my temples and fought the strong urge to shove George for going rogue, *again*, and making our situation even more complicated. "Are you kidding me right now? When were you going to tell me that?"

"Don't worry, this only happened, like a day or so ago."

I jabbed my finger into his chest. "Stop doing that! Stop barreling ahead without talking to me first! How can we be a united front if I'm always in the dark?"

George held up his hands and said, "Relax. Everything is under control." He grinned at me. "We will figure it out as we go."

"Oh my god," I tugged at my headdress, desperate to loosen the fabric before I started choking. "You cannot tell me to panic and then relax in the same conversation, while also giving me numerous reasons to panic and no reasons to relax. Do you understand?"

"Fair enough." He seemed unconcerned with how close I was to freaking out. "Which brings me to the most important task at hand. We need to figure out the rules of our particular kind of time travel." George tugged at his beard, a gesture I'd never seen him do before.

"What do you mean? What rules?"

He looped his arm over my shoulders so he could speak quietly into my ear. "Every time travel story must answer two questions: how does the time traveler get back home and how much impact do they have on the future, based on what they do while they're in the past? For example, in *Back to the Future*, they get home by powering up the DeLorean to eighty-eight miles per hour for the flux capacitor to work. And they establish that their actions in the past have a significant bearing on the future—including, but not limited to, erasing someone's entire existence. But other time travel stories, like *Outlander*, make it clear that you can't stop the inevitable. Thus, minimal impact caused by the time traveler's actions. So, we have to figure out exactly how the cottage works—because that tells us how to get home—and if anything we do here can negatively impact the future."

I considered this for a moment, soothed by having a problem to work on that didn't involve hygiene. "Well, the future impact thing is impossible to test out. We're six hundred years in the past, which means we have absolutely no way of knowing if what we do here will wreak havoc with the future. Or, on the flipside, if there's anything we can do now to make things better then. Since we have no way of knowing, I don't think we should worry too much about it."

George raised his eyebrows in surprise. I tended to be a stickler for the rules. But all rules have limitations, and we were confronted with a slew of them; it would be pointless to pretend otherwise. "Agreed. We don't have a photograph showing people fading into non-existence, so let's not stress ourselves out about that. As much as it sucks, there's no way to know for sure and I'd rather not twist myself into knots worrying about it. Ok, now the most important thing: how do we get back home?"

"We need to go back to the cottage. We've already wasted too much time being sick. What if there are additional clues we missed the first time because we were a bit ... distracted? What if your dad left us answers, somehow?"

"Fuck me," George exclaimed while rubbing his hand over his beard. "Do you know what this reminds me of?"

I nodded. "I do. And it's so, so expected if he had somehow mastered time travel. Right?"

Albert loved putting us through the ringer without our consent in the name of "adventure."

"Yes, absolutely," George sighed while scratching his face. I'd never known him to fiddle with his beard so much. "Back to the cottage, then."

"As soon as possible. Also, check your beard for lice. It's very common here. It's probably why they wanted to shave your face." Without waiting for his response, I darted back into the main corridor and made my way towards the great hall.

George trailed after me, calling out, "Wait, what about lice in my beard?"

12

RHIANNON

As we stumbled our way through the overgrowth to the cottage's front door, I could make out features of the landscape that were still intact when we inherited the cottage in our time. Most noticeably was the large oak tree that served as the cottage's northeast corner. While in 1420 the oak was considerably smaller, it was clearly the same tree. How it had managed to grow and support the cottage—rather than break the stone walls apart as the trunk expanded over the years—was a mystery. The vines overtaking the rest of the exterior somehow avoided the tree altogether.

We began by examining the front door: dark wood with chipped polish, cast iron hinges and door handle, wide breadth and made of thick planks. George ran his hands all along the edge of the door, framed in uneven stones, and along the threshold that was partially obscured by the creeping vines. There was nothing noteworthy—except that the door was locked. When I knew for certain we absolutely left it unlocked after stumbling out of the cottage a few weeks earlier.

After jiggling the handle fruitlessly, George shoved open the cottage's door with his shoulder, leaving it swinging on creaky hinges. We stepped inside to find everything completely undisturbed—even the missing blankets and rumpled mattress were exactly as we left them.

Using light streaming in from the open doorway, we went in opposite directions to find any clues that would help us understand how we got here and how to get home.

"You take the mantle, I'll take the bed," I said while kneeling next to the rickety frame. I ran my hands along the thin pieces of wood, pulled up the straw-stuffed mattress, and finished by pulling the linen mattress cover off and rooting through the straw itself for anything unusual. But there was nothing. I stood up and flopped down on the bed—forgetting the lack of foam and springs to cushion my fall.

"Any luck?" I gasped, shocked by the impact of my bottom hitting the hard slab of the bed frame. I was still getting used to everything being made of unyielding wood, metal, and stone. I had not realized how padded the 21st century was; everything seemed to be wrapped in memory foam, stuffed with polyester, protected by springy plastic, or bolstered with springs.

George was supposed to be checking the fireplace, but he stood with his back to me, head down and examining something. He tensed up before he looked at me from over his shoulder. "I don't think we're getting home anytime soon," he exhaled with a long breath.

"Why do you say that?"

He faced me and held up a blue velvet box, two pieces of parchment, and a skeleton key. "It's the stuff the lawyer gave me at the funeral. They were on the mantle, but we didn't see them earlier."

My stomach dropped as we confirmed, without question, that Albert had orchestrated this whole thing. The notes indicated he purposely lured us into this time travel escape room from hell and left us here to flounder with hardly any information to help us survive.

I rubbed my forehead, running my fingers under the edge of my tightly wrapped headdress. "What was he thinking?" I hissed. "We could die here!" My heart was pounding so hard I grew dizzy, despite still sitting down. I'd been nursing a lingering hope the time travel was an accident, or a fluke, or something that didn't involve someone who I thought cared about us shoving us backwards through centuries. A hope that shriveled into nothing when I saw the parchment letter in George's hand.

"You know what Dad would have said. You can die anywhere. Why not an on an adventure?" George shrugged defeatedly, like he'd already accepted this miserable fate.

I laid back on the bed, careful not to fall back too hard. I placed my hand on my forehead and exhaled, once again fighting the looming panic. "To think your dad used to be my favorite professor. How do you suppose the notes and key got here, but not any of our other stuff?"

George held the letter up to the light. "If I had to guess, based on how old this parchment looks, he used materials from this time period. Maybe things can only go back in time if they existed then? It would explain why my Norman coin is here, but its modern chain is not." He patted his chest where he now wore his coin on a leather string under his tunic. "I recall wondering why he wrote the notes on parchment in the first place. Maybe to ensure they came back with us? It's impossible to prove right now, but that's my only theory as to how they could be here, but nothing else."

Something else bothered me. I sat up and glared at George. "What did you mean you don't think we're getting home anytime soon? How could you possibly know that?"

George looked despondent. He shoved his hair out of his face with one hand and tilted his head at me. He'd been having Barrow shave his face, so now only a shadow of dark stubble lined his jaw. I hated how handsome he was. For a brief, stupid moment he reminded me of when we first met and how looking at him made me feel all kinds of distracting things.

He must've caught my expression because he cleared his throat and murmured, "I think I've already solved the riddle, if you could even call it that. Come look at these."

I stood up, steadied myself, and moved to George's side, taking the letter from him. The strange cryptic prose had a whole new meaning six hundred years in the past:

Dear George and Rhiannon,

What is life, if it is not filled with adventures? These experiences test our mettle, reveal our true characters, and teach us the unteachable.

You will find that humans haven't really changed at all. Technology, fashion, social norms and the like may change. But the big things—love, fear, joy, hate—they remain constant throughout the centuries. This should both comfort and terrify you.

But when you work together (and you must), you can handle anything.

You can even use it to your advantage. After all, Time has a way of repeating, of folding in on itself. But to do this, everything—and everyone—must be lined up perfectly, like the tumblers in a lock with the key *inserted.*

It is time for Plierton Cottage to belong to you. And if you want to come home, then simply stay put until the exact moment comes along again.

My Love Transcends Time,

Dad

P.S. The autumn equinox is a particularly lovely time of year to visit. I strongly recommend it.

I rubbed my temple; my headdress felt like a vice squeezing my skull. I'd have to ask Agnes not to wrap it quite so tightly. As I tugged on the fabric, considering what it meant to make an ongoing request of my personal maid, a nauseating realization crossed my mind. *Until the exact moment comes along again. The autumn equinox is a particularly lovely time of year to visit.* I closed my eyes and pictured the oak tree glowing with the light of the equinox hitting it.

"No." I could not accept that truth. It was unthinkable. "No," I said again, just to make my displeasure with this reality known to anyone who could help me. "George," I gasped, suffocating with the pressure of what we were facing. "Is this saying ..." I couldn't even form the words. "The note, the 'exact moment', do you think ..." I clutched my chest and heaved.

George gazed at me, lips pressed into a line, head tilted, eyes downcast. He knew. "Rhi, it's going to be awhile ... like, a year."

"I do not accept that!" I cried, though even as I spoke, I understood. The sun shines in a slightly different place every single day of an Earth year. Nothing would be perfectly lined up again until next year's autumn equinox, when the sun would once again line up perfectly with the tree. However this time travel worked, the sun and the tree lining up seemed to play a key role.

"No," I whimpered.

To be stuck here for a full year, without toilet paper and cozy towels and on-demand hot water for bathtubs, without cheeseburgers and chocolate bars and hot cups of coffee, without television I could watch while flopped on the couch after a long day. No. I could not accept that.

A year without my friends or colleagues or students. A year stuck with the one person I was working to remove from my life—my almost-hopeful-ly-soon-ex-husband.

A full year in this filthy, oppressive, cold, damp place where every meal tested my gag reflex and every trip to the garderobe made me want to die.

It was unthinkable.

"No," I said again as I stumbled over to the tree in the corner, grasped the trunk, and tried to catch my breath. My fingers brushed over straight grooves in the wood. I lifted my hand to reveal a small carving of a grid made of sixteen squares. The grid was small—only slightly bigger than my hand. And something about it was familiar. I placed the letter against the trunk, next to the grid. It had been folded so it made a matching grid of sixteen squares.

I held the parchment up to the light. The folding normally wouldn't be anything of importance, except for the fact that Albert had written the note *after* folding it. The words never crossed the creases, and in some places ink pooled in the crevices. As if the folds—which were clearly fresh as they weren't worn down to the point of tearing apart—were important.

A glimmer of hope sparked in my mind. "What if there's another way back? Look at these folds. What if it's a clue? What if we don't have to wait a full year?"

George came up behind me and placed his hands lightly on my shoulders. "Rhi, that's not what the letter says." He spoke gently, like explaining to a child that Santa wasn't real. "If there was another way back, don't you think he would have told us?"

"Maybe he did! We have to try!" I exclaimed desperately, shaking the letter. "There must be more clues! Remember our wedding gift? This can't be the last stop. Surely there's more." I started to cry. I had never felt so angry and helpless before. Which was saying a lot, given the trajectory of my life.

"Rhi," George wrapped his arms around me and pulled me against his chest. "He knew our capacity for problem-solving would be taken up by survival. I don't think he'd layer more complex riddles on top of that. He was selfish, but not a total psycho."

I shoved George away, wiped my cheek with the back of my hand, and held the letter up to the light so he could see what I was talking about. "Look how the words fit into the squares. He wrote this after folding it. Doesn't that seem unusual? Not to mention that it's a letter shoved into a little box instead of an envelope. That must mean something!"

He gave me a mournful look and held the velvet box up to his doublet. "Look, it's the same fabric." It was true. The blue velvet of the box was wrapped in the exact same cloth we'd been dressed in since we'd been here. "The folds, the fabric ... he's letting us know that somehow time folded, dropped us here in this specific place, and we have to work together to survive until the next equinox to get home again." He swallowed. "In about a year—"

"No!" I cut him off. "No! I am not giving up on this!" I began pacing around the cottage, reading the letter over and over, desperate for another clue that would offer some relief. I snapped my fingers. "They key! Try the key. Maybe it's that simple. It's another clue, the key!"

George huffed a sigh and went to the door. I knew he was humoring me. He carefully closed the door, making sure everything was lined up. He stood to the side of the lock so I could see him insert the key and twist.

Nothing happened.

He pulled the key from the lock and dropped it back into the box. "Rhi," he pleaded. "Do you understand now?"

"No! You always do this!" I exclaimed, my voice rising as I spit out words I knew weren't fully true. "You get us into these awful situations then bail when things get hard! And it's *always* on me to solve them. I should not be here. I can't believe this is happening." I began pacing around the cottage, shouting at George. "I never should have come on this insane trip, I shouldn't be here, this is *your fault*!" As I railed about the injustice of it all, about how it was all George's fault, he just stood there and took it. He said nothing, reacted to nothing, just let me vent.

I expected him to leave me there. I thought he would turn and run like he often did when things got hard.

Instead, he crossed his arms over his chest and simply watched me burn up my anger, giving me space until there would only be acceptance left.

But what George didn't know was that I'd woken up with a dull throb in my abdomen, a pimple forming on my forehead, and the irritated urge to murder someone. My period was looming. Which meant I still had a lot more anger to burn.

13

GEORGE

Happy couples are all alike; every unhappy couple is unhappy in their own way.

I used to run from Rhiannon when she cried or railed angrily or was otherwise pissed off. I didn't know what to do with her emotions. I'd learned to stuff mine down and ignore them, or to run as soon as they reared up; I was perplexed she hadn't learned that too. And the few times I would try to talk to her when she was upset, it seemed like I only said or did the wrong things.

So, I stopped altogether.

But leaving her alone to process the anger and fear she felt over our situation was unthinkable. I could not live with myself if I bailed on her during the worst, most challenging, fucked up situation we'd ever found ourselves in.

Instead, I took her hand and escorted her out of the cottage.

Rhiannon sobbed and vented about the injustice of it all and shook her fist at the physicists who never figured out time travel, the flawed scientists who should have been able to warn her about this very situation had they been better at their jobs. "How is it that a *history teacher* figured out how to time travel, but not Stephen Hawking or *literally* Einstein? The so-called best minds in the world obviously had a huge blind spot. It's insane that they could miss something like this, but your dad of all people solved it!" Rhi, a lover of science, took it personally that scientists had not thought to solve this specific problem before it negatively affected her.

I let her rant and panic and break down. I did not interrupt or run or argue or make it about myself (yes, sometimes I made it about myself). I simply held her hand and walked us back up the steep hill to the castle.

Clearly, Rhiannon had been holding a lot in. Her anger with the failure of scientists evolved into lamenting about the lack of quality skincare products and toothpaste and how much the shoes were destroying her feet (medieval shoes don't have a left or a right foot, no arch support, no grippy rubber sole—just flimsy leather and a dangerously pointed toe that caused you to slide and trip all over the place), and how she hated wearing a stranger's clothes and how much she loathed Agnes with all of her judgy comments about the color of her skin and how tightly she wrapped the fabric around her head and neck so she could barely breathe and how she yanked the comb painfully through her hair. Then she wailed about how every meal was a nightmare of organ meats and blood and so on.

At one point, Rhi demanded to know if I was listening to her, so we stopped halfway up the hill so I could give her my full attention.

As she lamented the lack of chocolate, she noted she would, "murder for some chocolate or a cup of coffee," then she realized that the reason we didn't have those things is because we were pre-colonization, and that meant at one point people literally did murder for chocolate, which made her feel guilty for wanting to do the same thing, which sent her off on a terrified tangent about how we may or may not get smallpox (a key weapon of the colonists, whose ancestors we were now living with), and were we even vaccinated against smallpox, because it had already been eradicated by the time we were born, but still.

I worked to keep my eyes glued to Rhi's face. To show her I was listening and not running away. That I was there for her.

However, behind her I saw a familiar gray cat with a white patch on his chest that may or may not have been in the shape of Texas (it was a little too far to tell for sure) jump up onto the back of a sheep grazing near the castle's wall. I thought the sheep would shake him off. Instead, the cat started kneading the sheep's back and the sheep bleated in what sounded like appreciation.

Desperate to stay focused on my wife and not the weird cat, I cupped my hands over my eyes like horse blinders and stared directly into her eyes.

This halted her ranting. "What ... what are you doing? Why are you doing that with your hands?"

"Because I'm trying to pay attention to what you're saying as I know it's important, but behind you there's a cat riding a sheep. Which I think we can agree is very distracting."

Rhi whipped her head around. We watched as the cat stretched out, then another sheep sidled up the first sheep, and the cat jumped gingerly to the new sheep's back and began his kneading routine all over again.

"What on earth," she muttered under her breath. The cat curled up on the sheep's back with such comfort, I knew this was a common understanding between them. "Doesn't that cat look like Gustav?"

"He does. Must be his distant ancestor."

"Those are incredibly strong genes if so."

We watched as the sheep held very still, careful not to disturb the cat curled up on his back. Before I could say anything else about it, I picked up the faint sound of horns and horse hooves pounding the earth in the distance. We waited another minute, letting the wind whip around us, before the horns sounded again, this time closer.

Rhi looked at me, eyes wide with fear. "Whoever that is, they're headed this direction."

"Come on, let's get back inside before they see us." I grabbed Rhi's hand and started pulling her up the hill, but she yanked it out of my grip.

"I can take care of myself." She glared at me before stepping in front of me to continue our ascent. Under her breath, just loud enough to carry over the wind, I heard her utter, "I've been doing it this long, after all."

I didn't reply, didn't try to defend myself. I knew if I was going to win her trust back, it would take time. Instead, I moved as quickly up the hill as my dumb shoes would allow.

There's a reason castles were built with thick walls and poop moats—and I didn't want to be on the wrong side of them if those were enemies advancing.

14

RHIANNON

The normally bustling castle was in an absolute frenzy when we returned. From what we gathered, a messenger sent ahead from the baron's party gave word that Lord Henry and his entourage would be arriving imminently and a slew of preparations needed to be made to accommodate them.

As we crossed the courtyard's expanse, I grimaced as Agnes swooped in. "My lady, no time to spare. We must get you dressed for dinner." She paused and assessed my face. "Ack, still as brown as a field," she chided.

As if I could change that. I rolled my eyes and let her drag me into the stairwell, still chittering about my complexion.

Behind me I heard George being accosted by Barrow, who was just as harried about the lack of time to get ready.

"The horns sounded far away," George tried to justify as Barrow pushed him up the stairs.

Alarmed, Barrow only squeaked, "You could already hear the horns?" This seemed to stress him out more than comfort him.

A cold dread settled over me. How draconian was this baron if the servants were in such a state over his arrival? Our plan to leave before he came back obviously failed. And now we had to keep our haphazard stories straight for *months* to survive.

We were to be scrubbed, oiled, hair washed and combed, dressed in the finest garments, and presented to the wealthiest couple in the region as if we were their peers. Which was wild, considering we were complete strangers who arrived clad in old blankets only a few weeks earlier.

Agnes ushered me into the bathing chambers where a wooden tub filled with hot water and lined with linen awaited me. Despite it being only my second time bathing in just over two weeks, soaking in hot water with real soap did little to ease my thoughts. I felt like I was being prepared for a ritual sacrifice.

I had no privacy. Agnes never left, didn't like that I wanted to wash myself, didn't like that my skin tone underneath my clothes revealed that staying inside would do little to make me pale. She didn't like how we showed up unannounced and with nothing, didn't like how my soft hands and feet made me look like a lady when she was suspicious I wasn't. I knew all this because she never shut up. Like, ever.

I sighed and sunk beneath the water, emerging only when I heard her squawking about not drowning myself with the baron's precious water.

For the night's occasion, Agnes braided the top part of my hair at the crown, but instead of the usual headdress, she allowed the rest of my curly locks to hang loosely down my back. The one compliment she paid me was that she admired my, "scarlet tresses."

She dressed me in a ruby colored velvet dress with sleeves so full, they dragged on the ground if I let my arms fall to my sides. The dress was trimmed with mink at the scooped neck and sleeves, providing a smidge of warmth. Agnes belted the dress above my waist with a sash that looked like it was embroidered with gold and hung all the way to the tops of my feet. She topped off the ensemble with a gold cross pendant that rested on white silk fabric covering my chest, and a gold ring she slipped onto my finger where my wedding band should be. "'tis an old piece, forgotten to most," she explained while patting my hand. "Cannot have ye looking unwed in the baron and lady's presence."

When I finished dressing, Agnes led me to the private dining quarters the baron used when he and his family did not wish to join everyone else in the great hall. A long, intricately carved wooden table sat in the middle of the room, flanked with formidable chairs, all decorated with what appeared to be a series of carved vignettes depicting hunts, parties, and various biblical scenes. An ornate silver chandelier bedecked with candles hung over the table, firelight reflecting off the shiny metal. Thick woolen rugs, a fire roaring in a fireplace so large I could stand inside it, and drapes flanking the glass windows added warmth to the room.

But what was most impressive was that every plastered wall had incredible scenes painted right onto it, like massive murals. Each wall seemed to show a slice of history from Kendal's formidable history—ancient battles, the building of the castle, and the wealth accumulated by the barons of this land. I had always believed medieval castles were dreary, cold, monuments to dull stone. But really, they were temples of color and life. Enamored, and briefly forgetting my misery, I let out a low whistle.

"Pretty cool, huh?"

I startled to see George standing off in a corner.

I was so taken with beauty of the room, I didn't notice he was already there. When he stepped into the light and I got a good look at him, my breath caught at how handsome he looked.

Barrow had dressed George in a perfectly tailored ruby velvet doublet that matched my dress. He wore tight black breeches and black calf-high boots polished so they glistened in the firelight. His shoulder-length hair was combed back, and his freshly shaved face revealed his pointed jawline. The deep flush of red velvet complemented his pale blue eyes and silvery blonde hair, making him glow.

One thing George always had going for him was his looks. As my students would say, "His face card never declines." It's annoying, actually. It's hard to be pissed at someone with a face like that.

I could not recall when I stopped desiring my husband. At some point the weight of our problems crushed my feelings for him and my heart had gone cold. I'd forgotten how attractive he was, how just being next to him could make all conflicting thoughts melt away.

But seeing him resplendent in these fine clothes sent a wave of warmth through my body. I ached to hold him, to kiss him freely like I used to. I knew part of it was simply my raging tangle of hormones. But it was also a shared history that would forever bind me to him—whether I liked it or not.

George stepped closer to me and held his hand out for mine, the way Agnes taught us was the proper way a lord escorted his lady to dinner. I placed my hand in his, reveling in the familiar touch.

"You look stunning," he whispered, though we were alone.

"You're quite dashing yourself."

He grinned. "Feeling better?"

"The bath helped." I shook out my loose hair. "And not wearing that awful headdress."

"Good. We will take this one day at a time. Okay?"

I nodded and took a deep, slow breath, never letting my eyes leave George. We stared at each other, fingers intertwined, letting the past fall away and allowing ourselves to be present.

Four servants we'd never seen before entered the room and flanked the two doors. Following them was Edward, dressed in a forest green velvet doublet over a black silk shirt, his dark hair falling in loose waves to his shoulders. On Edward's arm was a woman we'd never seen before but had been primed to meet, his wife, Lady Marguerite.

Marguerite was a pale, lovely beauty with large green eyes and a high forehead. Her rosebud lips were pursed in a slight frown, which somehow made her seem even more elegant and untouchable. She wore a deep aubergine gown, accented with gold thread at the cuffs and hem, that seemed to float around her as she moved into the room. Her hair was completely wrapped in a white silk headdress topped with a blue conical hat. Like something a princess would wear in a fairy tale.

Jesus, they were a gorgeous couple.

When she and Edward entered the room, we all grew quiet—as if the beauty and grace the two of them exuded together should not be disturbed by the rough noises of us mere mortals.

Edward led her to where we stood close to the fireplace and presented his wife. "May I introduce my wife, Lady Marguerite of Kendal, niece of Henry de Ros, the Baron of Kendal."

George gave my hand a sharp squeeze. He heard it too: de Ros. We were about to meet Henry de Ros's ancestor.

Marguerite placed her hand on her chest and dipped into a graceful curtsy, "It is my sincere honor to make your acquaintance," she greeted us with a French accent. Her words were as delicate and ephemeral as the rest of her.

As our medieval manners were rudimentary at best, George made the move to mimic Edward's introduction. But it came out clunky and stilted. We had no titles, no history other than having been found in distress on the side of the road. Despite our elegant clothes, we felt every bit the imposters we were. "I am George ... And this is my wife, Rhiannon." I imitated Marguerite's curtsy, hoping I was doing it right.

Though she was polite as could be, Marguerite looked especially shaken by George's presence. She turned to Edward, tilting her head in question, only for him to give her a curt nod of confirmation.

George and I glanced at each other, both confused by her reaction. Before anything else could be said on the matter, the four servants snapped their heels to attention and announced the arrival of the Baron of Kendal, Lord Henry de Ros and his wife, Lady Gwendolyn.

We all turned and faced the doorway as the couple entered the dining room.

I swayed where I stood, flummoxed by the appearance of the people who had just arrived.

Lord Henry and his wife Lady Gwendolyn were not the esteemed ancestors of the lovely couple we met in the year 2020.

They *were* Henry and Gwen de Ros, the lovely couple we would meet six hundred years from now.

15

GEORGE

Does time folding have anything to do with the fact that the esteemed baron we'd heard so much about was apparently also a time traveler? Or was there some other explanation for why a couple we'd seen just a few weeks—and six centuries—earlier were now standing before us, looking as shocked by our presence as we were by theirs?

Now before you think, George, obviously this is an ancestor with incredibly strong genes. Please consider the following two facts: Henry de Ros in the year 2020, in addition to looking just like my father, had a small mole at the corner of his left eye. As did the baron. And what are the odds that both Henrys married women named Gwendolyn who also looked exactly the same (strong Gwyneth Paltrow vibes, to be honest), but six hundred years apart? Nearly impossible.

On top of that, the mystery of why everyone in this damned castle acted like Rhiannon and I were cursed could be because Henry de Ros looked a hell of a lot like me—plus about fifteen years in age. Though that could be attributed to the rougher living of the medieval period.

I'd spent the past few weeks wearing the baron's clothes, wandering around looking like a slightly younger version of him, clearly scaring the shit out of the servants and clergy who had no explanation for my existence other than the fact that Edward told them we were "distant relations."

When they walked into the room, Lady Gwendolyn gasped and covered her mouth with her hands. Her wide eyes filled with tears as she stared at me. It was remarkably similar to how she greeted me in 2020.

Henry uttered, "Good God," under his breath before gently taking one of Gwendolyn's hands.

I felt Rhiannon grab my arm. I glanced to my right to see she'd gone completely pale and her mouth hung open in surprise.

Henry stepped forward and asked, "Is it really you?" His shaking hand extended as if reaching out to touch the face that bore a striking resemblance to his own. I took a step back, though I was not in proximity to be touched. My heart thudded heavily in my chest and a band of anxious tightness squeezed the breath out of me.

No one moved, nor said a word, for several moments.

Gwendolyn wiped a tear from her cheek before she asked me tentatively, "George?"

I swallowed. "That's me ... I'm, I'm ... George." I placed a hand on my chest, both out of courtesy and to make sure my heart was still functioning. "Have we ... have we met?" I was baffled by this woman from the distant past who seemed to not only know me, but clearly had strong feelings about it.

Henry turned towards Edward. "You rescued them on the side of the road, you say?"

He simply nodded in confirmation.

"Close to the old cottage?"

Edward nodded again.

"Well." Henry clasped his hands together as Gwendolyn full on sobbed. "You could say that we are well-acquainted with your father, Albert."

I felt like I'd been punched in the face. For every answer we received about what was happening to us, it only unlocked a thousand more questions.

"How?" I stammered.

"Yes, so many questions, I imagine. But for now, all you need to know is that you are most welcome here," Henry continued. "Fear not, for we will take good care of you, for as long as you need it."

Gwendolyn dabbed her wet face with a handkerchief and smiled through her tears. "A blessing. Truly. Please, let us eat." She gestured towards the table.

I could not move. Rhiannon gave my arm a gentle tug, moving us towards our seats. Despite the bombshells being dropped on us left and right, she'd gathered up enough composure to get me to the table.

I glanced at Edward, who wore an unreadable expression. He and Marguerite were lovely statues: immaculately dressed, smooth expressions that betrayed no hint of feeling one way or the other, both beautiful and untouchable in their own way. While Edward carried himself like a man who believes himself to be above others, it was Marguerite's delicate and frail beauty that kept her separate from the fray. Together, they seemed unfazed—almost bored, really—by this astounding development. They were a level of cool I jealously knew I'd never attain. I wondered what level of courtly etiquette demanded they stay this detached while the de Ros's were clearly jarred by our appearance.

Henry took his seat at the head of the table, not taking his eyes off me the entire time. But his gaze was neither hostile nor afraid; rather there was something warm about it. Almost like pride. I'd seen that exact same expression on my father's face. Not often, mind you. Pride was usually the last thing my father felt for me. Which meant Henry's expression unnerved me almost more than the hostile gazes of the castle staff.

After we settled around the table, a parade of servants carrying platters of food filed into the room. Henry raised his goblet—sloshing with the finest red wine imported from France—and said, "A toast, to our new friends, whom God has delivered safely to us."

The dinner was served in courses, each one a strange delicacy in its own way. Fruits and cheese opened the meal; followed by carrots cooked with raisins; a platter of eels simmering in broth; a savory fish and egg pie; finished with an entire lamb, head still attached, surrounded by what looked like haggis.

Rhiannon struggled through the meal. There was nothing I could do right then to help her, but I made a mental note of how little she ate.

As the evening progressed and the wine warmed over my shock over meeting the de Ros's here, my mind wandered to Gustav. I now wondered if it was the same cat that had barged into my cottage in the 21st century. Without thinking, I blurted out, "Earlier I saw a cat riding a sheep. Is that … is that normal?"

Henry snorted. "That's Gustav. The lazy beast hasn't caught a mouse in years, but the sheep love him, so he stays. He comes and goes as he pleases."

Under the table, Rhi pinched my leg, her way of letting me know we had a lot to talk about when we were alone later. So, so much to talk about.

16

RHIANNON

"I have a little present for you," George said while holding something behind his back.

"What kind of present?" I asked suspiciously. After the overwhelming day we'd had, I was in no mood for even more surprises.

"A present like this." He revealed his little gift with a flourish, pulling open a tied-up handkerchief full of crusty bread, a big hunk of white cheddar cheese, and an apple.

My stomach growled in appreciation. He must have noticed I nibbled at dinner, trying to eat as much of the lamb as I could stand before I just couldn't take it anymore. It tasted like I was chewing flesh off a live animal, like I could taste the grass and mud and filth it used to be covered in while looking it in the eye, of all things. Don't get me started on the eels.

The food, combined with the awkward and stilted conversation at dinner, made eating enough impossible.

Lord Henry and Lady Gwendolyn were keen on discussing everything but how they knew George's dad. We were too caught off guard, too bewildered by the events of the day, to press the matter. From our journey to the cottage, to the revelation we could be here for a full year (which I still had not accepted), to meeting odd people we thought were confined to the 21st century, I simply didn't have the mental bandwidth to figure out how to ask the right questions.

So, we let them ramble on about court, the journey, Edward's updates on the state of the castle, and so on.

It was awful and I was still hungry.

I grabbed both the bread and cheese, took a bite out of each, and asked George around my mouthful, "Where did you get this? I thought the kitchens were closed."

Every single person living in the castle had a specific amount of rationed food allotted to them, kept track of in Clifford's ledger. New people showing up and raiding the stores after hours was not accounted nor planned for.

"As it turns out I have some friends in high places. When I was poking around the kitchens to see if there was anything extra I could bring you, the baron himself, Henry, Lord of Kendal Castle, walked in and basically demanded that the servants open the kitchen for me. I didn't need them to cook me anything, of course, so I just told him that I would need a snack later as I had a big appetite, and he was more than happy to oblige."

"Hmm." I considered this while gnawing on the bread. "Speaking of Henry wanting to do things for you, are they not the exact same people we met back in 2020? The fact that you look just like him—and he looks just like your father—freaks me out. And the way Gwendolyn stares at you, with tears no less, is even more confusing. I feel like there's an obvious answer here we're missing because we're still playing by the rules of a reality that no longer exists. A reality where time travel is impossible."

George sat on the bed beside me and pulled out a small paring knife that had also been stashed in the handkerchief. He picked up the apple and slowly carved the peel away from the flesh, before slicing off one perfect quarter and handing it to me.

"Well, both versions of Henry mentioned knowing my dad. Since we've already established time travel is possible, let's assume anything is possible. Now we have a new mystery: who are Henry and Gwendolyn de Ros and how do they fit into all of this? All throughout dinner I kept trying to convince myself they were different people. And if it was only Henry we could say it's simply strong genes, handed down generation after generation. But it's Gwen's presence that gives me pause. She's the exact same person we met in 2020, right down to the tears."

For the first time since we'd read the note in the cottage, a realization sparked hope in my chest. I grabbed George's arm. "Let's ask them how they do it."

"Do what?"

"Travel back and forth through time." I stood and began pacing in front of the fire. "Obviously they know how to do it without an equinox or a cottage. Right? Maybe that's what the blue velvet box means. It's their fabric, maybe your dad wanted us to talk to them? Maybe this is the clue we've been looking for! Let's ask them. Do you think they're asleep already?" I was rambling, energized by this new thread we could follow to show us the way home. "They said they could help us. Maybe this is—"

"Rhi," George cut in gently. "If that were the case, don't you think the note would have said so? The directions were pretty clear on how to get home."

"Since when did your dad leave us a scavenger hunt with only one clue?" I was manic with the idea that there were more clues. There had to be. I could not accept it otherwise.

George stood, brushing breadcrumbs from his chest. "Since he planned all this while barely being able to breathe. Since he knew he had limited time left. Since he knew he was sending us on an adventure so intense, to layer in more clues would be cruel. Since then, Rhi."

"George," I took his hand in mine. "Please don't give up," I whimpered. "I will wait to ask the de Ros's if that's what you want. Because now that I think about it, I know where we might be able to find some answers."

"Oh?" He gave my hand a patronizing squeeze. George looked at me with something like pity in his eyes. But I was undeterred.

"We can look in Edward's library."

George handed me the last of the apple slices and tossed the core into the fire, where it sizzled and steamed. "Isn't the library off limits?"

Our first day here, after we were bathed and dressed, Agnes had given us leave to explore the castle as we saw fit—though warned us that the library was not to be touched. She said no one was allowed in but Edward. At the time we were so disoriented by the whole time travel thing that I didn't register why a library would be off-limits. At the time, we had bigger problems.

But those problems faded into the background as gathering information that could get us home became the only thing that mattered.

"Yes, according to Agnes, the library is off-limits. But why? Why make it off limits if there isn't something important being stored in there? Something that may provide us answers about how we got here?"

"It may be off limits because that's where they keep important documents, records, and even money. If it will appease you, I'll ask Edward if I can check it out."

"*Appease me?* I'm going to let that slide. But we need a plan." I resumed my pacing, tugging a lock of my loose hair, running through every scenario I could think of. This is where I excelled. I could solve this problem. I just needed more information.

George snorted. "What do you mean, we need a plan? That's it, ask Edward, then look in the library. Full stop. What more plan does there need to be?"

I exhaled the full extent of my exasperation. George had a habit of barreling into things without a plan, then being surprised when it all fell apart. "Okay, when are you going to ask him? And what reason are you going to give Edward when he asks why you need to look in the off-limits library that may be full of sensitive and important documents? And if he does give you access, where are you going to start looking? How are you going to recall, or even write down, anything important you learn? Do you even know what you'd be looking for? You don't even know how big the library is!"

George groaned and rubbed his face. "Oh my god, Rhiannon! There doesn't need to be a plan for everything. Especially not one for an imaginary scavenger hunt. Maybe the plan gets formed when I see what's in the library in the first place. Why can't you just let me handle this my way?"

I turned towards the fire, keeping George out of sight behind me. He had a long track record of relying on me to fix things when his plan (or lack thereof) didn't pan out. I glanced at him over my shoulder, to find he looked as annoyed as I felt.

"We shouldn't do it your way because your way frequently fails!" I seethed. "We may be running out of time to figure this out and I don't want to waste any more of it barreling ahead without a plan. Why are you so against just talking this through?"

"Because there's nothing to talk through! Why can't you just accept that we're going to be here for a year?"

I wanted to scream. "Because I do not accept that! I do not accept that we're trapped here for that long. I do not accept that I'm going to be stuck in this filthy, oppressive, cold, smelly place for one second longer than I have to be! Why are you so against trying to find a way to get home sooner?"

George wiped off the paring knife with his handkerchief, tossed both on one of the armchairs, and replied, "I'm not having this stupid fight right now." He huffed out an exasperated breath, grabbed his cloak, and swung it over his shoulders as he strode out of the room.

I rolled my eyes. George bailed when things got tough.

Which meant I would need to figure this out on my own.

Typical.

17

RHIANNON

George's car was already in the driveway when I got home. I tensed up, anxiety creating a slew of terrible stories about why he was here and not at work, where he should be. Despite heavy clouds blotting out the sun, there were no lights on in the house. My uneasiness grew.

"George?" I called out while setting my things down by the door.

"In here," he called from the dining room.

"What are you doing? Why are you home so early?"

He was wearing sweats and a ratty old Smashing Pumpkins T-shirt, barefoot, drinking a mug of tea. In front of him was a legal pad covered in notes and doodles.

"Hey," he said, avoiding eye contact.

I got myself a glass of water and pulled up a chair across from him. "Are you okay?"

George shrugged and gazed past me, towards the window. "I ... I don't think so."

"What's going on?" Fear burned in my chest. Something was wrong. Incredibly wrong.

He exhaled and shoved his hair out of his face. "I don't have a job anymore." When he finally met my eyes, George had a strange look on his face. Not sadness or fear or anger … just defeat.

"Why? What happened?" I placed my hands on the table, bracing myself. We were barely making ends meet and my mind was spinning with how we were going to manage if he'd been laid off. Or fired.

"I quit."

That's not what I expected. It was no secret to anyone that George hated his job interviewing small business owners and writing blogs for a local publication. But it was a desperately needed paycheck, and he hadn't exactly been working to find something new. The past year, George had slowly faded into the background of our lives while I ran myself ragged closing the gaps.

When I was a kid, a biologist came to speak to my 5th grade class. She explained that when we released balloons into the air, eventually they came down, often in the ocean, where they hurt a lot of animals. As she described sea turtles and dolphins choking to death on deflated balloons, I was horrified to learn I'd contributed to their demise. From then on, I regarded letting go of balloons as this terrible thing that must be avoided at all costs. If I was diligent and paid attention, no balloons would be released on my watch.

Over the past couple years, I felt like George had been holding a bouquet of balloons, and as he let each one go, I scrambled to catch the string, terrified of what would happen if I didn't. The first balloon he let go of was his once meticulously groomed beard. I said nothing, not wishing to cross a line where I critiqued his appearance—but I was concerned nonetheless when his unkempt beard made him look increasingly like he'd joined a cult.

From there, he let go of his role as the primary cook in the house. There was a time when George handled all the food, from shopping to meal prepping. But somewhere along the way we began subsisting on a steady diet of canned soups, frozen pizzas, easy salads, and takeout—most of which I procured or prepared.

Before I knew it, I was holding all the balloons, digging my heels into the earth, trying to keep it all from falling apart. I made sure the bills got paid. I scheduled oil changes and dentists' appointments and routine check-ups, called plumbers or HVAC guys or electricians or tree trimmers. I washed towels, vacuumed floors, dusted bookshelves, and took out the garbage. I loaded and unloaded the dishwasher, wiped the counters, and went grocery shopping when it became clear he was no longer going to.

While I was doing all of this, George took to disappearing for hours at a time. I was convinced he was having an affair; I thought it was the only logical explanation.

But when I worked up the courage to follow him for the first time (thanks to the handy Find My iPhone feature), I found him hanging out at a coffee shop, book in hand, paper cups accumulating on the table as time passed. I waited in the car, watching him through the window. When nearly an hour had passed, a pretty girl approached his table. My hands were clammy with sweat and I was dizzy with fear, waiting for confirmation of my worst suspicions. But after a brief exchange, he held up his left hand, showing her his ring, and she left. I was dumbfounded.

Another time he simply went to a park and read for over an hour until he passed out on the grass, book over his face. Again, I watched and waited, slouched down in my car, convinced a woman would show up to join him. But no one ever did.

The last time I followed him, he went to a sports bar late on a Tuesday night. Because there were no windows to watch him through, I decided to go inside to see what he was doing. George was sitting at the bar, drinking a beer, reading a book. Alone. The bar was relatively empty and he spotted me as soon as I walked in. The shock on his face, tinged with a little fear, was all I needed to know about whether he wanted me there. I walked right out the door as he called my name.

But he didn't follow me out.

When George got home later, his only explanation was that sometimes he just, "needed space."

I cried myself to sleep that night while he slept on the couch.

In the morning, I resolved to take care of myself. After all, I'd been taking care of myself for most of my life. George wasn't my prisoner; he could come and go as he saw fit. As could I.

But that meant the time we were spending together was dwindling. When I wasn't working, I was running errands, doing chores, or getting a precious few hours of sleep. No balloons would be released on my watch, no sir.

At the very least, George's direct deposit kept enough money in our accounts for me to keep handling all the things. Holding all the balloons gets expensive, fast.

That was the state of things when George was home early, newly unemployed, and unwilling to elaborate on it. In a home he barely helped maintain.

I massaged the palm of my hand, trying to calm myself, working through various reactions to this news. "I'm sorry, but I think I misheard you. You quit? Without talking to me first?" My heart hammered with some as-yet indecipherable feeling.

He dragged his hand down his grotesque beard. "I can't … " he started to say before just dropping the sentence and staring at me. We sat like this for several moments, not speaking, George offering no explanation for why he quit.

I'd been working all day—administering tests, grading lab assignments during my prep period, supervising the cafeteria during my lunch break—and knew when I got home, there would be a pile of chores for me to handle while I prepped my lesson plan for the next day.

I appraised our home. Dirty dishes were stacked in the kitchen sink. A pile of washed but unfolded towels languished on one corner of the couch where I'd had good intentions of folding them several days earlier, but never had enough energy to finish. George's shoes were piled by the front door. He'd brought in the mail but tossed it on the coffee table two days ago without opening a single thing.

He'd obviously been home for a while but hadn't so much as turned on the porch light for me.

It broke me.

Whatever bond we shared, whatever fragile threads bound us together, finally frayed and snapped. The balloons lifted into the air, taking with them any love or compassion I still felt for my husband.

I stood up. "I think I'm done."

George looked up at me, confusion barely registering on face. "With what?"

I met his eyes. "With you. With our marriage." I thought I should cry, but I felt numb. I paused to give myself space for tears. None came. So, I kept going. "I'm not happy and I don't want to be married to you anymore."

"Rhi, come on," he sounded exasperated, like he thought I was bluffing. I had carried the burden of maintaining every aspect of our lives, because at least I could rely on the extra income. But without that, without a partner in any sense of the word, I was done.

My numbness was quickly evolving into anger.

"You need to go, George. Right now. Go stay with your dad or something." I exhaled through my nose, controlling my emotions. "You haven't contributed jack shit to this home—or our lives—in a long time. And I'm done. I'm so, so over it. You are wildly self-absorbed and I'm just ... done."

"Rhiannon," he whimpered. "I'll get another job if it's that big of a deal." George didn't cry. His eyes were red, but whatever had shut down inside of him remained dormant—even as I severed our marital ties.

I shook my head and took a step away from where he stayed at the table. "If you think this is just about you quitting your job, then you haven't been paying attention. I can take care of myself, but I've been taking care of both of us for far too long. I am exhausted. And I'm lonely, George." I finally admitted. "You aren't my partner. You've become my dependent." I took another step backwards, adding more space between us. "I don't even know why I'm married anymore."

That was the core of it—I was incredibly overworked and lonely in my own marriage.

I didn't have a real family to speak of. My mother was a hot mess, I never knew who my father was, I had no siblings or cousins, no aunts or uncles to speak of. When I married George, I thought we would make a family together.

But after so much pain, so much disappointment, it became clear I was still on my own.

He stood awkwardly at the table, conflict flickering across his face.

I grabbed my purse. "I'm leaving for two hours. Please don't be here when I get back."

George could have stayed. He could have fought. He could have reached for me a thousand times before this.

But he never did.

When I got home, the house was still dark. He'd done the dishes and folded the towels. But he'd also packed a suitcase and left.

18

GEORGE

In my younger and more vulnerable years my father gave me some (bad) advice that I've been turning over in my mind ever since.

"Never show weakness, George. Never let them think they have the upper hand." He first said it to me at the edge of a soccer pitch when I was about to cry after a member of the opposing team hit me in the back of my calf with a cleat. I was seven. He repeated it after I got lost in the woods during a Cub Scout expedition; after my first heartbreak; and most notoriously, after my mother died.

Words like those, at such a young age, become tattooed on your heart and begin to define your personality. When I felt weak, the only way I knew how to hide it was to run.

The problem occurs when you can't run. Because you cannot run from yourself.

Depression is a bitch. Depression, stirred with grief, and topped off with the persistent feeling of failure, is a cocktail of drowning despair.

Every morning, I woke up gasping for breath, feeling like I was sinking and had no hope of floating to the surface. Like if I could just get more air, everything would be okay.

Then I would spend hours at work sitting in a tiny cubicle, writing inane little blogs that were hammered into unreadable garbage for SEO, and my soul died a bit each day. Every evening I would come home and half-ass my way through chores or cooking or some other necessary survival skill that felt increasingly meaningless as time persisted.

Until grief made it all impossible. Until the weight of my accumulating failures caused me to collapse under the pressure of it all. And I stopped doing anything.

Everyone copes with loss differently. Rhiannon retreated into her job. She took on extra tutoring and summer school classes, coached the debate team, monitored lunch, and seemed to say 'yes' to every single request. She immersed herself in work to keep her mind off everything we'd been through. At home, she filled every second with chores or mindless TV watching. The few times I reached for her, when I tried to explain that I was flailing and needed a hand, I couldn't seem to get her to hold still.

She was like a shark: if she stopped moving, for even a moment, she would die.

Where Rhiannon sunk into work to dull her pain, I dove into books. I always loved reading, but with every day that I thought about what we did not have and could not seem to make work, with every loss, I found reading to be the analgesic I needed to forget my life. However, if I read at home, then one glance up from the pages yielded reminders of the deep well of grief we were both drowning in.

So, I left. I went all over the city, just to read and get the air I had been desperate to cram into my lungs. Those hours spent exploring Atlanta with a book in hand were the only times I ever felt like myself. And like I could eventually, maybe someday, be okay.

I wanted to talk to Rhiannon about all of this. I wanted to tell her I was struggling and I knew she was too. But after a lifetime of disuse, the vulnerable words never formed properly. And I didn't realize how vital that context would've been for her to understand why I quit my job.

I should have told Rhiannon all of this. But I didn't.

Even when she was asking me to leave, I couldn't find the words.

I went upstairs to pack my bag as soon as she left. She didn't say goodbye.

When I was at the door, bag in hand, I saw the dishes in the sink. I imagined her coming home and dealing with those and everything else. I decided to do one last thing, to try and take one last little gulp of air before I let myself sink beneath the waves.

I spent the drive up to Athens blasting an old Ruby Haze album and thinking about what I should have said. I mentally wrote whole conversations where I explained to Rhiannon why I was dying inside and was justified in quitting my soul-crushing job. Why I couldn't contribute the way she needed. Why going out to read was crucial to my well-being. I imagined explaining this need for air … but no matter how I shaped it, spun it, worked it over … I felt wrong.

The imaginary conversation always came back to me letting the woman I love down in a myriad of ways.

When I pulled into my dad's driveway, I put the car in park and sat for a couple of minutes, considering what I would tell him about why I was there. He adored Rhiannon and would no doubt have an opinion about her asking for a divorce. I stayed in the car long enough for him to open the front door and watch me with one eyebrow raised. I got out, pulled my bag out of the backseat, and trudged up the stairs to where he was waiting.

"I figured this was only a matter of time," Dad sighed as he stepped aside and let me in.

"I'm not in the mood for your opinion," I snapped.

"Of course you're not. But if not now, then when?"

"When we can talk without you lecturing me."

He chuckled wryly. "Then I guess it will be some time. After all, the lesson gets worse every time you fail to learn it."

I dragged my hand down my face. "Fuck, Dad. Can you just be cool for once in your life? Can you not see that things are really shitty right now? I don't need you piling on."

He followed me inside and shut the door behind us. Dad was wearing a bathrobe over silk pajamas and drinking what smelled like ginger tea. On his dining table was a stack of half-graded essays where he'd clearly been working.

"Are you going to fight for her?" he asked quietly.

"I don't think she wants me to," I resigned.

He snorted. "You're too much like me, George. Which makes you a fool." He rubbed his hands together and closed with, "You know where your room is. Stay as long as you need, but not so long that I have to kick you out. Now, go, I have work to do."

I grabbed my bag and headed upstairs to my old bedroom. Dad was a bit of a hoarder and without my mom there, constantly curating his collection and staying his hand when he wanted to buy one more thing he didn't need, the house was packed with stuff. My old room had the same bed, bureau, bookshelves, and nightstand—but each and every surface was buried under piles of stuff. Books—both old leather-bound tomes and newer brightly colored paperbacks—were stacked everywhere. Piles of yellowing papers; old paintings leaning against walls and furniture; random detritus like rolls of tape, batteries, pens and pencils, dry erase markers, coasters, candles, tissue boxes (some empty); antique porcelain cups and pottery bowls; clothing including sweaters, neckties, folded pants, and single gloves—took up every inch of space in "my" room.

"Fuck," I muttered while wading through the crap. I would have to move most of it somewhere just to be able to walk into the room, much less live here.

As I began sorting and shifting things around, my mind wandered.

I pictured what Rhiannon was doing while I was out reading. I knew she followed me once, knew she thought I was having an affair. But we didn't talk about it, not after she confirmed I was still faithful ... if nothing else.

With each stack of books I cleared or each painting I moved to the study, I imagined Rhiannon folding towels, unloading the dishwasher, heating up cans of soup and frozen pizzas, and keeping everything running. Without me.

Every ounce of effort I put into clearing out this room could have gone into my own house, alongside my wife.

I was the fool my dad accused me of being.

I sunk down onto the floor and leaned against the bed, looking out the window where an old oak tree swayed in the late evening breeze.

And cried.

19

GEORGE

I needed to get out of that room and away from Rhiannon before I said something I'd regret.

I walked around the courtyard, enjoying the silence as everyone headed to bed. The afternoon's sharp winds had blown out the morning clouds, leaving behind a clear sky and a splash of bright and dense stars. But it wasn't the stars that halted me in my path and disrupted my irritation.

It was the shimmers of green and purple illuminating the sky. The northern lights. A bucket-list item Rhiannon had wanted to see for as long as I knew her.

Without hesitation, I bolted back inside, up the stairs, into our chambers. Rhiannon still stood by the fire, wiping her eyes. "Come quick! You gotta see this."

"What—" she started to question, but I grabbed her hand and pulled her towards the door.

"Trust me on this one, please?"

She furrowed her brow but still followed me.

Instead of the courtyard, I pulled Rhiannon out onto one of the tall parapets where the view was unmatched. A guard gave us a curious look before turning his attention back to the rolling hills outside the walls of the castle.

"Look," I placed my hands on her shoulders, turning her to where the northern lights shimmered above the castle walls, a dazzling light show that felt surreal and unworldly. The lights cast an eerie glow on the town of Kirkby Kendal below us. I inhaled the damp night air, wonder and awe filling my chest.

"Wow," she breathed.

Rhiannon shivered and leaned into me; I wrapped her up in my cloak, realizing too late that in my haste to get her out here, we'd forgotten her cloak, and she was underdressed for how cold it was. Holding her this close, I could feel she'd been losing weight. Between the meals she struggled to choke down and the corresponding sickness, Rhiannon was growing thin—too thin. I brushed my thumb along the top of her jutting collarbone, aware that our time travel experiences were markedly different.

Food aside, I didn't have to wear a headdress nonstop, nor did I have to contend with skirts dragging in the mud, or hovering over a chamber pot in the middle of the night, or having Agnes yank a comb through my long curly hair every evening, or worry about the leering stares of many of the men here. Nor did I have to contend with the monthly cycles that kept her hoarding linen rags nonstop, in nervous preparation for when the time came.

I understood then why Rhiannon was manic to get home, why the idea of spending an entire year in this time was terrifying.

I considered how I'd bailed on her earlier, left her alone to work out a problem because I didn't think it was valid or important.

Shit. I'd been given a second chance and was already ruining it. I could do better. I would make this right.

"Hey, I know this is terrifying," I whispered as I wrapped my arms tightly around her. "But you're not alone and I'm not going anywhere. I won't let anything happen to you. I won't let you out of my sight. I promise."

Rhiannon started shaking with what I knew were silent tears. "There has to be another way to get home," she sobbed.

"If there is, then we will find it."

"But you don't think there is, do you?"

I winced. "No, I'm sorry, but I don't. I know my dad's style. This is too big for him to have left it to chance. He would have told us if there was a way. In fact, I'm certain he meant for us to be here this long. Hence the letter emphasizing adventures and working together."

Rhi sniffled and turned around so she was facing me, still wrapped up in my cloak. Her face was only inches from mine. There was a time when I would have kissed her without hesitation. I resisted.

We stared at each other for several breaths, huddling close to stay warm.

She tugged on my hood. "You know, with this hood up and your hair like that, you're really giving Aragorn vibes."

I laughed. "That's a big compliment. Everyone loves Aragorn. If you'd like, I'm sure I can find a sword and really lean into it." I lowered my voice and whispered in her ear, her hair brushing against my lips. "Would that make you feel better?"

Rhi pressed her hands against my chest. A flicker of a smile crossed her face before her expression crumped into tears again. "I already miss movies," she wailed. "I miss my life. I can't believe this happening." She started crying again, pressing her teary face into my shoulder.

"I know. I'm sorry." I felt partially responsible for her being here, even if I'd had nothing to do with the time travel bullshit. I stroked her hair, letting my fingers lightly tug the ends just how she likes. "We'll be okay." I said it over and over, willing it to be true.

I was also terrified. But I would not let her see it. I would be the rock she needed, the safe place, the refuge in this wild experience. I would not let her down.

20

RHIANNON

During the early weeks of our stay at the castle, we were basically stray animals wandering around aimlessly, relying on the charity of Edward and the servants to feed and clothe us at the right times. Very few people in the castle seemed keen on getting to know us, and we were more than happy to give them a wide berth. Between the reoccurring stomach bugs, processing time travel-related trauma, and my newfound fear of smallpox, I had no desire to expend any energy getting to know—and having to pretend around—new people.

That all changed when the baron and his entourage returned.

The morning after our first dinner, Agnes dragged me from bed at an absurdly early hour to be groomed and dressed. "You've been summoned by the lady of Kendal Castle," she chirped, meaty hands dragging a comb through my hair before I even knew what was happening. She wrapped my headdress tightly around my throat, giving it a good yank across my windpipe, before roughly patting her hands down my dress as if I was coated in layers of dirt.

When Agnes felt I was presentable, she led me to Lady Gwendolyn's personal chambers where Marguerite was already sitting, holding what looked like an embroidery hoop. They stood, Gwendolyn smiling and Marguerite appearing pleasantly accepting of this new arrangement.

"Join us," Gwendolyn motioned towards a seat next to what initially looked like a massive woven blanket bunched up on the floor. The hoops they were working with were attached to what I realized was a tapestry in progress—and they assumed I knew how to embroider (like many ladies of stature) and would be assisting them.

"I'm afraid my skills with a needle and thread are lacking," I demurred before I could ruin what they were working on.

"Nonsense," Gwendolyn waved me off. "This is for practice. Look closer." She pointed to the fabric.

I knelt beside the tapestry and pulled up a corner to see what she was talking about. They had stitched images of battles with victorious heroes, idyllic farm scenes, drunken holiday celebrations, sumptuous feasts, bountiful harvests, and various other vignettes of life in both Kendal Castle and its adjoining town, Kirkby Kendal. Each scene was stitched with various degrees of skill, some rudimentary and simple, others so complex they were life-like illustrations made of thread. Some utilized multiple bright colors, the shading creating a three-dimensional effect. Others were simple black and brown threads creating rough outlines, reminiscent of the Bayeux Tapestry. Some of the scenes were so large, the figures were the length of my forearm. In others, the figures were smaller than my pinkie finger.

"What is this practice for?" I asked.

"We will begin a tapestry commemorating the recent victories in France," Marguerite answered softly. Her voice was breathy and gentle, like wind through flower petals. I picked up on a note of sadness—it was not lost on me that Marguerite herself was French, and this tapestry would celebrate the losses and humiliation of her people.

"I see," I nodded as Gwendolyn fastened another hoop to the practice tapestry and handed it to me. My sewing skills were rudimentary at best, but I was a fast learner and was being given the chance to practice. Plus, it's not like I had anything else going on.

The idea of being here with these ladies, learning about how noble women in 15th century England lived, and thus getting to reclaim some agency over my life, appealed to me. Perhaps if I was regarded as a lady myself, I could assert myself more effectively with Agnes. Or confront the hostile glares of the people who lived here. Or perhaps even request different food. I could gain some semblance of control back over my life, bring back some order to the chaos. And in turn, make the coming months more bearable.

I watched surreptitiously as they worked, mimicking the process as best I could. The ladies chatted about their summer at court, detailing who wore what, who had married and who was recently widowed, snippets of court gossip, and what not. Their questions for me were limited to how had we been treated since arriving, did I need anything they had not yet provided, and would I like some gowns of my own made so I did not have to keep wearing Lady Gwendolyn's. (Which, yes, of course.) That was all fine by me. I was there to learn.

And though I'd been nervous about the vague backstories George gave Edward when we arrived, Gwendolyn and Marguerite didn't ask me anything about it. I didn't know why. Medieval etiquette? This is what I was wanted to find out. Regardless, I was grateful to not have to fumble about for lies.

I practiced stitching simple flowers to get the hang of managing the various threads before I attempted something more sophisticated. Though I was often impatient and thought embroidery would be tedious, there was something about the repetitive stitching I found meditative and calming. As my first flower—a rough pink rose—took shape, the satisfaction of seeing it come to life soothed my mind and distracted me from the stress and trauma of the past few weeks.

Plus, I genuinely enjoyed hearing the women chat about King Henry's court. It was not lost on me that this was history; I was living out a scene from one of my beloved historical fiction books.

A servant brought us our midday meal in Gwendolyn's chambers. We paused our work to enjoy roasted chicken, mashed turnips, and bread—a blessedly simple meal I had no trouble eating. It was a rare sunny afternoon, and light filtered through the paned glass, warming the room. Combined with the goblet of Bordeaux I'd had with lunch, I was feeling toasty and content for the first time since we were dumped in 1420.

When I was so relaxed I was dozy, an insistent, "meow" startled me awake. Gustav, the strange cat we'd seen hanging out with sheep, appeared out of nowhere and brushed up against Gwendolyn's leg. He was wearing a bow made of frayed blue tartan.

"Oh look!" Gwendolyn exclaimed with a clap. "I wonder when this one is from." She picked up the cat, rubbed his ears, and inspected his bowtie before dropping him gently to the floor and retrieving a leather-bound book from a table in the corner of her chambers. She flipped open the book and scratched a series of notes on the pages before leaving it open to dry on the table.

Marguerite gave me a pointed look, the kind of look that said, *yes, this is kooky behavior and you're not imagining it.*

I gave her a nod and hoped I communicated that I understood. Which I did not.

Near the end of the afternoon, Marguerite rose and announced she was tired and would be going to her quarters to rest for a bit. She addressed me. "Tomorrow is market day in town. Would you and Lord George like to accompany us?"

"It would be my honor," I dipped into a slight curtsy due to a woman of higher rank than myself.

Marguerite smiled, gave us an almost imperceptible nod of her head, and floated out of the room.

"She is with child, of course," murmured Gwendolyn after she had left. "It is early, so she is quite tired most of the time." She yanked out a tangled stitch and reset it. "Do you and George have children?" She asked tentatively.

"We do not." I always hoped to sound light and unbothered when people asked me this question. But I feared I never did.

Gwendolyn only glanced at me for a second, long enough for me to see sadness and longing written on her face—an expression only certain women could understand. "We have not been so blessed either, my dear." She resumed her stitching. "This is not Lady Marguerite's first pregnancy."

My heart clenched. I did not need to ask any further questions.

21

GEORGE

Market day came once a week in the town square. It was a chance for all the various tradespeople, farmers, and peddlers to sell goods they'd spent the previous week harvesting, building, shearing, and so on. When Rhiannon told me we'd been invited, I couldn't hide my excitement. Yes, we'd had to deal with a stupid amount of gross and uncomfortable things, but the chance to witness a medieval marketplace almost made this catastrophe worth it. Almost.

Edward and Marguerite rode ahead of us on his massive black stallion. She leaned against his chest, her hands holding the reins and guiding the horse down the hill, while his hands were wrapped around her waist. I jealously watched as Edward nuzzled his wife's neck and they shared some quiet words, intended only for each other.

Rhiannon and I rode a gentle brown beast who trotted amiably along the path with very little command on my part. Rhi sat in front of me, but she kept her back straight and worked to maintain distance between us—unlike Marguerite who seemed inclined to press into her husband as much as possible. Though the cold had driven Rhi into my arms in bed, and though she occasionally grabbed my hand out of habit, most of the time she kept an untouchable distance between us. I knew she was torn between seeking out the comfort of familiar human touch in a wildly stressful situation and protecting her fragile heart. As was I.

We stabled our horses at an inn on the edge of town, leaving them in the hands of a boy who couldn't have been more than twelve years old, but knew Edward and was clearly familiar with the routine.

The packed-mud road leading into town was punctuated with jutting stones, and more than once I reached out to grab Rhiannon's elbow when she slipped or tripped over the sawdust-filled toe of her supposedly fashionable boot. With the stupid elongated toes, we both clopped around like ducks wearing flippers, marking us as clumsy and odd strangers.

The market itself was a bustling, loud, crowded, smelly affair—but it was also the coolest thing I'd ever seen. Stalls lined both sides of the road, selling everything from hats to raw wool to apples to tools. Performers juggled, told bawdy jokes, and played tunes on rudimentary flutes and stringed instruments. We were surrounded by the voices of people striking deals, haggling for lower prices, or bartering goods and resources like a real-life *Settlers of Catan*. It reeked of old cow, pungent cheese, and stale sweat. But I also picked up notes of honey, lavender, linen, and crisp wood smoke. It was October, and the low autumn sun shimmered over wooden and thatched roofs, backdropped by ruby, copper, and gold-leaved trees.

I watched as old friends reunited with hugs and slaps on the back, close friends commiserated with heads tilted to hear each other over the din, and adversaries lobbed various insults and complaints from across the stalls.

However, nothing prepared us for the reception Edward and Marguerite received.

The crowds parted as the couple moved through the market, many people bowing as they passed. But it was not fear, nor even simple respect of status that drove the behavior—it was clear the townsfolk loved them. Vendors smiled, dipped graciously, and were clearly excited when one of them would pause to admire the goods they were selling. They scurried over to show Margurite bolts of fine wools and silks, bakers offered Edward samples of their pies and tarts, and both were greeted warmly by everyone they encountered. Many paid special welcome to Marguerite, as she'd been gone much of the summer. In return, the two asked respectful questions, spent money lavishly at multiple stalls, and complimented the goods of many of the vendors who interacted with them—driving up business for all of them.

I was dumbfounded. Edward and Margurite were like rock stars in this town. They were easily the richest, handsomest, best dressed couple for miles. Even I briefly forgot who I was and what I was doing there, totally dazzled by these medieval influencers.

"Why do I want to ask for their autograph?" I murmured to Rhiannon.

"Because Marguerite is basically a Disney princess," she sighed adoringly. We both watched as the white silk veil Marguerite wore floated in the breeze, casting a pale halo around her face. "I didn't know loose veils were an option," Rhi grumbled under her breath.

Rhiannon and I were not getting the same response, despite being part of Edward and Marguerite's entourage. Much like in the castle, we were either ignored, shunned, or people made the sign of the cross and put space between us. "For heaven's sake," Rhi muttered after a fruit vendor slapped her hand away when she reached out to touch an apple.

After meeting the baron, my mind got to working out why people would be treating us like this. But it wasn't until seeing how Edward and Marguerite were treated that something occurred to me.

"Oh shit, I think get it now," I muttered under my breath.

"Get what?" Rhiannon asked, examining a bolt of burgundy velvet.

I took the bolt of fabric out of her hands and set it back on the pile (pretending to ignore the glare the vendor gave me) and pulled her down a quiet side street, removed from the dense crowd. "I think I know why everyone has been giving us dirty looks."

Rhiannon crossed her arms and glanced to her side where the market was fully bustling. "They probably think you're Lord Henry's illegitimate son," she replied before meeting my eyes. "A bastard. And thanks to you, I'm your, quote 'filthy Spaniard' wife. It's not a mystery. Just one more super fun thing we get to deal with."

"That's what I was thinking too, though it could be more than that. Lord Henry has no living heirs. Lady Marguerite is his closest blood kin, so she and

Edward are set to inherit the barony. And they are clearly well-loved by this town."

Rhiannon scratched the side of her tightly wrapped head. "And they think you're here to make a claim?"

"Yup. And who knows what kind of baron I would be. In this time, lords could be brutally unfair, greedy, and incompetent, making life miserable for everyone. As baron, Henry dispenses justice, collects taxes, solves disputes, and so on. He must be good at it because it's clear the people of Kendal are prospering, which means they don't want anything to change. As far as they know, Edward will continue whatever practices are keeping things peaceful and fruitful. Whereas I am an unknown quantity."

Rhiannon bit her lip. "And it hasn't been that long after recovering from the devastation of the plague. Succession battles are always a mess and the commoners get screwed." She glanced back at the market, as if considering it in a new light. "Which brings us back to why do you look so much like him? Do you think ... well, do you think you *could* be related to him? The names 'de Ros' and 'Rosen' aren't that all that different. Maybe these people have the right idea."

The question made me uneasy, so I waved it away. "I don't know and right now, it doesn't matter. We can ask them in 2020 when we make it home. That's what I'm focused on. Survival." I considered the stream of people walking past our little alleyway. "I wish I could tell them I have no desire to be the baron. It's too much responsibility."

Rhiannon snorted. "That could be the title of your memoir: It's Too Much Responsibility, a life spent avoiding hard things, by George Rosen."

I glared at her. "Hey, I don't avoid hard things. I married you, didn't I?"

"You know what? You can go to hell." Rhi snapped while turning on her heel. I grabbed her by the upper arm before she could take off.

"Wait! I didn't mean you personally. I meant marriage in general is difficult. Sometimes it's brutally hard."

Rhiannon stiffened but didn't pull away. I dropped my hand from her arm and stepped closer. "I didn't mean *you* are a difficult thing, not at all. Just that

I knew marriage would be hard and I did it anyway, okay? If anything, I'm the one who made it too difficult."

She met my eyes, chin jutted out. "How do you know it was hard, George? You checked out for big parts of it. I was doing it alone. And it *was* difficult. Too difficult to keep going the way things were."

"I know. And I regret it every day. I regretted it the very first night we were apart, and now I'm working to make it right. But," I gestured towards the medieval town, "I'm obviously failing miserably. I know this wasn't what you signed up for when you came with me on this trip."

I was trying to make it right, which was why she came with me to England in the first place, and why she'd ended up in the year 1420 where she was forced to eat organ meats and have lice picked out of her hair every night.

"You never even asked me if that's what I want. Which, I don't. All I want is for you to stop trying to make it right, okay? I'm exhausted and it's in the past. All I want is to go home. That's all you should focus on."

My heart sank but Rhiannon made no move to step away.

"However," she continued, "since we're stuck here together, and the letter implies we must work together to get home, then while we're here, we can pretend to be a happily married couple. At least by medieval standards. That's the best I can offer."

I shifted on my feet, hands tucked into my cloak against the chill of the shade we stood in. "I understand. I will do everything in my power to get us home safely. I won't fuck this up. I promise."

22

GEORGE

Call me Dumbass. Some days ago—never mind how long precisely—having little or no money in my purse, and nothing particular to interest me in the castle, I thought I would ride about and see the watery part of England.

Clifford informed me that a retinue of the baron's men were going hunting for stags near the lakes, and if I wished to take part in the bounty of the hunt, it was my duty to join them. Later that day, Henry pulled me aside and offered me one of his horses and some hunting garments. He looked concerned for me, as if he knew the man with soft hands and unmarked skin was in for something well beyond his ability.

Which, in retrospect, I was.

I'd intentionally waited until the morning of the hunt to inform Rhiannon I was going with them. It was purely strategic: I would give her as little time as possible to worry and to plead her case.

"Hunting? Are you insane?!" she demanded. "Do you know that hunting is one of the leading causes of death for men in the Middle Ages? Oh gosh let's see, you could be impaled by a boar, shot through with arrows, crushed by your own horse," she ticked off the grisly list of outcomes one finger at a time, as if reading through a data set. "Run through by a stag, knocked unconscious by a tree branch, disemboweled somehow," she continued, "And, by the way, we're not exactly in a time when medical intervention is all that helpful." Rhiannon jabbed her finger at me, emphasizing the seriousness of her point. "Do you want to deal with rabies or wounds in a time when antibiotics and anesthesia are *centuries* away from being invented? Do you want some medieval quack to piss on your wounds, slap some leeches on you, then leave it up to quote 'God's will' to save you?"

I listened, nodding along as if agreeing, keenly aware that interrupting Rhiannon when she was laying out her point of view only made her angrier and more insistent on winning her case. When she paused her opening statements, I placed my hands gently on her shoulders but didn't say a word, only held her gaze. She shoved my hands off but didn't look away from me.

"Do you know what else was a leading cause of death in the Middle Ages? Starvation. It isn't fair to drop in unexpectedly and cut into the rations of these people. We've completely thrown off Clifford's numbers for how food is distributed. Since we are most likely going to be here a full year, we must be prepared for anything. *Even if it's hard.*" I gave her a pointed look, and she cringed. "I am going on that hunt. And I promise I will be very, very careful." I lifted my hands to place them on her shoulders again (a force of habit) but refrained and let them drop to my sides. "You don't need to worry."

Rhiannon released a held breath and stepped back. "I've also had thoughts about the rations ledger. And I feel bad about it too. But I swear to God, George, if you die and leave me alone in this place, I will kill you! I'm serious. If you abandon me again, I will *never* forgive you."

I swallowed. "That's fair," I agreed. "But I'm taking on this responsibility to show you that I can—and will—do difficult things. Okay? As for the hunt, how hard could it be?"

Rhiannon scowled. "Seriously? Were you not paying attention when I told you exactly how hard it could be?"

"Sorry, I was just trying to ease your mind."

Truthfully, I was already thinking ahead to the hunt itself and trying to assuage my own fears. It would've been a lie to say I wasn't nervous. My general plan was to stay close to Henry, learn as much as possible, and kill something if—and only if—I was absolutely compelled to. Basically, a fake-it-til-you-make-it kind of plan.

"Okay," Rhiannon squared her shoulders and bit her lip. "I will do my best not to worry. Which will be very challenging given that my day is going to be yet more gossip and embroidery, and not much else."

"I thought you were enjoying the embroidery?"

"It's good. But not all the time. My back is sore from sitting on a stool, hunched over the tapestry. And it's getting tedious."

I patted her shoulders like a coach pumping up his star athlete. "Listen, we can do this. We can do what they ask of us, when they ask it. We can and will survive. We can and will get home. I will hunt. You will embroider. And we will survive."

"We will survive," she repeated back to me. But I could see the doubt in her eyes.

I met the hunting party of the baron's men in the courtyard, with me wearing Henry's clothes and looking alarmingly like him. When Henry gave me that proud father look again, grasped me by the shoulder and said loudly, "Lord George, I cannot wait to show you the lay of these lands!" the rest of the party shifted nervously and exchanged glances with each other. Henry must have sensed the shift because he leaned close to me and said, "Never show them weakness, George. They think they're wolves, but they're really vultures waiting for a carcass."

"Wait, what?" For a moment I was back in the 21st century being lectured by my actual father.

He squeezed my shoulder, gave me a wink, and stalked off to tend to his own preparations. It did not reassure me.

Medieval society was extremely stratified—there were literally laws dictating who was allowed to wear what, based on class—and Henry was upending the hierarchy with this behavior, by dressing me in his clothes and calling me "lord."

To signify their rank, the baron's men were dressed more as if they were going to a lavish party than to chase animals through the woods. They wore mink-trimmed cloaks and yards of velvet and silk and finely-spun, brightly colored wool—a marker of their wealth and power. And they were all strapped to the hilt with intricately wrought weapons, daggers, and bows plated in gold and elaborately decorated with the symbols of their success. Which I was not.

I stood awkwardly, twisting one of my gloves in my hand, when Edward caught my eye and motioned me over with a jerk of his head. He stood away from the group, adjusting his horse's supplies and checking his own weapons. His outfit was understated compared to the rest: a black leather tunic, with a hip-length black wool cloak secured with a ruby brooch, and a deep burgundy velvet hat.

"*Lord* George," Edward drawled, adding a derisive note to the title Henry himself had added to my name. "You shall stay close to me today. Given your unfamiliarity with these woods, of course." He gave my weaponless outfit one long look with his eyebrow arched. But didn't say anything else.

"Of course," I agreed with a slight bow.

Just as I considered how much I couldn't stand him, Edward added in a low voice: "Don't let the gossip and insecurities of mere squires trouble you. For they see you only as another rung on a ladder they cannot possibly hope to scale." He patted the flank of his horse. "You and I are above such things."

"Yes, naturally," I agreed, like this had already occurred to me.

In any other situation I would not give a shit about such things, except for the fact that being on the outside of the social core impacted our ability to survive. In the far north, on lands bordering dangerously close to the hostile Scottish, in a climate that dealt brutally cold and wet weather year round, having help when you needed it could literally mean life or death.

And, despite the baron obviously favoring us, I didn't want to rely solely on his generosity. I wanted to contribute, to help. Life here was already inconceivably harsh; adding to the challenges these people faced didn't sit well with me.

I glanced up at the sky where rapidly accumulating dark clouds, and the eerily silent morning, meant a storm was coming. It only served to confirm I was right to come on this hunt, to contribute to the gathering of scarce resources, to build potentially life-saving bonds with the other men—regardless of their rank or status or what they thought of me.

We mounted our horses, left the confines of the castle, and rode down the hill to the edge of the forest. A cacophony of barking dogs, trumpeting horns, and neighing horses interrupted my rumination and marked the start of the hunt. Henry reared up his horse and led the charge behind a pack of dogs who were furiously sniffing for a trail. The dogs had handlers who blew horns to keep the group moving in the same direction, adding to the din. I wondered how they managed to kill anything when every creature in the forest was essentially getting a significant head start because of the noise.

We followed the hounds deep into the woods, riding at a brisk pace, guided by a scent only the dogs could find. Once we were so deep into the foliage that only small amounts of cold light could be seen through the heavy branches, the hunting party dismounted and tied most of the horses to trees in a small clearing.

Despite the cold, Edward discarded his cloak and strapped a quiver full of arrows to his back, with a three-point leather baldric that crossed his chest and secured at the waist. He gripped his bow with one black-gloved hand while shoving a small dagger into a leather loop at his waist.

I'm not going to lie, he looked extremely badass. As much as I wanted to dislike him, I also wanted him to like me.

And I was a little envious that outside of a middle school archery unit and countless hours playing *Call of Duty*, I'd never shot anything in my life. So wearing that type of gear would have been wasted on me.

As if he could read my mind, Edward gave me one glance and smirked. "No weapons meet your lofty standard, Lord George?"

I pretended I didn't catch the insult. Tapping my forehead, I replied, "I'm still not feeling quite right since being hit on the head and left for dead, and I didn't want to risk accidentally shooting astray and frightening our quarry. Or, worse, accidentally shooting *someone*." There was no menace in my tone. I was truly concerned I could hit someone given my complete lack of training.

Edward squared his feet and examined me, arms crossed over his chest, one eyebrow cocked. He was clearly mulling something over. He leaned down and tugged at his boot, pulling out another dagger.

I was irritated at how cool that move was—a hidden boot knife. Damn.

"As you already know, this forest is full of dangerous things. Wandering around unarmed and defenseless as a newborn babe is ill-advised. Take this." Edward pressed the knife into my open palm. I clutched the handle, metal warm from where it had been stored against his leg. I considered storing it in my own boot, but the pair Henry lent me were only ankle-high and secured with worn leather laces. I didn't think the knife would stay put.

Edward reached out and tugged a loop on the leather belt secured around my doublet. "Store it here," he commanded.

"Of course." I was embarrassed at how inexperienced and useless I was here. I came on a hunt without a single weapon—just an old, slow horse and borrowed clothes. Why hadn't I asked for some amount of training before this? I felt stupidly unprepared. I could be such a dumbass sometimes.

Edward simply nodded and stalked off towards where the rest of the hunting party had gathered.

My fake it plan was not working. I looked even more like an outsider, dependent on Edward for help. Whatever I felt about him, he had filled the role of protector and guide for me and Rhiannon. Which I hated. Sighing, I followed him, uncertain what else to do.

23

RHIANNON

I dutifully followed Gwendolyn and Marguerite down to the kitchens where the cooks were preparing a great feast that was to be held after the hunt. If all went well, everyone would dine on venison and boar from the successful outing. If not, then it was up to Gwendolyn to dictate what the menu should be.

From a toasty corner where the stone walls had absorbed heat from the always-burning fires, I watched as Gwendolyn reviewed Clifford's ledger before issuing her directives. She gave specific orders for everything from the menu to how the great hall should be decorated to who she wanted sitting at what table. I leaned against the warm stones, admiring how she managed her staff with the precision of a seasoned general giving orders. Every so often she asked me or Marguerite to taste a sip of wine, give our thoughts about a tapestry she hung, or deliver a message to one of the many servants decorating the great hall.

To my relief, we took a break from embroidery while the men were out hunting. It was a welcome change to spend my time running around the castle instead of perched on a stool. And it was satisfying to be exhausted from the fruits of my efforts instead of the constant flow of cortisol through my veins. I was aching to learn as much as I could about the little ecosystem of the castle, keen on being useful by contributing.

Sometime in the late afternoon, when preparations were mostly settled and I could barely stay upright on my sore feet, I dragged myself up the stairwell to go take a nap. Before I ascended even one level, Marguerite came barreling up the stairs after me.

"Lady Rhiannon, you must follow me!" she implored, grabbing my hand and pulling me back out towards the courtyard.

Without letting go of me, she rushed us through the main gates, over the bridge, and to the top of the hill where a cluster of guards and a messenger nervously watched the edge of the forest.

I heard the dogs' furious barking before I saw the hunting party break through the woods into view. From my vantage point, I could see a group of men moving slowly, haltingly, up the hill towards the castle. But I couldn't tell if the frenzied shouts were telling of victory in the hunt … or something else.

However, Marguerite anxiously holding both my arm and her breath told me it probably wasn't good.

I gasped when Edward and Henry stumbled into view, shouldering George between them. Two other men held his legs aloft. His left leg was soaked in blood from the knee down, his leather boot shredded and dangling. His right hand, draped over Edward's shoulder, was also coated in sticky blood.

"What happened?" I cried, stumbling down the slope towards them, my list of ways to die in medieval times cycling through my mind.

"He was slashed by a boar," Edward grimaced while gently lowering George to rest on a jutting stone. The men were out of breath and Henry mopped sweat off his brow with an embroidered handkerchief. Though they had made it to the base of the hill, they needed to stop to rest before the ascent.

"Where are the horses?" I kneeled beside George.

He was conscious, but barely. George exhaled deeply as he extended his injured leg into full view.

"Spooked by the commotion," Edward replied, a note of bitterness in his voice. "Most of the party is still in the woods searching for them."

"We got him here as quickly as we could, with the one horse we had." Henry offered.

Behind him I saw the baron's large brown mount being led out of the forest by Angus, the castle's marshal and overseer of all things horse-related. A thick trail of blood dripped down the horse's flank, most likely from where they had George riding it while they walked through the forest. Who knows how long he'd been draped over the horse, leg dangling, losing blood along the way.

I crouched next to George, pulled the remnants of his torn leggings away, and gasped when I saw the extent of his wound.

Henry explained what happened: deep in the woods, a charging boar barreled towards the hunting party. George, unaccustomed to the protocols and gestures of a group hunt, didn't understand the calls to get out of the way, and the boar slashed right through his leg.

They put him on a horse to get him to safety, but quickly observed he was losing too much blood to stay upright like that, so they pulled him off and carried him the rest of the way, leg elevated. Someone had had the sense to fasten a leather tourniquet above his knee to quell the flow of blood. But that was the extent of the first aid they'd administered before rushing him back to the castle.

George leaned forward ever so slightly and rested his clean hand on my shoulder for support as I grasped the knee of his good leg to steady myself.

"Is it bad?" he whispered, out of breath.

"It's not great," I whispered back.

He winced and sighed deeply. Color had drained from his face, leaving him a worrying shade of gray. Sweat glistened on his forehead and his hair was damp.

"You should ... " he wheezed, tried again. "If you think this bad ... you should see other guy ... " George held up his hand, dried blood caked in the lines of his palm, grinning at me through his pain.

"He gave the boar a good stab, right in the neck," Henry said proudly while making stabbing motions with his hand.

"It wasn't a killing stab, though we did manage to take it down," Edward clarified.

Henry gave Edward an aggressively jovial slap on the back, then clutched his shoulder tightly. "He impaled the beast *after* his leg was torn to bits. That is enough." The meaning in his tone was clear: George's heroism was not to be questioned. "Come, let us get him inside."

The men hoisted George back up.

"Angus, fetch the barber-surgeon, quickly, before it is too late." Henry commanded his marshal. Angus rushed off without a word.

When I shot him a sharp look over his choice of words, Henry pointed up at the swirls of snowflakes peppering the air. "It's the first snow. It will make the roads impassable for the barber to get here. We best hurry."

As the men hauled George up the hill, I stood where I was. I can admit, panic had frozen me to the spot. I was in unknown territory.

As George was carried away from me, I heard him moan: "Stay."

"What?" I scurried to his side and grabbed his hand, now hanging over Edward's shoulder. Edward clutched George's arm as they took each cumbersome step up the rocky path towards the castle.

"Stay," George rasped again. He turned to his left to try and look at me, but before he could say more, his head rolled back and he lost consciousness.

24

RHIANNON

"Rhiannon, don't panic."

I tried to move but could not even open my eyes. Then, searing pain. I started shaking until something pressed against me, something warm and weighted.

"Help is on the way, honey. Just breathe. I'm here. Everything will be okay."

I could not feel my left side. To my right, a warm rough hand grasped mine. I clutched it as hard as I could, digging my nails into the calloused flesh.

"George?" the name sounded hoarse and rough in my mouth.

"I'm here. I'm not going anywhere. Breathe, honey, just breathe."

"Stay," I moaned. I didn't know why.

"I'm not leaving," he replied, stroking my hand. "I've got you. You're going to be okay."

I heard sirens, followed by voices, chaotic and unfamiliar. I heard George describe something to these voices, these intruders in my head.

Then blackness.

Beeping, more voices, and a white light slicing across my eyes so harsh I could not bear the thought of opening them further. Yet the desire to understand where I was summoned enough force to keep them open. I blinked rapidly as fluorescent lights singed my retinas. The work to keep my eyes open exhausted me. I closed them and decided to leverage other senses instead.

I inhaled sharply. Rubbing alcohol, cotton, and latex permeated my senses.

"She's waking up," a woman said.

"Rhiannon Rosen?"

"Hmmm?" I mumbled, still unable to open my mouth. It felt sealed shut, though I did not know why.

"Ms. Rosen, do you know where you are? Do you remember what happened?"

I tried to shake my head, only to find it immobilized. A warm hand rested on my thigh, gentle. Comforting.

"George?" His name was the only word I could form with this tongue that felt like it had been packed in salt for a decade.

"I'm here, honey. You're going to be okay."

"What happened?" I croaked. I cracked my eyes open for a few fleeting moments. Though the images were blurry, I could make out a woman with fine black hair wearing a white lab coat standing next to the bed. George stood opposite her, his hand resting on my leg. And behind them a nurse, clad in deep blue scrubs, tapped information into a machine on a rolling cart.

The doctor spoke: "You were in a car accident. For now, all you need to do is rest."

They put something into the IV bag hanging above me and all went dark again.

I opened my eyes again to see the room was darkened, the lights dimmed to cast a creamy taupe haze over everything. To my left, George was sleeping on a vinyl armchair, his long legs dangling over the armrest, his head twisted at an angle he would undoubtedly regret later.

I wiggled my toes. They responded accordingly. I bent my knees ever so slightly. Though the weight of the blankets and the compression pads around my calves made it challenging, I was relieved to learn my legs were in good order. I tried to move my arms, only to find the left one was in a thick white cast up to my shoulder and my right arm was wrapped in wires and the IV line.

I could not turn my head. My neck was braced in thick foam, keeping me immobile and staring straight ahead.

But there was no pain, only stiffness and a sense of floating beside myself. A plastic line ran oxygen into my nostrils. I took a deep breath, letting the cool air fill my stuffy lungs. I coughed, took steadying breaths, swallowed.

George woke up, stretched, blinked, and smiled at me. "Hey there," he whispered. "How are you feeling?"

"You stayed?" I rasped.

"Of course. I haven't left your side."

I observed him from the corner of my left eye as I could not move my head. George swung his legs around and stood up, shaking the stiff sleep from his limbs. He came around and perched on the right side of the bed where I seemed to be mostly unharmed, and grasped my fingers, mindful of the IV line taped to my hand.

"What happened?"

"We were driving home from dinner. Someone who was texting and driving ran the red light and T-boned us. They hit the left side of the car. You were driving. But the airbags deployed, which is why you avoided being more seriously hurt."

I grimaced. "What's the damage, doc?"

"Well, your arm is broken in two places, so you get to wear this awesome cast for a bit. But I guess that means you get out of dish duty for at least seven weeks." He grinned at me, relief lighting up his eyes.

I coughed out a weak laugh. George knew how much I hated doing dishes. But I did them anyway since he did almost ninety percent of the cooking in our home and it didn't seem fair he should have to clean up as well.

"They're keeping you overnight for observation, but there's no sign of concussion or spinal injury. Just lots of bruises. I already let Carmen know what happened. You're officially on medical leave for at least the next three weeks, so they got a long-term sub for your classes."

"You handled all that?" My words were weak, mostly whispers.

"I got you, Rhi." George squeezed my fingers. I wiggled my fingers back, letting the tips brush against the palm of his hand.

"Are you okay?" I asked. He was in the car with me, after all.

"Yep. A bit bruised and shaken up, but no significant injuries. And now that I know you're going to be okay, I'm feeling better."

"You should go home and get some sleep," I wheezed.

"Not a chance. We'll go home together, okay? I'm going to stay." He brushed his lips across my forehead, the only affection he could show me without disrupting the lines, wires, and casting cloaking my body.

I tried to nod but it was mostly a twitch given the neck brace. My eyes watered and I blinked back the tears. George thumbed away a tear that rolled down my temple.

"I'm going to stay," he reiterated.

Stay. He stayed for me. I'd spent so much of my life handling emergencies completely by myself, that I was unprepared for what it would be like to have someone here with me. "Thank you. Can I ask you something?"

"Anything."

"Earlier I remember starting to shake, but someone put something warm on me. What was that?"

"That was me. Before the ambulance got there, it seemed like you were going into shock. I put my coat over you and tried to keep you calm until help arrived. Which is a good thing, really, because I was in half a mind to drag the other driver from their car and beat the shit out of them."

I choked out a small laugh. "What happened to them?"

"They walked away from the accident uninjured, but the police came and there were many witnesses, so I don't think they're getting away without some legal consequences. But let's not worry about it right now, okay? All you need to focus on is recovering."

"I can do that." I inhaled deeply, starting to feel like I was occupying my own body again. I gazed at my husband, still holding my fingers, watching me curiously. "You stayed," I marveled again.

"I didn't want you to wake up and not know where you were or what was going on." George kissed my fingertips and gently pressed his stubbly cheek into my palm. "Plus, I wanted to stay."

I started crying then, the trauma and uncertainty of the evening washing over me.

But mostly, I cried for all the past versions of myself who experienced pain and didn't have anyone to stay with me.

The tears made me drowsy. I closed my eyes and slipped back into sleep.

Later. Someone took my hand in theirs. Stale cigarette smoke and Calvin Klein Eternity perfume—a painfully familiar combination—clouded my senses. I heard rustling and felt the bed shift.

"How's my sweet girl?" a voice with a Southern twang, the sound of fake nails tapping on something, and the crack of chewing gum roused me from my sleep. The sounds were also familiar—and unwelcome.

"Mom?" I cracked open one eye.

"I'm here, baby," she cooed, leaning forward from where she sat on the left side of the bed. Her weight pulled down the mattress and I began to shift painfully on my injured side.

"Stop!" I managed to gasp, before she could jostle me any further.

I opened both eyes to see my mother stand up and begin rummaging around in her sizeable shoulder bag. Her hair was dyed a brassy copper and teased into a crispy cloud around her head. She wore faded black leggings, her signature beat up motorcycle jacket, and a tight pink shirt. My mother may have been consistently inconsistent in my life, but her familiar style remained firmly rooted back in the late 80's of her glory days.

I hadn't seen her in several months. While we'd spoken a few times over the phone (mostly when she needed money), for the most part my mother lived her life, and I lived mine.

From her bag, she pulled out a pack of nicotine gum and added a piece to the wad already in her mouth. She tossed the empty foil tray at the trash can, where it missed and hit the floor. She made no move to pick it up. If I hadn't been anchored to the bed with various tubes and lines, I would have picked it up for her.

Instead, I tried to ignore the litter.

"What are you doing here?" I rasped, voice still hoarse.

"A momma can't visit her baby in the hospital?" she asked defensively. As if this wasn't the same woman who missed my high school graduation because she was partying with a group of Hell's Angels in a Motel 6 in Macon.

I sighed. "It's not serious. I'm going home later today."

She hoisted the bag up on her shoulder and cracked her gum. "You should get a good look at yourself before saying that. You're a real mess, babe."

"Mom," I groaned. "Just tell me what you want."

"Well, firstly I came to see you to make sure you're okay." She tilted her head down and smiled up at me, mimicking Princess Di's signature look. I think she was hoping to channel some sense of authenticity, despite being completely full of crap.

Before I could begin to entertain ideas of what she might want from me, George pushed open the door with his foot and entered carrying two cups of coffee and a tower of chocolate pudding cups stacked precariously atop them. When he saw my mother standing over the bed, he stopped short.

"Candace." He scowled, furrowing his brow. "Did Satan accidentally leave the gates to Hell open again? What are you doing here and what do I need to do to make you go away?"

George absolutely hated my mother and made no show of hiding it. It didn't help that she had a long and sordid history of being a perpetual gambler, drunk, liar, and occasional con woman.

And he knew too many stories of her forgetting me in some fairly precarious situations when I was a kid.

She gave him the same coquettish smile and replied, "George, you can call me Candy." She licked her lips. "*Ya know, 'cause I'm sweet.*" This last part came out so menacing, I felt a chill crawl up my arms.

Mom turned towards me and lit up with her most inauthentic benevolent smile. "Sweet as in, I have somethin' for you this time." She wagged her finger at me, winking like she held all the cards and then some.

George set the coffee and puddings down on my bedside table. He stood to my right, staying close, protective. "Whatever it is, we don't want it. Now please, leave Rhi alone. She needs to rest."

Mom shook her head. "You know, there could be a big settlement for you kids. Rumor is the driver was a bit, shall we say," she tipped her head back and used her hand to mimic drinking, "and she may or may not've been textin'. That'd be a pretty big settlement if you decided to sue her ass. Of course, you'd be needing a witness and all to testify. One that I may or may not know." She smirked at George, declaring victory.

He took one step forward and narrowed his eyes at her. "What's the catch?"

Mom faked indignation, placing her hand on her chest. "There's no catch. Just an arrangement ... of sorts. Bonnie will testify she was in the car with the driver—which she honest-to-God was—and when you get your settlement money, you give her just a tiny ... well ... really just a smidge, of a cut." Mom paused to fluff her hair. "And you send me a little ol' finder's fee too, of course. For putting y'all together."

George laughed derisively and threw his hands in the air. "Oh, of course, *Candy*! We will just participate in bribery with you, of course. Because why wouldn't we want to pay off a witness, which, I'm pretty sure is a fucking felony!"

Mom looked truly indignant this time. "Who said jack shit about 'bribery'? It's just a little tit for tat. That woman was Bonnie's best friend! Why shouldn't she get a little somethin' out of the deal? She's ending a friendship to help your sorry asses! She doesn't have to say nothing. But she will and for just a tiny cut! As for me, I'm the one settin' up the whole deal *and* I'm your momma, which apparently doesn't seem to count for much these days."

"Get out." George pointed at the doorway. "Before I call security, get the fuck out of here."

I used to intervene in their blow ups out of some misguided need to keep the peace. But I was too tired, drugged, and sad to do much besides lie on the gurney. My head throbbed, my arm felt like it had been split in two and taped back together, and I just wanted to go home.

And honestly, I was glad George called her out on her shit. My mom had been taking advantage of me in one form or another since I was small, and I wished I had the courage—or at least I wished I could give up on the idea of her ever being a loving mother—to stand up for myself.

Mom heaved her bag up on her shoulder. It was so large, so brimming with stuff, that I briefly wondered if she was living out of it. I had to push that thought out of my mind before I offered something stupid—like for her to come stay with us.

She stared at me. "Bonnie said that bitch is rich. You're leaving money on the table, babe. That's real dumb. You going to let this man tell you what to do?" Mom snapped her fingers in George's general direction. "I thought you was one of them feminists," she smirked and headed for the door. With her hand on the doorknob, she glanced at George and said with aspartame sweetness, "You could use that money to get yourself a haircut."

He clenched his fists at his sides. "We both know you're jealous because I have better hair than you."

Mom flipped him off then slipped out the door without saying goodbye to me.

George exhaled, shook out his hands, and ran them through his (admittedly, great) hair. "This is why I got extra pudding. I had a feeling we'd be needing it. How did she even know you were here?"

"She's always had her ways," I sighed. Mom always had this sixth sense when it comes to me possibly getting money that she wants a piece of, combined with numerous means and methods of gathering intel. If she wasn't so committed to a life of debauchery and crime, she probably would've been a hell of a CIA agent.

George cracked open one of the pudding cups, stirred it around, and offered me a bite by holding the laden spoon up to my lips.

Before I took the bite, I held his gaze and said, "Thank you for making her leave. I don't think I had it in me to do it myself. Even if her presence always makes my life worse."

He nodded. "I may or may not have some experience with a narcissist for a parent. Though admittedly mine is at least gainfully employed and a law-abiding citizen. But it doesn't matter. You've had my back with him, and I've got yours. We're a team."

"A team," I nodded savoring the pudding, still basking in the warmth of the fact that he stayed. *He stayed*.

25

GEORGE

Growing up, Rhiannon's mother was a literal criminal who moved them all over the place to evade authorities when her stolen checks eventually bounced, or she was caught using someone else's identity, or when she'd simply pickpocketed someone who noticed in time.

Her only redeeming quality was that she never left Rhiannon alone with any of the thugs and criminals she liked to hang out with—nor did she ever let them touch her. For all of Candace's (excuse me, *Candy's*) neglect and selfishness, she drew the line at letting others hurt her daughter. Which is the only reason she had even a smidge of a presence in our lives.

At our wedding, I caught her going through my dad's wallet, which she'd dug out of his suit pocket while he was dancing. I grabbed her wrist before she could pocket a wad of cash. If she had been any other guest, I would have kicked her out. But I didn't want to humiliate my new wife, so I let her mom stay (with a few threats about what would happen if she tried that bullshit again) and I never told Rhiannon about it.

But it made Candy and I lifelong enemies and we didn't even try to hide it.

Nor would I want to. Rhiannon had been through enough because of that woman and she'd been dealing with her all alone, until I came along.

At every new school she attended, Rhiannon watched as all the other well-dressed, well-fed, well-loved little girls got into their mother's minivans and

SUVs and went home to a place where they undoubtedly had warm beds and full bellies. Which she rarely had.

Rhiannon spent her childhood wearing clothes fished out of lost and found bins, sleeping in the backseat of her mom's Buick when they couldn't afford a motel room, and sometimes having nothing but a bag of chips for dinner—or nothing at all.

So, she resolved to have a family and a home of her own, one filled with good food, clean clothes, and loving gestures.

Because I had grown up as an only child, and lost my mom when I was in high school, I too wanted the family Rhiannon described in her aspirations. I spent many evenings home alone while Dad worked, wondering what it would have been like to be eating dinner with parents and siblings like a normal kid.

But even if I hadn't already wanted it, I was crazy about Rhiannon and would have done just about anything for her. When we got married, we resolved to be the family each of us longed for growing up. We made a point of eating dinner together most nights, showing up for each other's special events, and protecting each other from the uncertainty and chaos of the world.

Which meant there was no way I was going to let Candy come into her life and mess it all up with her outrageously self-absorbed and generally shitty self. Especially when Rhiannon was already in pain.

I had her back because I knew she had mine.

We were a family.

26

LATE OCTOBER 1420

RHIANNON

"Angus informed me that the weather has turned and the barber-surgeon cannot get here until morning … if not later." Clifford looked grim. He pursed his lips while twisting a wooden rosary between his fingers.

The men brought George inside the gatehouse and into a lower-level room, as hauling him up the narrow, steep, curving stairs to our quarters would only worsen his injury. They laid him out on a small wooden bed, stoked a fire, and quietly conversed over what should happen next. Icy, dense snow was already heaping into piles along the castle's steep path; no one could safely come or go until the weather cleared.

George's gray face was slick with sweat, his hair in a tangled mass. I clutched his hand, feeling helpless. There were no ambulances to call, no doctors dispensing pain meds and antibiotics, no nurses bearing trays with sterilized suture materials. No one other than the ill-equipped, ill-informed people of the castle to help.

Upon hearing of the injury, Gwendolyn and Agnes had rushed into the room, Gwendolyn in a near-panic. Henry embraced her and stroked her cheek, offering low words of comfort, before heading off to monitor the return of the hunting party and the horses.

George opened his eyes, winced with pain, and closed them again. "Stay," he murmured.

"I'm here," I leaned close to him. "I'm not going anywhere."

"Good," he breathed.

I squeezed his fingers, which were growing increasingly warm as a fever developed. I wracked my memory for some know-how of what to do to help him. All I could think of were basic steps, without time-period specific instructions on how to accomplish them:

Prevent infection.

Check the bone for any breaks.

Clean and stitch the wound.

Wrap the leg.

Do whatever it takes to save George's life, even if it means improvising along the way.

I ran through the process again, mentally making a list of what supplies I needed that they could provide. I could do this. I was terrified, but the thought of losing George was enough motivation to push through the fear.

I stood up and addressed the group. "I know what to do." Everyone paused their mutterings and looked at me curiously. I considered a viable reason for why I'd have any knowledge in medical arts. I wasn't as good as George at spinning helpful stories on the spot; I mainly dealt in facts and evidence. But I did know history. "I, uh, spent quite a bit of time helping the barber-surgeon in our village." I swallowed and smoothed my headdress nervously. "He was quite successful treating injuries such as this. I ... I think I can manage."

No one objected, so I proceeded with my plan. "Agnes, please fetch a pot of water and bring it to a boil. As much as you can."

Agnes looked to Gwendolyn, confused. She nodded at the maid. "As fast as you can, Agnes. Do whatever Lady Rhiannon asks." She turned to me. "We are at your service. What else do you need?"

"I need clean cloths, a needle and thread," I glanced at George, who seemed to be unconscious. "As well as brandy. Lots of it. Plus, uh ... honey and garlic." Those were the main antibacterial agents I could think of that would be easy enough to procure.

There was also vinegar, but I suspected George would rather die than have vinegar poured into his gaping wound.

Edward, who silently watched from the corner, stepped forward. "I'll summon the kitchen staff for the rest of these items."

After everyone departed to gather supplies, I knelt beside George and grabbed his hand.

"I'm going to stitch you up." I didn't know if he could hear me, but I had to tell someone, anyone, before I did anything else. "I'm going to figure this out. But ... I'm really scared." I wiped a few loose tears away with my free hand. "I'm terrified I can't do enough. Or, worse. I'm scared I'll make it worse," I confessed quietly through my tears. "Just please don't leave me here alone. Please do whatever it takes to survive."

George's eyes fluttered and he gave my hand a weak squeeze. It seemed like he'd lost a lot of blood, but there was nothing I could do about that. I could only get the wound closed, hopefully quickly enough to ward off infection.

"I'll do my very best," I promised through tears. I kissed the palm of his hand and rested my forehead against it. "I'll stay and I'll do anything I can to help you," I vowed. "Just ... please don't leave me."

Edward returned first. He showed me a glass bottle with a cork stopper. "I believe this may be a bit better than brandy. Aqua vitae. The water of life."

One sniff of the acrid stench of distilled alcohol told me it was exactly what I needed. "Yes, perfect," I graciously accepted the closest thing to antiseptic in Kendal Castle.

"George, you need to drink this." I commanded. Edward put his hands under George's arms to help lift him up into a sitting position so he could drink from the bottle I held up to his lips.

He had been in and out of consciousness since being carried back from the hunt, and I'd hoped he'd stay blissfully unaware of the pain that was coming.

But no such luck. I held the aqua vitae up to his lips, giving him just enough to dull the pain, but not so much as to thin his blood to a dangerous level. He drank from the bottle, coughed and wheezed, then resumed taking slow breaths between each sip of the liquor.

"That's enough," I said gently when I estimated he'd had about two shots.

Clifford returned with a pot of honey and several cloves of garlic, followed by Agnes and Gwendolyn with a team of kitchen maids hauling a bucket of water and a cauldron for boiling, plus several linen cloths. They set everything up in the fireplace, stoked the flames so they burned hotter, and began mashing the honey and garlic into a poultice on my instruction.

Once the rest of the supplies were gathered, water was coming to a low boil in a pot hanging over the fire, and I'd determined the ideal order of operations, I allowed myself a slow steady breath to calm my nerves. "I can do this," I muttered under my breath.

I had Edward and Clifford gently roll George over, so his injury was facing up, giving me easier access. They held him steady and put a small wooden stick in his mouth to bite down on—a centuries-old battlefield ritual performed by men when a gravely wounded comrade was about to undergo an extremely painful procedure without any kind of numbing. George groaned into the pillow, but didn't protest.

I swirled the aqua vitae around in the bottle. "George, this is going to hurt." I spoke so softly, I almost wished he couldn't hear me.

Edward held George's leg steady as I poured a considerable amount of alcohol over his wound, making sure to disinfect every little jagged gash.

He roared in pain, face buried in the pillows, panting and spluttering very modern sounding expletives.

While we disinfected the wound, Gwendolyn and Agnes boiled the cloths, squeezed them out with hands that had been doused in aqua vitae, and hung them over a rod by the fireplace to dry. When they finished with the cloths, they boiled the needle and thread according to my specifications. "'tis a bit odd," I heard Agnes murmur to Gwendolyn as they worked, but she followed my directions precisely, nonetheless.

When I was satisfied with the sterilization of my tools, I took one of the cloths, doused it in freshly boiled and cooled water, and began cleaning George's leg. The tourniquet had caused the stream of blood to taper off enough so I could clean and sew him up. I dabbed at the dried blood, careful not to exacerbate his jagged wound any further. As I worked, I could see that the boar had gouged a Y-shaped tear along the underside of his calf muscle.

I felt along his leg; nothing seemed to be broken. It was a miracle the bone wasn't shattered in the process. I whispered thanks to any deity who may be watching over hapless time travelers that I didn't have to set a bone. Basic first aid and stitching I could handle. Setting a bone correctly? Not likely.

However, I still had to sew up a gruesome wound.

I rinsed my hands in aqua vitae again and took up the needle and thread.

"I'll go as quick as I can," I said more to myself than to George. I squeezed the base of the wound, at the bottom of the Y torn into his leg, while pushing the needle through his flesh. George mumbled a combination of prayers and curses around the stick in his mouth, but he didn't move or jerk out of my grasp.

Edward and Clifford continued to hold him, both refusing to watch the procedure.

I worked quickly, sewing up his wound as carefully and as disconnected as if I was simply embroidering an unpleasant tapestry. A tapestry that occasionally stretched and oozed blood and smelled like copper and soil. My complaining about the time spent tediously working with a needle and thread gave way to gratitude for being able to tend to George adequately. I made even loop stitches up one side of the Y, then the other. I didn't know what would happen to his muscle long-term; it pulled up in a huge flap, and I didn't have the medical knowledge to do anything more than sew the skin back together. Hopefully it was enough.

When George was fully stitched up, I poured another dose of aqua vitae along the seams. I dabbed the poultice of mashed garlic and honey all along his incision, praying again and again to what I decided were the Gods of Time Travel that it would be enough to stave off infection.

Agnes helped me wrap clean bandages around George's leg to protect the wound and keep the incision clean. "This is very important, Agnes." I explained to her. "Any time we change his dressings, we must boil the bandages first, clean his wound with the aqua vitae, and check for any swelling or pus before reapplying the bandages."

Agnes nodded, "As you wish, m'lady."

The men rolled George back over, careful to keep his injured leg elevated. His breathing was quick and shallow, and he clutched the edge of the sheet in his fist, twisting it as if he could channel his agony into the fabric for some relief.

I perched on the edge of the bed and took George's free hand in mine. It was warm and clammy, but mercifully the heat of the fever he'd been experiencing earlier seemed to be subsiding. "I'm here, I'm not going anywhere." I spoke quietly.

George nodded—a flicker of a gesture—though enough to know he heard me and understood.

"Lady Rhiannon, do you require anything else?" Edward moved towards the fireplace where Clifford and Agnes waited at attention for their next instructions. Gwendolyn stood facing the fire, murmuring quiet prayers and occasionally crossing herself. At some point, a kitchen maid had retrieved the soiled rags and left another stack of clean linens. I'd been so absorbed during the stitching process, I'd completely forgotten they were in the room with me.

"No, I will tend to him tonight." I said protectively.

"As you wish. We will move him upstairs in the morning." Edward bowed slightly to me, then with a flick of his finger motioned for everyone to leave.

Gwendolyn hesitated before following Edward out the door. She opened her mouth as if she had something she wanted to say but reconsidered. It wasn't the first time I'd observed such behavior of her. Though it was the first time I was too distracted to care.

I sat in silence for several minutes, eyes closed, hand on my chest, listening to the crackling flames of the fireplace, calming the copious amounts of adrenaline rushing through my system. George's survival wasn't certain yet, and my body seemed to understand the predicament we were in because I simply could not calm down.

George groaned and shifted in the bed, breaking my reverie. He was awake.

"How does it feel?" I asked as calmly as I could.

"It'd be less painful ... cut my leg off," he rasped. George was pale, though color was returning to his face. The gray-green pallor of earlier was fading away.

With a shaking hand I held a cup of water up to his mouth. "I think you lost a lot of blood. We need to give you plenty of fluids to recuperate."

He nodded and took slow sips. While he drank, I took one of the clean cloths and gently washed his face, hands, and chest. He was splattered with dried blood, dirt, bits of leaves, and sweat. Agnes had offered up a rare lemon, deemed immensely precious for its cleansing and healing properties, to soak in the water. As I dragged the citrus-infused cloth up and down George's arm, pausing to scrub his elbow, he stared at me.

"Hey." He wheezed. "Not going ... anywhere ... Ok?"

"What?"

"Earlier ... I heard you ... not die ... not leave you here ... alone." George took a slow breath, continued. "I couldn't talk. But ... can now. And ... promise ... not leaving you. Ok?" He took another deep breath. "I do ... whatever it takes ... survive." He started coughing, lungs spent from vocalizing his pain earlier.

I clutched his hand and started to cry. Not the whispers of tears I'd fought back earlier, rather a full deep sob of both fear and relief. George was alive. And he almost wasn't.

After so much time spent keeping all the terror of the past weeks locked up for my own survival, I finally let go and let myself feel it all.

I curled up next to him in the rickety little bed, burying my face in the covers next to his side. He moved his hand so he could clumsily stroke my shoulders, lifting and dropping his limp fingers with the meager burst of energy he had left. "We will survive ... okay?" His voice was no more than a fierce whisper, but I heard it clearly.

"Okay," I mumbled into the blanket before sleep came for me.

27

RHIANNON

The night of George's injury, he slept so deeply, I worried he might actually be in a coma. Every so often I'd jerk awake in a panic and jab him until he groaned. Satisfied, I'd flop back onto the straw-stuffed mattress and marinate in my neuroses about his prognosis. Though grateful he was able to sleep through the pain, I was concerned about how much blood he'd lost and whether he was actively fighting off an infection and if his bone was broken but I'd missed it because I'm a high school biology teacher and not a doctor. Not even the unholy medical trinity of Google, YouTube, and WebMD could help me in this situation.

In the morning, Edward arrived with three men of Henry's retinue, ready to transport the fragile patient on a stretcher made of dusty canvas stretched over two sticks. As carefully as possible, they hoisted George onto the contraption. As they trudged across the snow-covered courtyard, up the narrow winding stone stairwell of the main tower to where our room was, he made whimpering noises but did not wake from his sleep.

Once George was settled in bed, I checked his bandages and felt his forehead—no blood, mild fever—before taking a seat by the fire to consider what my priorities now were.

I could not accept that Albert would put us in this situation without an immediate exit strategy. Surely he knew that injury and illness were rampant here; forcing us to stay a whole year was completely insane.

We'd been lazy about trying to decipher the letter he left us. I was sure the answers were probably obvious, but without being able to hash it out on paper and with a pen, without being able to look anything up online, and having no clue what cryptic and unscientific phrases like, "time has a way of folding in on itself," meant, we were stuck.

Watching George sleep, his chest rising and falling with each breath, sharpened my resolve to figure this out. There was nothing I could do for him while he rested, so I decided to head out and look for clues on my own. I would go back to the cottage, letter and key in hand, to figure out what we'd missed.

I could do this. I could—and would—solve this. I'd make it happen.

Determined, I bundled up in a heavy fur cloak and hood and slipped out the door.

My progress was short. Before I even left the stairwell, I heard Henry and Clifford discussing something intently. It was not my intent to eavesdrop, but there was nowhere for me to go and once I heard George's name, I had to listen.

"... I have had enough of the squibble squabble about this. George is *not* my son and he has no intention of challenging the succession." Henry's voice rose an octave. "But I knew his father well and would have done anything for him. *Anything*. I owe him that much. And so it goes for his son. Do you understand?"

I couldn't make out Clifford's quieter response, despite leaning as far as I could into the hall to catch every snippet of sound. This was the second time Henry claimed to know George's father—and his words rang true. Given our presence here, it was entirely possible that Albert had traveled before us and developed a relationship with the baron.

Or at least, that was one of hundreds of potential explanations for the strange tangle of relationships we found ourselves in. Since my understanding of what was possible had been upended in the last few weeks, it meant anything was possible.

The voices and steps receded into the stones, cutting off my source of information.

It didn't matter. I had a new plan.

28

RHIANNON

George had a restless night, where it seemed like he kept trying to turn on his side to get comfortable, only to be met with pain from his injury. I was helpless. There was nothing I could do for him, no place to go, no one to call or consult. We were snowed in and everyone in the castle was hunkered down. At best I could rub his arms and uninjured leg, trying to soothe him in any way I could.

After overhearing the conversation the day before, I returned to our room and spent the day practicing my needlework (which had proven its value when I had to stitch up George's leg) and considered my next moves.

George didn't wake to eat anything; I only managed to get a bit of broth down his throat before he fell back into that deep—yet restless—sleep. His fever came and went, escalating and then tempering my fears as it rose and fell.

Another day passed.

I stayed by his side. Servants brought me food. Agnes came and went, poking and prodding me into various outfits along the way. Gwendolyn stopped by and sniffled into a handkerchief while staring at George. Gustav appeared at one point, dressed in a pink silk bow. He brushed along my legs before slipping out the door. Marguerite came and sat with me, stitching lace and chatting about various things I knew were meant to distract me from worrying, like how she'd witnessed soldiers recover from far greater injuries. I found her voice strangely calming and was grateful for the company.

The following day, when the glazed window yielded just a bit of frosty light, I got out of bed and was tugging my dress over my head before Agnes could come and manhandle me, when the door of our chambers burst open.

I managed to yank my dress into place before Henry, followed by a servant carrying a platter of cooked meat and a flagon of something that steamed in the cold air, barged in.

Henry made straight for George, the servant trailing after him. He sat on the edge of the bed and took George's hand in his. "Come now, son." He said gently, reaching over to pat the side of George's face. "You need to eat something."

I watched wordlessly from where I stood by the armoire.

George groaned and cracked open one eye. Upon seeing Henry sitting on our bed, he blinked open both eyes and sat up a bit, wincing as he registered pain from the movements.

Henry tore a chunk of meat from the slab on the platter and held it up to George's mouth. "Feast upon the flesh of your vanquished foe and make his strength yours," he commanded.

"What?" George rasped, grimacing at the meat being held in front of his face.

"This is the boar who gored you and whom you slaughtered in return. Eat of his flesh, drink of his blood, and revel in your victory." Henry practically shoved the meat into George's slack-jawed mouth.

After George chewed and swallowed, looking completely bewildered, Henry motioned the servant over and took the steaming flagon. He held it up to George's lips. "This is a broth of the boar's blood and bones. You must drink of it to restore your own blood, your own bones."

George obliged, drinking several gulps of the revolting concoction. Henry continued to feed him the meat and broth, giving him soothing words of encouragement.

When he was satisfied, Henry turned to me and said, "You too, my lady. Eat of this flesh, drink of this blood."

As I started to decline the horrific breakfast, Henry leapt to his feet, grabbed a hunk of meat, and strode over to me, holding the boar up to my mouth just as he had done for George. "You are wasting away before my very eyes, girl." He pinched my jutting collar bone with his free hand. "I won't have it. Eat. Now."

I looked at Henry's bare—most certainly unwashed—hand gripping the boar steak and reluctantly opened my mouth a polite fraction to take a bite. Henry shoved the chunk in with such force, I had to take a steadying step backwards, bracing my feet. The meat was smoky and greasy, probably because it'd been turning on a spit all night. But it was also tender and reminiscent of a gamey bacon. I chewed and forced myself to swallow, controlling my gag reflux with every ounce of will I had. Henry continued to feed me; thankfully, he did not make me drink the blood broth.

When he was satisfied we'd eaten enough, Henry handed me the flagon. "See that he finishes this. Before it gets cold."

"I will," I nodded with a slight dip to my knees.

Henry gave me a decisive pat on the shoulder before he and the servant left as abruptly as they'd arrived.

George, awake and flushed with color for the first time since his injury, raised his eyebrows at me. "That was ... something." He chuckled wearily.

I perched on the side of the bed and raised the flagon to his lips. "You heard him. Drink. Baron's orders."

George grasped my wrist and held my gaze. "No soup in bed," he said seriously.

Without thinking, I burst out laughing.

Years ago, when we were first married, I came home sick with a severe cold that'd been circulating my school. I passed out in bed, exhausted and depleted, too tired to even change my clothes or feed myself. Hours or minutes later, George came to see if I wanted something to eat. He'd prepared a hearty chicken and rice soup from scratch and wanted to help me to the table to eat it. But I resisted, desperate to stay in bed.

"No soup in bed," George insisted repeatedly. But back then, we were newlyweds, and I could still wear him down with my charm and stubbornness. I convinced him I could be trusted to eat in bed.

He brought me the soup, on a lovely tray with a roll and a mug of tea. Roughly two seconds after he set it in my lap, I burst into a coughing fit so intense, my knees jerked up and caused the entire spread to go flying. Soup went everywhere. It looked like a Campbell's factory exploded in our bedroom. Bits of starchy rice, buttery chicken, and sticky carrots adhered to every fabric-covered surface within a four-foot radius of the middle of our bed. Broth dripped from the end of my ragged braid. The bowl was face down on the carpet. The tea bag had landed on my pillow, leaching out a brown stain I never did get out of the pillowcase.

George (whose black joggers were coated in rice from the knee down) clenched his jaw and flared his nostrils. He took in the crime scene (which he must've known he would be cleaning up alone) before seething, "*No soup in bed.*"

He won the debate … in the worst way possible.

Helpfully, I started to cry. It was years ago, and my memory has omitted some of the scene, but I do remember George put me in the bath while he stripped the bed, shampooed the carpet, and wiped down a myriad of soup-stained surfaces.

"*No soup in bed*" became a hard, fast rule we never broke. Over time, when we disagreed about something and it was escalating into a fight, saying, "No soup in bed," was George's way of breaking the tension.

If George was recovered enough to invoke the "No soup in bed" rule, then it meant he was going to be okay.

I laughed so hard the flagon sloshed blood up to the rim and tipped dangerously to the side. George grabbed it from my shaking hands and set it gently on the bedside table. He groaned as he twisted, bearing weight on parts of his body he probably didn't think he would have to move so soon after being torn apart.

"I'm sorry," I wheezed, hand on my chest, still laughing, relief washing over me.

"Why are you apologizing? Being gored by a boar was like, literally the first thing on your list of things to avoid on this hunt." He took my hand in his. "Are you okay?"

Catching my breath, I nodded. "I will be. I'm glad you're awake."

He raised his eyebrows. "Are you? Is it just so you can tell me how right you were about going on the hunt?" George's voice had regained some depth, some smoothness now that he'd rested and eaten. He sunk back into his pillows. "I'm such a dumbass," he sighed.

"No." I shook my head and wiped my eyes with the fabric of my sleeve. "You're not. But you definitely scared me."

"I'm know. I'm sorry."

"Don't be. I think you've suffered enough."

George huffed a breath, blowing a lock of hair out of his eyes. "Still. I realized too late I was totally unprepared for the reality of the hunt."

"How do you feel, now that you've eaten the flesh and drank the blood of your vanquished foe?"

He coughed a laugh. "Better. At least I stabbed the fucking thing. I can hold my head up high in front of the other men." George shifted in bed, clutching the edge of the blanket in his hands. "Someday, but not today, you can tell me all about sewing my leg back together."

"It's best if you don't hear about it until you're healed."

He smiled, eyes dropping, head sinking down into the pillows.

"Get some rest," I patted his hand.

Relieved, I curled up next to him in bed and passed out as he stroked my hair.

29

GEORGE

I woke up with a gasp, the pain in my leg so sharp and unyielding, I had forgotten what it felt like to be without it. The pain had no beginning and no end. My forehead was slick with sweat, a damp linen nightgown was twisted around my waist, and my tangled greasy hair fell over my eyes. When I tried to speak, nothing came out of my mouth but a dry rasp.

In short, I was a real fucking mess.

Outside I could hear the white noise of wind whipping around the castle's stone walls. Given the dark and quiet of the normally bustling estate, I assumed it was late at night.

The pain was disorienting. At one point in my haze, I knew I was being carried upstairs to our quarters. I recalled being fed by Henry and talking to Rhi, but that was the extent of my memories. I didn't even know how many days it had been since the hunt. Only that I hurt, was desperately homesick for my real life, and it was quiet.

Beside me, the bed was empty. Rhiannon sat in an armchair by the fire reading what appeared to be an unfolded piece of paper—probably the letter.

She didn't seem to realize I was awake, so I watched her for a bit. Her auburn hair, unwashed for weeks and under wraps most of the time, now fanned around her head like a wild ruby halo. She was cocooned in a wool blanket from the bed, feet up on the edge of the chair, one arm wrapped around her knees while the other held the parchment up to the firelight.

She looked as beautiful as I'd ever seen her, undone, with her guard down. The only thing stopping me from going to her was my mangled shambles of a leg.

I reached out to her in the only way I could in this state. "What are you reading?" I asked, voice hoarse, my throat coated in sandpaper roughness.

Rhiannon startled and twisted to look at me, eyes wide with concern. "The letter your father left us. Given the state of your leg, I think we need to get serious about finding a way to get home. As soon as possible." She secured the blanket around her shoulders and lowered her legs so her bare feet rested on the rug. "How are you feeling?"

"It feels like I'm being actively mauled by a bear," I wheezed. The pain from my wound worked its tendrils down my shin and up my thigh. It felt like claws scraping up and down my flesh—burning, acid claws.

Rhiannon stood, placed the letter on the chair, tightened the blanket around her neck like a cape, and padded towards me. She came to my side of the bed and felt my clammy forehead. When she pulled away, her fingers brushed down my cheek. "No fever," she whispered, relief threading through the words. I knew every minute I eluded infection meant a greater chance I would survive this ordeal. I clasped her hand in mine, kissed the back of it, and pressed it to my chest. She gave my hand a squeeze before withdrawing and ambling back to the chair by the fire.

She glanced at me from over her shoulder. "You should rest. You're not out of the woods yet." Rhiannon adjusted her blanket. "You've been fighting an infection and lost a bit of blood. Even with the boar's meat, I don't think you've been able to eat or drink enough to fully recover." She picked up the parchment, sat down, and resumed her study.

"How long has it been?"

"Four days. You've been asleep most of it."

"A blessing," I whispered. But she was already engrossed in her study again. "Is that how long you've been studying that thing?"

Rhiannon gave me a small nod but didn't answer.

"And? Any magical revelations we hadn't thought of before?" Despite the roughness of my voice, I somehow summoned just enough sarcasm for Rhi to glare at me.

"I'm doing this *for you*, you know. I'm trying to get us home so you can get real medical attention. Did you know that we finally got a physician to come and he wanted to cut your wound back open so he could stuff it with some weird, gross poultice? If it weren't for me, you probably would have lost your leg. So let me handle this." She gave the letter a single shake to indicate she was getting back to work and I shouldn't interrupt.

I clenched my fists. "Rhi, how long have you been at it? And, in all seriousness, are you understanding something that I didn't?"

"Are you asking for a status update?"

"I'm asking if it's worth you losing sleep over something we've already figured out."

Rhiannon inhaled slowly. When she was challenged or contradicted, she'd slow her breathing. Either to (ideally) manage her temper or (usually) to figure out how to eviscerate her opponent. "You're asking if trying to find a way to get home to the 21st century where there are antibiotics and sterilized instruments and real doctors using them is worth it? What if your infection returns and you lose your leg? Or worse? Do you want to undergo amputation without anesthesia?" She glared at me. The fire illuminated her from behind, casting her face in shadow, giving her a menacing appearance.

I sighed, my breath rattling through my spent lungs. "I'm not trying to fight with you. And I'm aware of the dangers. I just think ..." I started coughing. "I think this isn't worth it." I finally spit out.

"You would think that," Rhiannon muttered under her breath, focus entirely on the parchment held up to the firelight. "I can handle this."

Her last statement dredged up something deep in my mind, memory fragments of not wanting to deal with things, but being both relieved and ashamed to have Rhiannon work it out on her own. She was so smart, so capable, so *on top of things*, my dad had once observed. The memory scratched at my mind.

That comment wasn't a compliment for Rhiannon; it was a criticism leveled at me.

Shame burned down my throat, right into the shredded leg I knew she'd had to sew up while terrified and inexperienced. Because I was stupid and stubborn and went on a hunt totally unprepared for the reality of it, wearing dumb shoes and carrying no weapons and having taken no time to learn or practice or anything—anything that could have prevented this. And now she was powerless to do anything more to help either of us, so she was clinging to what little she could.

I thought the great mystery of the time travel note was resolved. But she clearly did not. And if I left her on her own to figure it out, she'd never forget it.

I dragged my hand down my face. "Fuck. Then let's do it together. Come over here. Let me see it."

"It's too dark over there."

"Let's light this candle then." I gestured at the taper on our bedside table. "I want to help. I really do." I practically gasped those last words. Leaning to reach for the candle had caused my calf muscles to shift and the pain nearly knocked me out.

Rhiannon looked back at me, frowning. "It won't help either of us if your wound doesn't heal. You're going to tear your stitches if you keep moving like that." She turned away from me.

"Rhiannon." I swallowed, working up my last bit of energy to sound calm and resolute instead of like the mess I was. "We. Are. Doing. This. Together. Okay?" I jabbed my finger into the mattress so she would know I was serious.

But she ignored me, lost in thought. I watched as she angled the letter higher into the light of the fire, working out how she could squeeze additional meaning from the sentences.

Frustration welled in my heart. This was my problem too. Hell, the only reason she was even in this mess was because of me.

I flung back the covers, revealing my bandaged leg elevated on a pillow. My exposed toes were bruised a frightening, corpse-like purple. Though I could feel my toes, I didn't dare wiggle them for fear my calf muscles would get involved and the pain would be too great. It occurred to me then that pain relief options were slim here: a shot of alcohol, a paste made of mashed poppies I didn't dare try, and perhaps a little bit of heat in the form of a fire-warmed brick wrapped in fabric ... and that was it. As far as I knew.

I would have to live with it.

Undeterred by this revelation, I took a deep breath. "Rhi, please. Let me help." My voice was thin and raspy, dragged down with pain. It also occurred to me I was miserable with thirst. "And can I have some water, please?"

That got her attention. "Of course," she murmured, clearly still distracted. Rhiannon padded towards the table beside the bed, filled a clay cup with water I knew she had boiled and let cool, and handed it me.

After I drained the cup in one gulp, Rhiannon refilled it. She watched me, head tilted to the side, eyes narrowed, biting her bottom lip. Her debate face, as I liked to think of it.

It was the face she made when she was getting ready to pounce on her opponent like a tiger snagging prey. Motionless as a predator, carefully weighing out her strategy, summoning the alpha energy she must channel to manage unruly high schoolers holding scalpels.

My heart pounded. I felt a serious fight developing.

"George," she whispered. "I know you want to help. But right now, all you need to do is recover. I got this. I can handle it." Rhiannon licked her lips. "If something happens ... if you re-open the wound or it gets infected ... do you even have an idea of what a terrible situation we'd be in? What kind of situation it would put *me* in?" She turned away, shaking her head.

I grabbed her hand while trying to ignore the shooting pain lancing down my leg. "Listen," I wheezed. "I never said you couldn't do it on your own. Only that I wanted to help." I grasped the blankets, teeth clenched together, huffing with the effort of the words. I forced my mouth into some semblance of a smile that I hoped said *I'm okay and can do this!*

"Jesus, George," Rhiannon sighed. "You can barely see straight, much less help solve one of your dad's stupid riddles. It's the middle of the night, you lost a lot of blood and almost *died*, in case you forgot, and right now all you need to do is rest." She yanked her hand out of mine and went back to the chair.

Her dismissal was clear.

I opened my mouth, words on my tongue, an argument forming about why I should be allowed to help do something I thought was dumb in the first place.

Frustration and pain melded into rage. I needed air. I needed to get out of this room. I needed space and time to process everything. Normally when I felt like this, I could escape. I could drive around for a bit, go for a run, or hang out at a park.

I could run away.

I remembered sitting in a coffee shop, drinking a series of hot cocoas to avoid going home, leaving a line of empty paper cups on the table, chocolate and remnants of whipped cream lining the rims. How long had I been gone to have had that many drinks? What had Rhiannon thought about my absence? And before you wonder what kind of man uses hot cocoa as a crutch, consider this: growing up, my mother used to make me mugs of cocoa and tuck blankets around me while I was reading. It became a comfort drink, a liquid hug I needed when life felt overwhelming.

I hated that things had gotten so tense with my wife, I drank that many cocoas—using it as an avoidance mechanism instead of a salve.

I closed my eyes and inhaled slowly. The air smelled of firewood and wool and garlic. I breathed again. I could not run, could not drown my feelings in chocolate.

My father—though he truly loved my mother—could also say cruel, cutting things in the heat of his rage. Words that broke her down and left her feeling small and unimportant. I didn't want to do that to Rhiannon. I couldn't do that to her. So, when I couldn't handle the anger (anger that was often a poor substitute for sadness or grief or frustration), I fled. When I felt sharp words form in my mind, I would bail. Better to leave than say something I'd regret, right? Especially if it was something I could never take back.

Better to run than to fight. Or cry.

But now, I was literally hobbled. Fuck.

I inhaled slowly again, the pain so bad I thought I would pass out. It was the only thing stopping me from leaping out of bed, grabbing my cloak, and getting out of the stifling room where I was on the verge of hurting Rhi in a way I knew I'd regret forever.

The thoughts came fast, zipping across my mind. *When she tries to control me, then dismisses me when she can't, I am flooded with rage.*

Breathe in, breathe out.

Why does she do that? A voice somewhere behind the rage asked.

God, there were too many answers to that. And so many of them reflected the mirror of my anger right back at me.

Amidst chaos, she's trying to get ahold of something—anything—to regain her footing. She feels helpless and alone when I flee. Perhaps she thinks if she can solve the problem on her own ... well, she was the only one who could answer that.

I kept breathing, moving air in and out of my lungs, watching Rhiannon hunkered down by the fire. She sat hunched over, an occasional sniffle the only indication she was still awake.

I knew that sound too. My anger broke open and began to dissipate.

"Are you crying?" I asked softly.

She wiped her face with her sleeve before she turned around to face me. "Maybe," she admitted.

My anger softened further. I hated the thought of her suffering too.

"Come here, please," I patted the bed beside me. "No letter. I just ... I just need you."

"George," she sighed.

"I'm going to play my I-almost-died card. Will you please just sit with me for a bit? That's all."

She seemed to consider this. After a beat, Rhiannon rose from her seat, folded up the letter, placed it on top of the fireplace mantle, and came back to bed. She slid in next to me, curled up on her side, resting her head on the pillow. I stroked her hair with my free right hand, letting my fingers drift into her messy curls.

"We can look at it tomorrow. Together." she murmured into the pillow.

"Tomorrow," I agreed, running my fingers through her hair and down the side of her face until she breathed in the steady rhythm of sleep.

30

RHIANNON

A rooster crowing in the distance pierced my dreams. Asleep, I was home again, tucked into five-hundred thread count sheets, a coffee maker prepped with a French roast brewing downstairs, and a fresh novel waiting for me. My ideal Sunday morning.

But the pervasive smell of damp stone and unwashed linen made the reality of our circumstances hit me like a water balloon to the face. I sighed and shifted against our dense mattress.

Beside me, George slept soundly, gently snoring. I reached over and felt his brow—normal warmth. A quick glance under the covers showed his wound hadn't leaked through the bandages—a good sign healing had begun.

After a few minutes of resting under the covers, the anxious stirring that routinely kept me from sleeping in too late caused my legs to itch. I needed to get moving.

George's injury renewed my sense of urgency. I'd become consumed with the daily rhythms of keeping myself relatively clean and fed, pushing everything else to the back of my mind. It had been too stressful to think of anything beyond the constant battles of keeping lice off my scalp, or maintaining enough linen rags for my period, or finding food that tasted halfway decent and didn't make me sick. How could anyone solve an irritatingly vague riddle under these circumstances?

But when I was stitching up George's leg, I realized survival meant more than just staying alive—it meant getting home.

I had been going about it all wrong. George is the writer; he would naturally want to approach every aspect of this problem as if it's simply a riddle to solve. A letter is a very literary clue, and we thought it's all we had.

But I'm a scientist. My approach to solving this mystery had to be different.

My favorite thing about science is it gives us a process to find answers to the greatest mysteries facing humanity: the scientific method. I decided it was my job to work out a hypothesis I could test. This, of course, was where I got stumped. How could you even develop a hypothesis related to time travel with minimal clues as to how you time traveled in the first place? The only way to gather enough information to formulate a theory was to do research on the cottage, the castle, and the surrounding area for any mention of what could be causing this strange phenomenon.

Overhearing Henry in the stairwell triggered the idea. It was entirely possible he did know Albert, which meant Albert was a time traveler, which meant there should be evidence and clues as to how he did it. He must've known he was sending us to a place where people would recognize us and help us. While he probably embedded clues in the letter, there had to be other evidence of this as well. There had to be more to this story than what was contained in the little piece of parchment.

And as far as I knew, there was only one place in this entire village where I could do anything close to real research: Edward's mysterious library.

George would be upset I left without him, but if I was successful, he'd get over it. Waiting until he healed enough to navigate the stairs was out of the question. That could be weeks.

I slipped out from under the covers and padded to the table where our toiletries were laid out: fine tooth comb carved out of wood, a ceramic basin full of fresh water for washing hands and faces, and a clove tonic for cleaning our teeth. I splashed water on my face (while wishing for a toothbrush and paste for the thousandth time), twisted my hair up into some semblance of a bun, and wrapped it in my white silk headdress. It was a haphazard mess—Agnes would undoubtedly accost me if she saw me wearing what looked more like a lopsided turban than a fine lady's headdress. I pulled on my simple green wool day dress, knotted a leather belt high on my waist, and slipped on my boots.

As I dressed, I glanced at George, still asleep. He'd wanted to help decipher the note, despite his pain, despite his skepticism. And I wanted his help. But what I wanted even more than that was for him to heal. To focus on recovery.

I knew George well enough to know that when solving a complex problem, he veered from getting excited and easily distracted, to swinging all the way to the obsessive end of the attention spectrum. He could go from flippant and barely interested to staying awake for hours on end to understand something. With this letter, if he was bored (which he would be, given he thought it was already solved) he would slow me down by trying to distract me into doing something he thought was more interesting. And if he was obsessive about it, he could exacerbate his injury when he inevitably decided to try walking or staying up all night in service of solving the riddle.

I grabbed the letter off the mantle, tucked it into the pouch hanging from my belt, and quietly left the room.

My first thought was to head to the great hall to try and intercept Edward before he began his rounds of the castle. I considered asking him for access to his library. I didn't know why it was off limits, but I was hoping if I asked him for help, he would be willing to let me examine his collection. And possibly point me in the direction of some of the history of Kendal Castle. Our only lead was tied to the cottage, and the cottage was sitting on Kendal Castle's land.

Early in the morning, the castle was a bustle of activity. Servants were scurrying up and down the stairs emptying chamber pots, stoking flames and adding wood to fireplaces, gathering up linens for the wash, serving the considerable cadre of staff their breakfast before they headed off for their respective work, and tending to the baron and baroness of the castle.

When I reached the great hall, Edward was wrapping up his breakfast. We learned the first few days we were here that only workers and servants had breakfast. Apparently, noble classes avoided the meal entirely as it was a sign of wealth to not need food in the morning—unlike those preparing for a day of labor. The only non-servants in the castle who took breakfast were Edward, George, and me. I simply could not be up for hours without even a cup of coffee before the midday meal.

From across the room, I saw Edward rise from the table, stop and say something to Clifford who'd entered from another door, and walk towards where I was entering the hall.

"Lady Rhiannon," he nodded while sweeping past me out the door.

"Lord Edward," I curtsied. I watched over my shoulder as he made his way up the stairs at the north end of the hall. Weighing my options, I decided to follow him. When I ascended a floor, I was surprised to see Edward still in the stairwell, reading a note, illuminated by a narrow window.

I paused, waiting for him to notice me so I didn't startle him. When that didn't work, I took a few heavy steps as if I'd just been lumbering up the stairs.

He tucked whatever he was reading into his doublet and turned towards me, surprise gracing his features.

"Lord Edward, a moment please." I was a bit out of breath and leaned against the stone wall, realizing too late it wasn't how a proper lady conducted herself.

"Yes?" he paused, squaring his shoulders, regarding me curiously.

I stood up straighter. "Given the state of George's injury, and that winter is here, I fear we cannot impose on your hospitality any further." I paused for a moment to catch my breath. Edward raised one eyebrow but made no attempt to interject. "When George and I … " I fumbled around for a plausible story. In all my haste to get to work researching, I hadn't formed a plan for this conversation. The irony! I cleared my throat. "There is an old cottage at the bottom of the hill, and I think it may be of … importance for how we got here and why we're here. And I was wondering if, perhaps, there was documentation regarding its existence, then perhaps we could get answers." I was rambling. Most likely incoherently. God, how I missed mind-clearing coffee.

Edward gazed at me, his espresso-colored eyes boring into mine, unblinking. A slight twitch in his jaw the only indication he was processing what I'd just told him. "The old game warden's cottage?" he finally responded.

"I, uh, I would not know." I answered meekly.

"Ah," he shook his head as if chastising himself. "You would not know that. If we are thinking of the same cottage, it has had many uses over the years. It is old, but has not been in use for, oh, perhaps a decade now? It has been a small hunting lodge, a game warden's cottage, and I think even a chapel. But, that is all before even my time." Edward leaned against the wall, crossing his arms over his chest. "And what of this cottage?"

"Well, we stumbled across it after we were attacked, right before we ran into you on the road. Perhaps we were there for a reason? The cottage felt familiar. Perhaps we'd been there before." I paused, pinching the bridge of my nose so I could think clearly, unsure where to take this reasoning next to get access to his library, desperately trying to recall what stories George had already spun about our presence here. I vaguely recalled a backstory about Germany and a head injury, of course. I was irrationally annoyed with George and his stupid stories I couldn't remember.

Edward raised his eyebrows then waved his hand, motioning for me to continue.

"I'm trying to learn as much as possible about it, to see if it stirs up any memories. Does ... does your library perhaps contain any documents pertaining to this ... area? Kendal and its surrounding lands?"

"You would like to see what is in the library?" he asked.

I nodded. "I would, if that is acceptable to you." I dipped my head and gave a slight curtsy in deference to him and his rank. I kept my gaze to the floor as he considered it. But I didn't have to wait for long.

"Of course." Edward fished in the leather pouch attached to his belt, procured a key, and held it up to the light of the window. With a jerk of his head he commanded, "Follow me."

He grabbed a blazing torch from its sconce and held it up to illuminate our way. Edward led me up two more twists of the spiral stairway and towards the end of a narrow hall where a door, smaller than the ones leading into various chambers along the corridor, stood. He handed me the torch, which I held aloft while he twisted the key into the door's lock, pushing it open.

"After you, my lady."

I took a few steps into the room, letting firelight wash over the walls. Edward strolled in behind me, took the torch out of my grasp, and used it to light tapers on an iron candelabra sitting in the middle of what appeared to be a table made of marble. The room itself was smaller than the chambers George and I occupied, no larger than an average bedroom from my time. Besides the candles, the only other light came from a sliver of a window. The room was lined with shelves built of iron and marble. Shelves were stacked with leather-bound books of various sizes, all with ornately stamped spines, scrolls assembled into pyramid-shaped piles, and layers of incredibly old looking parchments.

Edward stood beside me, so close I could brush my hand across his if I wanted to. This morning he smelled of cinnamon and smoke, a warm and alluring scent. Edward's beauty was such that I observed the noticeable effect he had on others. Maids blushed when passing him; the baron's knights liked to crowd around him as if angling for a selfie; and on more than one occasion, I even saw Clifford gaze at him longingly from across the room.

I'd never been alone with him before, had never stood this close without others acting as buffers for whatever inappropriate thoughts might invade my mind.

He gave me a slow, sideways feline look that increased my heart rate before leaning against the table and facing me. I felt like I was being appraised, but I could not tell for what. I swallowed and patted my sloppy headdress, suddenly wishing I'd let Agnes do my hair for this endeavor.

Edward gestured to the stacks. "When I first came to Kendal, there was no library. As you know, Henry has no children. Not a single heir to speak of." He gave me a pointed look. "Not a single legitimate one, that is." I bit my tongue to keep from blurting out how it was impossible for George to be the illegitimate heir of someone who died hundreds of years before he was born.

"When I arrived," Edward continued, "I found many things to be in disarray. Priceless codices were strewn about the keep, stacked on top of ancient maps, records, and loose illuminated pages, all piled up in corners and on tables; it seemed the scribes simply abandoned their work to roving mice. Many things had been left to rot where they were, as if the absence of an heir also meant a complete abandonment of one's duties to the crown." He shifted his gaze to the precious stacks. "I took it upon myself to gather everything I could find and put it somewhere safe. And thus, the library of Kendal Castle came to be."

Edward must have commissioned the furniture in here—all stone and metal—not a splinter of wood to burn.

"Lord Henry allowed such a thing to be done?" A newcomer messing with the valuable belongings of a baron probably wasn't normal. Or allowed.

"He not only allowed it, he encouraged it. Lord Henry and Lady Gwendolyn had lost interest in doing much of anything besides the occasional leisure activities and attending the required court events during the summer. Rents were only sporadically collected. The castle was falling into disrepair. Manners and customs regarding one's station had been completely ignored. Everything was a mess. After Lady Marguerite and I were married, I took over management of the barony. I spent a year having the entire estate cleaned, organized, documented, and put back into shape. Even now, the baron is content to let me manage affairs." Edward regarded me with a tilt of his head. "And up until now, no one has shown hardly any interest in the contents of this library."

"Well, Agnes told us it was forbidden," I remarked. "Your library doesn't exactly have a welcoming reputation."

He chuckled. "I once caught Agnes getting ready to use a series of three-hundred-year-old maps—the original Norman surveys of this land—as kindling. She cannot read, so what use does she have for a library? It is forbidden to *her*." Edward pushed off the table and headed to one of the shelves. He pulled a worn leather book from the stacks and laid it open on the table. "This is the first of the records about the history of this castle, beginning near the end of the 12th century. However, there is no mention of the cottage until about a hundred years ago in a land survey. Even then, it is referred to as 'the old cottage' and nothing more."

I came to his side and scanned the pages. Much to my dismay, I realized everything was written in Latin, using a letter style that made it almost impossible for my 21st century eyes to decipher. It was complete gibberish. But I pretended otherwise. "Do you know where the other mentions of the cottage are?" I asked, leaning over the open book. I was determined to make this work, to find the information we needed.

Edward nodded. "Most mentions are in land surveys. None specify a date or purpose for the build. However, I do have one thing that may interest you." He pulled another bound leather book from the shelf. When he flipped it open, I could see that each piece of paper had writing formatted as a letter, written in what must be an older form of English.

"These are the gathered personal correspondences between Lord Henry and Roger Martin, who was the steward of Kendal Castle before Clifford. Roger wished to either demolish the vacant cottage or rent it out, as he felt it had become an unsightly—and dangerous—blight on the road up to the castle. But Henry adamantly refused. He would not say why, only that the cottage was to remain untouched." Edward flipped through a few more letters. "Later he consents to have the cottage repaired and upgraded, but that is all."

The letters were dated with the year 1408, about two years before Edward said he'd arrived. And mercifully, they were written in a script that while ornate, was at least decipherable if I studied it long enough and sounded the words out in my head. Holding the letters up to the shard of window light, I pored over each one, gathering as much understanding of the debate over the cottage as I could. Henry's responses, from the few bits I could make sense of, were almost overly emotional considering they're about a rundown little pile of stones sitting on his property. At one point, Henry is so enraged by Roger's refusal to relent on the cottage issue that Henry threatens his steward's life.

"Wait, why are Lord Henry and Roger corresponding via letter if they both live here?" I asked.

"Because Lord Henry was in London, serving the King at court, when this all happened. And," Edward flipped to an earlier letter we'd skipped and pointed to a specific line, "he was terrified Roger would simply tear down the cottage in his absence." He pointed to a line where Henry emphasizes that the cottage is to remain untouched. Here, the emotion is almost fear-like: he references "grave and terrible consequences" should the cottage be "defiled in any manner."

What did Henry know about the cottage that would elicit such a reaction?

I flipped to Roger's response, and from what I could make out, it was clear the steward was baffled by his lord's stance. The tone and language indicate they had an amiable relationship, and Roger is surprised by Henry's outsize reaction. Which is why he kept pressing the matter in further letters. He frequently mentioned how bandits and other outlaws had been caught in the building before, as a legitimate reason why he wouldn't relent on the issue.

No wonder Edward genuinely believed we'd been attacked and robbed. But why leave such a blight standing, vacant and unused?

Unless Henry knew what the cottage was truly capable of.

"Have you ever asked Lord Henry about his insistence on maintaining a vacant cottage on his property?"

"No. Though it became my business, I was fine leaving it as is. Roger Martin passed of a fever the following summer and from what I understand, when Clifford took his place, he was not remotely interested in reviving the debate. Roger had already commissioned the allowed repairs to the cottage, and that was that. My time, as you now know, was dedicated to getting other aspects of the castle in order."

I rubbed my temples. I'd developed frequent little headaches—most likely from endless wine and tightly wrapped headwear. "I find I now have more questions than answers, I'm afraid."

Edward closed both books and reshelved them. "Would you like me to escort you to the cottage, Lady Rhiannon? I do not know what you should be looking for, but perhaps the tour will coax some memories."

I couldn't admit we'd already done that, so I had very little choice in the matter. "I accept, and am gracious for the offer," I bowed.

George wasn't going to be thrilled when he found out.

31

GEORGE

"Where were you?"

I'd woken up to find Rhiannon missing, along with the velvet box and its contents. I was afraid she'd gone to the cottage, alone, down an icy snow-packed hill wearing flimsy and stupidly shaped shoes, surrounded by unfriendly faces who knew I was out of commission.

By the time she slipped back into our room, I'd told myself a thousand stories about all the terrible things that could have happened to her without my being able to find or help her. I scooted up in bed, suddenly furious she was totally fine.

Rhiannon pulled off her shoes and set them next to the hearth. I watched as she wiggled her toes and fingers in front of the fire, undoubtedly chilled from her adventures. "I see you're feeling better."

"I'm conscious, at least."

She took her time before replying. "I went to the library," she answered. "With Edward."

I tried to scoot up in bed to face her fully, but the pain lancing down my leg paused my motions. "You did what?" I grimaced while bearing all my weight on my elbows. Holy fuck I was in pain. "What happened to the part where we agreed to be a team?"

Rhiannon turned so her back was to the fire, hands clasped behind her, still warming up. "We need to get home, George. Your injury changed everything. You can think what you want about the possibilities of doing so. But I'm going to research this place to try and find answers, okay? That's how I'm being a good team member."

"You may not know this since you've never played a team sport before, but doing shit without telling your teammates what's going on is generally considered bad form." It rankled me that she was once again barreling ahead without including me. I leaned down to rub my throbbing calf, hoping the pressure would relieve both my frustration and pain.

"Oh, you mean like telling stories about how we're from Germany or Spain without giving me a heads up? Or how you agreed to go on a hunt and didn't tell me until the morning of? Like that?"

Ah, I'd forgotten the ground I stood on was as thin as a melted sheet of ice.

I cleared my throat and decided not to press the issue. "And did you? Find answers in the library that is?"

She rubbed her hands together. "I've learned a few interesting things since you've been unconscious. First, I overheard Henry vehemently insist to Clifford that you're not his son. But he knew your father and would do anything for him. He emphasized that word, '*anything*.' I believed him. I think he really did know your dad."

I raised my eyebrows. That was certainly something. "What else have you learned?"

Rhi turned back towards the fire. I noticed her usually secure headwrap was listing to one side and some of her curls were busting loose. "Some years ago, before Edward came here, the old steward wanted to have the cottage torn down because it had become a haven for bandits and outlaws on the run. But Henry adamantly refused. Like, he was super emotional about it."

"How did you learn this?"

"Because in the library there are letters between him and the steward." Rhiannon crossed her arms, turned again, and put her back to the fire. She bit her lip and gazed out the window where snow was beginning to fall. "What's also interesting is that in the letter your dad left us, the cottage has a name: Plierton. But that name is nowhere in the documents I found. So, that's next on my research list. When the weather clears, I want to go back down to the cottage to have another look. Maybe there's something buried or hidden that could help us?" She was almost talking to herself at this point, lost in thought.

I shifted against the pillows. "Will you wait for me to heal enough to go with you?"

Rhiannon considered this. "We don't have the luxury of time. But we can talk about it again when the snow stops." She shifted on her feet and said the next part without looking at me. "Edward offered to escort me down there, to help me look for anything that may be useful."

I scoffed. "Of course he did. So helpful, all the time, that Edward."

Was I jealous? Maybe. I didn't know why; he seemed happily married. And (as far as I knew) hadn't made any overt passes at Rhiannon.

"Yes," she replied seriously. "He has been exceptionally helpful. You would have *died* without his help, if you'll recall."

I sunk down into the pillows. She was right and I knew it.

"Fine, but can we go back to the being a team part? I'm not comfortable being left out of this."

"We can be a team. But I'm still going to figure this out, with or without you."

I exhaled and shoved my hair out of eyes. Rhiannon could be brutally stubborn. Even when she was wrong, she could find ways to justify it. And since my shredded leg kept me bed-ridden, my options were limited.

So, I acquiesced. "Fine, we do it your way."

32

ATLANTA, GEORGIA · DECEMBER 2015

RHIANNON

George said very little on the drive home. Every so often I glanced to my left to see he was white-knuckling the steering wheel, staring straight ahead, scowling.

He was angry with me, but I thought he was overreacting.

Earlier in the evening, we'd been at a staff holiday party thrown by the principal of my school. Carmen's Decatur home was gorgeous: a massive Tudor-style house with floor-to-ceiling windows and a swimming pool. Administrators are paid far better than teachers, but even so, I knew it was her husband's finance salary that funded this level of lifestyle. When we walked in, I'd had one of those small twinges of jealousy where for a moment I wished I'd married a lawyer or a doctor (or really anyone with a bigger salary than my teacher's paycheck) instead of a blogger … who made even less than me.

As much as I loved George, I didn't love living paycheck to paycheck, with every unexpected extra expense loading up our credit card balance. I wondered what it would be like to not worry about money, to have so much extra you'd spend it on an extravagance like a high-maintenance pool.

I also wondered how we were going to afford a baby when I finally got pregnant—though that wasn't top of mind this evening.

The party itself wasn't lavish, just a catered buffet with lots of booze and Christmas music playing in the background. I grabbed a handful of sugar cookies and a glass of cabernet before parting ways with George to mingle with my coworkers. After my second glass of wine, George found me and handed me a plate loaded up with cheesy potatoes, roast chicken, and various salads before he headed off to the kitchen to do something I didn't catch over the music and conversation.

I wandered outside into the strangely warm, balmy night where several members of the science department were circled up and talking. Blue light from the swimming pool reflected off everyone's faces, giving the group an ethereal appearance. Sam, the chemistry teacher, waved me over.

"We're discussing the science fair for next term, thinking of moving it up to March so it doesn't overlap with finals again."

"Won't that interfere with spring break?" I asked between bites of potatoes. I was already feeling buzzed on wine and sugar, so was focused on getting real food into my system. "They'll have to work on it over break if they want to make the deadline."

"Not if they plan accordingly," he replied, which elicited a laugh from all of us. No student (except the rare teacher's pet) ever planned their time properly for major projects.

George had been gone awhile, so I took a few steps back to glance into the living room window where I could see he was talking to Jennifer, the new English teacher—and a very pretty blonde. I watched as she laughed at something he said, reaching out to touch his upper arm. Something about the gesture made my stomach plummet and my head grow light.

I headed back to my little cabal of science teachers. "Let's go ahead and move it."

We spent the next few minutes verbally agreeing to a rough plan for the science fair when Rebecca, a veteran physics teacher, asked about spouses helping to set up, judge, etc. "That's Rodney's busy season, so he's out," she nodded towards her husband, who gave us a thumbs up from where he lounged close by on a deck chair. "What about George, can he help? Does he have a busy season?" she asked me.

I shrugged. "George doesn't have a busy season. He writes blogs about laundromats and mom-and-pop restaurants. A sixth-grader could do his job. Not even an especially talented one."

Sam chuckled awkwardly, but Rebecca looked uncomfortable as she gazed past me.

I felt someone touch my shoulder before handing me another glass of wine. George had come up behind me and the expression on his face—grim smile and narrowed eyes—told me he heard everything.

"I guess it's at least one step up from a trained chimp," he remarked.

I winced. "You know I didn't mean it like that. Only that they make you dumb everything down for the wider audience."

"Sure," he said without looking at me. To everyone else he offered, "I can help with the science fair if you need it."

Sam and Rebecca both nodded solemnly, as if he'd offered to help us plan a funeral.

To me, George simply said, "I'm going back inside. It's too cold out here."

I sucked in my breath through my teeth. "How bad was that?" I asked the group after George was out of earshot. Both Sam and Rebecca had been married to their spouses for years, and teachers for just as long, so I often went to them when I needed advice or input.

"It wasn't great!" Rodney called out from his deck chair.

"Thanks, Rodney," I called back.

He gave me another thumbs up.

I cleared my throat. "In my defense, he's used those exact words to describe his job before."

Sam looked down at his brown loafers and mumbled, "But it's different coming out of your wife's mouth, isn't it?"

I didn't necessarily agree. But knew I needed to at least go talk to George. "Shit," I muttered. "I should go handle this," I said already heading towards the door.

Inside I found George in the kitchen talking to Jennifer again, along with a few other English teachers. His people, I realized, as he was a Lit major and (kind of) a writer.

"Can we talk," I whispered in his ear while sliding my hand through the crook of his arm.

George nodded and excused himself, following me into a hallway.

I crossed my arms over my chest. "Are you mad at me?"

He looked at me like I was insane. "You talked shit about me in front of your colleagues. And it was clear I wasn't mean to hear it. You could say I'm a little peeved, at the very least. Plus finding out my wife thinks my job is a joke is not the best feeling."

"Well, you were hitting on one of my colleagues. How do you think that makes me feel?" I deflected.

George raised his eyebrows incredulously. "What are you even talking about? We're literally discussing essay writing—the most unsexy subject ever."

"Well, whatever it was, she seemed to be enjoying it."

He snorted. "God forbid someone enjoy talking to me and not an—how did you put it—untalented sixth grader? Or a trained chimp?"

"You know I didn't mean it like that! I used *your* literal words to describe the job *you* make no secret of hating. How am I in the wrong here?"

George placed his hands on my upper arms and pulled me closer so he could speak softly without anyone hearing. "The difference, Rhiannon, is that you weren't joking. And everyone knew it."

I tightened my crossed my arms, creating a shield over my heart. I felt slightly off, like my words weren't totally lined up with the movements of my mouth. "No one thinks less of you. They all know and like you. What's the big deal?"

George dragged his hand down his face and glared at me. He wore several silver rings that glinted in the Christmas lights strung everywhere. "The big deal is you humiliated me in front of your coworkers. I'm not sure how else to phrase it so you understand why I'm pissed. If I had done that to you, you'd be furious. And hurt. Rightfully so. We always say we have each other's backs, but now I know what you say behind mine."

"Well, it obviously wasn't behind your back as we're having this conversation right now." I snapped.

"Wow." He shook his head and turned away from me, already glancing towards the front door. "I think I'm done with this party. I want to go home."

"Jesus, George," I muttered. "We give each other shit all the time. And it's just joking."

"This is different," he insisted. "And you playing dumb is making it much, much worse. You're the smartest person I know, so this is all just bullshit." George's eyes flashed and I realized just how angry he was.

But I was not ready to back down. Something within me, something linked to the constant stress about our financial situation and his endless complaining about his work, kept me tethered to the failing argument.

"Fine," I sighed, still not convinced I was (totally) wrong.

As we said our awkward goodbyes to my colleagues, I realized the third glass of wine was making me woozy. I wobbled to the car, George supporting me with his hand on my elbow, yet somehow keeping me at a distance.

The drive home was quiet, tense. I contemplated the various things I could say to ease the tension, but nothing seemed right. So, I said nothing.

When he pulled into our driveway, George put the car in park and asked, "Are you embarrassed by me?"

"What? No, not at all!"

"You don't wish I was a CPA like Rodney? Or had a finance job like Carmen's husband that could pay for a house like that? Would you like me better if I wore blue button-down shirts and khakis and worked in Buckhead?"

I rubbed at my temples, feeling a headache coming on. "Khaki pants aren't really your style." I quipped. George was wearing a black blazer over a white henley shirt and a red tartan kilt. Yes, an actual kilt, paired with combat boots. The thing is, his style is so authentically his that it worked—he looked great. George wearing khakis would be as tragic as RuPaul wearing Costco pants.

"*Rhi.*"

"Fine!" I defended. "Listen, it would be a lie to say I didn't wish you made more money. But I'm certainly not embarrassed by you."

"That doesn't sound very reassuring. Especially because you have yet to apologize."

"Why should I apologize? I'm not in the wrong! Just because I didn't fawn over you like Jennifer—"

"Nope, fuck that nonsense." George shoved his door open and stormed towards the front door before I could process the string of incendiary things I'd said that'd infuriated him so much.

"*Come on,*" I groaned. I'd made one dumb, unfunny comment and it was snowballing into a major fight. I sat in the car a few minutes to give George time to cool off.

Inside, he was banging around the kitchen, unloading the dishwasher so furiously I was afraid he'd break something.

I stood in the doorway for a couple minutes, still unsure what else to say. My scalp was throbbing, so I pulled the bobby pins out of my tightly-wound bun and shook my hair loose. The release of tension helped me think clearly. "You know, if you loved your job, I wouldn't care about your low salary." George paused tossing dishes around to stare at me. "What I don't like is that you both hate your job *and* make peanuts. I'm a teacher, God knows I have no ground to stand on when it comes to paychecks. But at least I *love* my job. And that balances it all out. I love you, and it's clear you're unhappy much of the time. You hate what you do, and you're always stressed about money, and that affects me too. So, pick one: love your job and manage the low salary, or find something you still hate but at least pays the bills."

George glared at me, eyes narrowed. "Again, that's *not* an apology." He grabbed a handful of silverware from the dishwasher and started slamming forks and spoons into the drawer, making it clear we weren't going to discuss anything else until I apologized.

And God help me, I was just as stubborn about not giving him an apology as he was about getting one.

I was still a little drunk, still smarting over seeing him receive attention from another woman, and still convinced I wasn't wrong as I was simply using his own words. *Using his own words against him,* a little voice nagged in the back of my head. *Using his own words to make fun of him in front of your coworkers.*

I flicked away my conscience's voice as if it was no more than a nagging grasshopper on my shoulder. After washing up and changing into my pajamas, I turned on the TV to a reality show where women wearing too much makeup screamed at each other the whole episode. Though I was trying to distract myself, all it did was make me self-conscious. Had I behaved this badly at the party? Surely not. George was being dramatic.

He didn't come to bed until well after midnight, long after I'd turned off the TV. But he stayed inched over to the edge of our king-sized bed, instead of cuddled up against me, how he normally likes to sleep.

"Seriously?" I said into the dark.

"Still not an apology," he noted.

I grumbled something about being treated unfairly while tucking the blankets under my chin, noticeably cold without his body heat warming me.

George didn't respond, didn't even shift in the bed.

We'd had standoffs before. Often it was about dumb miscommunications we both felt justified in battling over.

But this felt different. I wrestled with whether I was wrong. I liked to think that when I was genuinely wrong, I was big enough to admit it—to gracefully acknowledge I'd made a mistake. But I clung to this stupid idea that I wasn't wrong, that George was just being overly sensitive. Or that this was just another miscommunication we'd laugh about later.

I decided sleep would make everything better. In the morning, I would be sober and he would realize he'd overreacted, and we would laugh about it. And it would be okay.

⪼⧫⪻

When I woke up the following morning, George had gotten up before me and made only half a pot of coffee—enough for just himself. If I thought a little sleep would smooth this all over, I was wrong.

I added more grounds and water to the coffee maker and sat down at the kitchen table. While the coffee brewed, I replayed the previous night's fight in my mind ... and no matter how I spun it, I wasn't looking great. If I had to be honest with myself—and I did—then I had to admit I was wrong. I'd really hurt him. Even Rodney could see that from his deck chair.

In the morning light, sober, and admittedly feeling a bit chastised, I was willing to consider the possibility that I may have been, ever so slightly, possibly wrong.

I poured myself a cup of coffee and made my way into the living room.

George sat on the couch, writing in his journal. He didn't look up when I sat down next to him. But he paused writing, pen hovering over the page, waiting for me to speak.

I set my mug down on the coffee table. "Look, last night I may have ... accidentally said some hurtful things. I'd had too much to drink ... well, no matter the reason, I want you to know that I'd never intentionally hurt you or try to embarrass you. So ... so, I'm sorry. I'm sorry I said those hurtful things. I'm sorry I embarrassed you."

George closed his journal and tossed it on the table. He took one of my hands in both of his and began stroking my palm. "Do you want to know what hurt the most?" he asked.

I nodded.

"You know I already have those same insecurities about what I do. I already feel like a failure. Having you express that to your coworkers made me think you feel that way too—that I'm a failure."

"I'm really sorry. I don't think you're a failure." I paused, weighing how to add the next piece, before deciding honesty was best. "But I do think you're unhappy. With your work, that is."

He traced little shapes on my palm with his fingertips but didn't look up at me. "You're not wrong. And I've spent this morning thinking about what I'm going to do about it. But I'd rather keep it quiet until I have news to share."

"Does it involve you wearing khakis?" I joked, hoping to lighten the mood.

George smiled. "We'd both be unhappy then, wouldn't we?"

"True. At least right now you get to wear whatever you want to work."

"At least there's that. Now, come here." George pulled me onto his lap and wrapped his arms around my waist. "Your opinion matters more to me than anyone else's, you know that right?"

I rested my head on his shoulder and draped my arms around his neck. "I do. And I'm really sorry," I emphasized again. "I didn't want to admit I'd hurt you because it's the last thing I'd ever want to do."

He tightened his grip on me. "I love you a lot, Rhiannon. More than anyone else."

"I love you too." I breathed into his neck, inhaling the scent of cotton and George's specific scent that always smelled like everything I wanted. "You're my favorite person, you know that right?"

He nodded. "I do."

"Good," I smiled against his shoulder, relieved we were working through it.

When Monday morning rolled around, George left earlier than usual for work. By that evening, everything had changed.

He came home with a bag of groceries that were mostly treats we could rarely afford: fancy cheese, a couple of steaks, chocolate cake, and bottle of wine.

"This," he gestured towards the bounty, "is for a celebration meal. Because today I asked for a raise. And I got it."

I set down the mail I'd been rifling through. "Wait, seriously? You did?"

He nodded. "I went in early to check some things out and verify what I'd already suspected. Which means I came equipped with data showing my blog was the most trafficked section on the website, and views—plus ad clicks—had increased by 26% since I took over. When I presented my findings and asked for the raise, Gail didn't argue with me. She agreed! It's not a huge raise, but after taxes it will be about an extra six hundred dollars a month."

I squealed. When you're living on the edge, an extra six hundred smackers a month was life-changing. "Holy crap! George! That's huge! That extra money will make a massive difference."

I jumped into his arms and gave him a tight hug. We started jumping around the kitchen, laughing and celebrating with a happy dance.

When we'd calmed down and cracked open the wine to toast George's success, he pulled me against him and nuzzled my neck. "You know, now that there will be more money coming in … perhaps we can … well, maybe it's time to pull the goalie. If you know what I mean."

"The goalie that keeps your balls from getting into my nets?"

George laughed. "Yes, I believe those are the correct scientific terms. What say you?"

He knew I'd been wanting to start a family. But up until then, it felt impossible.

I wrapped my arms around his waist and squeezed. A family. A real family. The thing both of us missed out on growing up and had promised would be a priority in our marriage.

"Let's do it!"

33

RHIANNON

Edward strolled into the great hall, dressed in his riding clothes, clutching leather gloves in one hand. He tossed them on the table next to his plate before taking a seat for the early meal. "How is poor George faring this morning?"

I stirred my bowl of stewed oats with apples and cinnamon. "It'll still be some time before he can walk normally again, but the physician believes he will recover."

After the snow stopped and paths had been cleared, the village physician made a second visit to the castle to check on George. It took quite a bit of self-control on my part to not challenge or contradict his woefully inaccurate diagnoses and treatment plan. We were adamant—again!—about not re-opening the wound to stuff it with a poultice, so he'd reluctantly prescribed some herbal teas, a salve that seemed to have some merit, and a few specific prayers and rosaries.

George spent quite a bit of time sitting by the fire, stretching and massaging his brutalized muscles to aid in the healing process. Though with a cane he could navigate the stairwells and make short journeys around the castle, he was still a long way from being able to hike up and down the castle's steep, icy hill anytime soon.

I didn't look up from my food, simply offered the report on George's condition while attempting to control my emotions. To let myself feel anything about his injury would open the doors to every emotion roiling in my heart about the sheer terror of our predicament.

Edward took a bite of stewed oats the servant set before him. "And you? What will occupy your time today? More stitching?"

While I enjoyed the time spent with Gwendolyn and Marguerite, I needed a break from embroidery. My distracted mind weighed on me, and I found myself pulling out more errant stitches than I was adding to the piece. The visit to the cottage with Edward had been fruitless (as I knew it would be) and I was stuck in my search for clues and evidence on how to get home. I needed to expand my search.

"No, I expect I will tend to George today. Then perhaps I will explore the town a bit. If the weather holds up, that is." After several days of snow, a brief warm spell turned everything to mud, followed by another freeze. Though it was still bitterly cold, the sun was shining and the winds had calmed. It was my best chance to go back into town to learn more about the history of this place.

"Nonsense," Edward declared resolutely. "I fear you have only seen the worst of what this land is. But you will find it is quite lovely. It is decided. You shall accompany me today. We will be traversing the barony, checking on our tenants and collecting rents on behalf of his lordship. It will do you good to leave the castle for a spell."

"But George—"

"Will be well-tended to by the servants." Edward cut me off with a wave of his hand. "Agnes will bring you adequate riding attire. We leave shortly." He scraped the last of his oats out of the dish, dabbed his mouth with a napkin, then shoved his chair back while grabbing his gloves. "As soon as you are dressed, meet me at the stables," Edward commanded.

I could only nod meekly; it was clear I had no say in the matter. I found the loss of my autonomy more difficult to get used to than the lack of technology and physical comforts of my own time.

In the stables I found Edward stroking the nose of a grey mare, already saddled up and ready, waiting patiently next to his black stallion. I was relieved it wasn't the cumbersome sidesaddle I'd witnessed Gwendolyn using, rather a traditional saddle that granted me a bit more stability. Moreover, I relaxed when I learned I'd be given my own horse for this excursion, rather than sitting wedged into Edward's lap like on our first journey up to the castle.

Because if I wasn't distracted by noodling on how the time travel cottage worked, or stressing out over George's injury, or panicking when contemplating how to maintain basic hygiene in a world where no one had heard of germs, then my thoughts were commandeered by Edward and his obscene handsomeness.

His thick, dark hair that had the wave of a Pantene model. His full lips, often arranged in an arrogant sneer, which somehow made him more alluring. The entitled swagger, where he tossed his cloak over one shoulder before issuing a command that sent everyone scattering.

And the persistent mental nagging that I knew him from somewhere but (obviously) couldn't place it because, no, he did not go to any of the schools that I did, and no we did not have a class together in college, nor did we ever work side by side folding pants at the Gap or bartending at Grindhouse or any of the other jobs I'd worked over the years. It was a complete mystery as to why he was so familiar. At the time, I chalked it up to his being the first person we encountered in the 15th century.

Edward was decked out in black and burgundy velvet, trimmed with gold—the livery colors of House de Ros. Agnes had dressed me similarly, complete with a jaunty velvet hat with an ostrich feather sticking out of it. My hair was done up in braids and she'd wrapped a piece of silk from the base of my chin, tucked into the neck of my dress, so no gust of wind would disturb me.

The whole traveling ensemble was strangely comfortable, like being wrapped in blankets.

We trotted down the hill in silence and looped around town, my mare following so dutifully behind, I barely had to tug the reins. Once we reached the outskirts—the furthest I'd ever traveled from the castle—Edward called out over the whip of wind, "Though we are far from London, I think you will find the beauty of these lands unparalleled."

He pointed towards the horizon. Ahead of us stretched increasingly rugged rocky hills, frosted with remnants of snow, and a clear blue-gray sky stretching above us. The forests thinned out a bit, revealing rolling hills that dipped into clear lakes. It was a landscape that made you feel blessedly small and insignificant.

Beyond the chaos and fear and filth, there was true beauty here. I released a full breath I didn't realize I'd been holding. In some ways, it felt like a clean slate.

Without all the connective tissue of the modern world—asphalt roads, train tracks, electric lines, barbed wire fences, billboards, streetlamps—the isolation made me feel like I was on another planet. Years ago, I'd read that the population of the world in the early 15th century was less than four hundred million people; humanity still hadn't recovered from the bubonic plague. So, in a sense, I was on a totally different planet. One where humans had barely made a mark.

This version of Earth was utterly unrecognizable to me.

We worked through the outskirts of Kirkby Kendal and rode west. My idea of medieval rent collecting was like something out of Robin Hood: I thought we'd be unwelcome and met with resistance as Edward conducted cruel shakedowns of those who couldn't pay. I'd mentally braced myself to remain passive in the face of human suffering, powerless to interfere in events that happened six centuries before I came along. I even envisioned myself, maybe once or twice, putting my hand on Edward's arm and imploring him to show mercy to the good people of the land.

But it was nothing like that. Most families welcomed us in. While some committed to paying with giant wheels of cheese or bags of raw wool that would be collected later, and others with coins in leather pouches they handed to Edward—they all traded in information. They wanted to hear news of the court, the young king and his new French bride, the baron and his family. They shared their own stories of tending unpredictable crops; brought Edward's attention to conflicts needing intervention; and told us stories ranging from folklore to village gossip while they served us pieces of honey cake, clay mugs full of mead, or bread slathered with butter.

They showed a great interest in me but refrained from asking questions once Edward informed them my husband was a distant relation of Henry's and we were visiting for only a short while.

This far north, the thick rolling grasses were perfect for tending flocks of sheep. Stone cottages dotted the landscape, often flanked by small scraps of tended land and ample paddocks. Edward explained that much of Kendal's wealth came from the wool it exported to the Italian states for spinning and dyeing. Italians spun wool into the finest cloth, imbued it with vivid colors, then sold it back to the nobles and wealthy merchants of England. Wool that was spun, woven, and dyed in England had a rougher texture and was colored a woodsy green; it made up much of the clothing the peasants wore. Regardless of who bought it, ample wool production in this part of the country had made the de Ros family startlingly wealthy.

Up until then, I hadn't considered how the de Ros money impacted my time travel experience.

For all my kvetching about the damp noisy castle, my complaints were silenced when I was welcomed into homes of common people, where pigs and cows were brought inside to keep everyone warm, entire unwashed families slept piled into one sagging bed, and sometimes dinner was little more than stew made of boiled turnips and not much else. We did not stay long in these homes, and we made sure not to impose on anyone's hospitality in such a way that would wreak havoc on their meager food stores during winter.

We went from tenant to tenant, making a wide loop around town, staying close enough so it was a short journey back to the castle. The following day, Edward would continue rent collection on his own, accompanied by two guards, as he worked further away from Kendal Castle and would need to spend the night in inns or the homes of some of the baron's knights along the way. Without the gravity of the castle providing safety, it would not be wise for me to join.

Despite having been resistant to collecting rents in the first place, I found myself disappointed I wouldn't get to finish the job. The thought of having to go back to the castle—which was somehow both stuffy and freezing at the same time—stifled me. Out amongst the windswept hills and broad lakes, I felt free for the first time since we'd been dumped in the 15th century. I had work to do; it gave me purpose beyond changing George's bandages. I desperately wanted to keep going.

I tugged lightly on the reins, pulling my mare to a stop as we crested a hill.

Edward pulled up next to me, gazing at the low winter sun with a strange look on his face. "Is it at least half as beautiful as I promised?"

I inhaled a gulp of cold, pristine air before replying. "There is no comparison to what I imagined. It is everything you promised and more."

He dipped his head in agreement. "When I first came here, I longed to be back in London, which seemed to be the center of everything important and interesting. But after spending time traversing these hills, the city no longer beckons me as it did. If anything, I prefer the quiet of this place."

"Why did you stay?"

He gave me a surprised sideways glance. "Lady Marguerite, of course." When I cocked my head in question, he continued. "Much like you and George, I was traveling here for the equinox when I was attacked. Lady Gwendolyn found me just as I found you. I had no intention of staying more than a night, but my heart had other plans." He cleared his throat. "Marguerite is Henry's niece. When her parents died and her older brother inherited everything—which at that point was not much more than a title and a small bit of land—he sent her to live with her aunt and uncle in hopes of making a fortuitous match in England. She was only sixteen. I came along a few years later and ruined those plans. It was a true love match and the de Ros's, having plenty of fortune but no heirs, supported the union."

"Lord Henry and Lady Gwendolyn seem quite kind."

"Yes, they are. That is not always common for people of their rank. But I am sure you noticed that the people of their lands hold kind regards for the baron and lady."

I nodded. "I'm glad I came today. That I got to see this."

It was true. In my impatience to get home I was not paying attention to my surroundings. I felt a tremendous sense of peace out in the open landscape. The craggy hills and sweeping moors were soothing; I felt small and insignificant in their presence, which was strangely a relief. Not to mention that by getting out of the castle, I got to meet people living in a world I'd only read about. I'd been so obsessed with staying clean and comfortable and safe, I was missing out on the incredible experience of witnessing history.

"What then, do you believe your plans to be?" Edward glanced at me. "I am certain Lord Henry would be happy for your continued presence at the castle. If that is what you choose, of course."

I tilted my head slightly but did not look at him. The sun was obscured by a mist of clouds, turning it a vibrant orange. "As beautiful as this place is, as calming as I find the solitude to be, this is not where we belong. As soon as George's leg heals, we should be on our way."

"But after the thaw, yes?"

I did not answer, for the truth was I still had no idea how to get back to our own time, I still hadn't accepted we would have to wait, and there wasn't a way I could explain this to him without making it sound like I was crazy.

I appraised Edward, taking in his form, refined and elegant atop the stallion. A breeze lifted his hair off his shoulders, like he was posing for the cover of a romance novel.

I shifted my focus to the less-distracting landscape ahead of me. "It would be unwise to travel before the thaw, given the state of George's leg. So, I will be patient."

"Until then, how do you plan on spending your time?"

The question surprised me. It was the first time Edward took any interest in my daily habits. "I ... well, I would like to contribute," I answered honestly. "It does not sit well with me that we have little to offer the residents of Kendal, who have been exceptionally generous."

Edward waved me off with his gloved hand. "Nonsense, you are clearly relatives of the baron's, and he has made it clear your welcome will not wear out. Besides, Lady Marguerite has been most appreciative of your company. She says you are quite talented with the needle and she enjoys getting to chat with a lady who is not her aunt." His restless horse scratched at the dried grass, but Edward ignored him. "I believe she has benefitted from your presence, offered her a necessary distraction."

I'd picked up on snippets of conversation and the occasional shift in tone, indicating Marguerite was anxious about her pregnancy and impending birth. Given that this was not her first pregnancy, the lack of children was enough to prove her fears weren't unfounded.

We had that in common.

I shook off those memories and tugged the reins of my mare, sidling up to where Edward's horse had meandered down the hill. "Regardless, if I can find a way to be of some use, then I will do it. It will be good to have something new to focus on."

"I have a task I believe you may be interested in," Edward said casually while giving his reins a sharp tug.

"Then I will be most glad to assist with it," I found myself agreeing before I even knew what it was I was agreeing to.

34

GEORGE

Of all the things that drive husbands to change, the most common disaster, I've come to learn, is wives.

Rhiannon climbed into bed and handed me what looked like a little clay ball with nubby feet. I gave it a little shake. It had a metallic rattle ... coins, perhaps?

"This is the precursor to the piggy bank," she explained, giving it a little tap. "They're called 'piggies' and at Christmastime, it's customary for nobles to hand them out to the poor. They're full of gold coins, so people smash them open to get the money inside. Like a piggy bank—that's where the term comes from. Isn't that cool?"

"It is," I agreed. Despite the physical discomfort, I was in awe over what we were learning about life in late-medieval England.

"I thought you'd like it," Rhiannon smiled at me.

"I do." I turned the piggy over in my hands until I found the slit where the coins were put in. Candlelight illuminated a glint of gold within. "Can we keep this one?" It was not lost on me that we qualified as broke. Broke, though we had high-ranking friends supporting us. Regardless, it made me uncomfortable to be so dependent on them.

"We could, but I'd always wonder if there was someone who needed the coins more than us. Someone who belongs in this time, someone who may be one expense away from disaster."

Though we had no way of telling what kind of impact our presence was making, we were trying to disrupt as little as possible. I would never want to cause undue hardship for someone else. "That makes sense," I agreed.

"I helped fill them with coins. Edward told me that only the baron and his family are allowed to do that. Isn't that cool?"

"It is."

Rhiannon put her hand on my knee. "Do you want to help us distribute them? We do it outside of the church after Christmas mass. It'll be a lot of work, but—"

"I would be glad to help." I put my hand on top of hers.

"Really?"

"Yeah, why wouldn't I?"

She looked away. I could tell she wanted to say more, but hesitated. Instead, she casually traced the embroidered flowers on the quilt of our bed, saying nothing else.

Rhiannon had been distant the past few weeks. When I awoke in the mornings, she was often already gone, her side of the bed long cold. When I asked how she was spending her time, she would either be evasive about her schedule or prattle off a list of castle-maintaining duties normally reserved for someone in Gwendolyn or Marguerite's position. Not a short-term guest.

The brief closeness we'd rekindled after my injury seemed to have evaporated.

There was no animosity, just ... distance. Like she was still working to extricate her life from mine, even here.

My leg healed enough that I could hobble around the castle and its grounds with a cane. It still hurt like crazy, but I'd learned to live with the pain. I focused on doing things like walking short distances without a cane, standing on my toes to build up my leg strength, and stretching as much as I could. When I wasn't doing that, I was limping to the great hall for meals (where I caught fleeting glimpses of Rhiannon running around). And that's it.

I was going stir-crazy with the simple routine and limited company.

Getting to go into town to interact with the townsfolk, while engaging in an ancient and generous tradition by Rhi's side, sounded incredible.

Christmas was a rare sunny day in December; the frosting of snow coating everything lit up and glowed, giving the town a heavenly appearance. As we rode down the hill to the chapel for mass, I found myself shielding my eyes with my hand, wishing for a pair of sunglasses while also marveling at the pureness of unpolluted light.

"These are my favorite mornings," Henry commented from where he rode just ahead of us. "The whole town looking like it is bedecked in silver and diamonds, gathered to celebrate with a mighty feast." He paused his horse at the edge of the hill, gazing wistfully over the land. "It is times like this I wish ..." he trailed off. Henry glanced back at us with a sad smile and nudged his horse forward without another word.

Rhiannon gave me a pointed look from over her shoulder, indicating we'd discuss Henry's odd behavior later. Not that we had any definite conclusions, just an ongoing catalogue of strange things the baron and baroness said and did. Much of our limited conversation, confined to evenings in bed, was about the de Ros's.

Henry often spoke words meant to convey happiness but were shellacked with sadness instead. Gwendolyn was no better; her being constantly on the verge of tears when she saw me was becoming more grating than confusing. She'd often reach her hand out to touch me, not in a romantic way, but as if I was a child she wanted to comfort. They both left sentences unfinished, memories unshared. They veered from being overly familiar with me to recalling we were technically strangers and should behave accordingly.

Rhiannon thought I should press the matter. She wanted me to talk to them; she was convinced they had valuable information about how to get home.

But I resisted. I could not even begin to form a rational question to open that conversation. There were no words that could bridge the strange gap between our centuries, only phrases that would make us sound insane and compromise our safety. My only goal was to make it to the next equinox in one piece so we could go home and be done with it.

On the nights I couldn't sleep, I wondered if this disagreement was yet another wedge we were shoving between us.

As we rode into town, Rhiannon held the reins and nudged the mare on with gentle taps since my leg was still too weak to guide the horse. I kept my arm around her waist, surprised to find her purposely leaning against me. I tried not to think about how she'd become an adept rider; she'd apparently been spending quite a bit of time in the saddle without me.

At the edge of town, we left our horses at the livery and ambled down the main street towards the chapel. Each of us, including me, carried a heavy basket full of clay piggies to distribute after mass. Upon my request, Angus fashioned a leather strap so I could wear the basket across my body instead of carrying it, allowing use of my hands to manage my cane.

We were slow going as I hobbled along the icy road—though I noted we'd left early enough to allow time for me to make this journey. Rhiannon had wrapped my leg tightly, turning the bandage into a compression sleeve, helping with both pain and movement. As we walked, crowds once again parted for us, though this time everyone was all smiles, even for me.

I'm sure it helped they knew we were carrying quite a bit of money we were planning on handing out later.

Kendal was not a bishop's seat, so it did not have one of the elaborate medieval cathedrals I'd hoped to see. But the Parish Church of Holy Trinity featured stained glass windows, a carved altar piece, and the warm smell of incense throughout. Rainbow light flooded through the windows, bathing the finely dressed congregation in a kaleidoscope of jewel tones.

The service was entirely in Latin, with no magic overlapping voices trans-lating the dead language for us. One scan of the room indicated no one else understood what was being said either. People fidgeted with their fine cloaks and hats. They closed their eyes and leaned their heads on loved ones' shoulders. Most of the congregation was standing in tightly packed crowds, so they held low conversations or managed bored children or stole glances at unrequited loves.

The expressions, movements, and whispered words were all so familiar, the part of my dad's note that said humans haven't changed at all rang true. Bored, restless crowds were apparently universal throughout time.

Though there was a chapel within the castle's grounds, it struck me that we hadn't attended any services. The chaplain was known to struggle with alcohol addiction (making his commitment to holding services inconsistent at best) and the de Ros's didn't seem particularly religious—yet another odd behavior for the 15th century. I'd assumed everyone was still fervently devout. It seemed our presence here on Christmas was mostly symbolic, as the de Ros's were the leaders of this region.

When the service ended and the clergy streamed out, we followed behind, into the frosty sunshine where tables filled with little clay piggies were guarded by several of the baron's men.

Rhiannon brushed my elbow with her fingertips as she took up her post next to me; I had to resist the urge to return the affection. It could have been an accident, after all.

Before Christmas, my only experience interacting with people of this time and place were limited to the castle's occupants and our foray into the market. But I was startled by the reality of what life was like for those who did not work in the castle or have the cushion of a merchant's resources. An old man missing an eye and dressed in threadbare linen clutched his piggy and thanked me profusely. A haggard-looking woman holding a baby, with two more children with tangled hair and dirt-smudged faces clinging to her skirts, took the coins without making eye contact with me. People using rags wrapped around their feet in lieu of shoes, wearing cloaks so thin you could see daylight through them, held out bone-thin hands for the tiny bit of relief I was offering them. It is one thing to read about what life was like for many medieval peasants ... it is quite another to witness their suffering firsthand.

Something occurred to me. While I knew what it was like to be broke, I had never been poor. Being broke meant that even when my checking account was running low, I still lived in a decent house and had food in the fridge and a closet full of nice clothes. If I ever became destitute, I knew my dad would help me. I had a support system, a safety net.

But Rhiannon has known true poverty. She has known what it's like to be hungry and without a home and with very little to call her own. Because her support system was nonexistent.

And when we separated, her support system—the family she thought she had with me and my dad—all but vanished, leaving her on her own once again. Sure, she had friends. But they had their own families, jobs, and homes to tend to. It's different asking a friend for help versus a family member.

I was her family.

And I'd left her all alone.

More than once.

Even here, I understood she believed she was on her own. While I recuperated from an injury caused by my own negligence, I watched passively as she worked and worked to become invaluable so she wouldn't be turned out in the literal cold. I watched as she obsessed over the letter and the cottage to get us home; as she tended to my leg as best she could so I wouldn't have to deal with the village physician who was an absolute maniac about cutting my leg back open; as she embroidered for hours and ate things that made her sick and let Agnes dictate what she could wear—even though she hated all of it.

My heart clenched in my chest. I wondered if she'd thought I'd bail on helping with handing out the coins, blaming my leg and the cold for my lack of participation. Those would have been good—even valid—excuses. I'd been watching from a distance this whole time, so why should today have been any different?

Rhi's words about my avoiding difficult things had been playing on a loop in my head since that day in the market. She'd voiced my greatest insecurities about myself, the deep dark thoughts that kept me awake at night. The thoughts that always circled back to my dad insisting I lean into the difficult things, and my stubborn resistance in doing so, in some misguided attempt to assert my independence.

Rhiannon didn't believe my words. And I'd given her many reasons not to. She had many experiences to draw from where my words were as hollow as wind through a tunnel and she was left to fend for herself.

But I could no longer bear the thought of someone I loved so much doing this all on her own. I resolved then and there that those days were over. Only my actions mattered now.

35

RHIANNON

George trudged up the stairs, leaning on his cane, keeping a frozen smile on his face to mask what I could tell was considerable pain. His still-healing injury was pushed to the limit by the distance we'd traveled, in frigid weather, weighed down with heavy baskets.

A kitchen maid brought him a hot brick wrapped in fabric that he used as a heating pad; he alternated between massaging his leg and pressing the brick against his ravaged muscles while sitting on a rug by the fire.

I plopped down next to him, pulled my shoes off, and wiggled my numb toes in the warmth.

"I enjoyed that," George mused.

"I'm surprised you came."

"Because I avoid difficult things, right?"

I opened my mouth, ready to eviscerate him with evidence of his past failures, ready to justify my beliefs about him. But an inkling—like a gentle hand on my shoulder—stopped me. He wasn't being defensive. His words were simply stating a fact.

He'd had Angus fashion a strap for him so he could carry his own heavy basket. He'd ridden a jostling horse down and up a steep hill, walked all the way to the church and back over a muddy and icy road while carrying a heavy weight, followed by hours of standing. All without complaint.

Knowing this shifted something in my heart.

I stared at George until he met my eyes. "No, that's not why. It's because your leg still needs rest. It's clear you're in pain. That's all."

He considered this while kneading his calf muscles. "I can be in pain and still contribute."

Again, too many cutting comments were fighting to be said, to validate my own old pain and frustrations. I too, had had to do far too much while in pain. I could lead with that, but a pressing voice in my mind asked, *who would it help, to minimize him again and again, to continue rubbing his nose in his past failures?*

Instead, I simply replied: "That's true. I won't underestimate you again."

George raised his eyebrows at me and blinked. He stopped massaging his leg and rested it gingerly on the warm brick, not breaking eye contact. "And I won't give you a reason to."

I scooted closer to him and pressed my shoulder against his upper arm.

We sat leaning against each other, grins spreading across our faces, aware that some big thing had shifted between us. Something we thought was forever damaged.

I grabbed clean bandages and kneeled before George to wrap his leg. Though the gash was healed, the pressure of the tightly wound cloth kept his leg steady and eased his persistent pain.

He watched me, head tilted to the side, something unreadable in his eyes. When I finished, I rose from where I knelt and extended my hand to George. "Come on, put your hose back on so we can go eat this fine Christmas banquet I helped plan. I'm starving."

He stood up, shook his leg out, and worked his dark blue woolen hose over his wrapped leg, attached them with ties to the bottom of his doublet, and held his arm out for me to take. "To dinner then, Lady Rhiannon."

36

JANUARY 1421

GEORGE

Whether I shall turn out to be the hero of my own marriage, or whether that station will be held by anybody else, these pages must show.

January was a cocoon of snow and darkness; the sun rose late and set early, giving us only a few glimpses of light each day. Everyone in the castle hunkered down and seemed to go into hibernation to survive the heart of winter. Marguerite went into her confinement for the last few months of her pregnancy; Edward stayed by her side. Henry and Gwendolyn spent their days in their chambers, occasionally summoning us for meals or to sit quietly by the fire. The servants tended fires and prepared meals, but they too had more time on their hands, which they used to sleep or attend sporadic services in the chapel or play games of dice in the kitchens.

Everyone went into hibernation, that is, except the two people who were used to the constant stimulation of a post-industrial society. Rhiannon and I, both bored and fidgety, took to entertaining ourselves. We got wine-drunk (easy to do when all there was to drink was wine) and played cards, or made up medieval dances based on movements we witnessed at banquets in the great hall, or told stories pieced together from our favorite books and movies.

We explored the castle, often walking the length of the curtain wall along the parapets, high above the courtyard. Rhiannon would lean against me, closing the distance between us she'd been diligently maintaining until Christmas. I would wrap her in my cloak and kiss the top of her head. It was as if those calm days created space for her to reach out to me again.

We had not kissed—or done anything else—since we separated over a year earlier. Though I still desired her, I was aware we were rebuilding a broken bridge, and to rush it would be to plunge everything back into confusion and pain. So when she reached for my hand, I grasped hers. When she cuddled up to me in bed, I wrapped my arms around her and kept her warm. And every so often, when one of her curls came loose and brushed across her face, I would reach out and twirl it around my finger like I used to. She never pulled away; if anything, she leaned into my touch. But I did not take it further than that.

We needed time.

And it felt like those calm, quiet days gave us just that. They were a respite from the discomfort and pain we'd been wading through. I began to think that perhaps we would be okay. That we would spend the rest of our months here hunkered down, drinking wine and eating cheese, learning how to love again.

But the Gods of Time Travel, those prickly sadistic bastards, had other plans.

37

RHIANNON

Brace yourself, because this next part could use what my students call a "trigger warning." But guess what, kids? That's bullshit because life doesn't come with warnings. You don't get advanced notice to detour around the hard things. No, life barrels ahead, and sometimes traumatic stuff happens, and you go through it because you have no choice.

When Agnes shook me awake in the middle of the night, I understood it was going to be one of those times.

"Lady Rhiannon!" Agnes's voice was urgent and tinged with fear. She shook my shoulders until I sat up, disoriented, heart pounding from having someone's voice break through my dreams.

"What on earth," I muttered, rubbing sleep from my eyes.

"Come quickly," she implored. Agnes held up my simple wool day dress, motioning I should raise my arms so she could pull it over my head. "Lady Marguerite needs your help. Quickly now."

Beside me I heard George stirring. "Rhi?" he croaked. "What's going on?"

"None of your concern, my lord," Agnes replied while yanking the dress over my head. She was rough with me on a good day when we had plenty of time.

During a late night emergency, she almost took my head off trying to get me dressed. She'd left our room's door open and echoing through the corridor I heard a woman—Marguerite, I realized—emit a bloodcurdling scream. Agnes said nothing, only dragged me out the door, to the stairwell, taking the uneven stone stairs two at a time while looking back to make sure I was following at her pace.

When we reached Marguerite's chambers, I found her lying in bed, bed-clothes drenched in sweat and blood, Gwendolyn stroking her hand.

Gwendolyn stood and motioned me over. "The baby is coming too soon and she is in a great deal of pain. Our messenger said the midwife is with another birthing mother." Gwendolyn's voice barely rose above a whisper. She gave Marguerite a worried glance. "And the snow would hamper her considerable journey regardless. Given your expertise with the barber-surgeon, we need you to tend to her. Do whatever you must to save them both." Her tone was resolute, the true baroness of the castle who would not take no for an answer.

The room was unusually hot from the roaring fire and the coppery smell of blood was nauseatingly overpowering. I could barely breathe; I steadied myself with one hand on the post of the bed, swallowing and trying not to gag.

Marguerite whimpered, twisting the linen sheets in her hand. Tears streaked down her alarmingly pale face. Her normally ivory complexion was ashen and dark circles under her eyes had deepened into bruised smudges. Based on the state of the bed, it was clear she'd lost a lot of blood.

Right. Time was once again a scarce resource. I pressed my hand to my forehead and closed my eyes. *I will not panic*, I thought, returning to the mantra I had to abandon because overnight (and six hundred years) I became a person who panicked. But I could not panic here. I could not abandon Marguerite to this hell all alone.

I summoned Agnes. "I need hot water, boiled and cooled. As much as the kitchen maids can bring. We also need clean bedclothes, some thread ... and ..." I was wracking my memory and limited knowledge for how to handle this particular medical emergency. "That's all for now, until I can do a thorough examination, that is."

I began by placing a shaky hand on Marguerite's forehead. Her skin was cold and clammy, mirroring her deathly pallor. Despite my limited (okay, nonexistent) experience tending to a pregnant woman who'd gone into labor too early, I determined we had to stop the bleeding and fast. I held a candle up to Marguerite's face to see her eyes were unfocused. She didn't even acknowledge my presence. My stomach dropped and my heart rate accelerated.

She was in bad shape. Really bad shape.

"Help me pull back the covers," I instructed Gwendolyn, who cooperated without hesitation.

Marguerite whimpered as we exposed her lower body. After pulling back the sheet, I saw the devastating problem: the baby, come too soon, was trapped exiting the birth canal. Its tiny head was somewhat emerged and nothing more. My fear melted into rage at whatever misguided beliefs had led to this moment, to this woman being covered up while she was in labor and struggling.

Bile rose up in my throat, and it took every ounce of my strength to hold it back and show no reaction. Sweat dripped down my sides, dampening my dress. It was too much. My first instinct was to curl into a ball and cry. I was also tempted to run. God, it would have been so easy to just hurl myself out into the snow and give up entirely. But that wouldn't help anyone. And Marguerite desperately needed my help.

I took a deep breath of humid air laced with wood smoke, shook off my fear and revulsion, rolled up the wide sleeves of my gown, knelt in front of Marguerite's legs, and got to work. I could not wait for the clean water at this point. The chance of either of them surviving now depended on helping the baby out as quickly as possible. My hands were shaking so hard I had to clasp them for a moment to steady myself.

"Gwendolyn, I need you to comfort her while I do this," I instructed as calmly as I could. She nodded and scooted up onto the bed, cradling Marguerite's lolling head in the crook of one arm and stroking her hair with the other.

"Where is Edward?"

Gwendolyn grimaced. "This is no place for a man."

Right.

"How far along is she?" I tried to ask smoothly, like this was all very ordinary and there was no cause for alarm.

I placed my hands on the baby's head only to find it was cool and firm. It felt wrong. All of this was terribly wrong.

"Perhaps seven months?" Gwendolyn choked out. In the flickering firelight I could see the tracks of her tears as well.

I nodded and moved my fingers further down into the birth canal, driving all coherent thoughts from my mind and focusing on the task at hand. If I thought too much about what I was doing, if I let my own memories and traumas take root, everything would fall apart.

Once I felt like I had a solid enough grip, I gently pulled. Marguerite convulsed and shuddered, letting out another rattling scream. Her body seemed to be producing contractions again. As I gently worked, terrified of causing more harm to either of them, Agnes rushed in with a bucket of water and two kitchen maids carrying heaps of clean linens.

"My lady!" Agnes cried, falling to her knees and beginning to wail.

One of the maids got to work stoking the fire while the other soaked a rag in warm water and began cleaning Marguerite's face.

"Go get Chaplain Bell," I commanded Agnes. She leapt to her feet and scurried off without hesitation. I did not know if Marguerite would survive the night, but I knew she was a French Catholic who would probably want last rites performed for both her and her child ... if it came to that.

Moreover, I knew Agnes was in a terrible state and needed tasks that would take her out of the chambers and doing something important instead of freaking out next to us.

The baby came free, into my hands, and I knew immediately she was already gone. Trembling, I cradled the tiny girl. "Tie off the cord and bring me some cloth," I shakily instructed the maid who was cleaning Marguerite's face.

"Let me," insisted Gwendolyn, taking the twine from the maid.

I wrapped the baby and carefully set her in front of the fire, covering her face with the linen. I was moving in autopilot, dulling my thoughts and senses, because to acknowledge what was happening would have destroyed me.

I looked at Gwendolyn and shook my head.

She gave me a single nod and looked at Marguerite. "Save the girl," she commanded me, far more confident in my (again, nonexistent) medical skills than I was.

Marguerite had lost consciousness and was sprawled across the bed. The only mercy of this situation was that her tremendous bleeding seemed to have subsided. I checked her pulse: slow but stable. I knew we had one more trial left before we could let her rest. The placenta.

"We must massage her womb," I told Gwendolyn.

She nodded, understanding what I was getting at.

Together, we managed to guide Marguerite through the last painful aspect of the stillbirth.

I could scarcely breathe, could hardly process everything my shaking hands were doing to try and save this woman. I felt useless: we had no medicine, no way to give her a blood transfusion, no way to alleviate the pain or see inside to determine what the problem was. I had very little clue what I was doing, but everyone was counting on me, so I leaned into the worst kind of imposter syndrome possible. Gwendolyn had put her trust in me, and I was terrified that I was failing miserably.

Afterwards, we had the maids pull the stained bedclothes off the bed, cleaned Marguerite using linen cloths soaked in lemon and lavender water, remade the bed, and dressed her in a fresh nightgown. Her consciousness came and went as we worked, and I was feeling slightly better about her chances of survival.

Through all of this, I forgot I'd sent Agnes for the chaplain. When I noted it had likely been well over an hour, they finally entered the room and I immediately understood the delay.

Chaplain Bell was seriously drunk.

I didn't know how long I'd been in the chambers. I'd forced myself into a dissociative state, acting on instinct, stuffing my own feelings deep into the recesses of my mind so I wouldn't faint or vomit or flee.

But seeing the drunk chaplain standing (no, swaying) before me—reeking of cheap ale and smoke, rosary beads clutched in his hands—broke the spell.

"I need air," I mumbled, reaching for the door. My tears came hot and fast. I emitted a sharp sob before stumbling into the cool corridor to escape the oppressive heat of the room and the distinct smell of blood and the feel of death that clung to everything. I stumbled out of the room, right into George's open arms.

"I got you," he said as he wrapped his arms around my waist and pulled me into his lap while lowering us both to the floor. "I got you, I'm here," he kept repeating as I unleashed a flood of tears into his shoulder.

"The baby," I sobbed into his shoulder. I tried to form more coherent words, but grief slammed against my heart and stopped up anything else but tears.

George stroked my hair, clutched me tightly, and rocked us back and forth while murmuring, "I'm here, I've got you, I'm not going anywhere."

When Marguerite woke up, she would feel a pain I knew all too well: the pain of losing a baby before it even had a chance to be a part of the world.

38

GEORGE

Did you really think I wasn't going to go find out why my wife was dragged out of bed in the middle of the night by a panicked Agnes? Both of my legs could have been cut off and I still would have found a way to get to her. Whatever was happening, I knew Rhiannon needed me. And I would never let her down again.

39

ATLANTA, GEORGIA • APRIL 2018

RHIANNON

I was dressed in all black. And it was Friday the 13th.

In retrospect, these were bad omens.

Sometimes I wonder if I'd scheduled the appointment on a different day, or had worn pink corduroys instead of black jeans, or had done a million things differently, would the outcome be different? If I'd made different choices, would it have made a difference?

Sometimes I rewound my life back years instead of days and wondered if having a mother who blew second-hand smoke in my face during my formative growth years was the problem. Or perhaps the steady diet of Doritos and Diet Coke she fed me was to blame. Maybe it was the sleepless nights curled up in the backseat of her Buick parked behind various Walmarts, or the stress of being shuffled around to every public school in the state of Georgia, or the fact that I once left a tampon in far too long because I didn't have money for more.

Maybe, if as a child I'd known better and had advocated for myself, I could have prevented this mystifying problem in the first place.

Maybe the root of the problem was six hundred years in the past and I simply hadn't been planning ahead long enough.

Regardless. This is what happened.

The ultrasound tech slid the wand around my abdomen, occasionally stopping to take a screenshot of the brutally silent monitor. She said nothing, just tapped info into her computer and frowned. The clock on the wall ticked and ticked and ticked.

I clenched my fists at my sides and closed my eyes, pouring every ounce of my concentration into willing the sound of a thudding heartbeat to materialize, indicating the life growing inside me was healthy and thriving.

But this was not my first time staring at an empty, eerily quiet ultrasound monitor. This was not the first time I was giving every prayer in my soul to magically conjure up something that was not there.

One glance at George, who sat with his hands clasped and his head hanging low, hair falling over his face, told me he was doing the same: offering up an impossible prayer to any god who would listen.

The tech finally clicked off the ultrasound wand and placed it back in its holder. She replaced her studious frown with her best expression of condolences. "I'm sorry, Mrs. Rosen, but I'm afraid there is no heartbeat. I'm going to send in Dr. Golding to speak with you about your options."

Two days later I woke up at 4:00am to scrub my entire body with a fierce antiseptic wash in anticipation of the procedure I was about to endure. For an unconscionable third time.

Normally, doing something repeatedly makes you better at it. Your brain creates new neural pathways that makes each experience easier to navigate and less anxiety-producing, which ultimately makes you better at doing the thing. Since increasing neural pathways in a specific area makes you better at something, eventually, when those pathways are well-worn and familiar, it makes you an expert.

This is when people bust out phrases like, "This is not my first rodeo," and they typically mean it in a positive, you-can-trust-my-expertise kind of way, because they've done the thing repeatedly enough to not get thrown off the horse too soon. Or at all.

This was not my first rodeo.

But I found that every time I got thrown off this particular horse, what followed was a thousand times worse in every way. Because every attempt was laced with more hope, more determination, more care. And every failure echoed with the futile attempts to get my body to do this basic thing bodies are designed to do: reproduce.

The nurse was gentle with me while she wrapped my legs in compression pads and covered me with an extra heated blanket to ward off the distinct chill of the impending operating room. A second nurse came in and hooked up my IV, followed by an anesthesiologist who immediately dosed me with a nice combination of meds meant to temper my anxiety and dull any pain.

"You get the good stuff today," he winked at me, like he was offering me a vacation from my present misery and that was somehow enough.

George was slumped in the armchair beside my gurney, absently flipping through cable channels on the muted TV. He briefly landed on an HGTV show until a heavily pregnant, pert blonde showed up to pick out tile patterns. With a derisive grunt he clicked off the TV and tossed the remote on the little table between us, clasped his hands over his chest, and sunk further down in the chair.

When the anesthesiologist returned, with a medical student in tow, he explained that this time, I would be under general anesthesia and all that that entails. I didn't care. I mercifully wouldn't be awake for any of it. He had the student pump another round of meds into my IV line before he patted my wrapped legs and said he'd see me in the OR.

When we were alone, George leaned forward and brushed his fingers over mine. He'd said almost nothing since we woke up.

The first time we went through this, he'd been doting and caring—to the point I told him I felt suffocated. While I was heartbroken, I was still optimistic. Dr. Golding assured me miscarriage was common and we would most likely go on to conceive a healthy baby the next time around.

The second time, George looked as if he'd been slugged in the gut with a sledgehammer. He still doted on me, cooking my favorite things and making me a pillow pile on the couch to watch TV while he worked from home. But he was distant—like he was afraid to say or do the wrong thing, so he added protective space between us. I would reach for him, desperate for connection, only for him to kiss me on the forehead, pat me on the hand, and go handle another non-urgent chore.

Our baseboards were spotless, but I was traumatized and lonely.

We gave ourselves time after that one. We went on an Alaskan cruise. We worked and paid off medical bills and threw pennies into our anemic savings account. We watched movies that made us laugh. We kept our plans close to our chest because we were embarrassed to share even a shred of optimism with our friends—especially the fertile ones who were populating daycares like it was their full-time jobs.

Then, because we were ready to participate in the rodeo again, we would nervously say things like, "Third time's a charm!" And, statistically, getting thrown off this horse a third time, especially when no medical professional had ever figured out why you got thrown off at all, seemed impossible. I would cling to that fucking horse like my life depended on it.

Getting pregnant was easy. "The third time's a charm," I muttered while looking at the positive test. I could make this work. I had to. I always did. Well ... almost always.

I read all the books about what to expect and what not to expect and how to expect better; I ate an abundance of vegetables to compensate for my piss-poor diet as a kid; I took folic acid and choline supplements and the most expensive prenatal vitamins I could find; I quit drinking altogether, save for an occasional sip of wine, because European women drink wine throughout their pregnancies and somehow they turn out better than okay; I went to yoga and took long walks and did cardio and stretched and read every study showing how much easier it is to give birth if you're physically fit; I stood in the baby aisle of Target and just let the baby-ness of it all wash over me, like I could immerse myself in this world of powder smells and diapers and tiny onesies, and that would coax an embryo to hold on, to stay on the horse with me, until we could dismount together.

But, as it turns out, that is not how any of this works.

The third time the horse bucked us off (after twelve weeks no less), George became a ghost going through the motions. He wandered around our house, looking haunted and grim.

After we got home from the procedure, he set me up in bed with a cup of green tea and a grilled cheese sandwich. He said very little, just went through the motions we'd established as a tragic routine.

At some point, he disappeared. I woke up and he was gone.

But I was still amongst the living, nursing the wounds of my latest fall off the horse, navigating a trauma that compounded with each rotation through the experience.

40

GEORGE

I stood in the doorway and watched Rhiannon slip into a deep nap. She was curled on her left side, clutching an old stuffed bear—an object of comfort from her tumultuous childhood, one of the few things she owned. I'd spent the better part of the last hour puttering around the house, restless with grief, trying to find something—anything—to ease the tension in my chest.

I needed to get out of the house that had become a paragon of our suffering, down to the third bedroom we'd kept empty in anticipation of putting a nursery in it. When I passed the doorway in the hall, I found myself blocking my sight with my hand so I couldn't see the bare wood floors or unassembled crib in the corner.

There was nothing I could say or do to fix this situation, to make it better. Worse, Rhiannon was the one who carried the physical burden again and again. It was impossible for me to lighten that load for her. Making tea and propping up her pillows felt performative at best.

Wracked with guilt and grief, feeling like I was coming out of my skin, desperate for anything to clear my mind, I got in the car and left.

It doesn't really matter where I went or how I spent my time. Hours compressed into minutes as I aimlessly wandered all over the labyrinthine roads of Atlanta. When the sun hung low in the sky and the gas light pinged, I realized I'd been gone a long time.

I'd forgotten my phone was on *do not disturb* from when we were at the hospital earlier. When I checked it, a slew of texts and missed calls flooded in. Rhi was looking for me, was worried about me. My dad had even called, letting me know my wife was looking for me and how could I leave her alone in such a state and didn't I know better than that?

Shit.

When I called Rhiannon to let her know I was okay and heading home, she barely responded.

By the time I got home, the sun had set. Rhiannon hadn't closed the curtains or turned on the lights. The house was dark, quiet.

"Rhi?" I called. No answer.

I found her in our bedroom, lying flat on the bed, spread out like a starfish, staring at the ceiling.

"Where were you?" she asked without looking at me.

"I just ... needed some air. I needed to get out of the house and clear my head."

"That must be nice," she whispered. "How nice you got to do that."

Rhiannon turned on her side and curled away from me.

Shit.

41

RHIANNON

When my crying subsided and my panicked breathing reduced to hiccups, I got a good look at George. He'd hiked up two flights of steep stairs, using his cane, where he'd been waiting for me outside Marguerite's door.

"When did you get here?" I asked between gulps of air. Though he'd been able to navigate the stairs, he usually waited until daylight as one slip on the uneven stones in the dark could prove fatal.

"When Agnes dragged you away, it seemed like an emergency. I needed to know you were okay. I've been waiting out here for you the whole time." George rubbed his injured leg over the bandage and carefully flexed his knee joint. He winced but otherwise seemed okay. "It's bad, isn't it?" he asked softly.

"It is."

We sat in the corridor for several minutes, me in George's lap, catching bits of Chaplain Bells's slurring prayers through the door frame. My eyes grew heavy as the adrenaline wore off. I needed to get to bed—though I doubted I'd be able to sleep. I grasped George by the upper arm to steady myself. "I can't believe you came for me."

"Of course I came for you. I told you, I've got you. I'm not going anywhere. Okay?"

I nodded and wiped my face with the sleeve of my dress. "Come on, let's get back to our room and I'll tell you what happened."

We got to our feet, holding each other for stability. I grabbed his hand and together we navigated each uneven step down to our room.

In our chambers, the light of the waning fire revealed George's face was slick with sweat and his breathing was labored. It was clear he was in a great deal of pain.

"You didn't have to do that, you know. I wasn't in any danger." My words were meant to be reassuring, but my voice came out wobbly and false.

George looked at me like I was crazy. "You were summoned from bed in the middle of the night by a frantic Agnes. I had no idea where she was taking you or what was going on, but I could hear screams. And," he limped to my side so he could take my hand. "And I swore I'd never let you handle this kind of shit alone again. We're a team."

From above, we heard a woman's deep wail. Gwendolyn's voice. A great commotion stirred the castle, followed by more shrieks. George and I stared at each other, wide-eyed, too familiar with the sounds of grief.

"Should ..." I gulped. "Do you think I should go back up there?" I had a devastating feeling the cries were not related to the baby.

George wrapped me up in his arms and spoke quietly into my ear. "Rhi, I know you want to help. But this may not be something you can fix. Or solve. Or manage."

Tears spilled down my cheeks as I choked out short breaths. "Marguerite ... she ... she..." I couldn't even begin to form a sentence that would suffice in this situation. My hands grew numb as I was lightheaded with despair, trying to process everything that had happened since we'd been here. I gestured to my face, words caught in my throat, hoping George could understand what I was trying to communicate.

How it was my fault, that I hadn't done enough, that I'd let her down. Let them all down.

He sat in one of the armchairs, pulled me into his lap, and held me as I gasped and cried. He stroked my hair, kissed the top of my head, and just let me cry.

When there was a break in my tears, when the flooding of my emotions seemed to crest and recede, I cupped George's face and gazed into his eyes. He had been crying as well, and though his eyes were red-rimmed and wet, he was calm and his breaths were measured.

"I'm sorry," he whispered.

I rested my forehead against his. "What are you sorry for?"

"Running. All the times I ran when it got too hard." He tightened his grip around my waist. "Mistaking your ability to take care of yourself with thinking you didn't need anyone to take care of you."

I exhaled slowly, letting my fingers drag down the side of his face. "How can I ever trust you again?" I hiccupped. "You left me and I *needed* you."

George just held me, stroking my hair. "You can't," he finally murmured. "That's how trust works. I'll have to earn it back. But I'm going to. I promise."

42

RHIANNON

The days after Marguerite died were a blur. I didn't get out of bed for three days, laid flat by my own despair and shame as a barrage of relentless memories played my various traumas and failures on a loop. I could not save them. Any of them. My efforts were a meaningless sieve.

The headaches I'd been suffering from since we arrived intensified; I'd assumed it was due to having my scalp wrapped in a vice-like headdress every day, but after several days without it, I was still in pain. I added it to the mental list of painful things I could not solve.

George brought me food and forced me to sit up so he could feed me pieces of bread or sips of soup broth. Everything tasted like dirt and nothing mattered. But I still ate. In between bites of cheese or sips of watered down wine, he reported what was happening in the rest of the castle while I was sequestered.

He told me that the dreamy haze Henry and Gwendolyn seemed to occupy had morphed into a heavy cloud that settled over everything. Gwendolyn could not seem to stop crying and Henry was in an unresponsive stupor, barely uttering a word, often sitting with his eyes closed, tapping his fingers on the armrest of whatever chair he occupied.

She had been like a daughter to them and the loss was immense.

Edward completely retreated into his chambers, with only servants scurrying in and out to confirm he was still alive.

Long, dark days dragged by and George constantly voiced his worry for me and the desolate hole I could not seem to climb out of. Eventually, I let Agnes wrestle me back into gowns and headdresses so I could eat in the great hall, where the de Ros's looked like slumped over puppets in their chairs, untouched food growing cold in front of them. Edward never joined us. The general mood was somber, quiet, and hopeless.

Winter persisted. If it wasn't snowing, then the temperature dipped so low it was dangerous to be outside. "I'm sure missing those extra layers of carbon dioxide making everything warmer," I muttered to George one night while huddled in bed. My breath clouded above us as the fire struggled to warm the room.

"You don't really mean that," he replied. We were both wearing knit hats, thick woolen socks, and mittens in bed. So yes, I did mean it.

My headaches persisted, with nothing but herbal teas and warm compresses to relieve some of the pain. And though George's wound had healed, it was clear his muscles were still recovering, causing him a great deal of pain. His exercise options were limited to hiking up and down dark stairwells and limping across the frozen courtyard with his cane—though that didn't deter him from working his leg every day.

At night we lay awake in bed, tossing and turning, desperate for some kind of relief from the endless gray choking out all thoughts, all action, all life. We both felt trapped, with the pressure building daily.

"We should not be here," George lamented more than once. "I'm going crazy feeling bored and useless. Plus, these people should not have to grieve around us. They should have the privacy to feel it all, without us strangers in the way."

"Where would we go?" I asked one evening, only half-listening while stitching a chain of limp-looking sunflowers along the border of a linen cloth.

George was startled by my question and the realization it held: we didn't have to stay in this castle. We were guests, not prisoners. Technically, we could go wherever we wanted.

Without thinking, I'd pushed his rhetorical complaints into the ability to make a choice.

A couple days later he had an answer: "The cottage. We should move into the cottage."

"The dirty cottage with one window and no servants? Hard pass."

But George was undeterred. "You mean our cottage, the place that dropped us in this time, the most likely way home? Look, I know what I said about needing to wait a full year. But what if we've been missing opportunities to go home? What if we should have stayed put the whole time? What if," he made sure he made eye contact with me, "What if you were right all along?"

I rolled my eyes. I'd accepted we were going to be here the full year, and this felt an awful lot like he was dangling an imaginary carrot to get me to move. "I know what you're doing. And it won't work."

George got down on one knee and took my hand in his, like he was getting ready to propose. "Rhi. The letter explicitly says to 'stay put.' Maybe there's more to this than we thought. Maybe just by living in the cottage, we'll unravel more of this mystery. Don't you at least want to find out? Aren't you at least a little bit curious about the possibilities of our haunted time travel cottage?"

I set my stitching in my lap and glared at him. "We both know you're full of shit. You don't really think there's more to the riddle."

"Maybe. But I'm not full of shit about needing to get out of here. Out of this depressing as fuck castle. What are we even doing here? I'm losing my mind with boredom and it just feels, like, why go through all the trouble of sending us back here just to have us sitting around doing nothing? Surely there's more to it than this."

I'd already had too much time to overthink and come to similar conclusions. We felt stuck, but the way out was unclear.

"George, you might be right. But I've never wanted you to be more wrong." I closed my eyes and rubbed my jaw joints where another headache was forming.

"Do you know how long it has taken me to accept we would be here until the autumn equinox? Do you know what we'd be taking on, to try and live down there, by ourselves? No servants? No money? Heck, no indoor garderobe?"

"I do. Honestly, it's all I've been thinking about for the last two days, as soon as you wondered where else we could go. And, I'm sorry, but I don't think I'm wrong about this. I think we need to move."

"It's at least six months until the autumn equinox. That's a long time."

"What if we could have gone home on the winter solstice? Or, what if the spring equinox springs us forward?" George countered.

"What if the spring equinox doesn't send us home, but rather another point in time? What if we get sent back even further in time?"

"We can't go back before this cottage exists, right? At least, it's a safe assumption. You didn't find any mention of it prior to, what, a hundred years before this? So, what if we do travel again, but in the right direction? What if spring sends us to 1520? Or, hell, 1820? Wouldn't you rather hang out with Jane Austen in the Regency era for a few months before the autumn equinox sends us back home?"

"Jane Austen died in 1817. Also, don't try to use my love of *Pride and Prejudice* against me," I sighed. "As tempting as that is, it's all just guesswork." I was frustrated with the lack of solid, provable information. "With massive risks attached to each wrong guess."

George clasped both of my hands in his. "Then let's take a risk. I can't stay in this castle much longer. Everything feels wrong here. And it's not just because they're grieving. Henry and Gwendolyn have always been ... off. I can barely think straight, and not just because of this injury. It's like there's a cloud constantly fogging my thoughts. Tell me you don't feel it too."

I squeezed his hands but didn't pull mine away. "I do. Feel it too, that is. But I just assumed it's because we have alcohol with every meal, so we're always slightly drunk."

"Maybe. But, Rhi ... have you noticed there are no children in this castle? There are, like a hundred people, all adults. I noticed it when we were at the market and then at the church. We went from a place where everyone seemed to be at least twenty-five years old, to the town where suddenly there were families again. It was jarring."

I closed my eyes and mentally walked the grounds of the castle, searching my memories for anyone younger than in their twenties. There should be lots of kids running around, but I couldn't picture a single one. "Jesus," I exhaled and opened my eyes. "No kids, just one specific cat."

"Right. Gustav. That's also weird. I don't even know where to start with him."

"I really want you to be wrong about all of this. But once again, there's evidence." My stomach twisted considering the possibility of trying to survive without the help of everyone here. "I'm terrified of what we'll have to endure down there! You barely survived your injury and I've yet to get a handle on the food situation. And that's with the help of a staff of servants and a wealthy baron. How will we survive completely on our own?"

"I know," he said solemnly. "We'll have to figure that all out. We won't rush into it. We will make a plan, okay?"

I raised an eyebrow. "Wow, look at you with all the carrots today. Telling me I'm right and we get to make a plan? Is this your way of persuading me?"

He grinned. "I know how much you love being right and making a good plan. And if I could offer you a nice spreadsheet to organize it all, I would. But alas, no Excel in the 15th century."

I gazed at George, kneeling before me, illuminated by firelight, his blonde hair brushed back over his shoulders. He always had this strange effect on me, like I wanted to follow him wherever his stupid ideas led us because it felt right—even as logic and reason screamed at me to not go. I sighed, defeated. "It's annoying how charming you are. Because I'm actually considering this awful idea."

He lit up. "That's all I ask. Just consider it. We have time to figure it all out."

43

GEORGE

Once Rhiannon was willing to consider moving into the cottage, I got to work on a plan. We would need to be able to feed ourselves, bathe semi-regularly, and keep the cottage clean and comfortable. We'd need supplies. And a lot of clean water. With no access to the well. All of which meant we'd need money.

That's where my planning ended. I had no idea how to get a medieval job, how to grow a single vegetable or tend to chickens or milk cows or dig a latrine ... my thoughts would spiral off at that point. At how overwhelming the tasks at hand seemed.

I considered that maybe the effort wasn't worth it, that perhaps I had been wrong to want to leave the castle. Who cared if there were inexplicably no kids? Or that its lone cat had a strange habit of popping into rooms with closed doors wearing a variety of bowties? What did it matter if Gwendolyn burst into tears as soon I walked into a room? We could manage it all as long as someone came to tend our fire and clean our chamber pots and do our laundry.

I'd almost convinced myself to stay until one evening, when Edward joined us for dinner in Henry and Gwendolyn's private dining room—the first time we all gathered for a meal since losing Marguerite.

The food was simple: roast lamb, baked root vegetables, and bread. We ate, drank wine, and engaged in subdued conversations about daily minutiae and nothing else. After the dishes were cleared and the conversation wound down, a servant brought Edward something he must have requested earlier: a lute.

He sat by the fire, idly plucking the strings. After he strummed a series of chords, I realized he was tuning the instrument. When Edward was satisfied with the notes coming from the lute, he began a song ... a song of love gained and love lost, of yearning for the days when everything was pure and happy, before sorrow stained the memories forever. It was a song I knew well. It was the song I listened to when I drove from my house to my father's after my wife asked me to leave. A song that brought me to my knees with despair as I contemplated losing the most important person in the world to me: Rhiannon. And it was a song I'd listened to probably a hundred times before that because it was by one of my favorite bands, Ruby Haze.

And the man singing it, perched on a stool with his long hair falling over one eye, executing every note and lyric flawlessly, was the exact same man who would write it hundreds of years later.

Holy shit.

I leapt up from my seat. Everyone but Edward stared at me. Unsure what to do next, I sunk back down and started shaking my good leg, bursting with nervous energy over this wild revelation. Rhiannon tore her attention away long enough to shoot me a look that said, *get it together and stop embarrassing us.*

But I couldn't help it. From the first moment I met Edward, I knew there was something familiar about him, something that scratched at my memories, begging me to make the connection. It had bothered me since he found us on the side of the road, that nagging familiarity with no answers.

I glanced at Rhiannon to see if this song—and the man playing it—stirred any memories. But she seemed to be lost in the melody, her eyes glazed over with tears. When Edward finished singing, she clapped, wiping a stray tear from her cheek.

I braced my hands on the table to steady myself. It was strange enough that we'd met Henry and Gwendolyn in our time, but to have Edward here too? Before I could process the impossible sequence of events that had to have occurred for all of us to be in this room, at this time, Edward began a new song.

If I had any doubt that Edward was from our time, the next song put it to rest. It was "Eternal Flame" by the Bangles.

This time, Rhiannon tilted her head, narrowed her eyes, and bit her bottom lip. She knew this song. We'd danced around our kitchen to this song, wine-buzzed and madly in love, serenading each other off-key (ok, technically only Rhi was off-key as she's totally tone-deaf). She knew this song because I'd put it on more than one playlist for her, a declaration of my love unending. This wasn't just any song. It was *our* song.

The lilting melodies and heartfelt lyrics transported me back in time, to when we couldn't get enough of each other, to when we'd spend entire weekends in bed holding each other.

I stared at Rhiannon, willing her to look at me, to confirm what was happening.

She acknowledged me only once, giving me her best *what in the actual fuck* expression, before staring at Edward, unblinking, brow furrowed.

When he finished singing, I limped to the other side of the table where Rhiannon sat and extended my hand to her to indicate I was ready to leave. She did not hesitate to take it. We expressed our admiration of the music, bid our evening farewells, and hurried outside to the courtyard.

In the bracing air, with a blanket of vibrant stars above us, Rhiannon grabbed me by the cloak and demanded, "Be honest with me, George. Am I losing my mind? Or is that ..." she couldn't form the words. "Is that ... our song? And if it's our song, was that really Eddy Fox playing it?"

"You aren't losing your mind. It's definitely him. Wow," I exhaled. "What does this mean? Did he come here through the cottage as well? Should we ask him about it? I have to admit, this is uncharted territory. I have no idea what to do next."

Rhiannon said nothing, only blinked at the sky with her arms crossed over her chest. I tightened her cloak under her chin and rubbed her shoulders for warmth.

"On a lighter note—pun intended—can you believe I was right about this one stupid, crazy thing? I mean of all things!"

She leveled her gaze at me, eyes round with the terrible realization that a bonkers theory I'd had years and years ago (and six centuries in the future) turned out to be true. Under her breath Rhiannon acknowledged, "Yes, of all the things for you to be right about, I did not have my money on this one." She shook her head and looked back up at the stars. "I know it took, like a decade, but you can gloat now."

"You better believe I will. In the history of husbands and wives, this is the most right a husband has ever been about anything, ever!"

She rolled her eyes but could not disagree. Because we were both remembering our first date.

44

GEORGE

"Dad?" I knocked on his rarely-closed office door. No answer. A quick check of the knob revealed the door was unlocked and easily swung open. A folded note resting atop a stack of books had my name scrawled across the bias.

I dropped my work bag on the floor and scanned the note, which simply said: "George, had a history emergency. Let's reschedule. Love, Dad."

"What the fuck is a 'history emergency'?" I muttered to myself while crumpling the note into a ball. I was still out of breath from dashing across campus so as not to be late for our standing lunch date. I swung Dad's cracked red leather desk chair around and flopped into it, spinning so my back was to the door and I could look out the window, contemplating what to do next.

In an attempt to recover and reconnect from the tumultuous few years after Mom passed, Dad and I started having weekly lunches where I'd meet him at his office and we'd walk to a nearby burger place or Greek café for lunch and small talk. He'd recount the latest history department gossip while I nodded along, chewing each bite as thoroughly as possible so it seemed more like I couldn't contribute to the conversation because of my food, as opposed to the reality, which is I could not get a single word in.

This was my father—entertaining, charismatic, loquacious—a gifted story-teller always in search of a captive audience.

And a son whose phone bill and lunch you're paying for is as captive an audience as you can get.

But Dad had always been a degree removed from the audience, as if bright stage lights in his eyes always kept him from seeing the person sitting right in front of him.

I considered waiting for him to return from this supposed "history emergency" and hold him to our plans. The thought of staying here until he got back to make him feel as guilty as possible for the cancelation (and not even with a text, but with a note after I drove all the way from Atlanta!) tempted me. I love having the upper hand.

Outside, students hung out in the green, shoving bare toes into fading summer grass and turning faces up to the waning September sun. There wasn't much stopping me from joining them, from letting myself take an afternoon to pretend I could spend time tracing shapes in the clouds instead of meeting my deadlines. Before I could craft the perfect sick script to bail on the rest of my workday, the hairs on the back of my neck stood up. I perceived someone quietly stepping into the office behind me.

Given the high back of the chair, I was certain they couldn't see me, so I fully expected to swing around and scare the crap out of some naïve freshman.

When I rotated slowly towards door for dramatic effect, I was instead greeted with the sight of someone I thought I'd never see again: Rhiannon Keller.

We both gasped, but I like to think I gained my composure first.

"Well, well, well—" I began to say as I kicked my feet up on the desk and interlaced my hands behind my head in a move I thought appeared both cool and intimidating at the same time.

Rhiannon cut me off: "If it isn't the prodigal son, returned home to remind his father why he should've gotten a vasectomy."

Before I could finish delivering the opening line I'd been practicing for at least three years (in the unlikely event I saw her again), the girl who'd been the bane of my existence senior year beat me to the punch.

"Damn it, Keller! You ruined my opening line." I slapped the desk in frustration over her quick timing.

Rhiannon's sarcastic cackle sliced the air between us. She crossed her arms over her chest while eyeing me up, clearly daring me to insult her right back.

Which, I absolutely would. "So, still stuck in History 101? It's okay, reading is hard for people with single-digit IQs. But you not giving up is so inspiring!" I wiped a mock tear from the corner of my eye.

She rolled her eyes at me. "C'mon, tell me you've got a better line than that. I'm almost offended by your effort. Or lack thereof. An IQ joke is the lowest form of insult. Don't you think I deserve better? Of course, if that's the best you've got…" she trailed off, shrugged, and smiled at me with pity.

Rhiannon was infuriatingly right about that—but she ruined my initial opening line, so I went with low-hanging fruit because it's the best I could do on the spot.

I shoved my hair out of my eyes. "Listen, I haven't eaten lunch yet and it's difficult to think in the presence of someone who sucks all the joy out of the room. What are you even doing here anyway?"

She rummaged around in her bag and pulled out an essay. "Dr. Rosen asked me to re-do a few sections of this paper. He told me he'd be here at this time, so I came to get his feedback." Rhiannon started to set her paper on the desk but hesitated. She narrowed her eyes at me. "Can I trust you not to mess with it?"

I feigned insult. "Me? I take academic integrity very seriously you know." I leaned over the desk and snatched the essay out of her hand before she could pull back any further. "*Public Health Interventions During the Bubonic Plague in Medieval England*. Wow. You know, I've been praying for a cure for my insomnia and here you are, handing me the essay-equivalent of Ambien."

"Ha, ha." She replied sarcastically. "It's easy to find something boring if you're too dumb to understand it."

"Didn't we already establish that IQ jokes are the lowest form of insult?"

"We did, but you don't give me much to work with considering you wouldn't understand a more sophisticated insult."

I laughed. "Ah, Rhiannon Keller. Some things never change. In all seriousness, aren't you a biology major? Why on earth are you still taking history classes?"

"Why do you care?" She asked defensively. It was a fair question.

I met Rhiannon at a party the beginning of what was my senior year and her freshman year. She had long, curly, reddish-brown-copper hair, tawny olive skin, and big hazel eyes—an unusual combination I found intriguing. I recall moving through the crowd of familiar faces to talk to the one person I didn't know but was suddenly desperate to have in my life.

It should also be noted that at that point in the evening, I was fairly drunk. Like, I could still walk and talk, but I should've limited who I was walking towards and who I was talking to for my own sake.

I vaguely recall sidling up to Rhiannon and saying something that made her laugh, so I laughed too. We exchanged some witty banter, good enough that I remember she placed her hand gently against my chest and it felt incredible. Blood was rushing to all sorts of interesting places, leaving my brain tragically debilitated. Because after that it gets fuzzy.

The next thing I knew, she looked furious. She gave me a small—yet aggressive—shove away from her while some guy wearing an Ed Hardy T-shirt wrapped his arm possessively around her shoulders, glaring at me while pulling her against his side. I stumbled away from the two of them, towards the safety of a beer keg and friendly faces.

A few days later, I was waiting for my dad outside one of his classes. When most of the students had left, I peeked into the classroom to see it was only Rhiannon who remained, speaking to my father about one of his assignments. Dad waved me in. Rhiannon looked at me, but her expression was blank. For a moment I assumed this meant she didn't recall meeting me over the weekend. *Clean slate!* I recall thinking, relieved.

Dad patted me on the shoulder. "This is my son, George. He has a knack for storytelling, so I always recommend him as a tutor as he does a lovely job of bringing history to life." He turned towards me and said, "George, this is Rhiannon. She's pursuing studies in biology and is considering adding a historical component. She's keenly interested in the history of medicine, which can be a little dense. So I told her I have a few good tutor options in mind and here you are, just in time! Speaketh it into existence." He closed, adding his rarely-used British accent to really ramp up what he probably thought was drama, but made me cringe with secondhand embarrassment.

Rhiannon's smile was clearly false, as her eyes (more green than hazel in the fluorescent light, I noted) were unblinkingly cold, like they couldn't possibly occupy the same face as any smile—even the most insincere smile she was working with here. In fact, Rhiannon looked like she'd rather chew on old textbooks than accept my help. Perhaps the slate wasn't as clean as I thought.

"Oh, I'm always happy to help!" I exclaimed. I patted Dad's shoulder right back. Our arms became linked across each other's shoulders, like we were the idyllic father and son duo of any number of commercials advertising fishing or golf equipment—not two people fumbling through emotionally stunted conversations designed to mask the pain we were ill-equipped to process with only each other.

My smile was a rubber band, pulled taut with the tension of this situation. "Where are you headed, Rhiannon, was it? I'll walk you and we can discuss your tutoring plan."

"Okay," Rhiannon replied through bared teeth. "You can walk me to … there."

"Right."

"Right," she nodded.

Dad pulled his arm from around my shoulders, clapped his hands together, and said, "Splendid!"

Outside Rhiannon walked roughly two paces ahead of me, though her rapid gait was no match for my much longer legs. She was wearing cut-off jean shorts, a tight white T-shirt, and these incredible black cowboy boots with silver-tipped toes. Given how much she stood out in the sea of Ugg boots, pink velour pants, and straightened blonde hair most girls were wearing at the time, I wondered where she was from. Certainly not Georgia.

"Listen," I huffed, somehow out of breath despite playing soccer for years. "I think I may have said something stupid to you at the party the other night, and I honestly don't remember what it was. But," I wheezed and she slowed down a bit. "But I'm sorry, okay? I'd been drinking and that makes most people say dumb things."

Rhiannon came to an abrupt stop, causing me to almost plow right into her before I caught myself. Her back was to me, my hands hovered over her shoulders, not daring to touch her but prepared to do what it took to not knock her over either. She stood a few inches from me, her loose hair brushing against my chest.

She took one step forward, turned on one booted heel to face me, and replied: "Look, apology accepted. It wasn't that big of a deal. But that doesn't mean I want or need your help. Dr. Rosen assumed that's what I was asking for. Which, I wasn't. So, no hard feelings. You're free to go."

I crossed my arms and cocked my eyebrow. "I'm going to be honest. That didn't sound like there are no hard feelings. I'm genuinely willing to help if you need it."

"Well, I don't need your help. I'm not sure what else you want to hear from me." She shrugged.

"Okay, fair enough. See you around Rhiannon. And good luck with your class." I gave her a curt nod and started walking backwards away from her. She didn't turn away. She watched me expand the distance between us, our eyes locked, biting her lower lip. I continued walking backwards, praying people would get out of my way because I didn't want to turn around. I held her gaze for a stupid amount of time, like it was a challenge I couldn't lose. She didn't look away either, nor did she continue walking. She stayed and watched me.

When there were too many people weaving between us to maintain eye contact, I turned around and headed back inside, not daring to look back.

Throughout the rest of the school year, we'd catch eyes from across various distances. And we would just watch each other. No words spoken, no winks or smiles or anything like that. Just staring in a way that could have been creepy or intense or off-putting but somehow was not. It was simply an acknowledgement of a connection we clearly weren't ready to do anything about.

But the few times we ran into each other close enough to exchange words rather than glances, she had a cutting remark or pithy insult ready for me. And I happily dished it right back. It was the strangest, most undefinable relationship I'd ever had.

I learned through the gossip chain that Ed Hardy T-shirt guy was her boyfriend—hence her reaction to whatever I said at the party that upset her so much. She seemed to end it with that guy later in the fall, only to take up with some other jackass who was always drinking Red Bulls and liked to put his hand in her back pocket while they walked across campus. Gross.

This was unfortunate, because every time I saw Rhiannon my heart clenched up a little bit. I found myself scanning the campus, hoping to catch sight of her red hair and the black boots with silver toes she almost always wore.

I was crazy about a girl I barely knew, who seemed to loathe me, but who was constantly in my orbit, nonetheless.

Graduation was a relief. Leaving school would put healthy distance between us and I assumed Rhiannon being out of sight would eventually mean she would become out of mind.

So why, three years later, did I care about this girl still taking history classes? Because apparently, I still cared about her.

As soon as I saw Rhi, I realized my crush had only been dormant—never gone.

Before I could respond to her question, Rhiannon's stomach growled. Her eyes widened in embarrassment.

I smiled. "Come on," I snapped the essay out of her hands and slapped it on my dad's desk. "Let's go have lunch."

She scowled. "What makes you think I want to eat lunch with you?"

"Because I want to keep talking to you. And I think, despite your commitment to being as shrewish as possible with me, you want to keep talking to me too. And if that's not true, then at the very least I know we're both hungry."

"Did you just call me 'shrewish'?"

"I did. It's an underused word and seems to fit well here."

Rhiannon arched one eyebrow at me, though her scowl was now fighting its way into a reluctant smile. "For all you know, I have a boyfriend."

I stood and came around the desk, so we were standing only a foot apart. She smelled like honeysuckle and fabric softener. And I was grateful to be in the cloud of her scent because it meant she hadn't moved an inch, even as I came closer.

"I'm asking you to lunch, not to marry me. Besides, does this supposed boyfriend wear Affliction T-shirts? Does he have a tattoo in Chinese characters that he thinks says 'strong' or 'wise,' when really it says something ridiculous like 'hot dog'?" Rhiannon's eyes widened with this assessment. "Or perhaps over the years you think you've upgraded by choosing the kind of guy who wears boat shoes when he's nowhere near a boat. Yeah, I remember your type, Keller. Guys who aren't nearly as smart as you, thus easily controlled. But I'm going to be very honest. I don't care if you do have some douchey boyfriend." I leaned down so I was speaking softly right into her ear. "Because I think you're about to break up with him if you do."

I straightened and looked into her eyes, hovering over her. I decided since the universe dealt me a new chance with this girl, I'd be damned if I was going to let it slip away.

Rhiannon's cheeks flushed, though she didn't break eye contact with me, nor did she add space between us. She bit her lower lip, furrowed her brow. "Well George, you're right about at least one thing. I'm starving. You win. Let's go." She adjusted her backpack over her shoulder and stepped towards the door.

If there is one bright spot in losing a parent to cancer at a relatively young age, it's that you become fearless. Nothing can feel worse than that, so why not just go for it? As soon as I saw Rhiannon Keller again, I knew I wanted to be with her, and I was going to make it happen.

Because despite our prickly interactions over the course of my final year at UGA, I was certain she felt the same way.

One of the last times we ran into each other, during the end of my senior year, was between the stacks of the Roman Empire section of the library. I was flipping through a book, looking for the right quote to finish off an essay, when Rhiannon came barreling around the corner and almost smacked into me. Startled, she tripped on the carpet. I grabbed her upper arm, keeping her from crashing to her knees. When she looked up at me, adjusting her backpack behind her, I half-expected another cutting comment.

Instead, she said, "Thank you."

Rhiannon shifted her feet as if confirming the stability of the floor beneath her and continued to watch me curiously as I held her arm lightly. She was wearing a tank top, and it occurred to me too late that my fingers were clutching her bare skin, and she may not like that. Yet neither of us moved. I could make out flecks of green in her hazel eyes and the smattering of freckles across her face. She searched my gaze, breath held.

Then, she was gone. While I was still processing what to do next, Rhiannon had shaken free of my grip and scurried off.

I thought about that moment for days afterward, replaying the reel in my mind, searching for clues about what had happened. And what I could've done differently to make her stay.

Like she could read my mind, Rhi grabbed my upper arm. "Well? Are we going to eat or what?"

She had caught me standing in old memories.

"Yup, let's go."

I flung the menu on the table without opening it. "Order for me. I'm on decision overload."

Rhiannon snorted. "Are you serious? What if I get you something you hate? Aren't you concerned I might purposely get you something gross?"

I leaned back and spread my arms across the top of the booth. "You won't do that. You're an overachiever and a perfectionist. You'll get a lot of pride out of getting this order right. There's no way you'd fail on purpose."

Rhiannon scoffed. "Like you know me at all. We haven't seen each other in three years. And back then we weren't exactly friends. You have no clue who I am."

I leaned forward and clasped my hands on the table. "I observe more than you think. Did you know I was a Lit major? I spent a lot of time analyzing characters, then started doing it in real life. For example, very few students ever take my dad up on his offer to improve their essays for extra credit. But you did. What's more, you showed up to get his feedback on it. That's an overachiever if I've ever seen one. As for the perfectionist thing," I waved my finger in a circle around her face. "Your hair is done in two, perfectly even braids. Your white shirt has literally no wrinkles, which—side note, that's very impressive. What is that, starch? Anyway, you also got a manicure sometime in the last couple days. I could keep going, but you get the point. So, yes, Rhiannon, given your attention to details and results, I trust you to order me a cheeseburger without messing it up."

Rhiannon closed one eye and squinted at me as if examining me under a microscope. For a moment I thought I'd gone too far, and she was considering whether to bail. Instead, she laughed, closed her menu, and tossed it on top of mine.

"Coming from anyone else that little assessment would be creepy and off-putting. But somehow you have just enough charisma to pull it off." She leaned forward. "Though I could be projecting since I like your dad's teaching so much. I mean, my first impression that you're an unbearable asshole could be spot on. That said, I'll take the risk and get you what I'm getting for myself."

I grinned. "Even better. Also, you thought I was an 'unbearable asshole?' Rude." I didn't press it further. Sometimes I suspect I am an unbearable asshole.

Rhiannon laughed but didn't defend her position. "For the record, I gave myself the manicure." She held up her hand and wiggled her immaculately painted nails.

"Of course you did," I chuckled.

When the server came to take our order, Rhiannon got us both double-stack burgers with American cheese, grilled onions, pickles, and mayo. She added sides of both fries and coleslaw, then informed me she thought all meals should include vegetables.

"Of course," I agreed, completely unsurprised that her overachieving perfectionism extended to meals as well.

"So," she clasped her hands on the tabletop. "What are you doing these days with your Lit degree? Working on the next so-called great American novel?"

I snorted. "Not quite. I'm writing for a local business blog. It's mostly interviews with small business owners written at a fifth-grade reading level and chock full of keywords for SEO. So, you know, super high-quality creative output. Plus, some freelance stuff here and there. As for writing for myself, does making up stories in my head while bored out of mind at work count?"

I expected Rhiannon's trademark caustic wit in her response, but instead she looked curious. "What kind of stories?"

"Well," I glanced around the mostly empty sports bar we were sitting in for an interesting-looking person to craft a narrative about. No one fit the bill. However, there was an intriguing midday news report on the tv above us. A story I'd already been following. "Hold on, let's watch this for a moment and I'll give you an example."

A blonde, perfectly coiffed American reporter standing in the London rain recounted the following: *"The search continues for missing frontman Eddy Fox of the British band Ruby Haze. Fox was last seen leaving a pub in Windermere, which is in England's famed Lake District, around six o-clock the evening of September twenty-second. CCTV footage obtained from the day in question shows Fox getting into a cab that police haven't been able to identify. He has not been seen, nor heard from, since. Fox's bandmates reported him missing the following morning when he failed to show up for their rehearsal for that evening's show in Liverpool. That was four days ago, and investigators have few leads about what could have happened to him. A candlelight vigil is planned for this evening..."* The report cut to an interview with a teary fan clutching a candle and a giant homemade sign with Eddy Fox's face on it, begging for prayers for his safe return.

I pointed to the TV. "Okay, this is where the story begins. What are your best guesses as to what happened to that guy?"

Rhiannon took a sip of her iced tea, keeping her eyes fixated on the TV as they replayed the CCTV footage of Fox getting into the cab. It showed him stumbling off the first step of the pub's stairs but regaining his footing and lowering himself into the cab without further incident. The angle of the camera affixed to a building caddy-corner from the pub meant a low stone wall in front of the pub obscured the cab's front plates. When it drove off, the cab turned a corner, disappearing behind more stonework without ever revealing unique identifying features. At no point is the driver's face visible.

"Hold on," Rhiannon replied, still engrossed in the news report.

The desk anchor conversing with the on-location reporter closed the segment on Fox with a description of his appearance: *"Eddy Fox was last seen wearing black jeans, a Joy Division T-shirt, denim jacket, and several items of silver jewelry. Notable physical features include shoulder-length brown hair and a fox tattoo from his forearm to his upper right bicep. Scotland Yard is encouraging anyone with information on his whereabouts to call this number…"* The segment wrapped up by showing a photograph of Fox on stage at one of his most recent shows.

In the photo, he's swinging the microphone around by its cord and his eyes are rimmed with black liner, giving him a ferocious, animalistic appearance. He's shirtless, the stage lights illuminating the sweat across his muscular chest. And the noted tattoo is a bright red-orange fox curled from the fox's head at his shoulder, all around his right arm to the tail of the fox flicking his wrist.

Out of the corner of my eye I saw Rhiannon lick her lips before taking another sip of iced tea. She appeared completely enraptured by this report. For a moment I deeply regretted asking her to turn her attention to something that wasn't me—specifically, towards Britain's apparent rock-and-roll sex god. But when the report shifted to a food-borne illness outbreak, Rhiannon's spell seemed to be broken.

She glanced away from the television, leaned back in her seat, and tapped her fingertips on the table. "The simplest explanation is often the most likely. In this case, I'm guessing he was fairly drunk. Maybe he got out of the car somewhere near a lake, fell in, and drowned. The cold temps would cause his body to sink into the water. Perhaps there was even a current that dragged him from the shore, making it that much harder to find him." Rhiannon paused, took another sip of her iced tea, then clasped her hands again. "Why? What are your theories?"

The server came by with our food, sliding two plates laden with burgers oozing cheese onto the table. She dropped a basket of fries between us, slid a ramekin of limp-looking coleslaw next to it, retrieved a wad of napkins from her apron, tossed them on the table, then breezed off without a word.

I dragged a fry through ketchup and popped it into my mouth. It was so hot I almost spit it back out again, but Rhiannon was watching me with a sly smile. I would not give her the satisfaction of seeing me admit my hasty mistake.

Instead, my eyes watered and I had to inhale through my mouth to keep from sustaining a serious hot fry injury. "Jesus," I coughed out.

"Those fries a little hot?" Rhiannon's wide grin was pure schadenfreude. She took a giant bite of her burger and chewed slowly without breaking eye contact with me. I caved and chugged roughly half my ice water.

Once I regained my composure, I considered how to present my admittedly outlandish theory about what happened to Eddy Fox. "Well, while it's true the simplest explanation is often the most likely, it's not always what happened. I've been following this story in the news. They've dragged the shorelines of every lake in a thirty-mile radius of the pub. There was no evidence of him ever having been there. Not a single piece of jewelry, scrap of fabric, or so much as a footprint. Despite the Lake District being a popular tourist destination, and despite Fox's fame, no one has seen a hint of him since he disappeared." I rubbed my hands together and gingerly took another fry from the basket (and made sure it was cool enough to eat this time).

"It sounds like you have a theory you're dying to share." Rhiannon arched one eyebrow, letting her skepticism be known.

"I do. Promise to keep an open mind?"

"I promise to listen to your theory and apply sound scientific reasoning to determine its validity. How's that?"

"Good enough."

"Okay, lay it on me." Rhiannon paused eating and made a show of giving me her full attention.

"Don't you need to sample this incredibly healthy-looking coleslaw first? It's an important part of a well-balanced meal."

"Stop stalling."

"Right. So, you know how every so often people just vanish into thin air? Watch any number of episodes of *Unsolved Mysteries* and you can find several examples of a person who went missing without a trace. Years later these disappearances remain unsolved with little evidence to pursue. How can that be? How can someone just vanish without a trace? Now consider how physicists are learning every day that time is not flat or linear, but in fact rippled and possibly not happening in chronological order. Gravity pulls things this way and that, affecting how time progresses in different parts of the universe. For example, we know that time slows down the closer you get to a black hole." I paused to get a read on Rhiannon's thoughts. Her eyebrows were furrowed and she was biting her lip again. I hoped this meant she was still considering the possibilities.

I continued laying out my theory as if she was fully on board. "Given that, here's my theory: what if when people vanish without a trace, it's because they somehow stumbled into like, a rip in time, or something along those lines? Like, what if we can't find them anywhere because they no longer exist in our plane of time? I could go so far as to say a wormhole or something like that, but here on Earth."

Rhiannon picked up her burger and started eating again. I didn't know her well enough to know if this was simple hunger or an act of dismissal.

"Listen, I know it sounds absurd. But we've learned stranger things about the world around us. Is it really so crazy to think there could be rips in the fabric of time around us, and people occasionally fall through them? Perhaps it even explains how throughout history, we find people we consider to be 'ahead of their time' or people who just seem to know more or understand more about the world around them."

I paused my theory-sharing to eat my own lunch, suddenly ravenous from the unexpected series of events that led me to explain to my crush that I thought a missing British rock star time-traveled.

"You know, this sounds an awful lot like the plot of *Outlander*." Rhiannon grabbed a fry and chewed it slowly.

"I think you mean *Highlander*."

Rhiannon glared at me. "I most certainly do not. What kind of Lit major hasn't heard of *Outlander*?"

I sighed. "The kind who had to re-read *The Scarlet Letter* repeatedly. Why? What's *Outlander* about?"

"This exact theory. Claire Beauchamp is in Scotland post-World War II and accidentally travels through time to the mid-eighteenth century." Rhiannon took another fry and jabbed it in my direction. "You should read it. I think it's probably something you'd be into."

"Are you into it?"

"Of course. I love history and a good time-travel story. Though that doesn't mean I think your theory holds any weight. Only that I appreciate its creativity." She shrugged and popped the fry into her mouth. After she swallowed she asked, "Do you get the storytelling thing from Dr. Rosen?"

"If so, it's probably the only thing I got from my dad. I always felt I was a lot more like my mom."

"Really? Because you look just like your dad. And you both tell stories with the same enthusiasm and energy. Like, you both know how to perform it so people pay attention."

I furrowed my brow. "Wait, how do you know that? I don't think I've ever told you a story. Just deranged time-travel theories. We've literally spent more time together this afternoon than the previous four years combined."

Rhiannon averted her eyes and laughed uncomfortably. I realized she'd possibly been paying as much attention to me from afar as I had been paying attention to her.

"I mean, you're right," I added softly. "I just didn't think you knew that about me. Honestly, I barely know that about myself. It just kind of happens."

"Well, I ... guess maybe I assumed ... given your dad ..." she stammered, blushing, obviously not being fully transparent.

If I'd had any doubts before whether the feelings were mutual, realizing she'd been paying as much attention to me as I had been to her dispelled all of them.

"I'm glad you know that about me," I offered. I didn't want her to feel embarrassed. She was like a feral cat who was just starting to warm up to me—I didn't want to scare her off.

We ate in silence for a couple minutes before Rhiannon popped the last bite of her burger into her mouth, wiped her fingers on a shredded paper napkin, and said, "Speaking of parents, you should know my perfectionism is kind of like, balance in my life. My mom is chaotic and kind of unhinged, so keeping my life organized makes me feel like I have some control over things." She grabbed a fresh napkin to fidget with. "I didn't realize how obvious it was until now. So, feel free to continue psychoanalyzing me," she winced, clearly uncomfortable.

"No, not psychoanalysis." I shook my head. "Character study. Very different. And I'd rather get to know the real you instead of a character I invented in my head."

"I'm not all that interesting—"

"False. I think you're the most interesting person I've never been able to talk to."

We stared at each other. She held my gaze unflinchingly, yet without challenge or shyness. Eventually she smiled, an open lit up grin.

"What?" I asked, though I already knew I was smiling back. Her happiness was contagious.

"You were right"

"About?"

"You'll see."

45

EARLY MARCH 1421

RHIANNON

Multiple realizations slammed into me all at once, least of all that George was right about one of the greatest unsolved mysteries of our time.

"Eddy Fox has been missing for a decade and we found him. What does this mean? How is this possible? Did he come through the cottage? Did he try to get home?" I started pacing in a little circle in front of George, rubbing my temples, working out this new development. "Does he know we're also from the 21st century? If so, why wouldn't he say something? Should we tell him?" I switched to rubbing my palms with my thumbs, feeling panic once again rearing its unhelpful head. "What do we do with this information? Do you think your dad knew about him? Does he know that there's a Henry and Gwendolyn de Ros in the 21st century?"

"Rhi," George grasped me by my upper arms and pulled me closer to him. "There's nothing we can do about it tonight. So let's take a breath, get some sleep, and we can work it out in the morning."

But I couldn't calm down. I was spinning out. Any illusion I had had about regaining control of this situation was squashed by Eddy Fox crooning "Eternal Flame" to us.

"George, what if we're stuck here too?" My voice had an unusually high pitch, like I was lacking oxygen to my brain. "Eddy Fox has been here a decade. A decade! Do you know what that means? What if there's no way back? We need to go ask him!"

I loathe not knowing things. I hate feeling out of control and like I have no idea what's coming next. Information is power and stability and comfort. The worst part of our time travel hell wasn't the chamber pots or sporadic baths—it was that every answer only led to more questions. We were backsliding with every new revelation. Trying to get a handle on this situation was like trying to nail Jell-O to a wall.

"Rhi," George sighed, rubbing the bridge of his nose.

"We need to go talk to Edward right now!" I insisted.

"Are you serious? You want us to drag a grieving widower out of bed to see if he's a missing time traveling rockstar?"

"Yes! The stakes are incredibly high. For all of us! What if this means we're trapped here forever? How are you so calm right now!" The thought of spending the rest of my life in this century choked the ability to reason right out of my head.

George nodded and held out a hand for me. "I understand. But we can save that for tomorrow. Tonight, let's dance."

"What?"

He tossed his cane onto the ground and dipped into a low bow. "Let's dance."

"Are you insane? Are you not listening to me?" I glanced at the indent his cane made in the snow. "Aren't you in pain?"

He didn't respond. Instead, he swooped me up into a waltzing position and began singing "Eternal Flame," as he pulled me into the rhythm of the dance. I followed his moves on instinct, letting him whoosh us around the courtyard, my skirts dragging a looping pattern into the powdery snow.

"Do you not need a cane anymore?"

"Nope. I just like it because it looks dapper." He grinned at me, the moonlight illuminating his white teeth.

"And you chose now to Willy Wonka me?" I complained as he danced us around, keeping both the beat of our moves and the melody of the song.

That's right, George can sing. He's also a decent dancer; years of playing soccer made him light on his feet. He's one of those aggravating people who's great at just about everything he tries but chooses to be bad at things just because he can.

"Can you think of a better time for this dramatic reveal?" he asked while spinning me around.

"I don't know," I mumbled, refusing to admit that whatever this was, it was working. My panic melted away and I smiled against my will. We glided around the courtyard, cloaks flapping in the breeze, a billion twinkling stars and one luminous full moon shining down on us.

With his wavy blonde hair brushing his shoulders, decked out in blue velvet and gold jewelry, and the moonlight limning his features, George looked like a prince right out of a fairytale. He held me close, spinning me around every time he sang the line, "Am I only dreaming?" My heart started pounding for an entirely new reason.

When George could sing no longer, when our dance wound down and I fell into his arms completely out of breath, when he hugged me tightly and kissed the top of my head, I knew I was done.

My panicking thoughts dissipated; new thoughts consumed me.

I tilted my face up towards his and he brushed his thumb along my jawline before cupping my cheek. George rested his forehead against mine. He smelled like lemon and fire smoke, with a hint of wine from dinner, combined with his unique special George-scent that I adored. I wrapped my hands around his neck and pulled him down, brushing my lips across his.

He returned the kiss. Gentle at first, then hungry with desperation to make up for all the time we'd lost not kissing each other.

It was not enough. I needed him. All of him. I grabbed George by the edges of his cloak and started pulling him in the direction of our chambers. We stumbled up the stairs, groping each other, feeling our way to our door with more memory than attention.

George shoved open the door and pulled me inside before slamming it shut behind us. We started tearing at each other's clothes, fumbling with the knotted laces and the layers upon layers necessary to keep us warm. As I yanked his undershirt off, exposing his bare chest, George grasped me by the wrists. He had an odd expression on his face—pain, combined with something else.

"Is your leg hurting?" I blurted out. The dancing may have been too much.

"No. it's something else." He paused. "Rhi, what does this mean?"

He dropped my wrists and took one step backward, regret already registering on his face.

I was dumbfounded. Something shifted so suddenly, I didn't know what he was thinking.

"What do you mean what does this mean? We're adults. I think this means sex. Right? Did I misinterpret that?"

"No, not at all. What I meant is," George shoved his hair out of his eyes with one hand. "God, I'm probably going to regret this later. What I meant is that I can't do this if it's just physical. We haven't talked about our relationship at all. Our marriage. And what we will be *when* we make it home."

I stood there in my linen undergarments, wool dress pooled around my ankles, facing my half-naked estranged husband whose body I desperately wanted on top of mine.

But I didn't have answers to his questions. We'd gone from the Eddy Fox revelation to dancing in the courtyard to the bedroom with hardly any time to process. "I honestly don't know what this means. I just really want to get in bed with you. Why can't that be enough?"

"Because it's you. That's why."

"Well, I'm not sure what to say to that. Why can't it be just sex? Why can't we take a break from the endless drudgery of this life to feel good for a change?"

"Because it's never been *just sex* between us. That's why."

"Well, I'm not ready to be anything else with you. We're here, we're as married as we need to be to survive, and for now, that's all. Nothing else has changed." Even as the words left my mouth, they felt wrong. Everything had changed.

George winced. He turned towards the fire and closed his eyes, hands on his hips, clearly weighing something.

I fidgeted with the end of my braid, feeling exposed and annoyed.

"I'm sorry. But I can't do this." George picked his shirt up off the floor and pulled it back over his head. "I need some air," he explained before wrapping his cloak around his shoulders and brushing past me to the door. He paused in the doorway. "I know I fucked up. I know I needed to be there for you after … well, after the last time. But it was impossible to be there for someone who was always pushing me away. I could barely get you to stay still or focus on me as a person instead of just a warm body in your house. I can't do that anymore." He paused, eyes red-rimmed. "I can't just be a warm body you use when you need someone."

"A warm body?" I scoffed. "Were you even that? You say I pushed you away, but it's impossible to push someone away who's already running."

"I wasn't always running. I was grieving too. But you only ever cared about whether I was unloading the dishwasher or making money. Just a warm body doing chores and paying bills. I couldn't deal with that."

I rubbed my hands down my face. "We couldn't stop doing those things because we were sad. I was keeping everything together and I needed help!"

George huffed a breath. "As if it was just sadness." He tapped his fingers on the door frame. "For the record, right now, this isn't running. It's putting some space between us so we don't say things we will regret. But I will come back soon." He slipped out the door before I could respond, letting it fall closed behind him.

I wanted to scream. *Humans haven't really changed at all … love, hate, joy, fear … they all remain constant through time.* The words from Albert's letter echoed in my head.

We could not escape who we were and what we had gone through—even six hundred years in the past.

George came back much later and climbed into bed beside me. I hadn't slept a wink. I was cold. And devastated. But I did not huddle against him for warmth. He'd made it clear how he felt about that.

46

MARCH 1421

GEORGE

Henry rapped his fingers on the edge of the table, a rhythmic motion where each finger hit right as the other lifted, creating a steady beat. From the direction of his valet, I'd found him in his chambers, by himself, simply staring out the window. After I'd sat down and made a little bit of small talk about melting snow and what not, I got to the heart of the matter: moving into the cottage.

"I was wondering when you'd ask," Henry sighed.

That was the last reply I was expecting. "You were?"

He stopped tapping on the table and regarded me with a frank stare. "Tell me, how is your father?"

"He's …" I didn't know what to say. If I should lie or not. I ultimately decided to limit the number of stories we had to tell for our survival. "He passed away last year." I exhaled.

In saying it aloud, I recognized I was still processing the loss of my dad, on top of everything else. I held my breath and blinked rapidly, willing the tears to stay contained so I could focus on what I came here for.

Henry clutched his chest and closed his eyes. After several gasping breaths he replied, "I wondered. But I didn't want to believe it." He stared at me. "Yet, here you are. In the flesh."

I didn't know what that meant, much less how to respond to it.

"Lady Gwendolyn will be heartbroken, you understand. And to learn so soon after … so soon after losing our precious Marguerite." Henry grimaced. I noticed the red lining his eyes and the weariness that had settled into his posture. "I will tell her when the time is right. Let it not concern you."

I nodded. "I'm sorry. For your loss, that is." It seemed inadequate, but it was all I could say.

Henry waved me off. "It is your loss, too. It is no small thing for a son to lose his father." He began rapping on the table again. "Now then, the cottage. It is a very special place. Though I'm sure you already know that." He gave me a knowing look. "You and Lady Rhiannon are welcome to take up residence there. I will have Clifford get it prepared as it hasn't had residents for quite some time. Though I must let you know, very little can be done until late spring when the thaw sets in."

Rhiannon didn't know I was asking Henry about moving into the cottage. Things had been tense between us since the night we danced in the courtyard.

In her sleep she'd huddle against me for warmth, but if she woke still in my arms, she'd quickly scoot back to the other side of the bed. And she kept her distance the rest of the time.

She'd resumed rushing around the castle, taking on jobs and responsibilities as if she was once again trying to replace the vacancy left by Marguerite. That was what Rhiannon knew best: working to make herself useful to fend off both the intrusive thoughts of her own sorrow, combined with a deep desire to be needed.

The few times I tried to stop her, to talk to her, she'd brush me off before running off to do some other supposedly urgent task. In the evenings, back in our chambers, we exchanged brief pleasantries and bits of castle gossip. But that was all she'd sit still for.

We did not discuss what happened between us—nor did we discuss what we should do about Eddy Fox/Lord Edward. She'd gone surprisingly quiet about that development. Nor did we discuss the cottage, for that matter.

However, my mind was made up; I had to get out of this castle. I had to get away from the cloud of grief and loss hanging over everything. There was no privacy here—conversations bounced off the stone and plaster walls, echoing everyone's business throughout. People constantly barged into our rooms without knocking, for a multitude of reasons, at all hours of day and night. And there was no freedom—my daily habits were controlled by Henry and Clifford, right down to what I wore. I'd rather struggle in a cottage that was (mostly) mine than wither away in a castle where I was at the mercy of everyone else's actions.

I was tired of taking what seemed like the easy way out, only to find the consequences were disastrous.

The biggest challenge would be getting Rhiannon on board. Because no matter what was happening between us, I swore to never abandon her again. I would not leave her in this castle to waste away in despair.

But when she found out I'd made another life-changing decision without her input, I knew it wouldn't be good.

"That is not a problem as we are in no hurry," I explained to Henry. It would give me more time to figure out how to tell Rhi. "I'm simply aware that the time will soon come for us to be on our own." I rose from my seat. "We're sincerely grateful for your hospitality. Perhaps one day you can share with me some stories of you and my father. I am deeply curious to learn more about him."

Henry smiled sadly. "Likewise, my boy. Likewise."

47

RHIANNON

I had to know. Did Eddy Fox try to make it home and failed? Or had he stayed by choice, given that he'd found love?

I dragged my finger along a bookshelf in Edward's library. Every so often I paused, pulled a book from the shelf, carefully flipped through its delicate vellum pages, and returned it to its spot. I'd spent enough time there—both researching the cottage and trying to find a way to pass the time—that I knew each book, tome, and scroll by feel alone. Despite my show of looking for something new to read, I'd already read just about everything in the library that appealed to me (or that was written in some semblance of a language I could understand). After all, there are only so many religious books, wildly inaccurate medical texts, and epic poems you can read before the hand-scribed old English letters all blur together.

But I needed a safe way to approach Edward with our revelation. Though, surely he knew we were also from the 21st century; he'd seen George's tattoos, after all.

Why he hadn't brought it up himself was the real mystery. It made me nervous.

So, I settled on a strategy where I wouldn't approach Edward directly. Instead, I would take a page from George's book by telling him a story—the story of Eddy Fox's disappearance, wrapped up in the guise of a minstrel's tale—to see if it triggered any memories.

While I was working up the courage to speak, Edward had his back to me, examining a new map he'd found at a shop in London. It was unfurled on the table, the curled edges held down with two marble ink wells being used as paperweights. I paused my show of examining the bookshelf to watch Edward while he was engrossed in something else. He rolled the left sleeve of his linen shirt up to his elbow, moved to roll up his right sleeve, stiffened, then left it as is. Even distracted by the map, he was conscientious to leave his arm covered. He jotted a few notes on the map, while holding his sleeve tight to his forearm to keep it from dragging through the wet ink.

Eddy Fox had a massive, wildly conspicuous tattoo up his right arm, with sharp lines and vivid colors—the kind no artist could reproduce in the 15th century. Eddy Fox had the exact same high cheekbones, full lips, and dark hair as Edward. And Fox disappeared on the autumn equinox back in 2010, not far from the cottage ... and has not been seen since.

Lord Edward had to be Eddy Fox. I had no doubts about it. Only about his reaction to being confronted about it.

I'd hoped Edward would make my job easier and offer to help me find a book to get the conversation going. I had not counted on his being completely engrossed with the map.

When it was clear my strategy wasn't working, I tried a different tactic. "My lord," I moved slowly across the room until I stood next to Edward and gently touched his left arm above the fold of his sleeve. "Please forgive my interruption. But I am in search of information on something that has been on my mind."

Edward glanced up from his map, no trace of irritation in his expression from having been interrupted. Only curiosity. "What is it, pray tell?"

"I was at the market the other day and a minstrel in the square told a beautiful story that has haunted me. I think it might make a lovely embroidery. But I cannot recall the exact plot, only vague details. If I tell you what I remember, I wonder if you could tell me if you've heard of it, or perhaps know its origins?"

I swallowed, steadying myself. "Since you seem to have such knowledge of minstrel's songs, and all."

Edward slid both inkwells off to the side of his table, letting the map spring back into a loose roll. "I cannot say that I am an expert in the lore of traveling minstrels, but I will do my best." He perched on the edge of the table, arms crossed over his chest. "Please, what do you recall of this story?"

"Well," I moved slowly a foot or so around the table, away from Edward so I could gauge his expression accurately. "It was the tale of a minstrel, the most successful and handsome of minstrels. It is said that his songs were so alluring, so beautiful, they reduced even hardened kings to tears. Because of this, ladies far and wide offered him their hands. Though he had but one true love—a Spanish maiden." I paused and eyed Edward, looking for any kind of reaction.

He had none. Contrarily, he remained quite still, eyes on me, unmoving, blinking slowly, giving me his undivided attention.

I took a deep breath. "Though he loved the maiden more than anything, he told her he could not take her hand in marriage until he had traveled far and wide, playing music for the kings and queens of many lands. Despite his ambitions, he never forgot about his love, and he visited her as often as he could. When the maiden became with child, the minstrel vowed to finally stay by her side and marry her. However, not long after their son was born, the minstrel vanished into thin air!" I made a poof sign with my fingers, emphasizing the minstrel having simply disappeared. "All over the kingdom people searched high and low for him, desperate to hear the minstrel sing his heavenly songs again."

I paused for a moment, hoping for some tell from Edward that he understood this story was his, vague as it was. While he remained engaged with my words, Edward showed no trace of emotion or understanding that would reveal his thoughts.

I continued. "But, neither hide nor hair was ever seen of him again!" I held my hands out, as if to curtsy after a stage performance.

Edward gave me a small smile but did not say anything.

"So, is this a story you are familiar with?"

He remained still for another minute, then leaned on table, hands pressed against the polished marble, hair falling in a curtain over the left side of his face, obscuring his expression from me. "I am afraid I am not familiar with this story. Perhaps Lady Gwendolyn has the answers you seek."

I hesitated. I didn't have a follow-up plan. So, I gambled. "Why do you not roll up your right sleeve? Wouldn't that be easier than holding it away from the ink?"

Edward gave me a sharp look and tucked his hair behind his ear, giving me full view of his face. His eyes were red, and to my shock, he was blinking back tears. Though I'd hoped for some sort of reaction, it was still a surprise he responded so quickly—especially given his deflection. Of course, he was still in the throes of grief. "You know this story quite a bit better than you originally established. Tell me, do you recall what became of the maiden and their son?" He asked hoarsely.

"Well ... the maiden married another minstrel, one who had performed with her lost love. But he chose to stay close to home and raise the minstrel's son as his own." I pulled a newly embroidered handkerchief out of my sleeve and began twisting it into a linen rope, unsure what to do with my hands, resisting the temptation to touch Edward as a way of offering him comfort. "It is a sad story, is it not?"

Edward nodded solemnly. "Did anyone ever find the missing minstrel?" He grabbed the map and it unfurled it again, moving the ink wells back into place. Despite his forced nonchalance, I could see he'd gone pale and his hands shook.

"No. It has remained a great mystery for the ages. The famous minstrel, who legend has it was marked with the sigil of a fox on his right arm, simply disappeared, never to be seen or heard from again."

Edward didn't reply. When I mentioned the fox, I saw him visibly convulse for a second, before regaining his composure by smoothing his shirt with shaky hands.

We stood in silence, time stretching between us, neither attempting to speak or move from our places at the table. When the fraught energy became unbearable, I began to stammer out an apology before Edward raised one hand to silence me.

"Can we speak plainly, you and I?"

I tilted my head, raised an eyebrow. "Of course. Say what is on your mind."

He tapped the map on the table. "I know quite a bit about how this map is going to change over the years. Perhaps," he tapped a finger under my chin and tilted my head up, leaning down so his face was inches from mine, "perhaps you do too?"

His dark eyes were hypnotic pools I could not seem to look away from. This close, his cinnamon and smoke scent enveloped me.

"My lord," I spoke softly while placing my hand gently on his forearm, pulling his hand away from my chin. My heart quivered beneath my ribs, a combination of being keenly aware of the proximity between us and feeling the urge to flee. "I think you know what happened to the minstrel, don't you?"

Edward rolled his shoulders back and moved closer, so we were standing almost chest to chest. I held my breath and tried to take a step backwards, but he caught me by my shoulders and held me in place.

"Why do you think I know what happened to the minstrel? Is this not a clever bit of fiction you heard in a marketplace?" There was no malice in his voice or in his grip. Though he held me firmly, I understood I could break free at any time.

With one trembling hand I reached across my chest to where Edward held me by the shoulder, touched the edge of the sleeve on his right arm, and pushed it up to reveal the base of his wrist and the tail tip of the tattoo. I paused, fingers still resting on the skin of where the fox tail curled around his bones.

"Go on," he whispered. "I know what you're looking for." He kept his grip firm, his gaze focused intensely on me.

I shoved the sleeve up as far as I could, just above the elbow, before the fabric became too taut to reveal anything else. A bright red-orange fox tail appeared, wrapped around his forearm.

"How did you explain such a thing to anyone? Surely Lady Marguerite had questions." I queried in a low voice. "But more importantly, how did you end up here?"

Edward dropped his hands from my shoulders and turned back to his map. He carefully unfurled his sleeve, hiding the tattoo once again. "What do you remember of your own journey to this place?"

"Enough to know that neither of us belong here."

He sighed and ran his hand through his hair. "I wondered when this moment would come. Let's drop the pretense, shall we? Tell me your story and I will tell you mine."

"You did?"

Edward shot me an exasperated look. A look that let me know we'd been as terrible at blending in with these people as we'd thought.

"Fair enough. George's father died. He left us the cottage in his will, in the year 2020—"

"Hold on. It was 2020 when you left?" Before I could respond, he shook his head and laughed wryly. "I'm such a fool. I naively thought that if, or when, I finally made it home, it would be like I never left. But now I think I understand that the years are still rolling forward, progressing without me. Aren't they?"

I winced. "In our time, you've been missing for a full decade."

Edward shoved both hands into his hair before huffing a breath and staring at me, pale as the parchment of his new map. "Fuck me. It appears I truly am the ill-fated minstrel of your tale. I was hoping it nothing more than a mere coincidence, one that dredged up long-dormant painful memories." He stared at me imploringly. "Go on. How did two Americans—American, yes?" I nodded. "I thought so. I recognized the accent. Now, how did you two end up here?"

I recounted the will, our trip, and tumbling disoriented and naked into the cottage.

Edward didn't look especially surprised by what I was telling him. Instead, there was a wildness to his expression, a fierceness tinged with desperation.

For the first time, I was a little afraid of him. "Okay, that's how we got here. Now, your turn."

He covered his mouth with the palm of his hand and blinked rapidly. "I was in Windermere, in a small pub in view of the lake. As I was getting another pint at the bar, I noticed a pretty girl sitting right next to me, not talking to anyone. I believe we exchanged a few words before I went to the loo. When I returned, my pint was waiting for me. I downed half of it in one drink. Moments later I began to feel lightheaded. I think the girl asked if I was okay. I just knew I had to get out of that pub."

I was shocked. As Edward told me his story, his voice—no, his entire demeanor—transformed. His accent went from the deliberate and authoritative cadence I was used to, into what sounded to my untrained ear like the accent of someone from London in my time. His stiff posture relaxed into a loose swagger and he gesticulated wildly, acting out his misfortune. I could see it then, the man George remembered, the lithe and animated performer.

Edward exhaled and shook his head. "But no matter how many times I go over it in my mind, I cannot convince myself I was drunk. I hadn't taken anything, either. That was only my second drink—certainly not enough to be pissed. Either way, feeling poorly, I stepped outside to get fresh air. That's the last thing I remember. When I woke up, I was in that bloody cottage, memory blank, clothes missing." He stroked his chin. "Lady Gwendolyn found me, much like I found you, stumbling down the road, clutching a blanket. She was unsurprised by my presence when I told her I woke up in the cottage. In fact, she took it upon herself to care for me. And this is where I have been ever since, studying every map I can find for even a trace of how this happened and any clues to set it right again. This entire library," he gestured around the room, "is full of any documents I could get my hands on that might have an answer. And in all this time, I've learned less than I have in the few minutes we've been talking."

"When you found us, did you know right away that we weren't from this time?"

"Absolutely. That's why I helped you. I knew it had happened to you. I also knew that meant the cottage still worked and there was still a possibility of getting back."

"Why didn't you say anything?"

"George looks exactly like the baron. I didn't think you were here by accident. The way he treated you both confirmed my suspicions, so I thought it best I stay out of it."

"Holy shit," I exhaled.

"Holy fucking shit, indeed," Edward laughed wryly. "Now, tell me Lady Rhiannon, what is the world like in the year of our Lord, 2020." Before I could respond, he exclaimed, "No, wait, let's see if I have had an impact on your present. Where should we start? Perhaps we compare major historical events to see if they happened the same as I recall versus how you recall?" Edward seemed more excited about this line of thinking than any map or book we'd pored over before.

"Let's start with something that would have happened before you left. Like, do you remember World Wars?"

"Yes, absolutely!" Edward exclaimed. He began ticking off an encyclopedia entry highlight reel about World War II on his fingers. "Let's see, in my version there is Churchill, Roosevelt, Nazi air raids, atomic bombs … ringing any bells?"

"Yes, yes, that's all the same." I responded. "Everything you're saying is the same as what happened in my time. I feel like if anything had changed in this century it would have had a domino effect on the rest."

"Hmmm. How about British history a bit closer to now. What do you know about the War of the Roses? The Tudors? Queen Elizabeth?"

The part of my brain that lights up with getting to recite random trivia turned on. I rubbed my hands together. "The Tudors came to power because of the war between the Lancasters and Yorks, Henry the eighth had six tragic marriages, and Queen Elizabeth the first presided over England's Golden Age. The second Elizabeth is still alive and well in the year 2020. Does that line up with what you remember?"

Edward smirked. "Impressive for an American girl. And it does line up with what I remember. Frustratingly so. To think I'd spent so much time worrying I'd disrupt the future by being here. Only to find it's all the same. Okay, enough historical trivia. Pop culture? The Beatles? Madonna? Braveheart?"

"The same."

We went through a catalogue of history, art, literature, pop culture, politics, food, and so on. Nothing had changed with Edward's presence in the 15th century.

"All the same," I nodded. "Including Ruby Haze."

"Is that so?" Edward dragged one of the chairs out from under the table and plopped down, allowing his arms to fall to his sides. The longer this conversation endured, the more deflated he became. "It seems the world is little impacted by my presence in this time, and little affected by my absence in my own time."

I winced. "It seems you've had a great impact on the people of Kendal in this time. Perhaps there are smaller items that are different? We could explore those."

He shook his head. "No, I have long suspected there is something off about this time, this place. The de Ros's do not age and no one clearly recalls when Henry became the baron, or even how old he is. I've been here ten years and it's almost like being in a dream. I leave the castle often because when I get far enough away, it's like waking up again. When I am far from this place, people seem to move differently, speak differently. More urgently, as if they're aware they're short on time while everyone in Kendal Castle is blissfully unaware of time passing ... because it's not. Not in a meaningful way, that is." Edward slumped down in his chair. He ran both of his hands through his hair again, giving it an unusually unkempt appearance. Without his velvet hats and fitted doublets, wearing a linen shirt open low enough to expose the top of his chest, he looked like he'd just rolled out of bed.

I shoved that thought out of mind as quickly as it dropped in—Edward in bed.

I contemplated my choices. And made a decision without George's input I hoped I wouldn't regret. I cleared my throat. "There is one possible solution. George and I were given clues to how the cottage works. A note and a key. Would you like to see them? Perhaps working together, we can all make it home."

Edward rose from his seat, a new gleam in his eye. "My lady, I would like nothing more."

48

GEORGE

"**Y**ou did what? Fuck, that's *definitely* something you should have talked to me about first, as we don't know if we can trust him! The key, the letter, those are valuable tools and you don't know what a desperate man is capable of." I paced around the room, jabbing my cane into the floor, furious with Rhiannon for giving someone I don't trust incredibly sensitive information.

After dinner, as we ascended the stairs to our chambers, she nervously told me she needed to tell me something. The story of how she confirmed Edward was, indeed, the missing Eddy Fox tumbled out of her mouth quickly enough I knew she felt guilty. As she should.

"I'm sorry! But I felt bad for him. Edward just lost his wife, he's been stuck here a decade, and what if sharing info with him helps us get back? What if we can work together?"

"Work together to do what, exactly? Wait for the autumn equinox? What exactly were you hoping to accomplish?" I shook my head. "Something is off. If he knew right away where we came from, why not say something? He knew you were researching the cottage in the library, knew *why* you were doing so, and still said nothing? Why?"

"He said it's because you look like the baron and he was hesitant to get involved."

I clenched my jaw, debating whether that was a trustworthy reason to stay silent. Plus, on my end, I still hadn't told her I'd been making plans to move us into the cottage. The ground I stood on was nothing but thin ice.

Still. I ran my hand along my freshly shaved jaw and tapped my cane on the floor. "Regardless, did you forget the part of the letter that stated 'everyone must be lined up perfectly' as well? As in, no one missing and no one added. You shared that info with Edward and now he knows as well. What, exactly, do you think a desperate man might do with that information? Not to mention he now also knows a key is needed. And that we have it." I patted my chest where I wore the key, strung on the same leather strap as my Norman coin, reassuring myself it was still there.

It wasn't just that Rhiannon divulged critical info. It's that I suspected she was attracted to him and it clouded her judgement. I tried to tell myself I wasn't jealous; I knew Rhiannon was loyal and honest. But our marriage was in shambles and we'd made each other no promises except to help each other survive.

And I was genuinely worried about what Edward would do with this information. Where Rhiannon saw someone kind and helpful, I saw a shrewd and calculating man who now had nothing to lose and everything to gain by taking the two things that could get him back to his time. Leaving us behind in the process.

Rhiannon sat on the edge of the bed, watching me carefully. "He's been nothing but helpful, George. You could even say he saved our lives. More than once. Why not help him in return?"

"Because this isn't just about Edward. It's about the fact that we agreed to work together. You're constantly mad at me for not helping, not stepping up. But what about all the times you just barrel ahead without me? There have been so, so many times where I wanted to help, but you wouldn't let me! We're supposed to be a team, but you just handed the playbook to our opponent without even talking to me first. We're in a precarious, life-threatening situation and we need to proceed carefully."

Yes, I was aware of my hypocrisy. Still.

My leg started to throb; I limped to the bed and sat down next to Rhiannon.

"I'm sorry," she said quietly. "I know sometimes I can get ahead of myself. But I stand by my decision to tell him everything. The more information we have, the better our chances of success."

Frustration burned in my chest. "Did you even hear what I was saying? We had an agreement and you broke it. When I break an agreement, you unleash hell! But when you mess up, it's somehow justified?"

Rhiannon pulled a handkerchief out of her sleeve and nervously twisted the fabric into a coil. Competing thoughts flickered across her face as she weighed the validity of my point. "Okay, that's fair," she conceded. "I did break our agreement."

She looked up at me. I was briefly distracted by her big eyes, her ability to silence the noise in my head with just the sound of her voice. I brushed my finger down the side of her face and across her lower lip. She closed her eyes, leaning into my touch.

"We need to do this together. Okay?"

Rhiannon nodded. "Okay."

"No more making major decisions without talking to me first."

She nodded again, letting me stroke her cheek. My heart burst open and my desire to be mad at her dissipated. And I knew I had to be honest. If we were going to move forward, we had to be forthright. "Okay ... on that note, I have something to tell you as well."

Rhi jerked her face away from my touch and narrowed her eyes. "What?"

I cleared my throat and shifted on the bed so I fully faced her. "When the snow melts, Henry is going to prepare the cottage for us to live in." I clamped my mouth shut. To defend myself would make it seem like I felt guilty. Even if I did. A little bit.

"When, exactly, did you have this conversation?" Rhi's voice was low and menacing. I had done what I'd just flipped out on her for doing: barreling ahead with big decisions without talking to her first. "I mean, aren't we a *team*, George?" Her words were laced with resentful venom. Rhi stood up and put her hands on her hips. "Were you making these big decisions without me while I was also making big decisions without you?"

I swallowed. "Yes. But this is different. You put us in danger, while I'm trying to protect us. I was right about Eddy Fox and I think I'm right about this too. And if I waited for you to get on board, it may be too late."

"*Protect us?* Give me a break! You think leaving a nice castle with money and servants to go live in a hovel with nothing is *protecting* us?"

Rhi hovered over me. As I was sitting, I had to look up to meet her gaze. I could have stood up. I've got a good eight inches on her. It was tempting, to try and assert dominance that way.

Instead, I patted the bed beside me. "Sit down. Let's talk this through. I don't have the energy to fight anymore."

Rhiannon hesitated before flopping down next to me, crossing her arms over her chest and refusing to make eye contact. "You can't keep blaming me for trying to figure this out. For trying to survive, for trying to get us home. Especially when you keep saying we're a team but don't act like it either. I don't know what else to do. I don't know how to fix this, but at least I'm trying. It just feels like you gave up." She loosened up and began picking at a nub on the blanket. "You give up and then get mad when I keep trying."

I took her hand in mine. I expected her to jerk it away, but she didn't. "I know. I think I feel like you're always barreling ahead without pausing to check if it's the right direction. So I dig my heels in as a protest. And sometimes I do give up because it seems better than doing the wrong thing."

"Is this one of those times?"

"No. I've read the note at least a hundred times. I knew my dad. He meant for us to be here a full year. He had his reasons ... though I haven't figured those out."

She exhaled slowly. "I'm barely making it living in a literal castle. The thought of moving and making our situation much harder terrifies me."

"I know. And I promise I will do whatever I can to make it easier. But you need to know the only reason I'm asking is because I'm losing my mind here. Everything feels wrong. There's no privacy. We have no say in what we wear, or eat, or how we spend our days. Gwendolyn bursts into tears whenever she sees me, which is getting old. And Edward ... well, you already know how I feel about him. I'm bored and lonely and the stairs are a legit hazard. All I'm asking is that you consider it. Okay?"

Rhiannon nodded. "Honestly, I feel the same way about a lot of it—especially the part where I have no say in what I eat or wear. But my god, if you'd seen the way some of the peasants live," she shuddered. "You'd understand why I'm so hesitant to join their ranks. We will have to do everything on our own, from purifying water to cooking on an open flame to cleaning out our own chamber pots. Is that really better than hiking a few stairs?"

"I'm not going to lie, the chamber pot thing sounds awful." She cracked a smile at that. "But do you really want to spend the next six months moping around a cold, lonely castle? Do you really want to spend your time being pushed around by Agnes? Eating liver and blood sausage as a luxury? What if—hear me out now—what if it's better? What if we've been clinging to this old castle thinking this was a safe place, when really it'd be better to get out and see what our options are?"

Rhiannon squeezed my hand. "I'll think about it. But that's all I can agree to for now. Okay?"

"Okay. That's fair. The cottage won't be ready for us for a few weeks, anyway. We're not in a hurry."

49

RHIANNON

I had no desire to move into the dirty little cottage. While George had valid points, I knew that the intervening months of having to fend for ourselves would be brutal.

The sticking point I could not get over involved the garderobe—or lack thereof—in the cottage. It had an outhouse, roughly twelve feet from the cottage itself (or else the smell becomes an issue in the summer) and as of that point, it was completely covered in vines and debris. It would need to be cleaned and repaired.

I imagined myself, on my period, having to walk outside in the rain, in the middle of the night, to a separate little (literal) hell hole to take care of my business.

Every time I explained this to George, he would nod like he understood, then counter with, "In the middle of the night wouldn't you use the chamber pot anyway?" Which yes, I would, but that was only slightly better. He had lots of examples like this, of how it wouldn't be as bad as I imagined. For every legitimate discomfort I brought up, he countered it as if he were working through a list of my objections.

We were at an impasse. Briefly.

A few days after I promised George I would consider the move, I visited Edward in the library, Albert's letter in hand, cloak on shoulders, ready to trek down to the cottage to see about further clues that could help get us all home.

Edward's usual pristine and elegant appearance had deteriorated since Marguerite's death—and had unraveled even further after I confronted him about being from our time. He was leaning over the library table, greasy hair falling loosely over his shoulders, both sleeves of his wrinkled linen shirt rolled up, the neck ties undone, revealing his bare chest. He looked like a man on the edge.

"Rhiannon," he purred when I entered the room, his eyes glassy and red-rimmed. There was a solid chance he was drunk. Edward straightened up and let his hair fall over his eyes. "What brings you here today? More *research*." He coated the last word with enough innuendo that I took a step backwards.

I hesitated before asking, "You mentioned wanting to go back down to the cottage," I fumbled in my sleeve for where I'd stashed the letter, but reconsidered handing it over to him. "I came to see if you wanted ... company?"

As I spoke, Edward sidled up to me, invading my space and making me uneasy. A quick glance down revealed he was barefoot.

He placed both hands on my upper arms and leaned down so he could whisper in my ear. "I do want *company*." He sneered. "But no one will bother us here if you do not want to walk all the way down to the cottage." As he pulled away, Edward let his lips brush against my cheek before he pressed his forehead against mine, enveloping me in his wine-soaked breath.

I held very still and avoided making eye-contact.

In the 21st century, Eddy Fox was wealthy (and had been so since birth), attractive, famous, and charismatically intelligent. I knew he was used to getting what he wanted in every situation, was used to people bending to his will and complying with his wishes. In the 15th century, Lord Edward of Kendal was all those things and more—he was the heir apparent to a wealthy baron with a culture that supported his right to take what he wanted.

I gently pressed my hands against his chest and tried to step back. But Edward's grip on me was firm. "I think ..." I stammered, trying to gather the right words. "I think there has been a misunderstanding." I mustered. "I only want to get home. All of us."

Edward chuckled derisively. "Is that so?"

He did not release me, nor gave me any space to breathe. Edward's once alluring scent of cinnamon and cloves was laced with sour wine and sweat—a nauseating combination. I was light-headed and my heartbeat intensified with fear.

"Let go of me," I commanded in a falsely confident tone.

Edward moved his hands to my waist and pulled me against his body. "Is this not what you wanted, Lady Rhiannon?" he pinched my side and I grimaced. "Always flitting around me, pretending to be the lady of the castle, finding reasons to be by my side." He stroked one finger down the side of my cheek. "I'll admit, I have found your unique beauty to be quite alluring." He kissed my neck and I shuddered. "It took immense control not to take you when we were out collecting rents." He closed his eyes and bit his lip as if reliving this twisted fantasy.

I had to get out. I had to move before fear fully locked up my limbs and made me a sheep for the slaughter.

Don't panic.

Move! I silently commanded my body.

My only weapon was the element of surprise. I gave him one hard shove, enough to loosen his grip on me. "Stop!"

Edward stumbled back a step, briefly letting go of me.

Before I could move more than a foot, he grabbed my wrist and shoved me against the marble table. I gasped as my backside slammed against the cold stone.

Edward caged me in with his body, hands braced against the table on either side of me, his hips grinding against mine as I struggled against him. "Without me, you'd be *dead*," he hissed into my ear. "Now show a little gratitude."

Somewhere in my haze of fear a little candle of anger lit. Here I was, trying to help him, and he was turning it against me. I'd been running around this castle, working hard to contribute and help manage the chaos, and all I'd gotten in return was this disrespect. The candle blazed into a flame.

Fuck that.

As Edward fumbled around with my mercifully cumbersome skirts, I flashed to a self-defense and safety seminar my school hosted for the girls (we can unpack why a high school felt the need to host self-defense seminars for the girls—but not a corresponding please-don't-hurt-girls seminar for the boys—another time.) With his hand occupied under my skirts and no longer pinning me down, I was able to jab him sharply in the throat.

While Edward clutched his throat and gasped, I stomped on the instep of his bare foot with the wooden heel of my leather boot. He stumbled back, enraged, giving me enough space to run.

I burst into the corridor and didn't stop running until I was at our chambers. George sat by the fire, eyes closed, massaging his calf muscle, deep in thought.

"We have to get out of this place!" I choked out before bursting into tears.

PART II:

A COTTAGE REBUILT

50

LATE MARCH 1421

GEORGE

I knelt by the fireplace, stacking logs and sprinkling the pile with wood shavings, preparing to light our first official fire. While I tended to fire-building, Rhiannon organized our food on the recently-installed shelves: a loaf of bread, clay pot full of butter, wedges of cheese wrapped in cloth, venison jerky, a cured ham, several parsnips and turnips, and a bowl of pears and apples made up our first haul. If I could get the cast iron pan hot enough, I would attempt to make us sliced pear, ham, and cheddar grilled cheeses for dinner.

Moving into the cottage—after spending months of relative luxury as guests of the baron—was a risky move. We had to make our own fire (and keep it going nonstop), gather and prepare our own food (without refrigeration or electricity), empty our own chamber pots (as gross as you can imagine), and do our own laundry daily (either boiled in the cauldron or washed in the river, when weather permitted).

But being down here gave us more privacy and autonomy than we ever had in the castle.

When Rhiannon told me what happened with Edward, I did not confront him. Nor did I complain to Henry. As much as I wanted to beat Edward senseless with my cane, I knew doing so would only make our situation worse.

Instead, I immediately went to Clifford.

Henry told me that after the thaw would be the earliest the cottage could be prepared for us, but part of me felt like that was yet another stalling tactic to keep us close.

I had seen the way Clifford looked at Edward. The longing and admiration were barely concealed beneath his cold demeanor. I'd observed how Clifford blushed in Edward's presence, the way he adjusted his robes and tidied his hair when Edward walked into a room, and the way he subtly touched Edward's upper arm in agreement or to get his attention. Clifford did not lay hands on anyone else in the castle that way.

All I had to tell him was that I feared Edward coveted my wife (which, true) and we wished to move into the cottage as soon as possible to put some distance between us.

"Absolutely, my lord." Clifford quickly agreed. "I will have it ready without delay."

True to his word, Clifford spared no time or expense making the cottage both livable and comfortable for us. The thin grimy window was replaced with a glazed glass window that could open on a hinge, letting in necessary fresh air. The roof was re-thatched and the chipped stone floors repaired and thoroughly cleaned. Clifford had a new bed brought down, complete with a plush mattress and clean linen bedding. Fine woolen rugs, a chamber pot, a new carved walnut dining set, and a trunk full of our clothes were all hauled down and set up by a team of servants. They installed a cabinet with shelves next to the fireplace for dishes and kitchen utensils. Members of the kitchen staff hung a cauldron over the fire and placed a cooking pan on the hearth for preparing meals. Servants cleaned and repaired the latrine out back, built a small yard for chickens complete with a coop, cleared the path from the front door to the main road, and chopped a stack of firewood that reached to the ceiling. They placed a rain barrel in the front yard as the cottage had no well water and the river water wasn't the cleanest, given its location downriver of the town.

Clifford and his army of servants managed to make this all happen within two days, despite snow flurries and icy patches on the path down the hill complicating the work.

"Wow, Clifford really wanted to get rid of us," Rhiannon grinned when she saw the transformed cottage.

"And to make sure we never came back," I agreed. I had always picked up on some amount of animosity from Clifford, though it took me awhile to make the necessary connections to understand why.

After working the flint for several frustrating minutes, a spark ignited the wood shavings. As the fire roared to life, I felt a strange sense of satisfaction. I had done something myself—without modern technology or help from a servant—that contributed to our survival. My dad made me do Boy Scouts as a kid, but back then I thought it was all useless in a modern world. Now, I was grateful for the experience.

As I admired the growing fire, someone rapped on the door. Rhiannon paused her organizing and glanced at me with a worried frown. We were not expecting visitors and were still wary of strangers. And especially wary of Edward, who had gone suspiciously quiet in the aftermath of assaulting Rhiannon.

I motioned she should move away from the door, as a precaution. Rhiannon stepped towards the bed, handing me my cane to use as a weapon if need be.

"Hello?" I asked without opening the door.

"It's Henry. May I come in?"

It was strange having the owner of this cottage ask my permission to enter, but I appreciated the respect.

"Of course," I unlocked the door with the key I always wore on a leather string around my neck.

Henry stepped inside and handed me a large basket full of things, reminiscent of when he and Gwen (or at least, the modern versions of them) stopped by our cottage in 2020. I set the basket down on the floor beside the fireplace without checking its contents, more concerned with the man who had taken a seat at our dining table.

Henry stretched his legs out in front of him, crossing his feet at the ankles. He rummaged around under his cloak and withdrew a fat leather pouch full of coins, which he tossed on the table. "I expect you have many, many questions," he started before pausing and tapping his fingers on the table.

Rhiannon and I exchanged a look but said nothing in case he had more to add.

"I know who you are," Henry continued, "and how you came to be here. I even know when you will get the answers you seek." This was the first time Henry spoke plainly to us, as if he knew our story, and though unbelievable, understood it was true.

I raised my eyebrows at this. Henry waved a hand and I kept silent, letting him finish.

"I cannot give you much information right now. But I can help you, to the extent you will let me. There's enough money in that pouch to see you through a couple months, should you choose to use it." Henry leaned back in the little chair, straining the legs. "And there's more if you should need it."

I hated to admit getting the money was a little bit of a relief. I was fully prepared to find work right away, but this bought us some more time to get acclimated to life on our own.

However, it also rankled me. Somewhere deep in my core I wanted us to do this for ourselves. For the first time in my life, I wanted to feel the pain—and satisfaction—of overcoming harsh circumstances and surviving in the face of adversity.

"Thank you," I tossed the pouch of coins to Rhiannon who stashed it in a clay pot on the shelves.

"You are always welcome at the castle, of course." Henry continued. "I expect Lady Gwendolyn will long for company," he nodded towards Rhiannon. "And you should not hesitate to come and visit her."

Rhiannon gave him a small curtsy of acceptance. I knew she genuinely cared about Gwendolyn and wished to continue visiting her.

Henry appraised the room. "I see Clifford spared no expense nor detail in making this place accommodating. Marvelous." He stood and pulled his cloak tightly around his shoulders. He gave me a searching look, brows furrowed, before asking, "How did he die? Your father?"

"Plague," I answered honestly.

"Ah," Henry seemed especially pained by this answer. He closed his eyes and exhaled deeply through his nose. Without another word, he swept from the cottage into the swirling snow drifts.

The basket Henry brought contained two bottles of wine, a honey and almond cake, a wooden box of eggs, a jar of precious salt, a bag of hazelnuts, several little jars of dried herbs, two bars of lavender soap, a pack of hand-painted playing cards, and several linen cloths that could be used for just about anything. Going through the basket of goodies was like tearing open presents on Christmas morning, with each gift more exciting than the next. "Soap!" Rhiannon squealed with as much enthusiasm as if she were receiving diamonds.

That evening we feasted on unevenly cooked grilled cheeses, goblets of wine, and the honey cake. We played gin rummy, keeping score with loose hazelnuts as our limited quantity of paper was too valuable to waste. We climbed into bed, smelling of lavender soap, underneath thick quilts and woolen blankets.

In the castle, privacy was non-existent. But the cottage was quiet, secluded, and peaceful. I felt like I could think clearly for the first time in months and it affected how Rhiannon and I interacted with each other. I knew, despite how resistant she'd been about moving here, she was also feeling better than she had in a long time. She smiled easily. She ate more at dinner than I'd seen her eat during a meal in months.

And when we climbed into bed at the end of the day, Rhiannon sighed dreamily, covers tucked under her chin, and said, "Maybe you were right. Maybe this is better."

I kissed her head and cuddled up against her, feeling safe and content for the first time since we'd arrived in the 15th century.

51

RHIANNON

The first morning in the cottage, we woke up to snow drifts piled high outside our window and up against the front door. We were effectively snowed in. But it was okay. There was nowhere we had to go, no chores we had to do, no social obligations to fulfill. We had plenty of food and supplies, so we took a few days to cocoon.

After lazing in bed, uninterrupted by servants or bored barons, George got up and made us toast and eggs using the cast iron skillet over an open fire. He boiled water for chamomile and ginger tea—a welcome change from the endless booze being served at the castle—and with a drizzle of honey it was almost as good as a cup of coffee. Almost.

We hung out in our linen nightgowns and wool stockings, chairs pulled up to the fireplace, wrapped in blankets to ward off the ever-present chill.

I studied George's face as he sipped his tea, lost in thought. His ash-blonde hair fell in waves just past his shoulders. His beard had grown back but was neatly trimmed. There was a leanness in his face that had developed within the past few months—and with it a look of determination and resolve replaced the expression of checked-out despair he wore for months before we came here.

"What are you thinking about?" I asked.

He sipped his tea. "I'm thinking that this is the best I've felt in months. And I wondered why that was."

We sat in silence, drinking our tea, enveloped by the warmth of the flickering flames. I mentally catalogued all the changes in our circumstances that brought us here, having a quiet snow day. "Well, if I had to guess, it may be because today is the first day in months where we have no one to please, no stories to keep straight, and we don't owe anyone money."

George laughed. "Yes, the not owing anyone money definitely feels good." He glanced at me. "Who did you feel like you had to please?"

"Besides everyone?" I tightened the blanket around my shoulders. "I guess I spent a lot of time running from obligation to obligation, trying to be everything to everyone. I know why I did it at work, back in our time. At least then I could justify it because it was for my students and colleagues. I could say, this is what makes me a great teacher. But in the castle ... it was like, I didn't want them to think we were a burden. Especially after ... Marguerite. My greatest fear was that they'd kick us out and we'd either starve or never make it home."

"I had that fear too," George said softly. "Hence, the hunting fiasco."

I nodded, sipping my tea. "I've been thinking about this quite a bit. There were things Edward said when ... when he ..." I stumbled over my words, reluctant to relive what was a fairly traumatic experience. I took a deep breath. "When he pointed out everything I had been doing, like I was the lady of the castle. Things I didn't need to do, nor was expected to. It was startling to hear it like that from him."

George stood and moved his chair so it was right next to mine. He wrapped me into his blanket, sharing his body heat with me. "And now? Do you still feel like you need to please everyone?"

I rested my head on his shoulder. "Now, I don't know. My greatest survival instinct was being a highly capable, Type A, get-the-job-done kind of person who everyone could rely on. And for a time it worked." I looked up at him. "Who am I without that?"

"You're Rhiannon. And that's enough." George kissed the top of my head. "That's all you need to be. Just Rhiannon."

I exhaled, feeling the weight of tears pressing against my eyelids. "I'm not sure I even know who that is."

"Well, when we're not scrubbing out chamber pots and boiling endless gallons of water, we can figure that out. We can both figure out who we are now and what's important to us."

In the still quiet of the cottage, blanketed by insulating snow, with my head clear for the first time in months, I was no longer afraid of what was next.

52

MID APRIL 1421

GEORGE

It was a bright cold day in April, and there were no clocks striking anything. Mainly because we didn't have a clock.

Which was disorienting.

But we did have chores to anchor our time. So many fucking chores.

They fell into two rough categories: cleaning and eating. Cleaning chores involved doing the laundry by hand, washing dishes after every meal, handling the chamber pot, and keeping the cottage tidy and as dirt-free as we could get it. Eating chores entailed gathering food, washing and prepping vegetables and grains and meat, then cooking it over an open fire. All without electricity, indoor plumbing, or appliances.

Initially, we thought it would be smart to divvy up the work and take turns every week (so no one was stuck on chamber pot duty for too long). But since each activity was so labor-intensive, we ended up handling most of it together, working side by side.

Winter morphed into a damp, chilly spring. The snow melted, leaving behind muddy roads and ice-crusted puddles. It rained almost every day, though it often cleared out in the afternoons, allowing the sun to come out and offer us a brief bit of warmth. Slowly, the world became green again.

Through all of this we hauled loads of laundry to wash in the river and hung it to dry next to the hearth. We scrubbed out the cauldron and pan using dirt as an abrasive; chopped wood and tended to the fire; filtered water out of our rain barrel and boiled it for washing and drinking; and emptied the chamber pot in the latrine out back and rinsed it with a bit of vinegar to disinfect it.

For our meals, Rhiannon washed and chopped vegetables while I cooked stews and porridges and braises in the cauldron. When I ran out of the herbs Henry gave us, we walked to town on market day and used our coins to stock up on bread and cheese, salt and herbs, oats and barley, and occasionally cuts of (incredibly expensive) meat. Despite the lack of refrigerator, it stayed cold enough that we could keep the meat wrapped up and buried in the icy ground.

The townsfolk no longer seemed suspicious of us. Rather, they were eager to help the two strange idiots who moved out of the castle to make their own way in the world. They offered us samples of mead, advice about storing food for longevity, and recipes for baked goods sweetened with honey and dates.

Since we were subsisting on simple fare like chicken and turnip stew or braised ham and cabbage, Rhiannon slowly regained some of the weight she'd lost. Between the meals and the physical intensity of the daily labor, she looked stronger and healthier than I'd seen her in years.

When the weather warmed, Clifford brought us four chickens for eggs. We resisted naming them in case they needed to go into the pot at some point, but when I overheard Rhi chatting with them and referring to a couple of them as "Blanche and Sophia," I knew they'd never be eaten. We would continue to get our weekly meat from the butcher shop in town.

Every night we collapsed into bed, exhausted, but strangely happy.

I rubbed Rhiannon's back as she lied face down on the mattress. "We're still a good team, aren't we?" she mumbled.

I considered all we had gone through, all we had accomplished together. How we had been tested more than once. And how nothing, not even our wedding gift, was just handed to us. In a strange, soul-jarring way I began to understand how all these pieces came together.

"Yes, we're still a great team."

53

GEORGE

"So," Dad took a sip of his iced tea and wiped the condensation off the side of the glass before finishing his thought. "You're married now. Apparently, that means I'm supposed to give you a gift. That is the tradition, yes?" He pulled a small, glossy red envelope out of the briefcase he had resting on the booth seat next to him. It was quite thin, clearly not a card, and he wasn't the kind of guy to just write a check and shove it naked into an envelope.

He placed the envelope on the table, sliding it with one finger towards me.

Dad invited me and Rhiannon out to breakfast a few days after we returned home from our honeymoon. He'd been coy about a wedding gift for us ever since we announced our engagement; it felt like he wanted us to fish for information, only for him to keep yanking the line out of our grasp if we behaved too interested in what he had. I had to consciously refrain from asking any follow-up questions every time he brought it up as the push and pull only exasperated me.

"Dad, honestly, whatever is cool. Gift or not, I mean." I was, and had been, tired of this game.

He raised one eyebrow, looking on the verge of being offended by my words.

"But," Rhiannon added while resting her hand on top of mine under the table, "we're grateful for anything you've arranged, of course." Rhi was new to this game and fresh for the fight she didn't know she'd signed up for.

"Wonderful!" Dad replied, as if these were the magic words he'd been waiting for since he first mentioned this gift. He adored Rhiannon, most likely because she went from being one of his top students to his top daughter-in-law. Dad slid the envelope further across the table.

With an exasperated sigh, I opened it and pulled out a small piece of paper with a simple handwritten note:

> *V marks the spot*
> *ask Martha for one of everything she's got*
> *better eat fast while it's still hot*
> *your next clue is at the end of the lot.*

I groaned out loud and slid back into the vinyl booth. I knew exactly what this was. "Let me guess," I muttered. "Another scavenger hunt?"

Dad pretended he wasn't put off by my reaction. "Calling it a hunt for scavengers minimizes the complex thinking you need to solve each piece."

By then, he was used to my not fully appreciating his elaborate surprises. Growing up, nothing was handed to me. I always had to earn it, whether through a series of chores assigned by my mother, or through a series of clues assigned by my father. Imagine a thirteen-year-old, sweaty and exhausted after a soccer game, having to answer a Sphinxian riddle to get my Gatorade and orange slices, as my teammates watched curiously while sucking on their empty citrus rinds.

I was told this built character.

"Come on now, George. Remember what Emerson always said—"

"Oh, I know what he said. But I don't think he meant having to go on endless scavenger hunts for simple things like a wedding gift. You couldn't just give us a card like a normal person?"

Dad snorted. "When have I ever aspired to be normal? Regardless," he brushed his lapel off as if sweeping away these unsavory comments. "I think you'll like this series of puzzles. And I believe you'll especially like the treasure at the end of the hunt." He tapped his temple and smiled at me knowingly.

"Well, I for one am looking forward to it," Rhiannon chimed in, giving me a quick side-eye. "I already know the first location."

I was surprised. "That was quick."

"It helps that I love a good cheeseburger," she grinned.

"Quick is good," Dad said. "The hunt starts today at noon on the dot and ends at ten o'clock. You have ten hours to complete the mission."

"Or what?" I challenged. "Does the treasure—no scratch that—I mean does the *gift* simply disappear?" I was scowling, but Dad pretended not to notice.

"It might. I guess you'll just have to find out now, won't you?"

Two hours later I found myself waiting in line at The Varsity, Atlanta's iconic fast-food institution, marked by its giant "V" sign, a beacon for weary travelers stuck in traffic on I-85.

When we got to the front of the line, Rhiannon asked for Martha. The girl tending the cash register spoke into her earpiece, "Someone asking for Martha up here."

A tall, dark-skinned woman with her hair twisted into crimson braids came to the front—she was clearly the manager. "Someone is asking for me?"

Rhiannon held up the note. "We're supposed to order one of everything you got?"

"Oh yes!" she exclaimed clapping her hands together, clearly in the loop about all of this. "We've been waiting for you! Everyone wants to know what this is all about." As she spoke, Martha loaded a tray with a couple of cheeseburgers, two Cokes, and a heaping serving of fries. "And," she pulled a small red envelope from her back pocket, "when you're done eating, you're supposed to come get this from me."

We grabbed our tray and made our way towards a table. "This is hardly 'one of everything'," I grumbled, keen on complaining about something, anything, to prove how against the whole thing I was.

Rhiannon rolled her eyes and picked up a fry, holding it aloft to let it cool. "Obviously it was a code phrase so Martha would know it's us." When she was satisfied with the temperature of the fry, Rhiannon nibbled the end before popping the whole thing into her mouth. I watched as she carefully unwrapped her cheeseburger and took a massive bite, letting melted cheese catch at the corners of her mouth. Rhiannon is an incredibly picky eater, so anytime she genuinely loves a meal is a big deal.

"I suppose," I acquiesced, heartened by the fact that at least she was having a good time. "Why do you think he's having us start here?"

"We need to be fueled for the rest of this hunt?" Rhiannon shrugged, unconcerned with Dad's motives. "Are you at least curious about the next clue?"

"See, this is where you and I differ." I took a drag of the syrupy-sweet soda. "This is not my first scavenger hunt rodeo. In fact, when it comes to scavenger hunts created by my dad, I've been in far too many rodeos. Like, an excessive number of rodeos. And I'm telling you right now, not all his clues are going to be this straightforward and easy to figure out. He's just warming us up."

"Well," Rhiannon leaned forward and gave me what she thought was her most aggressive expression (but in reality was totally adorable). "I may not have as many scavenger hunt rodeos under my belt as you, but I know this city inside out. And unlike you, I'm not afraid of a good puzzle." She stared at me, unflinching, daring me to complain about this situation one more time.

Rhiannon knew I was competitive. She knew if she solved most of this on her own because I was being a pain, I'd never live it down. Nor would she let me.

I sighed. "I'm not afraid of the challenge. I'm just annoyed by it. Regardless, you know me well," I grumbled. "Fine, let's eat and get the next clue."

Several minutes later I showed Martha our empty wrappers and she handed me the next envelope, which I handed over to Rhiannon. "Doc Rosen says you have to go outside and look southwest for this one."

"What? Did he say why?"

Martha shook her head, "Nope. Hey, what's this all about, anyway?"

"My dad is making us complete a scavenger hunt to get our wedding gift." I worked hard to not sound completely exasperated by this, because apparently I was the only one annoyed by it all.

Martha looked ecstatic. She clapped her hands together and exclaimed, "How cool! Aw, I wish my dad would do something like that. All I get are gift cards, if anything. And congrats to you and your redhead there." She nodded towards Rhiannon, who was already engrossed in the contents of the next clue.

"Thanks," I nodded.

"Good luck, y'all!" Martha waved at us as we made our way outside.

"Thanks, Martha!" Rhiannon called over her shoulder as we shoved out the door.

We stood in the parking lot, facing our best approximation of southwest. I held my hand against my forehead, blocking the harsh sunlight bearing down on us. The next clue read:

> *Travel this direction to*
> *an artificial sea*
> *which is where you'll find me*
> *An eight-armed host*
> *with the most*

Rhiannon snapped her fingers. "The Aquarium. It's roughly southwest of us. The octopus exhibit, don't you think?"

I got it then, two clues in, what Dad had prepared for us. I laughed, shaking my head.

"What's so funny?"

"You know how growing up, octopi-slash-octopuses were my absolute favorite animal? I mean, they still are, really. But I can't recall if Dad knew that. It was my mom who kept track of that stuff. Anyhow, I guess my first instinct with these clues is they're going to be mostly things we can consider 'favorites.'"

Afraid of giving my father too much credit, I added: "Though it could just be random Atlanta stuff. We'll see."

Rhiannon wrapped her arms around my waist and rested her head on my chest. "You know, even if these aren't all about our favorite things, the scavenger hunt itself is still an act of love. He went to a lot of trouble to set this all up. Which means he was thinking about us the whole time. I know your dad is not great with expressing emotions, and I know he hasn't always been there the way you would've liked, but that doesn't mean he isn't showing you love in his own way."

"Are you saying my dad's love language is acts of scavenger hunts and riddles?"

"I'm saying your dad knows you're incredibly smart, creative, and competitive. He knows you get bored easily. I think this could be his way of bridging the gap between you: his inability to show his emotions and your inability to sit still long enough to have that conversation in the first place. Maybe this is how he connects with you."

I kissed the top of Rhiannon's head and rubbed her back, squeezing her tighter, despite the growing summer heat that made my shirt stick to my stomach. "You're pretty smart."

"I know. You really married way out of your league," she quipped.

"You're not wrong. Can I make one more complaint about this scavenger hunt before I put it to rest?"

"Go for it."

"He's making us go to the crazy busy, crazy expensive Aquarium on a Saturday. Like, what if we had plans? What if I had big plans to lie on the couch and do absolutely nothing?"

"You'll survive," Rhiannon replied. "Come on, let's go. We're on a time limit, remember?"

At the Aquarium we stood in front of the octopus's exhibit. At least, we got as close as we could considering the swarm of children around us. There were no obvious signs of one of the glossy red envelopes we'd come to associate with the hunt.

"Do you think we need to ask someone, like at The Varsity?" Rhiannon mused.

"Maybe?" I pushed my way through the crowd to the window of the exhibit. I ran my fingers along the frame, scanned the ground, looked for anywhere an envelope could be stashed. But there was nowhere to hide such a thing without it being disturbed. I was beginning to wonder if we wasted time and money coming here, my frustration rising the longer we stood there with no clear path forward.

Before I could voice my concerns to Rhiannon, I heard a man's voice behind me ask, "Can I help you find something?" One of the aquarium employees had materialized beside me.

"Yes!" Rhiannon held up one of the red envelopes. "We're on a scavenger hunt and we think the next clue is here. We're looking for one of these?" She waved the envelope like a fan.

"Oh! Are you George and Rhiannon?"

I was dumbfounded. "What?"

Rhi, who was quicker than me, exclaimed, "Yes, we are! Do you have the next clue?"

"No," the man shook his head. "But I know who does. Follow me."

A few minutes later we found ourselves standing in front of an open tank, in a private back room normally reserved only for the trainers and handlers. Shiny white linoleum and blindingly bright fluorescent lights contrasted with the darkened public area we just came from. A young man wearing knee-high rain boots and the same blue polo shirt as his colleague introduced us to the "host."

He pointed into what looked like an empty tank. "This is Inky. She's a giant pacific octopus."

Inky was wrapped around a reef of rocks, her coloring allowing her to blend right in with her surroundings. When the handler pointed to her, she moved a bit, revealing her location.

I had never been so close to an octopus before. I sucked in a breath. It was a childhood dream come to life.

The handler held up a small jar with a crab inside and showed it to the octopus. "Inky, do you have something for our guests?"

Inky waved one arm, floated down to the sandy floor of her tank, and started rummaging around under some rocks. After a minute, she pulled out a sealed jar with one of the red envelopes inside. Inky came to the surface and pushed the jar past the top of the water. Two of her arms opened the lid of the jar and tilted it towards us.

"No fucking way," I exhaled. I felt my eyes burning, welling with tears. It was the coolest gift I'd ever received. It was an answered prayer, twenty years after I first cast it. And yet my anger towards my father was only mildly dampened.

"Go on," the handler said. "Take it." Inky waved the jar a little, as if encouraging me to accept her gift.

Rhiannon pushed me towards the tank. "That's all yours," she whispered behind me.

I leaned over the tank and carefully pulled the red envelope out of the jar. As soon as I did, the handler dropped the small crab he had shown Inky into her jar. She immediately submerged it and retrieved her prize, sliding off to hide behind some rocks to enjoy her treat in peace.

"No fucking way," I said again, still in disbelief that my dad pulled this off. That he'd even thought of it in the first place. "That was extremely cool. I can't even ..." I shook my head. "How?" I asked.

The handler replied, "Dr. Rosen was one of my favorite professors at UGA. I was happy to help. And Inky could always use the enrichment."

Rhiannon squeezed my arm. "Are you going to open the next clue?"

"Right. Next clue."

The handler watched us curiously as I carefully opened the next envelope, making sure not to tear the paper. I already knew I was going to save this little memento of the time an octopus handed me something.

The next clue read:

Though made of bronze, I'm going for the gold
While this ring doesn't move, it's still a challenge to hold
This Flair is only for the best to behold

I folded up the clue and stuck it in my back pocket. "I know this one." I glanced at Rhiannon. "He's letting us know these first clues were softballs and it's about to get difficult."

"What makes you say that?"

"Because when I was a kid, Dad took me to this statue to give me a pep talk about the 'pursuit of excellence,' and perseverance and shit. You know why?"

Rhiannon shook her head.

"Because during a soccer game I didn't run as fast as he thought I should've, and my team lost. I was like, twelve. Whenever I didn't push myself as hard as he thought I should've, or worked as much as he wanted me to, I got a long lecture about pursuing greatness, excellence, and so on. It got to be white noise after awhile. And I rebelled by doing even less than I could, just to prove a point."

"The point being that you can fail if you'd like?"

"Yeah, something like that." The way she put it made me feel stupid. Like choosing to sabotage my life to spite my dad was really only messing up my own experience. There we were, in the middle of a hunt to get a wedding gift, and I'd been dragging my feet to stick it to my old man. Like always.

Rhiannon took my hand. "Come on, we're on the clock. Let's go get that next clue."

I was right, of course. About the hunt escalating in difficulty. Once we got to the statue *Flair Across America*, there were no more helpful employees dishing up cheeseburgers or talented octopi impressing us with her dexterity. There was only a signature red envelope, taped to a discreet underside of the statue, and a vague clue we deduced was directing us to the Margaret Mitchell house.

From there we made stops at the High Museum, The Cyclorama, Turner Field, and the sketchy grocery store Atlantans had christened "Murder Kroger."

It was there we found what we believed to be the last clue:

A red leather chair

Pales in comparison to her hair

This is where you two first became a pair

And where you'll find the answer to your prayer

Rhiannon studied the clue for a bit. "Is it just me, or is he sending us to his office, all the way in Athens?"

"He would do that, yes. And I think he did. Hence the time limit—wait too long and the building will be locked."

"But how did he know? He wasn't there that day we reconnected in his office."

"Dad has his ways," I sighed, exhaling years of frustration. After a hot summer afternoon running around the city, we were exhausted, sweaty, and hungry. The idea of driving all the way to Athens—a solid one-and-a-half-to-two-hours away—felt like torture. We would need to get there soon, which meant we had little time to contemplate our next move.

I sunk to my knees, right there in the cookie aisle of Murder Kroger. "Do you think this gift is good enough to warrant the drive right now? Because I really, really just want to go home. I had a long week at work and didn't think we'd be spending the weekend traveling to all of Atlanta's best tourist traps." I looked around at the seedy grocery store we were in. "Except this one, of course."

Rhiannon fanned herself with the envelope of the clue. Her normally pristine hair had battled the humidity and lost. Loose red curls framed her face, her mascara had smudged into black circles around her eyes that I found oddly alluring, and her white tank top was stained with sweat. She looked as spent and miserable as I felt. If we were going to give up, now would be the time. I bet I could persuade her to abandon this absurd quest to go home, shower, and order a pizza.

But I couldn't shake the image of watching my dad put this all together—the thought, the details, the goddamn octopus handing me the envelope as part of a trick she'd clearly been trained for. I thought of all the times I gave up, simply to get my dad off my back, so he'd leave me alone.

I thought of all the opportunities I missed out on because I'd stubbornly clung to having it my way, even when my dad did sometimes know better.

I exhaled and rubbed my hands over my sweaty face. He knew what he was doing. I held my hand out to my new wife. "Come on, I'll drive. We're finishing this, even if it kills us."

Rhiannon put her hand in my outstretched one. "Can we at least get something to eat for the drive?"

"Of course. You know feeding you is one of my top priorities." I kissed the back of her hand and led her out into the muggy summer evening.

Traffic was mercifully light all the way to Athens, a benefit of doing this scavenger hunt on a summer weekend. We made it in just over an hour, as the sun dipped below the brick buildings of campus.

When we burst into Dad's office, there was a single red envelope taped to his desk chair. I grabbed it—feeling it was noticeably thicker than the others—and tore it open. It was a standard congratulatory wedding card. But when I opened it, there was a check for ten thousand dollars taped to the inside.

"Jesus," I exhaled. "That was worth the drive." I handed the card with the check still attached to Rhiannon.

"The note says it's for a down payment towards a house."

I nodded. "I mentioned to him we were saving up. Hence, 'answered praye r.'"

Rhiannon flopped down into the red leather chair and swung around. Dad was so tall that her feet didn't even touch the floor; she was able to spin around freely while laughing, "That was so worth it! What a day!"

54

MAY 1421

RHIANNON

Growing up I couldn't control where I lived, or what terrible vending machine dinner Mom scrounged up for me, or how my classmates treated me. But I could control my grades. Losing myself in schoolwork gave me a reprieve from the reality of my situation, because iambic pentameter and algebraic equations are far less dramatic than a grifter feeling the heat of being caught. My overwhelming thoughts melted away when I was reading a good book or working out a problem in chemistry or putting the finishing touches on a diorama for history class.

Work was the soothing padding that blocked out the noise of my personal life.

After I lost my first pregnancy, I threw myself into teaching. Who has time to feel the pain of loss when there are lessons to plan and papers to grade and labs to prepare and cafeterias full of teenagers with bad judgement to supervise?

After the loss of my third pregnancy, I became so good at focusing on work, I stopped feeling anything at all.

When I asked George to leave, I struggled to cry what I felt should be the right amount of tears to process the end of my marriage. I even tried watching sad movies to coax out those elusive tears, only to find myself folding laundry or vacuuming or doing any number of mindless chores instead. I managed to watch (and re-watch) Littlefoot's mother die in *The Land Before Time* (arguably the most traumatic on-screen death, like, ever) without shedding a tear.

I felt broken—but somehow not broken enough to find a foothold towards healing.

When we tumbled into 1420, every minute became about survival. I was constantly terrified about any number of hazards facing us in the 15th century—which was compounded by George's gruesome injury. I refused to relax for even a moment, and it kept me from feeling a range of emotions. Fear called all the shots. The few times I cried, it was because fear had built up such a reservoir of distress, my nervous system had no choice but to release some of the pressure.

However, when we moved into the cottage, something unexpected happened: the ever-present hum of fear faded away.

Yes, the cottage was work and our chores took up an absurd amount of time. It would have been easy to drown out my feelings in the endless cycles of handwashing laundry and boiling water and feeding chickens.

But George and I did them together, working side by side, talking the entire time.

Early on, we reminisced about our favorite parts of the 21st century: how much we loved dishwashers and dryers and microwaves and blessed, blessed flushing toilets. We needed time to discuss benign things after stumbling out of our foggy castle lives, brutalized by trauma, carrying every type of pain. Bonding over how we'd give anything to complain about unloading the dishwasher again was a relief compared to the heavy things left unsaid.

That relief made space for different types of conversations. Without fear and pain containing our words, we began to talk about what happened.

When did we start to unzip as a couple? Was it when the sheen of invincibility that coats all new marriages finally wore off? Was it when the pressure of our mounting bills, combined with too little income, caused us to snip and snap relentlessly at each other? Was it when George resisted my efforts to get him to do more, like a knee-jerk reaction to his father doing the same? Was it when I started to overcompensate for my chaotic childhood by bearing down on our lives with an iron-fisted level of control? Was it when grief kept layering on, like coats of old paint, trapping everything we felt under an oppressive crust?

"Maybe," George mused while we walked to the market one morning, "it doesn't matter when it began, so much as what we do about it now." He stopped and pulled me off to the side of the road. "On that note, what do you want to do about it now?"

I saw the earnestness in his face. He'd already made it clear he never wanted to end our marriage.

In the evenings, exhausted from work, sometimes we only had energy to sit and hold hands while watching the fire. Other nights we'd dance around the cottage, singing off-tune songs to each other since we didn't have a radio. I consistently destroyed him at gin rummy, the only two-person card game we knew. On days when the weather was too terrible to do much besides hang out inside, George would reenact popular movies he'd seen a million times. My favorite was his one-man show of *Star Wars*, mainly because he did an uncanny Wookie impression with his hair over his face.

In the mornings, we gave each other big, enthusiastic bear hugs. We clung to each other, grateful we weren't going through this insane experience alone, before beginning our long list of chores.

Ever so slowly, I started to break open.

The first tears trickled down my cheeks while scrubbing linen nightgowns in the river. I chalked it up to my impending period and chose to ignore them. Not long after that, while gathering eggs from around the chicken's yard (Dorothy laid those eggs everywhere but the coop), grief slammed into me so hard I fell to my knees and began to sob. George ran over from where he was filtering rainwater into a pot and wrapped his arms around me. "I got you, I'm here," he said over and over. And he was.

We cried together, letting emotions flow through us.

We let it out, unimpeded.

Afterwards, I felt an overwhelming sense of calm and peace. Where dark, dull sorrow had been cloaking my heart, there was now the brightness of joy cracking open.

Over the ensuing days I cried. I laughed. I reflected on words spoken to me by friends and colleagues that I'd initially dismissed as superficial therapy-talk, letting the platitudes bounce off me unheard.

Yet those words must've made a dent. Using a stick, I scratched thoughts into the dirt outside our cottage like they were journal entries: *Love is not transactional. Control is an illusion. It's not my job to save everyone.*

I let go of the anger and resentment I had towards my mother. Holding onto to it thinking it was some twisted sense of justice, or that it was the only way to protect myself from her, was only hurting me.

I let go of the insane expectations I'd been putting on myself. I was exhausted and spent and lonely; that was enough evidence to show me it was not working.

And I forgave George for not being able to mindlessly ignore the pain the way I had.

When I woke up in tears in the middle of a cold spring night, George pulled me into his lap and rocked me back and forth while stroking my hair.

"I missed you so much," I cried into his shoulder, dampening his nightshirt. "But I was furious with you." I wiped my cheek with the back of my hand. "And mad at myself for being so bad at reproducing."

He chuckled mournfully. "It's a dumb thing to be bad at. But we have no control over it. And I'm tired of us beating ourselves up over it." George dragged his fingers up and down my arms with a soothing touch, calming my breathing. "I missed you like crazy. I was depressed and didn't know what to do about it, so I just stopped ... I stopped doing anything. I'm so—"

"Wait." I placed my hand on his chest.

George tilted his head at me.

"I think we both know we're different people now. It's impossible not to be after all of this craziness. Maybe it's time to set the past down. And just ... move forward. With clarity."

He nodded, letting tears slide down his cheeks.

I ran my hands through George's hair while pressing my lips to his. Months of built-up tension exploded as we tore at each other's clothes.

He rolled us over so I was on my back, my nightshirt shoved up around my waist. I lifted my arms, indicating I wanted him to take it off.

George obliged. I lay beneath him, naked except for my red woolen stockings. He inhaled slowly. "You're even more beautiful than I remembered," he whispered. "Especially now."

I knew what he meant. I was recovering my health, both physically and mentally.

"It's awfully cold for me to be naked by myself," I murmured.

George grinned before yanking his own nightshirt up over his head. He lowered himself down on top of me and I wrapped my arms around his neck. I had missed the warmth of his bare skin against mine, the way his lean and muscular body felt nestled between my legs, and his specific George scent that earned my devotion every time I smelled it. I kissed him hungrily, savoring the taste of cloves on his breath and the scent of lavender that enveloped us both.

When he pushed my leg up and pushed inside me, I clutched him tightly, letting the pleasure ripple through my body. In some ways it was like no time had passed—we were still the naïve, horny stupid twenty-somethings who couldn't get enough of each other.

And it was also better. Our love had grown deeper. We were different people who had gone through so much together, that our bond felt tangibly real.

He was the only man I wanted. I understood then that there was no one better for me than George.

So, standing on the road to the market, being asked what I wanted to do about it now, was not the confusing confrontation it would have been months earlier.

It was clarity.

"I want to be with you," I replied. "I think that's all I've wanted from the beginning."

55

RHIANNON

I pulled into the driveway, recognizing the car already parked there, relieved I had the right address. I tapped my fingers on the steering wheel, giving myself one more chance to bail on this evening.

After George and I reconnected, he put his number in my phone and told me to text him when I was ready. I knew what he meant—when I was single again and ready to see what this strange and unyielding attraction between us would become.

We knew, somewhere in the back of our minds and hearts, that this would be serious.

When I broke up with the placeholder boyfriend I knew would never have my heart, I texted George. It was so late at night, well after midnight (which is how long it took me to work up the courage), I realized he may have thought I was texting him for *other* reasons. But he seemed to know that wasn't what I intended.

Texting that first late night, he told me he wanted to cook for me—but only when I was ready. Every offer he made always finished with that phrase: "When you're ready."

After a couple of weeks talking on the phone for hours and messaging during the in-between, I decided I *was* ready. It was no small thing to commit to driving over an hour, from my studio apartment in Athens to his house in Atlanta, for a date. I spent the entire drive trying to talk myself out of it, trying to come up with reasons why this was a bad idea—only to have nothing solid to cling to. I liked George. A lot.

I got out of the car, smoothed down the dark floral dress I'd opted for over my usual jeans and T-shirt, and headed for the door. George opened it before I could ring the doorbell.

He was grinning, with his long hair tied back and the sleeves of his chambray shirt rolled up to reveal tanned forearms, dotted with a series of tattoos that had intrigued me ever since we first met. George was stupidly hot, with dark lashes that fringed his pale blue eyes and a warm smile that unnerved me—yet was comforting at the same time. He wore an apron that read, "He hath eaten me out of house and home," with a picture of a grinning cat on it.

"Shakespeare," he explained when he caught me staring at it.

"A gift from your dad?" I asked, stepping inside.

"Of course." He took my purse and jacket and hung them on a coat rack behind the door before appraising my dress. "You look beautiful. Welcome to Casa de George."

George lived in a craftsman bungalow in Decatur with two roommates. The living room had a giant beat up leather couch in front of a huge television, a couple of Ikea chairs, a sagging bookshelf crammed with books stacked haphazardly, and a stained ivory rug under a rickety coffee table. A bicycle leaned against the wall in the foyer, with a helmet dangling from the handlebar. Books were also stacked next to the couch, high enough that they made an end table, with a thick copy of *World Without End* serving as the top. Lining the walls were posters of various movies, bands, and museum exhibits, all hung haphazardly, some framed, some just tacked directly into the wall. Though the walls were painted black, the colors of the scattered posters and books added enough contrast that the effect was welcoming instead of morose.

The kitchen was in the back of the house, with windows looking into the lush backyard that appeared to be reclaimed forest. Pine, oak, and magnolia trees crowded each other right up to the edge of the deck that lay beyond the dining room.

"Something smells amazing," I breathed in. The room smelled of savory garlic, basil, tomatoes, and something meaty. From what I could see of the pots and pans cluttered all over the counters, it looked like George had been busy. The rest of the house, though messy, was clean and welcoming. I started to calm down, feeling like I'd made the right decision in coming here.

"Meatballs," he replied. "From scratch. Plus a few other things."

"Really?" I was dumbfounded. I didn't cook and had never really tried. Meatballs sounded like a complex recipe only a restaurant could manage.

"It's a specialty," George noted while leading me to a barstool at the island in the kitchen. "Have a seat. Do you want some wine?"

I nodded. All of this made me feel very adult. It was a long way from dinner at Applebee's followed by an action movie that most of my previous dates consisted of.

George popped the cork on a bottle of chianti and indicated I should choose a glass from the counter. He filled it up only a third of the way before pouring himself a glass. It wasn't lost on me that he showed me the corked bottle, let me choose my own glass, and didn't overserve me right away. I relaxed even more, letting my flight or fight instinct temper so I could enjoy myself.

"Where are your roommates?" I asked while taking a sip of wine.

George stood at the island so he was facing me, with his back to the stove, and started chopping carrots into tidy little sticks. "Steve is spending the night at his girlfriend's, and I think Adam went camping." He paused his chopping to smile at me. "I told them to get lost and didn't really pay attention to where they went."

I released the tension in my shoulders, secretly relieved I wouldn't have to interact with them when I was already so nervous.

"Who's birthday?" I asked, pointing to a stack of opened birthday cards on the opposite edge of the island.

George gave me a sheepish grin. "Mine, actually."

"Oh yeah? What day?"

He put his knife down and appraised me, like he was weighing out what information to share. "It's today."

"Really?" I squeaked, jumping off the stool, suddenly feeling like an intruder. "Wait, why didn't you say something? Wouldn't you rather be with your family or friends? Having a party or something?"

George laughed. "Relax, Rhiannon. This is exactly what I want to be doing on my birthday. I chose the date, remember? Which is why I told my buddies that the best gift they could give me was to not be here. I wanted you to feel comfortable." He resumed his chopping. "When's your birthday?"

"It's in May," I replied, climbing back up on the stool, still not convinced that cooking for a girl he barely knew and who'd given him hell would be what he wanted to do on his birthday.

"And what do you like to do on your birthday?" he asked, not looking up from his chopping. George gathered up a handful of carrot sticks and arranged them on a plate.

I debated how to answer this without revealing too much and making him uncomfortable with the reality of my past. However, I had a deep desire to be honest with George, like starting off with half-truths and obfuscations would hurt us in the long run. All the carefully cultivated stories I used with others seemed inadequate.

"Well ... I didn't really celebrate my birthday growing up. So, I stopped wanting to do anything. It's just ... it's just another day for me." George had stopped his chopping and was watching me with his head tilted. But there was no judgment in his eyes, only curiosity. "I think I told you that my mom was kind of a mess, and it was just the two of us, so at best I think I got like, a cupcake or something. And we moved around a lot, so it's not like I ever had good friends. Or ... friends at all." God, that made me sound like such a loser. I shifted uncomfortably on the stool. "Sorry, this is a lot to unload on you."

George held up his finger and said, "It's really not. But I need you to hold that thought." He turned around and used an oven mitt to pull something out of the oven. "This is baked feta dip," he explained while arranging the veggies he'd been chopping around a ceramic dish of baked cheese, as well as a handful of pita chips. "It has honey and pistachios in it. I hope that's okay. It's crazy hot, though, so let's give it a few minutes to cool and you can finish telling me about your birthdays." He stared at me for a moment before resuming his dinner preparation. "I'm serious when I say it's not too much. I genuinely want to know you. Even the not-great stuff. *Especially* the not-great stuff."

I raised my eyebrows. "You say that now. Let me have some more wine before I talk about my mom, okay?"

"Fair," he agreed.

"Can I ask about your mom?"

He stretched out his arm and showed me a tattoo of a raven on his forearm. "Her name was Eleanor, but she went by Lenore, hence the raven. She died when I was sixteen. Breast cancer."

"I'm really sorry," I offered softly. I could tell by the way his voice went low that he missed her. "Also, I'm sorry this conversation has gotten so heavy. I didn't expect us to be unpacking our mommy issues this soon."

"Don't be," he grinned, lowering his arm. "This is life, isn't it? Besides, I hate fake bullshit."

"Me too. Mainly because I'm so bad at it."

George laughed. "Me too. But we can lighten it up. For instance, you never did tell me why a biology major is still taking history classes her senior year." He plucked a pita chip from his spread, dragged it through the baked feta, and handed it to me. "Try this."

I obliged, popping the chip in my mouth. The cheese was incredible: creamy, salty, and decadent. The honey gave it a twist of sweetness and the crunch of the pistachios and pita was satisfying. I'd never eaten anything like it before. "Wow," I exclaimed between bites. "This is ... well, it's amazing."

"Good," he lit up, his smile crinkling at the corners of his eyes. "For some reason I have a compulsive need to feed you. Now, history classes. Why?"

I shifted on my seat, took another sip of wine, and considered how to answer this without sounding creepy. "I mean, I genuinely love the classes. But you're right, I certainly don't need them to graduate." I dragged a chopped radish through the feta and took another bite. It was so good, I sighed a little. "If I told you that I'm only taking history classes from Dr. Rosen, and no other history professor, what would you say?"

"I'd say you're a masochist but I'm guessing that's not what you're getting at." George tilted his head at me, tapping his fingers on the counter. He cocked one eyebrow. "Were you hoping you'd run into someone?"

Apparently I was more obvious than I realized. I blushed and took a big gulp of my wine. "I plead the fifth. Why do you care so much, anyway? My classes are my business."

George chuckled and sipped his own wine. "I'm just trying to figure you out, Rhiannon. Besides, you haven't asked me why I was willing to drive all the way to fucking Athens every week just to have lunch with my dad. Aren't you curious?"

Before I could answer, the oven timer chimed. George pulled two baking dishes out of the oven: the meatballs he'd mentioned earlier and what looked like some sort of casserole.

"Scalloped potatoes," he said over his shoulder, like he could tell I was trying to figure it out. "I like them with meatballs better than pasta."

"That all sounds amazing."

The warmth of the wine and cheese coursed through my veins, loosening me up further, calming my nerves. I couldn't recall the last time I'd had a home-cooked meal. I subsisted on a steady diet of take-out, deli sandwiches, canned soups, and frozen dinners. I was fine with it up until I tasted the feta dip. Suddenly my diet felt ... sad. Lonely.

After an incredible meal where we discussed nothing deeper than our favorite books and our controversial movie opinions ("*Revenge of the Sith* is a masterpiece and I'll die on that hill!" I exclaimed, wine-buzzed and opinionated), George went into the kitchen and emerged with a small, white cake with a swirl of chocolate ganache on the top.

"What are your thoughts on red velvet cake?" he asked, setting it between us on the table.

"Doesn't everyone love red velvet cake?"

"You'd be surprised. Does that mean you want some?"

"I feel like I should be asking you that. It's your birthday and I didn't get you anything."

He grinned at me before pressing a knife down the center of the cake. "I already told you, this is what I wanted for my birthday." George slid a slice of cake onto a plate and handed it to me. "Besides, if you really want to do something for me, you can help me with the dishes."

"Deal." I took a bite of the cake. It was chocolatey, dense, with a tang from the creamed cheese icing. "Did you bake this?" I asked with a contented sigh.

George chuckled. "No, this is from a bakery I love. A gift from a friend."

I tried not to think of what kind of friend would give him such a beautiful cake. I doubted guys gave each other cakes for any reason.

"She must be a very good friend," I mused, taking another bite, trying to nonchalantly feel out what other relationships George might have in his life. We weren't exclusive. I had no right to be jealous. Even if I was.

"She is, and *her wife* is the baker, in case you were curious," George responded with a sly grin. "You can just ask, you know."

"Ask what?" I avoided his eye contact.

"Whether I'm seeing anyone else. And the answer is no. I'm not talking to anyone else but you." He stabbed his cake with his fork and took a big bite, still watching me.

"That's cool," I choked out while shoving my loose hair out of my face. I'd forgone my usual braids and the humidity made my hair an unruly cloud around my face.

George laughed. "I'm glad you feel that way. I'm bad at multi-tasking, so I don't think I'm organized enough to date more than one person at a time." He sipped his wine and gazed at me with an unreadable expression on his face. "Besides, I'm trying not to scare you off. You're like a skittish feral cat and I'm trying to win your trust with good food."

I dragged my finger across my plate to get the last of the icing. Everything about George did scare me—but in a good way. He made me want to fight through the fear to see what was on the other side.

"This is new territory for me," I hesitated, considering what else to add. How else I could explain that all relationships were fraught for me, without going too far down a dark road I wasn't in the mood to travel down with him just yet. "But good food is a nice start." I smiled at him before popping my icing-coated finger in my mouth.

We did the dishes while debating the *Harry Potter* movies versus the books. When we moved to the couch, wine glasses in hand, George put on some music that sounded like a dreamy, multi-layered pop and lit a couple of candles in mason jars. The flicker of light reflected off the glass, casting a glittery glow over everything. I settled against the leather, George's arm around my shoulders.

"You know that party where we first met?" he mused while fingering one of my loose curls.

"Of course."

"I said something that pissed you off, but I honestly don't remember what. I'd had ... well, I was drunk. So, it was probably something stupid. But I was wondering if you'd remind me what it was."

I looked up at him. We'd never been this close before, so close our thighs were pressed up against each other and if I tilted my head just right, he could lean down to kiss me.

Which I realized I wanted very, very much.

"You honestly don't remember?"

He shook his head. "I honestly don't. And it's been driving me crazy ever since. Regardless, if it was offensive, I'm sorry. I can be an idiot sometimes."

I shifted so I was up on my knees, facing him, and placed my hand on his chest. I could feel his heartbeat underneath my fingers, felt him tense up with my touch, and could see his pupils dilate a bit. His hand slipped down so it was resting on my waist.

"It wasn't offensive," I offered. "But I'm not telling you. At least, I'm not telling you right now." I grinned at him. "I kind of like having the upper hand."

He laughed. "I absolutely believe that about you." George leaned forward a bit, close enough that I dragged my hand up, over his shoulder, and rested it on the side of his warm neck. He tilted his head down, and whispered, "As you have the upper hand, you should know that I'm completely at your mercy."

I fingered the collar of his shirt while gently pulling him down towards me. George brushed his lips against mine. I parted my lips, cupped my hands around the back of his neck, and gave myself over to the kiss. He wrapped his arm fully around my waist, and in one movement pulled me onto his lap so I was straddling him.

The kiss melted away any competing thoughts and simply replaced it with one: *Him. More. Now.*

He groaned a little as I shifted my weight so I could grind into him. He braced his hands on my waist, anchoring me against his body. George tasted like wine and chocolate, smelled like clean laundry and something unique—something that was entirely him and made me feral with need. I cupped his face in my hands, stroking his stubbled cheeks, and gave myself over to the deep kisses, parting my lips, letting him in.

When we paused to take a breath, George panted, "You're in charge. Tell me what you want."

"I'll try not to abuse my power," I said while tugging at the tie holding his hair back. George gave his head a little shake as his ash-blonde hair fell loose to his shoulders.

"No, no, by all means, take full advantage of me," George moaned as I ran my hands through his hair, dragging my nails along his scalp. He closed his eyes and took a slow, deep breath.

When I was debating coming here, I knew it was because it would be real, and that it would be more than dinner. I knew I wouldn't leave without knowing what it was like to be with him—in every sense of the word.

I unbuttoned his shirt while he ran his hands up my thighs, shoving my dress up around my waist. I parted the fabric of his shirt, revealing a lean and muscular chest dusted with a bit of blonde hair. George had a tattoo wrapped around his side that appeared to be two skeletons embracing. He watched as I lightly brushed my fingers over it.

"I'll tell you about that one another time," he breathed.

I nodded and continued my exploration of his skin. He wore what looked like a silver pendant hanging from a thin chain. I rubbed the disc between my thumb and forefinger. In the low light, I could make out a face in profile on one side—though it was incredibly worn—and a cross on the other, ringed with numerals.

George looked down to what had drawn my attention. "It's a Norman coin. A gift from my dad and apparently a lucky charm."

I leaned back on my hands and looked at him incredulously. "That's like, a thousand years old. Shouldn't it be in a museum? Or at least, somewhere safer, perhaps?"

He gave me his lopsided grin and ran his hands up my thighs. "Nah. They made a ton of these. Besides, I've had it for years and never lost it. I'm as good as any museum."

"Hmmm. And is it lucky?"

He leaned forward and brushed kisses along my collarbone, down my chest, between the slight cleavage that was exposed by my dress. Pleasant chills coursed through me, finishing with an exhale. George murmured into my chest, "You're here now, aren't you?"

"That *is* lucky," I breathed.

He ran his hands up my sides and tugged one of my loose curls of hair. "Like I said earlier, this is *exactly* what I wanted for my birthday."

"Better than red velvet cake?"

"Better than pretty much anything." He slid his hand up my abdomen. I arched my back into the touch, bracing my hands on his knees.

"You know, it's a long drive back to Athens," he murmured. "You can stay the night, if you want. I'll even sleep here on the couch, if that would make you more comfortable."

I cupped his face in my hands and kissed him again, leaning forward so I could feel his bare chest against mine. I whispered into his ear. "Is that why you sent your roommates away? So you could sleep alone on the couch?"

"Ha, no. But I don't want to assume anything. Like I said, I'm trying not to scare you off."

I kissed George again, wrapping my arms around his neck. "I'm not scared." I paused, looking him in the eyes. "Anymore, at least." He nodded, seeming to understand what I meant. "I'll stay the night. And I won't even kick you out of your own bed."

George chuckled. "I appreciate it."

We lost track of time. At some point, George pulled a quilt from the back of the couch and wrapped it around us. I rested my head on his upper arm, my back pressed against his warm chest, watching the candles flicker down into quiet darkness. He ran a hand lazily up and down my arm, occasionally tugging a lock of my hair, until I was so relaxed I was half dreaming.

"I was hoping to run into you." I whispered, mostly for myself.

He stilled behind me. "What?"

"That's why I kept taking your dad's classes. I was hoping to see you again."

George planted a kiss on my bare shoulder and tightened his embrace around my waist. "Good. And that's why I was willing to drive over an hour for lunch every week." He trailed kisses up my neck, nuzzling me just beneath my earlobe. I turned over so I was facing him. I cupped his face with my hands and pulled him down to kiss me, already aching to have him again. "It's why I'm still willing to make the drive. If you'll let me."

"Will there be more cake?" I grinned at him and tucked his hair behind one ear.

George smiled. "There will be more of everything."

"Good. I'm ready. For all of it."

56

JUNE 1421

RHIANNON

For several weeks, word spread through town that a famous traveling minstrel would be in Kirkby Kendal to perform at the local tavern. Up north, entertainment was limited and the best performers rarely ventured this far from the circuit of bigger, more populated towns.

Desperate for a break in our routine and completely fed up with telling each other rehashed versions of our favorite books and movies, plus exhausted from making every meal from scratch, George and I decided dinner and a show (as it were) sounded amazing.

We arrived early to get seats at one of several massive communal tables, knowing the tavern would be absolutely packed. A barmaid laid two thick bread trenchers on the table in front of us and ladled what appeared to be lamb stew on top. A young boy handed us two flagons of ale, foam spilling down the sides from his unsteady grip.

The food was good—better than I'd anticipated. I'd gotten used to lamb, and the savory stew was completed with parsnips, onions, and carrots. The beer was cold; the crowd was jubilant; and the thick bread, soaked with the stew's broth, was surprisingly tasty. George and I toasted to our rare date night and ate well.

After what felt like an hour later, the crowd was growing restless. The minstrel was delayed for reasons unknown. Everyone had been drinking heavily in anticipation of the entertainment, and combined with a desperate need for a break in the monotony of daily heavy labor, tensions among the crowd grew. Voices rose, some banged the tables in a show of frustration, and the air grew thick and hot.

When the mood shifted and it seemed like things were about to get hostile, George grabbed my hand from across the table and said, "Rhi, I'm about to do something either incredibly smart or really fucking stupid."

"What do you mean—" I started to respond when George stood and climbed on top the of the table, cane in hand, and flung his blue velvet cloak back with a flourish.

It's not every day that a newcomer dressed like a noble stands on a table at a tavern and waves a cane around. People hushed and gawked at George. I scanned the room for an exit strategy in case whatever he had planned went awry.

When George had the room's attention, he spoke in a booming voice. "Lords and Ladies of Kirkby Kendal, I have traveled far and wide, collecting stories from faraway kingdoms and distant lands. But there is one story above all that has regaled kings and queens, emperors and empresses, princes and princesses. It is a story with fencing," he wielded his cane like a sword and jabbed toward the crowd, "fighting, torture, revenge, giants, monsters, chases, escapes, true love," he smiled at me, "And … miracles." The crowd murmured and whispered amongst each other. "Would you be interested in hearing such a tale? What say you?" George pointed his cane in the direction of the mayor and his family, sitting in the corner.

"Let's hear it!" the mayor shouted, raising his ale in consent. Everyone else cheered and whistled, some slapped the tables, others jeered at George with indecipherable taunts.

When the crowd fell so quiet you could hear the rustle of a shifting body on the other side of the room, George began telling the story of *The Princess Bride*. "Long ago in a land far from here, lived a young farm boy named Westley and a lovely girl named Buttercup." As he described Buttercup's beauty, he gave her, "copper colored hair that fell in curls to her waist and pale hazel eyes," winking at me from where he stood on the table.

A scan of the tavern showed George had the room's full attention. He masterfully mimicked each of the character's voices, his voice carrying over the rapt masses. He emphasized the jokes about the Spaniard, much to the English audience's delight. During the sword fight between The Man in Black and Inigo Montoya, George wielded his cane like a saber, thrusting and parrying using his left hand. When the mysterious man revealed he was also not left-handed, George smoothly tossed the cane into his right hand, eliciting a huge gasp and cheer from the audience.

He was absolutely brilliant: charismatic, funny, and animated as he performed one of his favorite comfort movies for a crowd who'd never seen it before.

At the end of the sword fight scene, George surveyed the packed tavern and said, "My friends, this story is an epic tale and there is much, much more to hear. Who is The Man in Black and what does he want with our fair Princess Buttercup? Will she be rescued, only to have to marry the evil Prince Humperdinck? And is her true love Westley really gone forever?" He paused for dramatic emphasis. The crowd murmured, a few people whistled. "Well, you will have to return tomorrow night to hear the next chapter of our story!"

Everyone went wild, cheering and clapping, pounding the tables and shouting questions.

George hopped down from his tabletop stage, sweaty and out of breath, giving me a sheepish look, like he expected to be scolded.

"You were incredible!" I exclaimed breathlessly. I'd never been more attracted to him.

George raised his eyebrows. "You think so?" He leaned forward. "You're the only one who knows the real story. Did I do it justice?"

"Are you kidding? I'd rather hear your version any day!"

"I'm breaking it into three parts. It's too long for a one-man show to do all at once, without any kind of prep." As George explained where he'd go with the next two parts, the tavern keeper strode over and dropped a heavy bag of coins in front of him.

"Yer share," he said gruffly. "More tomorrow." He disappeared into the crowd before we could say anything.

"Wow!" George tossed the bag in one hand, marveling at how he had just earned his first wages in the 15th century—for storytelling, no less.

On the walk back to our cottage, we held hands and relived key moments of the story and speculated what it was like for a member of the audience to hear it for the first time. "You know," George ruminated, "I was a little drunk on ale and running the story through my mind while we waited for the no-show minstrel. I realized all the details completely fit this time—there were no parts I needed to adjust. And I've had this movie memorized, word for word, since I was in high school. It just went from there."

"It was perfect! It felt like I was watching it for the first time."

George smiled at me, squeezed my hand, and twirled his cane as we walked. We made our way home in comforting silence, the late summer sun casting shadows ahead of us on the road.

The next evening, we arrived at the tavern to find a long line out the door and a table reserved just for us in the middle of the room, where everyone could see George. As we wove through the crowd, people clapped him on the back and bowed slightly to me. Whatever ill-will they'd felt towards us when we first arrived had completely evaporated, replaced by awe and excitement over what we could offer them in the form of escapist entertainment.

After we finished eating, we noticed everyone had grown quiet as they waited for George to take the stage (or table, as it were) for part two of *The Princess Bride*.

George took a deep breath, winked at me, and hopped up on the table, giving his cane a twirl, like a baton. The crowd cheered and whistled, before quieting so not a word would be missed by even those standing in the back.

He glowed—a radiance I hadn't seen since early on in our relationship. We'd been beaten down and diminished by the pain of life's experiences, our happiness dimmed and almost extinguished entirely. But here was George, doing something that brought him joy, and coming to life again in the process.

He tapped his cane on the table's edge before opening. "When last we left, Princess Buttercup had been kidnapped by the Genius, the Giant, and the Swordsman intent on starting a war ..."

The audience booed and hissed for the villains, cheered for The Man in Black's success against the Giant, and laughed heartily over the battle of wits between the masked man and the so-called Genius. George held a flagon of ale in each hand to act out the Genius's dilemma, eliciting hearty laughs from the audience. When it was revealed that The Man in Black was in fact Buttercup's true love, Westley—now known as the Dread Pirate Roberts—the cheers from the increasingly drunk audience were deafening. George did a masterful job pretending to throw himself down a hill while calling out, "As you wiiiish!"

Though he played to the crowd, it was not lost on me that George saved the best of the lines about true love for me, and me alone. When he described the love between Westley and Buttercup, he looked at me—and only me. Whenever he uttered the line, "As you wish," he always turned to me.

And I found myself gazing up at him like a smitten groupie, ready to go wherever he wanted, only desiring to have him to myself.

The second night's bag of coins was even larger than the first, as word had spread about the must-see storyteller with an epic tale of love and adventure. George closed part two with Westley about to be tortured by the evil count and Princess Buttercup in the clutches of Prince Humperdinck.

Outside the tavern, several of the poorest residents of the town hovered near the door, hoping to catch snatches of the story, but unable to afford to buy a meal (and thus, a seat) for the show. As they bowed deferentially to George, he shook several coins into his hand. "Please, come early tomorrow for good seats," he explained while passing out his earnings from the night so they could afford the meal for the next day.

"That was very kind of you," I remarked while looping my arm into his for the walk back to the cottage.

"I know what it's like to want to forget about your problems for a bit by losing yourself in a good story."

I squeezed his arm. "You know, if we're stuck here for the rest of our lives, you have a bright career ahead of you acting out famous future movies."

"Oh, I'm already planning a thorough production of *Gladiator*. What do you think?"

"I think they'll lose their minds over Maximus and Commodus."

George paused his walking so he could face me. "Do you think they will be ... *entertained*?"

I shoved him playfully and strode past him, calling over my shoulder. "Does this mean you're about to become unbearable to be around?"

"Aren't I always?"

Normally I would have some snarky reply ready to keep the banter going. But the same shifts that were moving our relationship into its new iteration had shifted my words as well.

"No, George. In all seriousness you're my favorite person. And," I paused and looked him in the eye so I could see his reaction. "And I always want to be around you."

A slow grin spread over his face. "Well, that's very convenient, because I feel the same."

The third night of the performance, we arrived at the tavern to find a line down the street and crowds parting for us the way they parted for the baron himself. It seemed like all of Kirkby Kendal had shown up for the final night's show.

Our reserved table was now near the front door so they could prop the doors open for people listening from the street.

"Wow, I'm actually a little nervous," George whispered to me as we took our seats. Everyone watched us, eager anticipation written on their faces. "This has gotten much bigger than I intended."

"Title of your sex tape," I quipped.

George laughed, his nervous tension eased by one of his favorite dumb punchlines. "Thanks, I needed that."

"Good. You know you're going to be amazing, right?"

"Maybe. It helps that you're here."

"There's nowhere else I'd rather be." And I meant it, right down to the century.

After we finished eating and George felt like he had worked out the best finale, he hopped up on the table and turned to face everyone in the tavern, plus a nod to those gathered outside. His voice boomed throughout the room. "Tonight, we will find out: will true love prevail?" The audience whooped and pounded the tables.

George glanced down at me and smiled before launching into his finale.

He gave it everything he had, bringing to life Westley's dramatic rescue by Inigo Montoya and Fezzik; slightly modifying Miracle Max to be more of a religious figure (to play it safe, given the church's role in society); and acting out the final battles where the trio exacted revenge and rescued the Princess.

At the close of the story, George extended his hand to me and pulled me up on the table with him, where he gave me a deep kiss to the rousing applause of the audience.

The final bag of coins George earned was twice the amount Henry had given us. That night we spread them out on our bed and counted, did some fuzzy math about what things cost (medieval exchange rates were complicated), and realized we had enough money to easily sustain us for the next three months.

George let out a low whistle. "Even after giving away my take from the second night, we're good for quite some time. But just in case, let's not go crazy."

"Agreed. I mean, we probably won't need it much longer ..." I let the words ebb into a whisper.

We stared at each other, the unspoken dread of being here for the rest of our lives etched on both of our faces. But George's expression softened as he reached out and twirled one of my loose curls around his finger. "And if we don't make it home, will you be okay?" His voice was soft, tentative. He knew this was much harder for me than for him.

"I will have to be, won't I?"

He nodded. "Whatever happens, I'm here. I've got your back, okay?"

For the first time in years, I knew he would.

57

JULY 1421

GEORGE

"I have a surprise for you, when you get home later."

Rhiannon arched an eyebrow at me. She was in the process of dressing, the elaborate multi-step routine that involved donning and adjusting a series of cumbersome garments, all held together with various laces and ties. As she was readying to head up to the castle to keep Gwendolyn company over embroidery and gossip, she had to forgo her simple woolen work dress and once again dress as a lady of means. I was tying the ribbons on the sleeves of her undergarment as she no longer had Agnes to do it for her.

When I released her wrist, Rhi crossed her arms over her chest and gave me a searching look. "What's the occasion?"

"The occasion is I had an idea, I had the money, and I needed to make it happen. That's all." I could tell by her cocked eyebrow she was skeptical. I wrapped my arm around her waist and pulled her against my chest. "The occasion is that I figured out how to do something for you. Something I know you'll love. Does that make you feel better?"

I had the idea of a lifetime, combined with the money and confidence to execute it. The perfect gift for Rhiannon: a cheeseburger. In the 21st century, cheeseburgers were the way to Rhi's heart. They are her absolute favorite meal, and at that point, she'd gone months without any of her comfort foods. While I couldn't do anything about chocolate or coffee, I could do something about cheeseburgers.

However, in the 15th century making a cheeseburger was a series of herculean tasks, each one more complex than the last. It required a stupid amount of planning, and once I determined I wanted it to be a surprise, I also had to line it up with one of the rare days she wasn't working by my side in the cottage.

Rhiannon rested her hands against my chest and gazed up at me. "At the very least, I'm intrigued."

We'd been repairing our marriage through fits and starts, talking through things we should've been talking about all along. We'd dug up heartache that'd been left buried and dormant, brought it into the light, and reframed how it affected us so we could heal. Through conversations while hauling jugs of water and scrubbing laundry in the river and chopping vegetables, we'd processed much of the hurt between us, so it couldn't keep defining our relationship.

Words were a good start.

But I needed to make my actions count, too.

I kissed my wife, letting my lips brush against hers before she cupped my cheek with her palm and pulled me towards her. I felt myself respond to her touch as her body was pressed up against mine. "Listen," I gasped, pulling away just a bit. "As much as I want to take you back to bed, we just finished putting on, like a hundred different items of clothing, and neither of us has time to do it again."

Rhiannon smirked and took a step back. "Then let's hope your surprise later is worth it."

"Oh, it will be," I replied confidently. "I'm certain this is the best gift in the history of gifts." I paused for emphasis. "Not hyperbole."

"Hmmm. Those are big words, George. I'm looking forward to it."

After I escorted Rhiannon up to the castle and left her in Gwendolyn's care, I got to work myself. In the days leading up to this, I'd found the perfect skillet; unearthed a scantly-used meat grinder in the back room of the butcher's shop that had a courser grind than most (medieval people loved turning their meat into a paste); tested out frying chopped turnips in various oils like duck fat or beef tallow to get as close to French fries as I could; and found a baker willing to make me bun-sized bread loaves with a finely milled white flour. I'd procured mustard seeds and experimented crushing them with vinegar and white wine using a mortar-and-pestle to get some semblance of modern mustard; tried a disastrous take on mayonnaise (my whipping couldn't keep up with a modern hand blender, leaving me with a broken, soupy, eggy mess); and found a vendor with cucumber pickles that tasted even better than the soggy modern pickles Rhiannon loved to heap on her burgers.

And I'd bought wildly expensive beef. It wasn't very economical to butcher a cow that could give you years' worth of milk and cheese (and more cows), so medieval people rarely ate beef. They subsisted on lots of grains, vegetables, and occasionally fish or various types of fowl. And eels. Lots of eels—which even I had gotten sick of. Only the wealthy ate meat, and when they did, it was usually mutton or lamb, sometimes pork or venison. Beef was a luxury. And hard to come by in a region where everyone had lots of sheep and very few cows. But Rhi was never a fan of lamb, and the whole point was to create a real cheeseburger. So, beef it was.

I did all this during the rare moments we were apart, so the whole process was taking a long time. But I knew it'd be worth it.

While Rhiannon was out, I swept and tidied the cottage, gathered a couple eggs from the chickens as Rose clucked disapprovingly at me, and built up our pile of firewood. I prepped my ingredients and cooking station so when she came home, I'd be ready to get to work.

At one point Gustav appeared, wearing a red cotton bow, and sat next to me while I prepped, occasionally licking his chops and sniffing the air curiously. I scratched his ears and gave him a piece of cheese to nibble on while I worked.

Rhiannon came home, escorted by Henry, who stayed and made small talk for a few minutes before he left, the cat trailing him out the door.

She stared at my set up, my tools and ingredients under cloths. "What's all this?"

"You'll see." I led her to the table, tied a blindfold around her eyes, and handed her a full flagon of ale. "Have a little happy hour drink while I get things ready."

"I do miss a good happy hour," she sighed, taking a sip of foamy beer.

We chatted as I cooked, Rhiannon telling me about her day and the castle gossip as I assembled the meal of a lifetime. I buttered buns and toasted them on the skillet, beside beef patties topped with bubbling cheese. I fried turnip sticks in our cauldron, using beef tallow like an old school McDonald's. Occasionally Rhi paused, licked her lips, sipped her beer. But she didn't press me about the surprise.

When it was ready, I set two dishes in front of us. "Take your blindfold off now," I instructed.

Rhiannon yanked off her blindfold and gasped. On a wooden board serving as a plate, I'd laid out a cheeseburger, grilled to perfection, topped with sharp cheddar cheese, crunchy pickles, and mustard. On the side I had fried turnip sticks, coated in sea salt and perfectly crisped.

"George," Rhiannon exhaled in awe. "You did all this?"

"I did. Try it," I encouraged. I wouldn't touch mine until she had eaten first.

She lifted the burger and took a huge bite, chewing slowly, closing her eyes and savoring the taste. "Oh my god, this is the best thing I've ever eaten!" Rhiannon exclaimed between mouthfuls. She took a turnip fry and popped it into her mouth. "It's no potato, but it's still incredible!"

I smiled. "I'm glad you like it. But this isn't the gift."

"It's not?"

"Nope. Do you want to know what the real gift is?"

Rhiannon cocked her skeptical eyebrow at me. She took another huge bite of her cheeseburger. "And it's better than this? I find that hard to believe."

While the extensive work that went into making the cheeseburger could have been the perfect gift on its own, something else occurred to me while I was busy gathering and prepping everything. The reason all of this was so time-consuming and arduous was because cheeseburgers do not exist in the 15th century. They wouldn't exist for almost four hundred years, and in a very different form than what we had in our time.

I know my wife better than I know myself. And I know Rhiannon loves to know things. She hoards information like a Tolkien dragon hoarding gold. She's a wealth of random facts, bits of trivia, and secrets people have entrusted her with. We had to stop going to bar trivia because if she missed a question, she'd obsess over not knowing the answer for days afterward. If you could get a college degree in knowing tons of things, Rhiannon would have five.

The best gift for Rhi isn't a thing—it's *knowing* something.

I reached across the table and took her hand in mine. "Rhiannon, as of right now, in the year 1421, you are the first person in history to eat a cheeseburger."

Rhiannon stopped chewing and widened her eyes. I could tell she was considering the validity of this information, mentally wracking her memory for any instance of someone possibly eating a cheeseburger before this point in time. But we both knew not even sandwiches existed yet (which, why? Doesn't a sandwich seem like an obvious assemblage of ingredients? Not in 1421, that's for sure.) When it was clear she had no answer, she choked up a bit, taking a big swig of ale to clear her throat. Her eyes reddened as they welled up with tears.

"Oh my God, you're right! That *is* a better gift!" Rhiannon let out a little sob before taking another bite of her cheeseburger. As she chewed, she looked at the burger in her hands in awe. I let her eat a little longer before speaking.

"That's not all," I continued. "As of right now, you and I are the only ones in the history of the world who know that you're the first person to ever eat a cheeseburger. And because no one would ever believe us, you and I will be the only people in the history of the world to *know* that you are the first person to ever eat a cheeseburger. That's the real gift."

Tears ran freely down Rhiannon's cheeks. She stopped eating, just sat and stared at me, a peculiar look on her face. "You're right," she sobbed. "This is the best gift ever. Sorry, I don't know why I'm crying so hard," she gasped while wiping her tears with the edge of the linen tablecloth.

I knew why she was crying. I knew Rhiannon had spent a lifetime trying to be perfect because she thought that was the only way anyone could love her. Her childhood was an endless cycle of chaos, so along the way she was wired to believe that the answer to it all was to be an antidote to the chaos, that her life was only valuable if she could tame the storm. If she could control her surroundings, while maintaining an absurdly high standard for herself, then she could have the love she craved.

But as a result, very few people knew the *real* Rhiannon. She was a loner by practice, wary of showing vulnerability, convinced if she opened up and let everyone see her, they may not like what they see.

The real Rhiannon rarely received thoughtful, heartfelt gifts was because she was hidden under this façade of someone else. Without the distractions of our time—phones with their never-ending stream of notifications, the relentless demands of consumerism, and our respective careers keeping us chained to it all—we had the opportunity to get to know each other on a stripped down, authentic level.

In our time, I probably would not have conceived of such a gift; I was too lost in trying to make everything easy and convenient for myself.

There was nothing easy or convenient in 1421. Which I was strangely grateful for. The part of me that had wanted to skate by in life, to stay safe in the realm of not giving a shit, was dead.

I could never be that man again.

"Honestly I'd be bummed if you didn't cry over this," I laughed. "This was the reaction I was hoping for."

She gestured towards my untouched cheeseburger. "Are you going to eat?"

I still hadn't taken a bite. I was too nervous about Rhiannon's reaction. But once I saw I'd gotten the response I hoped for, I was famished.

"Yep," I replied, picking up my own burger. "Now I'm the second person in history to eat a cheeseburger." I took a bite. It was everything I'd hoped for: gooey, salty, crispy. Perfect. "God that's good," I murmured between bites.

"It is, isn't it? Now, do pizza!" Rhiannon joked.

58

RHIANNON

I watched George as he took the first bite of the cheeseburger he'd put an absurd amount of effort into. He looked happier than I'd seen him in years—bursting with pride and satisfaction, eating something amazing, toasty warm in our little cottage. In the firelight, I marveled at how his hair looked golden and his pale eyes glowed.

He was a different person. Every time I looked for George when I needed him, he was there. When I stumbled, he caught me. When I was hurting, he pulled me into his embrace and cared for me. And when I was sick of eating bland stewed barley and tough venison and bitter apples, he made me a cheeseburger. Whatever buried fears I had that this progress was only temporary faded away.

We ate quietly for several minutes, both of us grinning like idiots.

After we finished and cleaned up, we sat in front of the fire, watching each other wordlessly, sipping the last of our beers.

"You stopped feeding me," I said quietly. "Back in our time, you'd stopped feeding me."

"I know. And I'm sorry." In the past, George's apologies were despondent and reeked of hopelessness. This apology was resolute. He shifted in his seat. "Not to give my dad too much credit, but do you think this is why he sent us here? Do you think he knew what would happen?"

"I think he knew it would push us to our limits. Why else would he recommend coming during the equinox? He wanted us to have this experience."

George ran his hand through his hair. "He thought I was a fool for not fighting for you. For walking away instead of staying."

"Not a fool. We needed the time. We needed to know what it was like to be without each other. And apparently, we needed to know what using a garderobe in the middle of winter was like." I smiled. "It kind of puts it all into perspective, doesn't it?"

He laughed. "Yeah, there's something very humbling about dragging a full chamber pot to a latrine and cleaning it out. It's hard to complain about modern problems when you're dealing with ancient ones."

"Now that we're close to going home—and I won't entertain any other possibilities, by the way—I can honestly say I'm grateful we had this time. It was gross and awful and scary, but I feel like a different, better, person on the other side of it."

George grabbed my hand and brushed his thumb over my knuckles. "Just a couple more months left. I feel pretty good about our ability to survive, so there's no reason to think it won't be smooth sailing from here on out."

I smoothed my hand across an invisible plane. "It's all level from here on out."

Yeah, that's right. We tempted the Time Travel Gods again. Like fools.

59

RHIANNON

This was the plan: stockpile a week's worth of food and clean water; say our goodbyes to Henry and Gwendolyn (while deliberately avoiding Edward); hunker down in the cottage for the days leading up to the equinox and wait for the cottage to drop us back into the 21st century.

Though we knew what day the equinox was happening, and though we tracked it with tick marks scratched into a log by the fire, we weren't taking any chances. (You try and understand medieval calendars when you're used to a completely different calendar and a phone giving you all the answers. It's not easy.)

Even the weather cooperated with our plan to stay inside. Thick winds howled outside the window, lashing rain pelted against the door, and the sky remained dark even at midday. Inside we had a glowing fire, mulled wine, and warm bread slathered with butter and honey.

Easy, right?

We were ready for anything. Anything except three thugs kicking our door open in the middle of the night and dragging us out of our beds.

That evening, given the increasingly cold nights, we donned long linen nightgowns and woolen stockings before climbing into bed. We fell asleep ruminating on what it would be like to take a hot shower or ride in a car or taste coffee again for the first time in a year. I had dreams of pizza and HVAC systems and clothes with zippers.

Instead, I awoke to the sound of two heavy thuds, followed by a crack louder than lightning breaking overhead, and a crash as our front door hit the stone wall before hanging limply by one busted hinge. Beside me, George was already scrambling out of bed, fumbling for his cane to use as a weapon.

Three men stood before us. The youngest, hulking in size and reeking of rotten onions, moved to his right where George stood clutching his cane with both hands, like a sword. The other two—smaller, older, equally vile in smell and appearance—moved to their left to where I had leapt out of bed, trying to evade the attack. When the larger one lunged at George, I watched as he got in one good whack with the cane before the larger man wrestled him to the ground and twisted his arm behind his back.

We never found out their names, but for the sake of the narrative let's call the big, oniony one Ralph and the two smaller men Alfred and Edgar.

"George!" I cried out, distracted just enough for Alfred to grab my wrists, yank them behind me, and shove a burlap sack over my head. It smelled like manure and smoke; I started coughing and flailing around, but my defenses were cut short by my legs being knocked out from under me. I fell to my knees before I was yanked back to my feet from under my arms and shoved towards the cold, damp air of the open doorway.

"Wait!" George gasped. "Wait. We can make a deal with you."

Alfred snorted. "You think you can offer more coin than Lord—"

Ralph hissed, "Quiet!"

"Not coin. Cooperation," George replied. "If you were meant to kill us, we'd be dead already. You need us alive. Right?"

No one responded, but I felt the grip on my arms tighten.

"It's freezing outside. Let us put on our boots and cloaks and we will go willingly. No fighting. Deal?"

The only sound cutting through the silence was the shifting of feet. Alfred wrapped his greasy arm around my neck and I felt something sharp press into my belly. "Deal. But if there's any trickery, I will gut her like a fish."

"No trickery, on my life," George swore. "Let me dress her first."

The men didn't respond, but I felt George's hands give my calf a reassuring caress before he guided one foot, then the other, into my boots and tied the laces. The men held me at arm's length, still clutching my arms, when George draped my fur-lined cloak around my shoulders.

"Bind her hands," Edgar commanded.

I felt George's fingers brush my wrists as he tied a rope around my wrists. Though I couldn't see the knot, I knew something our captors didn't: George had been a Boy Scout. He knew knots. And he knew what knots looked secure but could actually be undone with one tug of a loose end. As he finished the knot, he gave my hand a quick squeeze, a gesture that conveyed enough information between us.

I understood that he was preparing for us to escape at some point. He knew we'd need to be able to shed our bindings and be at least semi-dressed to survive in the frosty woods.

George was planning ahead.

60

GEORGE

I finished binding Rhiannon's wrists with a fraud of knot and pulled on my own boots and cloak. Ralph put a hood over my head, shoved me through the busted-open doorway of our cottage, and guided me up onto what felt like a rickety cart attached to what I later figured out was a donkey. Rhi stumbled onto the cart behind me; I blindly tried to steady her with my knee until she was settled on the bench and leaning against my arm. With the crack of a whip we were moving.

Rhiannon and I sat side by side, our hands bound in our laps, huddling against each other.

As promised, we cooperated with our own kidnapping. By deciding not to fight, I got us dressed, bound in an advantageous way, and conscious so we could listen to our surroundings for clues as to where they were taking us.

After we'd ridden for what felt like at least an hour (though time was fuzzy and impossible to track), Rhiannon announced that she had to "relieve" herself.

Edgar muttered something, before halting the donkey and dragging Rhi off the cart, going somewhere I could not follow. Heart pounding, terrified they'd harm my wife and I could not get to her, I listened for sounds of a struggle. But the only sounds they made were leaves and twigs crunching underfoot. Off in the distance, in the direction they went, I heard water flowing. It seemed they took her to the riverbank.

"She's not to be marred!" Ralph called out, offering me some relief.

It also confirmed what I'd already surmised when they let it slip that a lord funded this operation: that piece of shit, Edward, was behind this.

To think I was ever a Ruby Haze fan.

Rhiannon heaved herself back onto the cart and brushed her shoulder against mine. Relieved, I rested my burlap-covered cheek against the top of her head.

We rode in silence. The few words our captors uttered were mostly drowned out by the increasing din of water flowing. Branches scraped against my arm and snagged on the sack covering my head. The cart bounced and jostled along, sometimes stopping entirely while the thugs cleared brush or worked together to shove the cart over tree roots; we didn't seem to be following a road. Rhiannon and I clasped our bound hands together, both as stability against the rocking of the cart and for warmth.

Though we'd been fast asleep when we were so rudely kidnapped, the adrenaline pumping through my system kept me from nodding off.

Which meant I had time to think. I thought about all the times my dad made me learn how to solve riddles and put together clues to reveal important answers and figure out locations. I mulled over his insistence I do Boy Scouts—especially the wilderness training aspects—and how I'd quit as soon he let me. He had wanted me to take Latin classes, but I'd adamantly refused, opting to half-ass my way through high school French instead. I considered how he drilled me with British history, literature, and culture, dragging me through museums and historical sites on his trips to England for work.

And I remembered, details clear and unmistakable, when he gave me the Norman coin and told me to wear it all times because it was a "lucky charm." It was the one instruction I followed faithfully, if only because it looked cool and the smart, bookish girls I was into seemed to like it too.

Every step of the way he was preparing me. As if he knew at some point I'd need to know all these things not just to survive—but to make it home again.

And I'd fought him at every turn, determined to live my own life, resistant to his surreptitious preparations.

When Rhiannon came into my life, she'd embraced his strange challenges, thrilled to be learning something new and happy to have a family.

I'd still resisted, caring more about being right than the way I was impacting those I loved the most.

Yet here I was, wearing a dirty burlap hood in the year 1421, grateful for all my dad put me through because we were going to need it all and more to get home.

The cart stopped. Before I could process that this stop was different than when we encountered previous obstacles, I felt a cold breeze where Rhiannon had been sitting as they dragged her away.

She didn't make a sound. Rhiannon, so smart and such a survivor, knew we needed to assess our situation before reacting.

When the thugs yanked me off the cart and shoved me forward, I also kept quiet, maintaining our earlier agreement to cooperate.

I tripped over a threshold and felt loose straw beneath my foot. The damp air reeked of rotting wood and mildew. A shack of some sort?

A rough hand shoved me down into a sitting position. When I leaned back, I realized I was leaning against Rhiannon. Relief coursed through me. I was terrified we'd be separated. But medieval thugs have a dearth of action movies in their repertoire, so they'd made rookie mistakes. Here we were, together, conscious, and with our hands tied in front of us. For a moment I thought escaping would be as easy as releasing a sham knot and walking out the door.

However, in situations like this, relief is always short-lived.

Mine dissipated when I heard footsteps followed by a familiar voice, laced with disdain and arrogance. "Apologies that it had to come to this. But I'm sure you understand. Now, simply give me the key and I will release you."

61

RHIANNON

We've already established that I hate being wrong, so having it rubbed in my face repeatedly was a special kind of torture.

Edward crouched down next to us and yanked the hood off my head. I took a deep breath of slightly fresher air, happy to be free of the itchy burlap on my face. More concerned with escaping than the man in front of me, I tried to look past Edward's shoulder to see where we were. It looked like some sort of small wooden shack.

Edward pinched my chin and turned my face towards him.

That beautiful face was ugly with rage. "Where's the key?"

I smiled. "What key?"

"If you think I won't kill you both, you're sadly mistaken," he snapped.

"But then you'd never find the key, would you?" I countered. I felt George repress a snicker behind me.

Edward slapped me. Hard. I yelped, surprised by both the gesture and the pain. Somehow, despite my lax parenting and unstable childhood, I'd never been hit before. I felt a strange affection for my mother, at the most inopportune time.

George tensed up behind me but didn't react. We both knew that was what Edward wanted—he wanted us unstable and vulnerable, wanted us to lash out so he could resort to violence sooner than later. George remained still, breaths measured.

"Where is the *fucking* key?" Edward seethed, face close to mine, the smell of cinnamon now nauseatingly close.

"It's back in the cottage," I lied. "We hid it before going to bed, as we always do, and your dumb thugs didn't think to check to see if we had it."

"Lies."

"How will you ever know if you don't go and check?"

Edward sighed and stood up. "I tire of this game." He yanked me to my feet by my unbound hair and wrapped one arm around my waist, so he was at my back, facing George. "You're awfully quiet, *Lord* George. Doesn't it bother you the way I'm touching your woman?" Edward nuzzled my neck, and I held back a gag, finding every part of him repulsive. He nipped my neck, sneering at George.

George held my gaze. I saw the fury in his eyes ... and the calculation. He raised an eyebrow and gave Edward a lazy smile.

"It's interesting, *Lord* Edward. You're so obsessed with getting back home, you haven't wondered what kind of life awaits you there."

Edward didn't respond, just dug his fingers into my side.

George continued. "For example, did you know that after you disappeared, Ruby Haze got a new lead singer and became exponentially more famous? Like, international stadium tour, comparisons to the Beatles famous? I bet you thought they fell apart without you. But they didn't. They *thrived*. And your fiancée—Marisol, right? Well, she married your drummer and they've been happy for years. And happily raising your—excuse me, *their* son together. So, you could say that everyone back in our time is happier *without* you." The way Edward's body tensed up behind mine meant the words hit their mark. "It kind of takes the shine off all the effort you put into this, doesn't it? Having us kidnapped so you can get back to a life where no one misses you anymore."

"Shut. Up." He hissed.

I couldn't see Edward's expression, but I saw a flash of guilt across George's face that told me all I needed to know. Because look, let's be honest, we both know that was an incredibly cruel (though true) thing to say. But if the choice is to be mean to a time traveling rock star trying to kill us *or* getting killed by said rock star, I think we can agree that George made the right choice.

When Edward squeezed me tighter, to the point where he was crushing the breath out of me, George shifted. "Look, Rhiannon is telling the truth. We don't have the key. We always thought it safer to keep it with the cottage."

Edward didn't release me. "Where is it hidden?" He slid his hand down, right above my pubic bone, daring that he'd go lower if he wasn't given the info he desired.

George exhaled, shaking his shoulders out, making it seem like he was about to reveal some deep, important secret. Instead, he addressed Edward with a controlled calm that gave me chills: "Take your hands off my wife."

Edward laughed and licked my neck. I shuddered.

"Or what?" he sneered. "I could take her right now, on the floor in front of you, and there is little you could do about it. But I'm a reasonable man. So, tell me where the key is and I'll release you both, unharmed."

George adjusted his injured leg, shaking out his foot. "You're already a dead man walking, so I might as well tell you. There's a loose stone in the floor. We put it under there. Now, release her."

Edward chuckled derisively and threw me down on the floor. I rolled up into a sitting position and backed up against George.

"Ralph and I are going to go look for the key. If it turns out you're lying, I will tear her apart until you hand over that key. And if even that doesn't work, then I'll just leave you both here to starve."

"If you say so," George replied sarcastically.

Edward gave a swift kick to George's scarred leg before storming out of the little shack, slamming the thin plank door behind him.

George inhaled sharply but contained his pain so we could hear what was happening outside. All we could make out were muffled voices followed by the sounds of horses riding off.

When it was quiet, George sighed. "I thought he'd been suspiciously quiet."

I leaned back against him. "You can say it. You were right."

62

GEORGE

"Listen, normally I love a good 'I told you fucking so' moment, but right now we have other things to handle." I already knew Rhiannon felt awful about her misjudgment, and at this point, I didn't care about it. I was laser-focused on getting us out and back to the cottage before the equinox, which according to our calendar log, was the next day. And I needed her feeling good about things to think clearly.

I whispered as loudly as I dared, not wanting to alert anyone who may be guarding us from outside. "See the end of the rope hanging off your knot?"

"Yes."

"Tug it until the knot falls apart. Once you're free, come over here. There's a knife in my boot that can cut my bindings." Within seconds Rhiannon scooted into view, hands free and gesturing for my feet. I held up my leg. "Left boot. I figured they'd never check, given the bum leg and all."

"It's clear they've never done this before," Rhiannon mused while pulling the dagger from my boot. She sliced through my ropes with quick, forceful movements until I was free. I grabbed the longest of the cut pieces and tied it around my waist in case we had need for it later.

"We do have an advantage there." I rubbed my wrists, paused, and held a hand up. I could hear voices coming closer. "I think it's the guys Edward left behind. Quick, give me the knife and get behind me. Pretend you're still bound."

Rhiannon tossed the knife into my lap and scrambled behind me, leaning against my back. I tucked the knife back in my boot and twisted my hands in my lap with the rope fragment draped over my wrists, mimicking my bindings.

The voices stopped outside the door and talked for what felt like an excruciatingly long time. While they spoke, I surveyed our surroundings. We were in a small, shack-like structure that seemed held together by only a few rusty nails and force of habit. Its wood planks were hammered together loosely, some overlapping like shingles, others with enough space between them that there were clear gaps in the thin walls. Shards of light streamed through the sparsely-thatched roof, the rough floor was simply packed earth sprinkled with straw, and a ring of stones and ashes in the center of the room made up a fire pit. Rhiannon and I leaned against the back wall, opposite the front door.

The shack was close enough to the river that white noise from the flowing water made it challenging to hear what the thugs outside were saying, their syllables drowned out and muddled. The voices finally went quiet, followed by the sound of a thud on the exterior wall, close to the ground. After several more minutes, I heard the faint rhythmic sound of snores. Only one thump, only one person snoring. The other guy left or was keeping watch while the snorer slept.

If it was just me, I probably would've tried to storm the door, slashing the knife back and forth to clear an escape path. But that chaotic tactic would put Rhiannon in danger and I just wasn't willing to risk it.

Given the rattling snores and the distance Edward would have cleared on his way back to our cottage, I felt safe enough to push against some of the weaker, rotting planks to my right. They were mercifully loose, the rusty nails crumbling with minimal pressure. One plank came free and plopped quietly into the mud outside the shack.

"What are you doing?" Rhiannon asked just above a whisper.

"I think we can remove enough of these planks to get out." I gave another plank a sharp, quick kick.

Rhi wrapped her hand in the edge of her cloak and begin punching out loose planks beside the one I'd kicked out. She made quick shallow jabs, forceful enough to loosen the wood, but not so loud that our guards would hear over the sound of the river. Working together we created a hole large enough for her to squeeze out.

I pointed to the gap and she nodded. Rhi pulled her hood over her head in case there were rogue splinters and shimmied headfirst through the opening.

Once outside, she handed me a piece of rope from our bindings. I wound it around the last two stubborn planks we needed to remove to make the opening big enough for me to escape. With both rope ends in her hands, she yanked until the rotting planks crumbled away, revealing a big enough gap for me to shove through.

I crawled out, careful to make as little noise as possible, until I rolled onto a bed of rotten leaves and mud. Lying on my back, huffing a relieved breath, I got a sense of our surroundings. We were in the midst of dense forest, though thankfully on a sunny enough day that pieces of light cut through tree leaves, helping us get our bearings.

Wordlessly, Rhiannon grabbed my hands and helped haul me to my feet. She jerked her head towards the sound of the river and hooked her finger indicating I should follow her. We stepped lightly through the underbrush, mindful of patches of slippery mud, avoiding dried twigs and their tell-tale crunch.

When we reached the river's shore, a safe distance from our captors, Rhiannon held her hand over her eyes to shield from the sun and pointed. "We go north."

"You could tell all that from the water's sound?"

"No, when I went to pee, I felt the water. We were heading downstream, which is south. So to get back to our cottage, we go north. We follow the river all the way there."

I wrapped my arm around Rhiannon's shoulders and pulled her into my side, kissing the top of her head. "You're so fucking smart," I admired while plucking a dead leaf from her curls.

"I know. You're very lucky I came on this trip with you." She grinned at me.

"I don't exaggerate when I say I wouldn't have survived without you."

"Same. But let's not congratulate ourselves until we're back home. Like, 21st century home, okay?"

"Agreed."

We walked in silence, hand in hand, following the riverbank north, occasionally checking over our shoulders to see if we were being tracked by anyone.

Between the rush of water and sun beating down on my face, I was parched. We hadn't had anything to eat or drink since the day before and it was already afternoon. Rhiannon was panting and pale; dark circles smudged under her eyes and more than once I caught her blinking herself awake. Despite her determination to keep up with my long strides, her pace lagged.

I pulled Rhi to a stop and gestured towards the river, whose clear rapids deceptively beckoned our thirsty selves. "Dehydration or giardia?"

She shoved her hair out of her eyes. It was rarely loose and I could tell it was driving her crazy.

I untied my makeshift rope belt and used it to braid (I use the word "braid" loosely here because it looked more like a deformed caterpillar) Rhi's hair behind her back while she considered the river. She patted the braid, seemingly aware of my terrible hair skills. But all she said was a grateful, "Thank you."

Rhiannon put her hands on her hips, ready to work out the water problem. "Okay, dehydration is guaranteed but giardia is not. Though both can be deadly." She spoke mostly to herself. "The water in the center of the river is probably cleanest but would still be full of waste from the town. However," she toed the mud beneath our boots, "if we dig a hole and let it fill, the sand will have filtered out most of the grossest stuff." Rhiannon crouched down and used a stick to start digging a hole. I knelt beside her and hauled handfuls of mud away until we hit a rocky patch that could serve as the bottom of our little well. Water seeped into the hole, filling it up, looking cleaner than I would have guessed. We dunked our hands in the rapidly filling hole, rinsing mud off our fingers, letting the sediment sink to the bottom.

"Hold on, one more step." I used my boot knife to cut a strip of fabric off my nightshirt. I lined the hole with linen so water could seep through one more layer of filtration.

We stared at our makeshift well, working up the courage to try it, knowing the consequences would be unpredictable and possibly awful. I blinked away flashbacks to our first gruesome nights hunched over holes in the garderobe.

"Here goes nothing." Rhiannon scooped her hands into the water and took several gulps.

I followed suit, desperately slurping the cool water dripping between my fingers.

After we'd satiated our thirst, splashed water on our faces and the backs of our necks, and rested on the riverbank for a few minutes, Rhi stood and offered me her hand. "We should get moving. Since we don't have anything to carry extra water, take the linen with you in case we need to dig another hole."

We ambled along the river, me clutching a wet piece of fabric, Rhiannon with her hair knotted up with a piece of rope, both of us wearing only dirty nightgowns, cloaks, and our boots.

When we came upon a wild apple tree, loaded with ripe fruit, we ate as much as we could. I grabbed a couple more apples and carried them in my sleeve in case this was the last food we would find.

The sun slanted low in the sky and a cool breeze caressed my legs. Given that it was late September, the nights were incredibly cold. Too cold for two inadequately dressed people to keep going. We needed to find shelter, ideally far enough away from the river that we wouldn't easily be found, but not so far we got lost ourselves.

I pulled Rhi into the forest. "Follow me." With the sound of rushing water behind us, I scanned the woods for a place we could hunker down for the night.

We came upon a giant tree whose roots split in such a way that two people could nestle against the trunk, relatively hidden, somewhat sheltered. We gathered dried leaves and piled them against the trunk for padding and warmth. I sat in the pile and pulled Rhiannon down so she sat between my legs, leaning against me. I wrapped my cloak around our shoulders and she draped hers over us like a blanket. We couldn't risk a fire, so this was the warmest set up we could achieve with what we had.

"I'll take first watch," I offered. "You try and get some sleep. Then we can switch."

Rhiannon nestled against my chest, my arms wrapped tightly around her. "Okay."

The sun set, allowing the moon to illuminate the forest with unnerving shadows and patches of silvery blue light, and the forest vibrated with the sounds of nocturnal creatures stirring as they prepared themselves for the impending winter.

Despite the late hour, I could tell by Rhi's breathing that she was still awake. When I rubbed her arms for warmth, she tilted her head up me. "Do you still want to know what you said at the party where we first met?"

She spoke tentatively, as if she was offering a final gift in case we didn't make it—whether that be home or something worse.

I kissed the top of her head. "Of course I do."

63

RHIANNON

We caught eyes from across the crowded dance floor. "Hips Don't Lie" blasted on the speakers, while my relatively new boyfriend Mike went to grab us a couple of drinks.

Back then George was lean and tanned, like he'd spent the summer soaking up sunlight instead of hunched over in a library cubicle like I had. I liked the way his shaggy ash-blonde hair fell to his shoulders and how his bronzed face contrasted with his pale blue eyes. When he brushed his hair out of his face, he didn't break eye contact with me. He wore a faded gray T-shirt, his arms were dotted with a series of tattoos of various symbols in thin black outlines, and he had a silver cuff bracelet on one wrist—a wrist I'd gotten a glimpse of when he took a sip of his beer ... still not looking away from me.

It was fall semester of my freshman year of college and I was feeling freshly bold and ready to embrace a new version of myself. I'd spent high school mostly avoiding eye contact with just about everyone. I kept my head down and did my work, nothing more. To make friends meant eventually having to explain my living situation—sometimes a motel room, sometimes a small apartment with cigarette-stained walls, sometimes the backseat of my mom's car—and facing the inevitable humiliation that came along with it. Dating was obviously out of the question.

But in college I could start anew, no longer tethered to my crazy mom, living in the dorms like everyone else. When I met Mike at my summer job and it was clear he was into me, I saw it as a way to reinvent myself beyond just my living situation: I would be The Girl With The Boyfriend.

When The Girl With The Boyfriend rolls into her freshman year of college, already taken, she creates an aura of mystery and untouchability about her. Other girls respect her because she's already locked down a committed relationship, and boys want her because she's off-limits.

Who cared if Mike wore a rotating series of obnoxiously bright polyester T-shirts and constantly smelled like Axe body spray and fried foods? I would make it work for as long as I needed to. I'd never had a real boyfriend before, so this seemed like a good plan.

That is, it was a good plan until I locked eyes with George on the dance floor and knew it would take my full effort to continue dating Mike.

When I didn't break eye contact, all through a full song and half of his beer, George cocked an eyebrow at me, grinned, and started making his way through the crowd to where I was standing.

At the same time, to my right I saw Mike winding his way back to me, two beers in hand, his highlighter-yellow Ed Hardy T-shirt a beacon of impending awkwardness.

George arrived a few steps ahead of him. Whatever pheromones he was emitting were working on me. I was completely sober yet wildly intoxicated on how attracted I was to him.

Just as Mike broke through the crowd, George leaned down and spoke right into my ear: "I'd marry you tonight if you asked me to."

Without thought, I shoved him away right as Mike came to my side and put his arm around my shoulders, still holding both beers.

George laughed, gave me a little salute goodbye, and faded back into the crowd.

"What was that?" Mike asked while handing me my drink.

"Just some drunk asshole." I shook my head and turned to my boyfriend, pulling him against my chest with one arm around his waist. But it felt ... off. Wrong. Like embracing a cold stranger.

Whatever lingering attraction I had for Mike faded in the minute it took for George to whisper his proposal in my ear. Because I would have left with him. I would have followed him wherever he wanted me to go. My entire body hummed when he drew close. I told myself it was most certainly a ridiculous biological reaction that meant nothing but chemicals and cells reacting to external stimuli.

However, as I lay awake in bed alone later that night, I knew that if Mike had not arrived when he had, I would have accepted George's offer. Biology be damned.

64

RHIANNON

When I finished telling the story in low whispers, George chuckled. "I stand by that. I would have married you that night. And," he kissed my cheek, "I'd marry you again. I have no regrets."

"None? Not even being in that stupid cottage on the equinox?"

He tightened his arms around me. "In a weird way, this specific experience aside, part of me thinks being in that cottage on the equinox is one of the better decisions I've made. I don't know what life will be like when we get home, but I do know you'll be in it. And really, that's all I care about."

"Me too," I reached up to caress his stubbly cheek. George pressed his face into my hand. "As hard as this has all been, I'm glad we did it together. I love you. I never stopped."

"I love you too. Always."

We cuddled like this, bracing against the increasing chill in the air, until I dozed off.

George gently woke me up what felt like minutes later, but the sky was already turning a pale shade of dawn. He whispered directly into my ear: "Don't make a sound. Stay calm."

Close by—too close—I heard the clear sounds of our captors crashing through the brushes, one of them shouting about having found our tracks.

My heart thudded against my ribs and a flood of cortisol burned in my chest. Despite the cold, I was sweating through my thin linen nightgown. I was out of breath yet holding completely still. After spending hours lying on the frozen packed mud, my bottom was numb and one of my feet had fallen asleep; if we had to make a run for it, I didn't know if I could keep up.

While I slept, George had pulled some dead branches and leaves over us. We sunk down against the tree trunk, hidden from view unless someone hovered directly over us. He held me tightly, not daring to move a muscle. I could feel his rapid heart beating against my back.

It was the day of the equinox. If they caught us, we would be trapped in the 15th century for at least another year. Or worse.

Alfred and Edgar's voices surrounded us, calling and answering; they'd found our tracks at the river but lost them again when we'd ventured into the forest. Despite losing the trail, they were gleeful about their impending discovery. The voices faded as they doubled back towards the river—though we couldn't tell what direction they'd headed after that. If they went north, we could run into them while trying to make our escape.

I kicked off branches and leaves and pushed myself up onto my knees before attempting to stand on my unsteady legs. I extended a hand to George, who winced as I pulled him up.

"My entire body is somehow both numb and sore from the waist down," he mused in a low voice. He handed me an apple from his sleeve. "Let's travel through the forest, just in case they come back this way. If they see us by the river, we're fucked."

When I bit into the apple, its sweet juice flooded my dry mouth and trickled down my throat. I coughed, muffling the sound with my sleeve.

George tilted his head at me. "You okay?"

"Yeah. It's just hard to eat and breathe at the same time when you're terrified for your life."

He grunted in agreement while biting into his own apple.

I wiped my brow with my sleeve and tossed my apple core onto the ground. "Let's get moving. I won't be able to relax until we're back in the cottage."

We picked our way through the woods, keeping the sound of the river to our left, indicating we were moving north, but staying out of sight of the riverbank. Every so often we paused to listen for any sound of our captors on our tail. Birds chirped and twittered around us, indicating no one else was stalking through the forest.

As the day progressed, clouds rolled in and obscured the sun and the information it gave us about how far we'd traveled and what time it was. I prayed to those fickle Time Travel Gods that we weren't too late.

Perhaps I was distracted by my worrying about the timing of the equinox.

Or maybe we let our guard down too soon. We'd assumed the thugs had gone in the opposite direction, and that if they did come our way, they would be loud enough to give us ample warning again. Whatever it was, when a hand reached out and yanked me, I was caught completely off guard. I squealed before falling backwards onto the leaf-padded ground.

George, who was only two steps ahead of me, whipped around right as Edgar grabbed him around the waist, trying to sack him.

"Gotcha!" he chortled with glee.

This time, George did not cooperate. Instead, he jabbed his elbow into Edgar's throat before grabbing his arm and pulling him down to the ground. He laid out the greasy little man on his back, gasping for breath, shocked he'd been overtaken so easily.

Alfred, who was pinning me to the ground by standing on my shoulder, was also surprised. So much so, he didn't notice when I grabbed a rock and slammed it into the back of his knee, causing him to collapse to the ground next to me.

George hauled Edgar up to his knees by his shirt and held his boot knife to his throat. "Tell your friend to go jump in the river, or I'll cut you wide open.

Understood?" He pressed the edge of the knife into his throat, hard enough that a drop of blood ran down his neck.

"Go—go jump in the river," Edgar croaked, flailing desperately for something to grab onto, finding nothing but damp leaves.

"He's lying," insisted Alfred. He was still on his hands and knees on the ground, careful not to make a move that provoked the guy with the knife.

"Am I?" George pressed the knife deeper, causing Edgar to whimper as more blood trickled from the knife slice. "I could kill him now, then it's two against one. And I won't hesitate to remove your head from your shoulders. Now, get in the fucking river before my hand gets tired and I have no choice but to finish this my way."

Alfred made to stand up, but George shook his head. "Crawl. Now."

He hesitated before crawling towards the river. George yanked Edgar to his feet, keeping the knife against his neck. "Rhi, bind his hands behind his back."

I did as he asked, using a real knot he would never be able to undo on his own.

George nodded his approval. "Let's go."

I could see George's discomfort with all of this in the way he winced before pressing his knife into Edgar's throat. He's a lover, not a fighter. But he loathes bullies and was just as desperate to get home as I was.

Nothing, absolutely nothing, was going to keep us from getting back into that damned cottage before the equinox. Which, at that point, could have been any minute. We had no time to waste.

Our awkward party stumbled to the riverbank, where Alfred hesitated.

"Get in," George commanded.

Alfred waded in, one tentative step at a time, pausing when the muddy bank caused him to slip in up to his waist. The thug looked back at us, uncertain. It occurred to me he probably didn't know how to swim.

"Lie on your back and float," George instructed.

Alfred hesitated, arms held aloft over the rushing water swirling around him.

George must have realized the same thing about his swimming abilities because he sighed before calling out, "If you stay flat on your back, with your arms and legs out, you'll float. Don't bend your knees or you'll sink. If you thrash, you'll drown. Stay calm and you'll live." I could see him working out how much of a swimming lesson he should be offering this guy before sending him down the river.

Alfred lowered himself into the river, hesitating and jerking up a few times, clearly afraid of the water.

"Move it!" George called. "Follow my directions and you'll live."

Alfred tentatively lifted one leg at a time to float before the water picked him up and carried him downstream. We watched as he thrashed a few times but steadied himself when George's instructions proved true.

When he floated around a bend and out of sight, George shoved Edgar to his knees. "Stay here and don't make a move until the sun sets. If you come after us, I will kill you. Do you understand?"

He nodded, sinking into the mud of the riverbank, shaking with fear. George wiped his blade off on the man's tunic before shoving it back into his boot. "Edward sucks but his boot knife trick has come in handy."

"At least there's that. Come on, let's get moving."

We hustled up the riverbank, moving as fast as our pointy-toed boots would allow, occasionally slipping in the mud, not taking a break for even a moment, George clutching my hand to ensure I didn't fall behind.

It wasn't until we finally reached the worn path leading from the river to our front door that we paused to catch our breaths. We stalked quietly up the path, familiar with each rut and stone, listening for any sounds of Edward or Ralph.

The woods thinned and our cottage came into view. We hid behind a bush to survey the situation before deciding on what action to take. George silently pushed me behind him before he pulled his knife from his boot and held it in front of him.

Our captors could be inside waiting for us to do something stupid.

It was clear they'd torn the place apart. Our rain barrel was turned on its side, the contents nothing but mud by the front door. Through the dark space of the kicked-open door, we could see our bedding and pillows piled on the floor in the middle of the room. Several logs that had been stacked up by the fireplace were now strewn all over the room.

"Rude," George whispered, scowling at the destruction.

"Very," I agreed.

He knelt down and removed his right shoe, felt around inside it, then shook out the sawdust stuffing that maintained the toe's point. Out fell the key. "Those stupid fuckers didn't even think to search us for the key. Here," George handed it to me. "Hold onto this. As soon as we get back inside, we must get that door set and locked. I can handle the door so you're in charge of locks."

I gave him a mock salute and clutched the key in my sweaty hand.

We watched the cottage for several minutes, with no sign nor sound of anyone being inside. Given that we were running out of time, we had to get moving.

George ran his hands through his hair, shoving it out of his face. "Ready?"

I let out a deep breath. "As I'll ever be."

65

GEORGE

I grabbed Rhiannon's hand and together we darted across our small yard into the cottage. As soon as we crossed the threshold, I lifted the door from where it dangled on its one remaining hinge and tried to close it so the lock lined up. But the heavy wood was cumbersome and the balance was off. Rhiannon came up beside me and together we worked to line up the door, but as soon as she let go to insert the key, it would fall just off kilter enough that the lock didn't work.

As we fumbled with the door, a leering voice from behind us asked, "Did you really think I believed you?"

We both turned to find Edward lounging on our stripped bed, muddy boots kicked up on the mattress, eating a piece of cheese. He tossed the wax rind onto the floor before brushing his hands together and clasping them over his stomach. Edward was dressed the same way he was for the hunt: black leather doublet, knife sheathed at his waist, hair tied back. Only now his sleeves were rolled up, revealing his tattoo.

I scowled at him. "Were you hoping to catch a ride home with us? It doesn't work that way."

Edward swung his legs over the bed and stood up. "I know that." He pulled his knife from its holster and flipped it over in his hand before pointing it at me. "You can choose. You or her?"

Rhiannon stood close enough to me that I stepped to my right to partially shield her. "Help me out, what am I choosing?" I asked, hoping to buy us time—if there was any time to buy.

If the equinox occurred while the door was loose on its hinge and all three of us were still in the cottage, there was a solid chance no one was making it home. And the clouds made it impossible to tell where the shard of light was traveling.

Edward rolled his eyes. "One of you gets to stay inside and go home, the other will be shitting in a chamber pot for the rest of your life." He gazed at Rhiannon. "Perhaps you should make the choice? We both know George is soft and thinks he's noble, so he will sacrifice himself to save you. Why not just skip that boring step and choose yourself?"

Rhiannon brushed my arm before taking a step away from me, closer to Edward. "If this was always the plan, why go through the trouble of trashing our cottage? There's debris everywhere." She used her foot to shove one of the stray logs from the fireplace towards me. "What a mess!"

I knew instantly what she was doing.

But Edward—who hadn't seen a soccer game in at least a decade—didn't.

He flipped the knife in his hand again, a taunt to show us he knew how to use it. "If you hadn't lied about the key, your precious little cottage wouldn't look like this. Now, like I said, I do not care who stays or who goes. We only have a couple minutes left. So, I will choose." He squinted one eye at me, then at Rhiannon, as if determining the best time travel companion.

I used his pause to move. With one motion I kicked the log at him like it was a soccer ball being launched into a goal. It slammed right into Edward's chest, knocking him off his feet, causing his knife to skitter across the stone floor.

Rhi didn't hesitate to pounce on him, pinning his arms to the floor with her knees on his shoulders.

Edward grabbed her by the waist and attempted to roll over, but she held on, using her foot to anchor herself from being steam rolled.

I stumbled towards them, grabbed another log off the floor, and held it over Edward's head. "Don't make me do this!" I commanded with a lump in my throat. I hate violence. I didn't like the idea of bashing his head in with a log any more than I liked the idea of cutting Edgar's throat by the river.

But when Edward's only response was to reach up to grab my wife by the throat, I let instinct take over.

I cracked the log down on his forehead. I didn't use all my strength—I was certainly not trying to kill him. Hell, I didn't even want him brain damaged. Just incapacitated. It was enough that Edward howled and struggled limply but was significantly subdued.

Edward blinked up at us, dazed; blood running down his face from the wound on his forehead told me I had used the right amount of force.

Rhiannon stood and stepped away from him. "Look!" she pointed at the tree trunk in the corner of the room. The clouds had parted enough to reveal the shard of tell-tale sunlight working its way toward the grid carved into the trunk. We had seconds before the equinox.

We didn't have time to get Edward out; we only had time to get the door in place, gambling the cottage's time travel magic would know who to bring home and who to leave behind. Adrenaline giving me more strength, I pushed the door closed and lined it up in the frame as best I could. Rhiannon shoved against it with her shoulder, helping the lock align as she inserted the key and turned.

The lock clicked into place.

She gave me a relieved smile as I reached out to caress her cheek. Before my hand made contact, I felt like I was being turned upside down and all went dark.

66

RHIANNON

I slammed into the unnaturally squishy bed and rolled onto the floor, taking blankets with me as my legs twisted in the quilt. Clawing at the wood planks as if I were sliding away, I opened my eyes to see sunlight pouring through sheer white curtains framing a clean, clear window. I sat up slowly and took stock of the room I was in. There was a little nightstand next to the bed, an alarm clock with glowing red numbers, and smooth wood flooring topped with a threadbare wool rug. The room—the clean, quiet, upper bedroom of the cottage—looked exactly how we left it a year earlier.

"Holy shit," I whispered to myself.

On the other side of the bed, George had also rolled onto the floor. He pushed himself up into a sitting position and stared at me from over the mattress, blinking away his stupor.

"We did it," I whispered, almost in disbelief that this wasn't a delusion brought on by lack of sleep and too many apples.

He nodded but didn't say anything. George reached up and ran his hand over the smooth sheets, seemingly marveling at the modern fabric beneath his hand.

I stood on trembling legs, still wearing the filthy linen nightgown and cloak I'd been wearing for the past couple days, caked in river mud, dead leaves clinging to the fabric. A quick pat of my head revealed my hair was still twisted into a knotted braid tied with a piece of rope. Dirt was caked under my fingernails, my torn wool stockings sagged around my ankles, and my boots had bent toes.

George groaned as he stood up and stretched his arms over his head. With his hair a tangled mess, his linen nightshirt filthy and torn, and his cloak hanging limply over one shoulder, he looked more like a hobbit who'd really been through it than Aragorn.

"What day is it?" he asked nervously. I knew what he wondered.

When had the cottage brought us back?

"I'm not sure." All I knew was that it was roughly after 5:00pm and the sun was starting its slide towards the horizon.

But I was startled to see my open suitcase sitting on the floor, its contents neatly folded and untouched. My shoes were lined up against the wall, my purse beside them. It'd been so long since I'd had my things that I hadn't even considered them. In two steps I was rummaging in my purse where I found my phone, somehow still charged. As I raised the screen to my face, it illuminated an image of me and George at a Falcons game, beers in hand, big smiles across our faces. It was an older pic, taken not long after we got married.

Though we were separated, I never had the heart to change it.

The date on my phone showed September 23, 2020. The cottage returned us exactly one day later than when we left—but so different, a lifetime could have passed.

"It's tomorrow," I breathed while dragging my finger over the unnervingly smooth screen of the device. Brightly colored little squares vibrated to life. But the answers I sought were not there. I tossed the phone on the bed where George sat, watching me fiddle with the phone.

"What do you mean?"

"Today is September twenty-third ... in the year 2020. It's like only a day passed." In fact, I had only one text message, from my substitute teacher, asking a clarifying question about the lesson plans I'd left.

George rubbed his eyes and ran his hands through his greasy, tangled hair. He bent down to take off his shoes and stockings, revealing the angry red scar twisting up his calf. "Let's get in the shower where we can discuss all the different fun stories we can make up to explain to modern doctors how I got this injury, never received proper medical attention, and somehow my scar looks like it's almost a year old, despite being, like a day old as of now." He rubbed his calf; his leg would probably never be the same again, regardless of what kind of medical treatment he'd be able to get now that we were home.

But something he said caught my interest more than anything else—a shower!

"Holy Gods, George! A shower!" I flung my cloak onto the floor, yanked my nightgown over my head, and kicked off the boots that had plagued me the entire previous year. My braid was too knotted for me to undo on my own, so George came around from his side of the bed and carefully worked the rope out of my hair. I stood there, naked save for my red woolen stockings, my matted hair just a clump of knots.

A mirror hanging over the bedroom door displayed the first clear glimpse of my reflection I'd gotten in a year. I was bruised and dirty. And despite eating better the last few months of our medieval adventure, I was still gaunt and hollowed out in places where I hadn't been before. "I look like I've been living in a ditch for the last year." I sniffed under my armpits. "Oof. I smell like it too."

George grasped my shoulders and turned me so we faced each other. "You just survived a year in the early 15th century. You don't look like you've been living in a ditch. You look like a warrior, fresh from the fight. Which, you are."

This is how you know you're loved: when they are looking at you at your absolute worst, and you see nothing but undiluted affection in their eyes.

I placed my hands over George's. "Do you realize we made it?" I wasn't referring to getting back home.

"I do," he nodded, tears filling his eyes. "We fucking made it!"

We started laughing manically, followed by shouts of victory, dancing around semi-dressed, flooded with relief. "We fucking made it!" we shouted into the ether, reveling in our victory.

I sunk to my knees and started sobbing. The reality of our success flooded me with intense joy—and grief. Dr. Rosen was still gone. Edward, despite all he'd done, clearly hadn't made it back with us. Who knows what sort of desperation of over a decade of missing his people had driven him to. So, I grieved for him too.

But, still. We made it!

I stood up and extended my hand to George. "Come on, let's get cleaned up. After that, let's go get some answers."

He put his rough, calloused palm against mine, never breaking eye contact. Together we removed his linen nightshirt, pulled off his boots, and tugged off his stockings. He was just as thin, bruised, and filthy as I was.

But we were alive. And we had each other. And I knew from this day forward, I was never letting go of him again.

George cupped my face with his hands and brushed his lips across mine. I circled my arm around his waist and rested my face against his chest. He kissed the top of my head and sniffed. "Warrior stuff aside, we do smell like barn animals. Come on, let's get in that shower. I don't even know how we've been delaying this long, as it's literally the only thing I've been dreaming about for a full year now."

The modern world turned out to be unexpectedly overwhelming. The shower, though glorious, stung. The pressure of the hot water scalded us pink and made my skin tingle. Our shampoo and conditioner's artificial fragrances were so overpoweringly cloying, they gave me a headache. Despite the discomfort, we stayed in until the hot water ran out, taking turns ducking our heads under the stream of water and scrubbing each other's backs.

"Why does everything smell like I got punched in the face with perfume?" George complained when applying deodorant.

My face creams had the same synthetic reek. They made my eyes water so badly, I had to wash my face again and use a little bit of olive oil I found in the kitchen cabinet as a moisturizer.

After showering, exhausted from our ordeal and running on fumes of spent adrenaline, we passed out until the next morning.

The 21st century wasn't just overwhelmingly smelly, it was brutally loud. As we trudged around the castle hill towards where Henry and Gwendolyn lived in this century, we were assaulted by an endless barrage of noise. Airplanes roared overhead. Cars honked. Trains whistled in the distance. Bass-heavy music thumped out of windows. Chainsaws and wood-chippers and weed-whackers grinded away. Endless leaf blowers disturbed the general peace. Plus, a litany of additional unidentified beeps and sirens and whirs marred the background and confused our senses.

The modern cacophony was layered with the thick scents of car exhaust and laundry detergent and cooking smoke.

"I forgot how much I loathe leaf blowers," George winced, pulling his shirt over his nose to dampen the smell of burning gasoline.

"It's a lot." I agreed.

Above us, the crumbled ruins of Kendal Castle gleamed in the morning sun. It had rained the night before and the castle's stones glistened in the light. Strangely, I felt an ache in my chest to see it in this state. I understood what kind of lives had been lived there—what kind of love and happiness and celebrations, as well as pain and grief—had been experienced within the circle of rubble that remained.

Even though the time we spent in the castle was the most agonizing, brutal, difficult time of my life, I still found myself grateful. Because I had survived. George was right. I was a warrior. If that year didn't break me, then nothing could.

"It's kind of weird to see it in that state, isn't it?" he remarked as we walked past the ruins. "It's like a dream now, to see how much it's changed. And for us, it was overnight. Like all we had to do was wake up." George gestured towards the city of Kendal. "Do you think they think about the people living here six hundred years ago? We just spent a year with their ancestors and can't even tell them about it."

I paused and admired the view of the city set into the river valley. "I bet they do." I glanced over my shoulder at what was left of the ancient castle. "However, the ruins are a nice reminder not to live in the past. Life happened here, but it's over now. And that's okay."

We took another moment to survey the land before George tugged my hand and we continued our trek to the de Ros's house.

When we crested the cobblestone drive up to the de Ros's elegant estate, following the directions they'd left in a note in the basket of goodies they'd brought us, Henry flung open the door before we could even knock. We paused our ascent and stared at each other for a moment. Though he looked older than the last time I saw him, it was clear this was the same man we knew in 1420. He had the same mole at the corner of his left eye, the same height, the same ice blue eyes.

"Lord Henry," I curtsied.

He smiled. "Well then, you made it," he replied as if we'd just stepped out to run a quick errand. Henry turned and gestured that we should follow him inside. "I know you have questions, and now is the time for answers."

Inside, Henry led us down a long corridor lined with paintings that appeared to be by great masters including a Monet-esque landscape, a portrait that was most certainly a Rembrandt, and several medieval religious scenes painted on wood panels interspersed with modern works. George paused to examine a painting with the name "Artemisia Gentileschi" scrawled on the corner, letting out a low impressed whistle. Henry glanced back to confirm we were still following him, a proud smile on his face.

At the end of the corridor was a massive library, two stories tall, brimming with books stacked along elaborately carved shelves that soared to the ceiling.

Mounted on the walls interspersed with the shelves were antiques including ancient looking rifles, swords, and framed documents. A faded globe with a visibly inaccurate map stood in a corner to my right. In the middle of the room was a sitting area comprised of burgundy leather armchairs circled around a coffee table. One side of the room was lined with floor-to-ceiling glass windows overlooking Kendal and the rolling green hills beyond.

Gwendolyn was already sitting in one of the armchairs, a cup of tea in her hand, and a stack of books and papers on the coffee table in front of her. Though she also looked older than I'd last seen her (like, a week before this), it was clear this was the same woman I'd spent hours embroidering with, the same woman who gleefully decorated Gustav with various bows, and the same woman who often burst into tears whenever she saw George.

Henry took the seat beside his wife and indicated we should sit in the chairs facing them. Gwendolyn poured us each a cup of tea without asking, placing the cups gently in our outstretched hands. As she handed me my tea, she held my gaze for a moment with a strange smile on her face. "It's so much nicer seeing you with your lovely hair undone instead of under that dreadful headdress."

I stared at her. "I guess if I didn't have questions before, I certainly do now."

Henry clasped his hands and looked to Gwendolyn for confirmation. She gave him a short nod. "Yes, I'm sure you have plenty of questions indeed. So, if you are ready, we will tell you a story."

We both nodded, sipping our tea quietly, neither of us wishing to delay with any further interruptions.

Henry took a sip of his tea, rested the cup on the saucer, leaned back in his seat, clasped his hands over his midsection and began to speak. "I wonder, then, what would you do for someone you loved? How far would you go? And what would you give up? Because it is time you understood what we were willing to do." He shifted, took a slow breath, and continued. "I was a warrior general who served under William of Normandy. Because I was instrumental in the success of his English conquest, I was gifted a very sizeable parcel of land, right here where we are currently sitting." Henry paused, letting us absorb those words.

George touched his chest where his Norman coin rested under the fabric of his shirt. Neither of us flinched or showed the smallest sign of incredulity.

Henry nodded, satisfied we believed him, and continued. "To fortify my holdings, I built a castle. Originally it was built out of wood, high up on the hill. It was not far from the river and not all that far from the ocean. The land was fertile, trade routes accessible, and I knew I could build a lasting legacy in this place. The kind of legacy that would be handed down to my heirs, generation after generation. But most importantly I was allowed something that very few men—or women—of my time and status were allowed. I was also able to marry the woman I loved." He reached over and squeezed Gwendolyn's hand before resuming his story. "I believed God himself had blessed me, that I was in his eternal favor. That is, until Gwendolyn and I began having children. Our first child was a boy, also named Henry, who was quite small when he came into the world. It seemed that he struggled to draw breath, and less than a month after he came into this world, he exited it again."

Henry paused, inhaled slowly, continued. "The second child was a girl. She, too, failed to thrive and died within the year. Our third child, another girl, lived to be almost three years old before she too passed away. All three children had the same affliction: they simply could not breathe. They turned blue and choked and gasped and there was nothing anyone could seem to do to help them. To watch our babies die in such a manner was worse than any battlefield I had ever been on." His eyes reddened and his breathing grew shallow. Even a thousand years later, it was abundantly clear Henry still grieved the loss of his children.

Gwendolyn picked up the story's thread as Henry paused to brush a tear from the corner of his eye. "In those days there was very little science; the main source of answers about the mysteries of life came from the church. But the only thing the priests could tell us was that we must have offended God somehow. We were being punished for something we had done, but we did not know what. We prayed and prayed and prayed. We sprinkled holy water, tithed generously to the church, gave alms to beggars, did everything we were told to, everything we could think of—and yet none of our children survived past the age of three.

"In those days it was vital that Henry have a legitimate heir to inherit the land, wealth, and title he had amassed through battle. I even wondered if perhaps the problem was me, and I offered to step aside so a more suitable woman could bear his children, but he was having none of it. We waited several years after the death of our third child—our daughter Mary—before we decided to try one more time. At that point I was already in my late thirties and I knew we were almost out of time.

"Our fourth child was a boy whom we named Albert," Gwendolyn gave George a knowing look, "who was born just shy of my 37th birthday. As soon as I saw him, I knew that if we didn't do something drastic, we would lose him too. Little Albert was born quite small and his lips were blue. The midwife managed to revive him, but I knew the same affliction that had plagued my earlier children would eventually claim his life as well. I had to take drastic measures right then, or my baby would not survive. And, though this is heresy, I also knew I was done with the church telling us it was our fault our children were dying."

Gwendolyn took a sip of her tea. The cup clattered against the saucer as her trembling hands lowered both to the coffee table. "I will never forget the look of pity in the midwife's eyes upon seeing the state of my fourth baby. And I knew she could see the look of terror upon my face, that we would once again endure the loss of a child. So, one night while she was helping my ailing son latch to my breast, she whispered into my ear. She told me there was another way—but I would have to be discreet, and should I be caught, she would deny ever revealing it to me. In a village not far from us, there lived one of the last druid priestesses. She would be able to save my son."

Gwendolyn inhaled slowly and reached for her teacup. I could tell from their shaking hands and tear-filled eyes that the de Ros's had never told anyone what they were sharing with us, that even though the story was now centuries old, the secret had been weighing upon them the entire time.

Henry reached over to squeeze his wife's hand again. "By this point in England, paganism was outlawed. When Gwendolyn came to me with this plan, she knew just considering it and having the church find out could mean certain, painful, death. We were both in a precarious position. I was a baron, and thus our church's most loyal benefactor. But I was also a father—a father to no living children, save for a frail babe. I, too, was ready to exhaust all options. Even dangerous options. Our decision was sealed the night we could not calm Albert's coughing. We had run out of time. Gwendolyn and I wrapped up our baby, put on dark cloaks, and on foot we travelled all the way to the druid priestess's cottage.

"We walked for hours, arriving at the priestess's door as dawn broke, to find she was waiting for us. She led us inside and took the baby from our arms. The priestess immediately rubbed something on little Albert's chest—something I now know to be eucalyptus—but back then it was unfathomable how she even got such a plant. His coughing was immediately soothed. For the first time since he had been born, our baby appeared peaceful. His cheeks even gained a little bit of color as he was able to take deep breaths that had been elusive to him before. I knew then I would do whatever the priestess asked of us to save my son's life." Henry leaned back in his chair again and nodded to Gwendolyn. This story belonged to them both, and they were both going to tell it.

Gwendolyn continued with her right hand over her heart. "The priestess gave us a little jar of salve and instructed us to use it on Albert's chest whenever the coughing fits began. But she warned us that it was only a temporary solution—the cure was incredibly far away. Perhaps impossible to get. 'What are you willing to do to save your son?' she asked. I told her that I would go to any end of the earth and would do whatever she asked to save him. There is no limit to the love I have for my boy, therefore no limit to what I would do for him. Convinced, she asked us to meet her at a specific place exactly three days from then. It was a small oak tree, standing by itself at the base of the hill, within sight of our castle.

"The priestess carved a grid into the tree trunk and instructed us to build a small stone hut, using the tree as one of the posts. We were to use no hired labor, and all work must be done by hand, at night. We only had seven days, and given that I was no stone mason, we knew every minute counted. But we did it. It was a haphazard little structure, yet it would work. The priestess came back on the seventh day and gave us an iron lock and key to complete the building. On the afternoon of the autumn equinox, we were to wrap up little Albert and put him in the hut by himself, with the key inserted into the lock. We were told he was going on his own to a place where he would be treated, and that we would meet him there." Gwendolyn swallowed. "And that is all she told us."

The de Ros's both had tears streaming down their faces. Henry pulled an embroidered linen handkerchief from his pocket and handed it to his wife. She used it to gently dab her cheeks, careful not to smudge her eye makeup. "What we did not understand back then was that Albert would have to travel to a time when they could treat him, because all our children were born with what we now know to be severe asthma. And it would be hundreds of years before the right treatments existed for such cases. What we also did not realize is that when she said we would meet him there, what she really meant is that we would live all these years, tied to this land, tied to that cottage, until he reappeared as a baby in the year 1950."

They quieted for a moment to let us absorb that information. George glanced at me, a stricken look upon his face, before addressing the de Ros's. "Are you trying to say," he asked with a rasp in his voice, "are you trying to say that my father was born almost a thousand years ago?"

Henry nodded and continued. "Once we put your father in the hut during the equinox, we watched as a shard of light lit up the tree and made the stones glow. Where we'd once heard his cries, there was only silence. He was gone. I almost went mad! I didn't think he'd disappear. I don't know what I thought. Only that my son was gone and the priestess was to blame. She was waiting for us on the path back to our home. She told us he was safe—alive, getting the help he needed. And he would return to us. We were to wait here for him, maintaining the hut that over the years became a cottage. That was critical—he'd only make it back if the foundations of the structure stood." He patted Gwendolyn's knee. "We told everyone we sent him to France for warmer air and treatment. And we didn't know when he'd return, which was true. A year passed. Then two. Then three. We worked on the hut—expanded the footprint, built new walls, added a fireplace, strengthened the roof—at a loss for what to do next, but keen to make sure the building survived."

Gwendolyn grasped Henry's hand and intertwined her fingers in his as he handed the story back to her. "The priestess, of course, never volunteered anything on her own, only gave us vague information until she too passed away. Eventually we learned we were now tied to this island, England, but could roam no further."

"Wait, how did you figure that out?" George asked.

"Years into our ordeal, we tried to travel. When you have nothing but time, why not see the world? But we could not leave. If we boarded a ship, something would always happen. A fire. A storm that marooned us in port. Tickets declined, carriage wheels broke down, and so on. Always. For hundreds of years. When air travel was developed, we thought we would try one more time. But an engine burst into flames before we'd even left London, and the plane had to turn around and make an emergency landing. We didn't want anyone to come to harm because of us, so we stopped trying."

Henry smoothed his hand over his face. "And we ceased to age—we were frozen in time until our boy came home. No one remembered anyone being lord of these lands before us, and no one could recall how long we'd been here. The information simply doesn't stick in anyone's minds. Generation after generation lives here, knows us, but never questions our lack of aging."

"This is a lot to process," George muttered while rubbing his hands over his own face that looked so much like Henry's. "Dad always told me he grew up in England for a little bit, but was a military brat so wasn't here for long. And ... he also told me that his parents were both ... gone. That he had no siblings or close relations. What happened? Why have I never heard of you before now?"

The de Ros's glanced at each other. Gwendolyn raised one eyebrow. "Perhaps this is your part to tell, my love."

Henry considered for a moment. "We begged the priestess to give our little boy life—not just to be alive, but to live! My dream for him was that he would take up his sword beside me and lead with me. That he would be a great lord of these lands and would be blessed with a large family. Most of all, that he would be robust of both body and spirit. And he was, my God he was. But Albert chafed at never being able to leave this island, because we couldn't leave it. And he figured something out: with the key, he could walk between times, untethered to the equinox."

Gwendolyn nodded. "During the year 1340, a thirteen-year-old Albert walked out of the cottage and into our lives. We were surprised of course, and back then we assumed it meant he had come back to us. He stayed for a few months, but it was clear he missed his life in his time. He missed what he called 'television' and his friends and the modern house we were all apparently living in then. So, he left. The key allowed him to travel back to his time whenever he wanted. From then on, he came to visit us over different years and at different ages. He experimented with the key and the various equinoxes and solstices and what not, trying to understand this incredible gift.

"It was Albert who realized that somehow the cottage existed in a place where—even without the key—time folded in on itself. It was the language that gave it away: the layers of different Englishes from different times layered on top of each other when we spoke, so he could understand us in any time. It was Albert who gave the cottage the name 'Plierton,' from the French word for 'fold.' And he recognized it only folded when certain elements were perfectly lined up. But he knew what it would mean to reveal this secret to the world, so it was contained within our family. Fame and fortune never appealed to him, only learning and exploring."

Henry added, "His wanderlust was not limited to the centuries. When Albert was about sixteen, he snuck out with a friend and took a ferry to Ireland. Once he figured out he could leave, he did. Your father chose to go to America for university, and though he came home to see us often, the visits dwindled in lieu of trips around the world during his school breaks. There was always a restlessness in his soul—that boy could never sit still! Even his leg was always shaking."

"Oh man, that used to drive me crazy!" George said while wiping his eye. I didn't realize he'd been crying. "Why do you think he didn't tell me about you?"

"Ah, well he met a girl, of course." Gwendolyn chimed in. "An American girl. But how could he explain his parents who could not travel outside of England and who did not age? I know he didn't intend to cause pain. Only that he wanted to have a full life, even if it meant seeing less of us. We still talked often, and he came by once a year or so. But ..." Gwendolyn choked back a sob. "But I knew what I was missing because I had already known you both in the fifteenth century. It pained us greatly that we could not be there for you as you grew up."

My eyes welled up with tears as I considered the implications. All this time, just across the ocean, there was this thing I'd craved my entire life: a family. Real grandparents, who had lived through the most incredible history, and had innumerable stories to tell about it. I felt blessed and cheated at the same time. Thrilled they were here, furious we hadn't gotten to meet them earlier. Though I could perhaps understand why Albert felt the need to keep these two parts of his life apart, I knew I would add this to the list of things I may never forgive him for. Right behind depriving me of toilet paper for an entire year.

That made me remember someone—someone who somehow got tied up in the cottage's spell and knew the de Ros's ceased to age. "May I ask you something?" I asked, voice shaky with harrowing memories. "What ever became of Edward?" I clenched my hands in my lap, only to find that George had reached over and intertwined my fingers in his. I rubbed the pads of his fingertips, calming my breath, letting myself accept we were truly home and no longer in danger.

Henry stroked his chin. "We knew, you know. That he also came through the cottage, ten years before you. We could never figure out how, though. He was the only one for almost a thousand years! Your father tried to bring him back right after it happened, but he failed. Poor Edward never made it back to his own time. He did live a long life though. He remarried and eventually moved to London when it was clear I'd never die and pass on the title." Henry gave us a grim smile. "The priestess once told me that this land would stay in our family's hands for over a thousand years. At the time I thought it a blessing. I simply did not imagine it would be like this."

"Do you regret it?" George asked. Then winced when he realized he effectively asked them if they regretted saving his father's—and his—life.

"Not for a second," Gwendolyn smiled weakly. "Though many of the years have been arduous at best, I have known great love in all of them. And in the end, that is all."

George stroked his thumb across my palm and smiled at me. In the end, that was all that mattered.

67

GEORGE

We stayed with Henry and Gwendolyn all day, talking into the late hours of the night, pausing to eat a dinner of pizza delivery (the pepperoni was so salty it burned my mouth, but was heavenly nonetheless) paired with a bottle of Bordeaux. We learned Agnes eventually married a young farrier, left the castle to live in town, and had twins of her own. Angus never married and worked as the castle's groom until his death as a hunched-over octogenarian. Barrow passed of a fever not long after we left. And Clifford took up another position as the steward of an estate in York, after meeting the enigmatic and charming lord who wooed him away.

While we lounged in front of a fire, comforted by the familiar warmth, a tufty gray cat with a white patch in the shape of Texas on his chest wandered in and flopped on the rug in front of us. I reached over to scratch under his ears as his purrs rumbled to life. "Okay, I have to ask. What's up with Gustav?"

Gwendolyn clasped her hands and grinned. "Oh! We don't precisely know. Gustav was a barn cat back before we ever met the priestess. Our best guess is he was in or near the cottage when it first folded into time. He seems to be able to come and go as he pleases, to whenever he pleases. I started tying various bows on him and recording them in a book to keep track, as he'd pop up wearing something unfamiliar, from a different time period, often—as we eventually learned—from the future. That's how we figured it out. But yes, this cat is at least a thousand years old."

I laughed. "So Gustav doesn't seem to follow any rules of physics or time travel, and that's all we know about it?"

"Yes, that's the sum of it." Henry replied. "Though I will say he did start aging again as we did when Albert passed. He's thinned a bit and has slowed down considerably. He mostly stays with us now, for the first time in a millennia." Gustav stretched out before curling into a little ball at Henry's feet. "'tis a strange thing to go from having all the time in the world, to facing the end in just a few short months. Which reminds me, there are a few matters of the estate to settle."

Henry slowly rose from his seat, clearly fighting newly achy joints. He retrieved two envelopes from a desk in the corner of the library. "Now, most of this," he gestured around the room, "has already been left to the National Trust. The house and all its contents, plus funding to maintain the lands, that is. The Barony of Kendal has long since been extinct, so there is no title I can leave you, though you are my rightful and sole heir. However, I found something in your little cottage after you left. A sack of coins. I'd heard about your performances at the tavern. I assumed the money was from that, so I saved it. Then I invested it. And over six hundred years it grew. It is now in a bank account under your name." Henry handed me one of the envelopes.

I opened it and motioned for Rhiannon to come and look with me. She hovered over my shoulder as I withdrew documents showing an account in my name with well over seven figures in it. We looked at each other, wide-eyed. Stunned. Rhiannon wrapped her arms around my shoulders and kissed my cheek. It was life-changing money.

Henry cleared his throat. "Every member of my household receives wages. Lady Rhiannon, I was not aware of how much you had done for both Marguerite and the castle in the wake of our loss. It was Clifford who informed me of the role you played when Gwendolyn was indisposed. So, these are your wages for your service as the Lady of Kendal Castle. Just as I did for George's money, it was saved and carefully invested over the years." He handed Rhiannon an envelope just like mine.

Together we opened the documents detailing a bank account in Rhi's name with a comparable sum of money. She let out a whoosh of breath before folding the papers and returning them to the envelope. "It's family money," she whispered into my ear.

I knew what she meant. Money for our family, for however our family grows. For each other.

We thanked them profusely. Henry waved us off. "You earned it. You deserve it. For the first time in a thousand years, I wish we had more time. With you, with our son. But I am also relieved to see you happy, healthy. I can go to my grave knowing I took care of my family in the only way I could. And that is enough."

"May I ask why you couldn't tell us any of this back in 1420?" Rhiannon queried.

"Strict instructions from your father," Gwendolyn nodded in my direction. "He always went on about adventures and what not and he wanted you two to figure it out. To struggle and learn and grow. He was adamant about it, despite my objections." She placed her hand against her forehead. "I'm not sure he knew the full extent of what you two would have to go through, but as he had seen the future and I had not, we did not interfere. Much, that is. Painful as it was."

"Yeah, that sounds about right." I was about to roll my eyes, a knee-jerk reaction to things planned by my father, but hesitated. On the other side of the struggle was victory. Through our perseverance Rhiannon and I had both grown, evolved. We were different—better—people on this side of it.

Rhi seemed to have the same revelation, because she looked at me and stated, "It was a gift then. A real gift."

I laughed. "Well, obviously we can't sell the haunted time travel cottage now."

68

GEORGE

The baggage claim of the busiest airport in the world was blessedly subdued when we arrived back in Atlanta.

All around us we watched as people—all masked, some wearing plastic visors, most ignoring social distancing—connected with their loved ones. They fist-bumped, gave air hugs, or in some cases leapt into each other's arms with reckless abandon. They laughed and cried and gesticulated wildly while telling stories; more than once I heard someone exclaim about how crazy the past few months had been. Families navigated a new world driven by the competing needs for connection and the desire to keep each other safe.

Rhi and I hung back while we waited for our bags, leaning against each other, still reeling from hurtling through space at six hundred miles an hour, after a year of not traveling faster than a horse could trot. Rhiannon interlaced her fingers with mine. I ran my fingertip along the ancient gold ring she'd been wearing on her left hand since the 15th century. The ring that matched mine and that I hadn't taken off since Barrow (of all people) shoved it on my finger right before that fateful dinner.

"You know," I glanced down at my wife. She was watching an older woman stoop down to hug a young boy before straightening up and patting his head. "There are many ways to have a family. We can do whatever we want. We can choose what happens next."

"We can," she murmured. The boy had a toy truck he was diligently driving up the woman's pant leg. Rhi smiled and glanced up at me. "Are you ready to go home?"

I squeezed her hand. "I'm ready for anything."

THE END

Behind the Book

and Acknowledgements

Back in 2020, I had an idea for a story about a millennial couple that somehow ended up in medieval England. At the time I had no interest in writing a novel; I had a thriving career as a public speaking coach and trainer and didn't think I had it in me to write a full novel, from start to finish. But this idea stuck with me, and I found myself mentally working it out while daydreaming. Who were these people? Why were they in the past? What would it be like to deal with the lack of technology, questionable hygiene, and a different culture when you're from the 21st century? What conflicts can they be working through that would be impacted by the setting?

Then I had a strange dream about a place in northern England I'd never heard of before: Kendal Castle. Yes, it's a real place! I found it on Google maps and spent quite a bit of time zooming around, fleshing out the story in my mind.

In October of 2022, my husband ran the London marathon, so we, along with my sister Brianne, took the opportunity to travel north to visit Kendal Castle in person. I walked around the ruins in the pouring rain, just like George and Rhiannon, letting the story take shape. You can see some of our video clips of the visit on Instagram.

Many versions later, including completely starting over at the beginning of 2025, yielded the story you just read. It's been a labor of love with over six years of research and writing and revisions, to bring the Rosen's story to life. In the interim I've written a separate novel (one with far less historical research required!), transitioned out of my coaching career, and completely pivoted into becoming a full-time author. Though I've technically been writing in some form or another my whole life, this is the first time it's been clear that this is my divine path.

I could not have done this without the help and support of my dedicated and loving crew of family and friends, whom I wish to thank profusely. First, my husband Shannendoah has been my scene partner, sounding board for ideas, and self-esteem champion when I wanted to give up. He's been unfailingly supportive of this venture and I'm eternally grateful to have him in my corner. My mother, Regina Puccetti, reminded me constantly of the book I wrote in the 4th grade and how she knew this is what I was meant to do. She read early versions, funded the first round of publishing expenses, and let me vent/rant/cry/laugh/celebrate/etc. depending on my mood at the time.

My best friends in my book club were my first beta readers and gave me valuable feedback to make the story and writing as strong as possible: Talia Pindyck, Stacey McGahee, Nicole Rateau, and Janet Cheng. My aunt, Mary Muramatsu, an avid reader and retired lawyer, made sure there were no continuity errors, plot holes, or grammatical weirdness. My dear friend, Chris Butsch, read from a male perspective and helped me make sure the ending landed with the impact I intended. My dad, Ron Chapman (a fellow author), supported me in numerous ways including and beyond being a reader, from providing cheeseburger inspiration to invaluable emotional support. And my sister, Brianne Solomon, has been instrumental in helping me grow my audience for this book. Beyond this, my good friends Joanie Twersky, Mara Krier, Louise Cohen, Aarti Sekhar, Smitha Kommareddi, Diana Stoian, Chuck fox, and Amy Fox, have been in my corner for this author adventure and have provided enlightening literary analysis of other books and emotional support along the way.

I'd like to thank Caitlin B. Alexander for her gorgeous cover design and artwork; in a world full of soulless A.I. it's refreshing to work with a real human artist!

Finally, I want to thank you, dear reader, for going on this journey with George and Rhiannon. I hope you enjoyed the adventure as much as I did!

ABOUT THE AUTHOR

Natalie Sol Gallagher wrote her first book in the 4th grade (*A Tree of Oranges Grows in the City*) when she should have been doing math worksheets. Fortunately, she had one of those rare teachers who encouraged her creativity, which inspired a life-long love of reading. Since then, she's earned undergraduate degrees in English Literature and History from Eastern New Mexico University and a graduate degree in Education from the University of St. Thomas. After a career teaching creative writing, narrative design, and composition at the university level, she spent a decade as a public speaking coach and speech writer before getting back to the business of writing books. This is her debut novel.

To learn more about Natalie's upcoming projects, enter contests, and get access to deleted scenes and extras, join her email list at NatalieSolGallagher.com or follow her on Instagram @natsolgal.author